Praise for *In This Ravis*

"*In This Ravishing World* also won The Prism Prize for Climate Literature. The judge for that contest wrote: Three pages into reading this fascinating book, I knew it was the clear winner of the third annual Prism Prize for Climate Literature that I sponsor through Homebound Publications. Not only does it cover every facet of the climate issue and the ongoing efforts at dealing with or denying/undermining what needs to be done, Nature's presence embraces the entire narrative and lends a sense of enchantment. Riveted, I could barely put it down for the three days it took to read the compelling stories of a diverse cast of characters: there is someone in these pages for every reader to relate to. Hooked by the older woman in the opening pages who was exhausted and discouraged after years of climate effort, and eagerly following her through to the final pages' plausible outcome, I applaud and admire Nina's skill at creating characters and plot that pull readers into climate awareness, while simultaneously acknowledging those of us who have tried to move the needle through non-fiction offerings. This book made me laugh and cry, and gave me a ray of hope."

—Gail Collins-Ranadive, author of *Dinosaur Dreaming, Our Climate Moment*

"In this ravishing book, you will find stories that lift your heart and stories that break it. Powerfully beautiful and beautifully powerful, Schuyler has written exactly the book this moment needs."

—Karen Joy Fowler, *New York Times* bestselling author of *Booth*

"A wildly inventive plot that keeps you turning pages, characters who steal your heart, big ideas that engage your mind, and gorgeous prose that delights your senses."

—Ellen Sussman, *New York Times* bestselling author

"With a surgeon's precision, Ms. Schuyler has written another exemplary story."

—Devi S. Laskar, *The Atlas of Reds and Blues* and *Circa*

"With astonishing dexterity and deep empathy, Schuyler takes the readers on a capacious journey with people from all walks of life: environmentalists, families, children, dancers, workers, hackers, and many more. Her spellbinding prose and unflinching vision overwhelms me with contrition for our prodigal past, trepidation for our fraught present, and hope for our perilous future on Mother Earth."

—Yang Huang, author of *My Good Son* and *My Old Faithful*

"*In This Ravishing World* is a magnificent story of hope and despair, love and fear, and the ongoing quest for personal and planetary survival. Both scientifically accurate and emotionally compelling, this book is necessary, timely, and wise."

— Lucille Lang Day, author of *Birds of San Pancho and Other Poems of Place* and coeditor of *Fire and Rain: Ecopoetry of California*

In this Ravishing World

Nina Schuyler

Regal House Publishing

Published by
Regal House Publishing, LLC
Raleigh, NC 27605

ISBN -13 (paperback): 9781646034420
ISBN -13 (epub): 9781646034437
Library of Congress Control Number: TBD

Cover images and design by © C. B. Royal

Regal House Publishing, LLC
https://regalhousepublishing.com

Printed in the United States of America

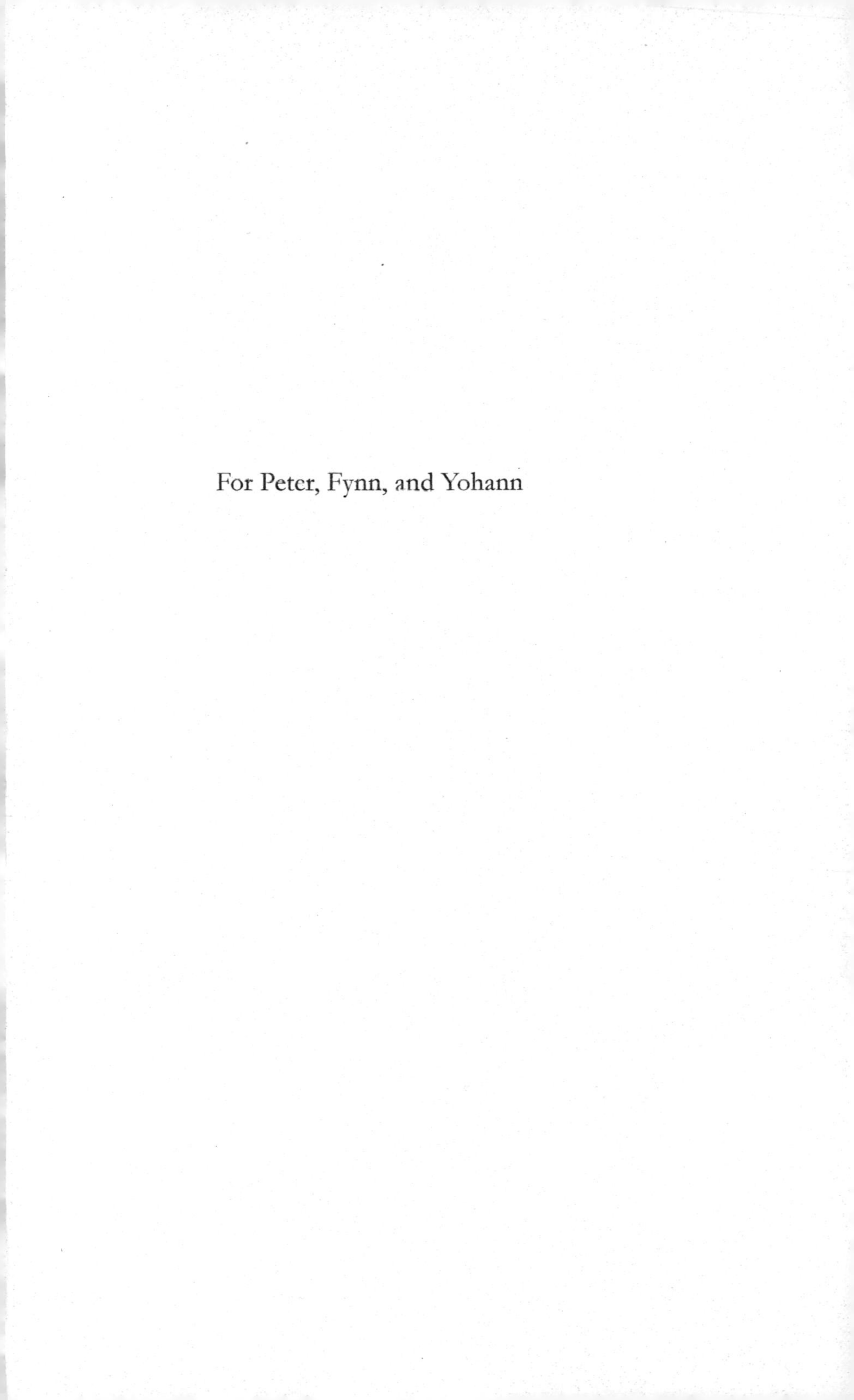

For Peter, Fynn, and Yohann

So much is unfolding that must
complete its gesture,

so much is in bud.

- Denise Levertov

The human ear can hear a sound wave as low as 20 hertz, the lowest pedal on a pipe organ, or pick up a pitch as high as 20,000 hertz, a soprano singer's C7. This might be the problem: I don't speak in your range.

If I say: the world can give you more than it should, do you hear me?

Or: the air will become so sluggish, so hot and heavy, clogged with pollution, eyes watering, burning, a constant cough, constant sickness, malaria, dengue, cholera.

Or: the sunlight filters through a green oak leaf on a hot June day, revealing an inner map of light green veins that lead to another shade of green, one that speaks to something deep inside, something that only green soothes.

Or: in the west, the land is so dry, the cracks scribbled in dirt spell the word "desperation."

Or ask: what do you care about?

Or: you will miss everything, always, painfully.

Or: what do you owe an egret? A jaguar?

Do any of those words spring up and flame? Maybe I need to say something comforting so you relax, and the words slip in like beautiful music. I've heard humans can't stare directly at it; it's like looking at the sun. How about, Once upon a time, a man and a woman had a child. They lived in a little house with a stone fireplace and a yard filled with Queen Anne's lace. Then one day, something terrible happened.

I've been trying to speak to you for years, and despite wildfires, droughts, and floods, I haven't gotten through. I know it's enormous and terrifying, and I wish I could think about dirt and new leaves sprouting, horses galloping in open fields, and spiderwebs woven in a rickety fence. Such fragility in all this wonder. For you, there are infinite ways to fill your ears, with melody and money, loneliness and love and envy. Stories, so many stories, you stuff your ears with romance, affairs, falsehoods, jokes, trivia, and mysterious struggles between humans. Amazing what the human ear attends to—and what the ear is flush with swims through the brain like a fish, or so I imagine.

The other day, I heard someone say, *Nature will have the last laugh*, but I don't want it. We're enmeshed, we always have been, tightly knitted together whether you like it or not. Our lots are cast together, and as things have become more urgent, we've become even more entangled, fine threads connecting us, billions of them. I'm not sure what to do because the alarm bell is ringing. Do you hear it? I know the sound waves are in your frequency.

What you listen to matters because each sound creates a visible pattern. Note A's pattern, for instance, is distinct from D minor's, which is different from C's. Like matchless snowflakes. And, most astonishingly, sound waves can change matter, water, blood, salt, oil, and fire. Like wind blowing waves in sand.

Maybe other voices are needed: human voices, a chorus, a concerto of joy and terror, hope and despair and pleasure. Someone honey-mouthed and persistent, someone full of sorrow, uttering the words "catastrophe" and "cataclysmic"; a voice angst-ridden and hopeful. Others scrambling to escape the despair of being human, another self-absorbed and, surprisingly, attuned to others, someone who loves freely and deeply anything that isn't human. Maybe these other voices will have sound waves you can hear; maybe they'll rearrange you.

Hello? Hello? Tell me, can you hear me?

Please, climb down the stairs and open the door.

On the Brink

I've been thinking about Eleanor for many years because she's someone I think I understand. She's sunk into the mood I'm in. There she is, standing at her mailbox, looking through her stack of mail, not seeing anything worthwhile, only bills and flimsy fliers, until at the bottom of the pile her fingers find an envelope of high-quality paper. She's in her front yard, and at this time of day the neighborhood is quiet, with those who had to head to work leaving long ago and only older people and women with small children in strollers passing by. At least she lives in a place with beautiful trees, so when she steps outside her mood lifts slightly, with the trees and green opening her up.

When she sees who the letter is from, she's sure it's a plea for money, and she'll gladly give as she does for every environmental group. Over the years, as the government has cut back on environmental protections, their requests have become more desperate, and her motivation to give has intensified. She recently revised her will, allocating the proceeds from her house to five such organizations.

But it isn't an appeal for money. As she reads the letter, her heart flutters like a bird spreading its wings, preparing to soar, and it does soar; flying high to the tops of the trees, reaching the puffy clouds, darting, diving, spiraling, but then, as if it's been shot, it falls to the ground with a thud. It takes a moment to realize her phone is ringing in her pocket. She glances at the screen—her daughter.

There is a confusion of noise and static. Ava is probably rushing from her office to the classroom, crossing the crowded university plaza. "Mom! I just saw the news. Congratulations!"

Of course Ava knows. In this age of information, everything is instantly known; it is an intoxication, this insatiable desire to know. If Eleanor checks her computer, she'll most likely find an email about this, and perhaps a press release has already been sent to the newspapers.

"It's probably the first time they've honored an environmental economist," says Ava.

Eleanor folds the letter and shoves it back into the envelope.

"It's such an incredible honor," says Ava.

The wind picks up and knocks down a handful of Japanese maple leaves, a flurry of red in the air. She'll have to rake soon, she thinks. A baby cries, followed by a mother's soothing voice, and Eleanor closes her tired eyes.

"Sure," says Eleanor.

"You don't sound very excited."

Eleanor used to fantasize about this moment, this very letter, and even imagined what she'd wear to the awards ceremony: a forest-green dress, sleeveless, with a scooped neck. But Arthur died, and her work unraveled, with fewer companies interested in her views on sustainability, and the earth tipped closer to the point of no return, and she slid into a different vantage point where the collective mind is deranged. Gloom has crowded into her being and made itself at home. Amidst the rubble is her dream, which the letter now hands her, the Goldman Environmental Prize.

"I guess I'm not excited," says Eleanor.

"What are you talking about?" Ava's voice pitches high with incredulity.

Eleanor heads down the stone path to her front door, where her dog, Blue, is waiting for her, tail wagging. She pauses and watches an egret pass over the neighbor's roof, white and enormous. She once saw a pair of egrets fight in midair. Inside, her house looks like it's fallen into a torpor, with the deep shadows from the oak and birch trees and her realization that life is not what you dream.

"Empty. There's an emptiness to it."

"No, it's something," says Ava. "It's the Green Nobel Prize. I called Ed and told him that I'm calling everyone I know."

Despite her fifty years of work trying to convince corporations that so-called external costs are, in fact, not external at all, despite endless meetings with CEOs and government officials explaining if they don't move to zero-carbon emissions operations, their company will go bankrupt, despite it all, her work has not averted what she most feared. She's seventy years old, and the world is precisely positioned where she worked all those years to avoid. Growing old has brought the inevitable, the body working furiously at demolition; she knew she would not escape that. But she wasn't prepared to experience it at the same time as the planet's demise. It was never her future because in her future, in her imagination, her work counted. Her life—what she devoted herself to endlessly—counted.

"We're on the brink, love," says Eleanor. She closes the front door and sets the mail on the front hall table.

"You just need to let this sink in," says Ava. "You used to say if you won this, you'd have more access to the corporate bigwigs. You'd get more done."

Ava, with her photographic memory. When she was a little girl, she suffered a series of frightening seizures, limbs shaking uncontrollably, eyelids fluttering rapidly, eyes rolling back. The doctor said she'd outgrow the episodes, and she did, but Eleanor always suspected it changed her brain somehow. Ava has the uncanny ability to remember the most minute, mundane detail. No one else in the family has such a skill. The things she remembers—what gifts she received for her birthday five years ago, seven years ago, ten; what her brother promised he'd do and never did; and what they did for July Fourth when she was thirteen.

Eleanor sighs, and Blue flops to the floor, picking up her mood. The house smells of coffee and toast, a hint of dust. On the front table is a catalog of colorful, expensive clothes. If she opened the kitchen window, she might coax the scent of honeysuckle to come inside. "That was a long time ago," she says, "and now everything is in bad shape."

She will not mention the bad shape of her mind, the ever-present sense of dread. How it makes her feel older than her age.

And she doesn't need to tell Ava, a professor of microbiology, the kind of shape the Earth is in, though Eleanor finds herself mentally ticking off the horrific details—up to 150 species lost per day; with global temperatures rising about 1.8 degrees Fahrenheit, the global sea level rising six to eight inches in the last century. Enough. No need to speak of it because everyone has heard it too often and tunes it out. Or goes numb or scrambles for a distraction. The litany of the catastrophic has turned into a tired old story, the meaning dried out, moth-eaten. But she can't help thinking—here's the punch to her gut—all of it could have been avoided.

"No one declines this award," says Ava in a deadpan voice. "It would be a slap in their face."

"You're right," says Eleanor. She sits on the floor and puts her head in her hands. Blue comes over and rests his chin on her thigh. Her pants hike up, and she sees pale blue veins stretched taut over her bony ankles, a map of old. "But I can't in good conscience accept it."

A stunned silence. "The prize comes with significant money."

Eleanor pets Blue's squarish head. "I don't want the money."

In the long awkward silence that follows, Eleanor wonders if Ava was counting on the money, at least a fraction of it. If so, Ava must be recalibrating all the things she will not be able to do or buy, the places she was planning to travel to—probably Berlin, which she loves, or Russia, where her husband was born—because there won't be any award money.

If she thought Ava truly needed money, Eleanor would take out a second mortgage, or she'd sell her house and move to something smaller. Ava, her brilliant daughter with her wispy blond ringlets, thanks to Arthur, and thanks to Eleanor her tall, wiry, boyish frame, and sharp points of cheekbones and chin, her soft, loose-lipped mouth; Ava, her firstborn, who, like a bloodhound, sniffs out inconsistencies in logic. But Ava doesn't need money. She's a professor at Stanford, and her husband teaches Russian literature. They earn enough to have a very comfortable life. Her son, too, is doing well as a professional dancer with the San Francisco Ballet. It's what he always wanted. And Eleanor's wants and needs are slim and becoming slimmer by the day.

"You're not thinking straight," Ava says flatly.

It's probably true. Her sluggish thoughts made so by despair. Did she even make coffee yet? Eat anything? Eleanor is aware of her heart beating fast like a trapped, anxious animal clawing to escape. Her daughter lately seems to view Eleanor as not so quick. Ava's concern about Eleanor traveling to Vietnam last summer, that pointed question: are you sure you can handle such a long flight? Followed by a flurry of other nervous inquiries: Where will you stay? You're going alone? Is that wise? As if Eleanor had never flown before, as if she'd never flown for her work to Vietnam, or Cambodia, Indonesia, Japan, Botswana, or South Africa, alone. As if all of that has vanished; and in some ways, it has.

Eleanor gets up and begins to walk the halls of her house, with Blue, her loyal black lab tapping the floorboards behind her, passing through the threshold of her study, back down the hall to the sunlit living room, the kitchen, and the front entrance. Their house, hers and Arthur's, where they spent their long marriage. She stops and looks out the window. The light shines brightly on the rhododendron leaves and an empty plastic cup sits in the gutter. It's true: some have a wonderful dream that they never accomplish. "But see, if I accept it, I'll have to give a speech."

"It's usually the way these things work."

"But I don't have anything to say. At least nothing anyone wants to hear."

There are days she can barely speak, her voice wheezy and faint. Where did she go wrong? What approach should she have taken? How come her work has come to nothing? Her throat tightens, clamping down her next words because she refuses—a rule she gave herself long ago—to burden her children with her inner angst, her vulnerabilities and fears. Lately, the slightest thing—the squawk of a scrub jay with the faint pink of its beak; the air all over Fort Funston, heavy with the sea's brine and seaweed; the morning glories, the lovely light in their center like a slow secret—makes her weepy. A mix of deep pleasure and deep sorrow. Somehow, to receive this prize now feels like a cruel joke. Absurd. The letter seems to have loosened something inside because before she can stop herself, she says, "I feel like a failure."

"Oh, Mom," says Ava.

Eleanor can hear the puzzlement and exasperation and hint of concern in her daughter's voice.

Eleanor steadies her voice. "I'll be fine."

Ava says she must head into the classroom but will call after she finishes teaching. This semester, in addition to Microbiology and Introduction to Biology, she is teaching a new class on Fertility and Technology. If she had a different disposition, Ava said she would teach elementary school and rekindle the children's philosophical and scientific minds. As toddlers, they ask why, why, why? But as they grow up, something goes haywire, and the philosopher/scientist is murdered. Ava's use of the word is intentional. She means to alarm, Eleanor knows, because it is alarming. Today's education system is about 200 years old and designed to churn out obedient, docile, punctual factory workers. Obscenely, devastatingly obsolete. What is needed are thinkers, questioners, visionaries, and leaders who can forge a path out of this mess.

The silence in the house stabs her. The tick of the clock sounds foreboding. A fatality to the space. She should get outside before she ends up with bad thoughts clamoring, persecuting. She hunts for Blue's leash and grabs her old *Economist* and the *New York Times* to drop off at her neighbor's house. Ilana, who is older than Eleanor and wasn't feeling well yesterday, is also a widow. Eleanor will bring her a bowl of vegetable stew and maybe a little gift. "You're a relentless gift giver, aren't you?" Ilana said the other day, smiling as she donned Eleanor's handknit pink scarf. "I'm the lucky recipient."

The phone rings again.

"I've only got a second," says Ava breathlessly. "Don't accept it."

A past Goldman prize recipient was murdered for his work to stop old-growth logging in Mexico. And the Honduran activist Berta Cáceres, another prize recipient, was murdered. She helped stop the building of a dam along the Gualcarque River. Gunned down.

"I'm the policy wonk, not the person on the front lines," says Eleanor. "They're the true environmental heroes putting their lives at risk."

"It's not true. He did policy work too."

After all these years, why does she continue to be alarmed at the forces working against nature? The forces willing to kill another human being, for profit, for established systems, for what's called progress? Despite her knowledge, she feels as if a bulldozer rolled over her again.

After stopping by Ilana's and the corner grocery store to buy eggs and bread, and for Ilana, her favorite bar of dark chocolate, Eleanor hears again from Ava, who says she's analyzed the pros and cons of accepting the prize, and now she thinks it's imperative that Eleanor accept it. "It's the most prudent thing to do," she says.

Eleanor cringes, hearing her own words thrown back at her. She's to blame for her daughter's pragmatic, realpolitik style. Over the years at the dinner table, Eleanor told stories about traveling to meet with CEOs dressed in dark suits and starched, blindingly white shirts, glancing at their expensive watches as if they held the answers. Eleanor perched on a leather chair, calmly showing them that their bottom line is inextricably linked to clean water, clean air, and the natural weather cycle. Eleanor would explain to her family, "You can't appeal to their emotions or the concept of public good or morality. You need to show them it's in their self-interest. A straightforward utilitarian, pragmatic approach—this benefits you—with valid premises and conclusions. That's how they're trained to think."

"Un-train them," said Arthur. "Assumptions can be brought to the conscious mind."

"That's your job as a therapist," said Eleanor. "My job is to recognize what's there and work with it. I have to play in their playground, and slowly, maybe, they'll find a new way to see things, such as the common good, but I can't worry about that. Above all, I can't become hysterical or too emotional." She directed this last declaration at her daughter. "As a woman, you've got to be the most level-headed, reasonable person in the room, or they'll discount you. No tears, no hysteria, no heightened emotion, no screeching, or they won't hear a word you say."

Eleanor has made up her mind. She won't accept the award. But she knows herself too well, so she's not sure this decision will stick beyond an hour. She's always played the role of mediator, the one who finds middle ground so everyone, the corporations and the environmentalists, can get along and something is accomplished. If she refuses the prize, she'll undoubtedly cause a scene, and tempers will flair, along with incredulity and disbelief. Just imagining this makes her uncomfortable. She doesn't want to argue anymore with her daughter, though there is an urge, new and foreign, to sob and tell Ava that her heart hurts because this award has, ironically, made more poignant all that has been lost.

"Okay, I'll think about it," says Eleanor.

Fortunately, she forgot to buy coffee, which gives her a reason to leash up Blue again and head outside. Soon she finds herself heading not to the grocery store but to Union Street because she wants to hear people chatting as if everything is fine. She wants to walk by the soapbark trees and let them wave their branches at her. Blue stops in front of a store and sniffs the dirt around a boxwood bush, and she looks in at the store's window display of golden slippers. She likes shoes and clothes. She owns an $800 camel-colored coat because she fell in love with the lines and soft fabric, and she couldn't leave Freda Salvador's shoe shop without a pair of long black leather boots. Nor did she let her hair go gray or cut it short. It's shoulder length, ginger-colored with a natural wave to it, because, she told Arthur, I don't want to look in the damn mirror and be frightened and baffled: how could this be me?

She passes by people eating big bowls of ramen at little round tables. A girl is making a tower of sugar cubes. People are digging through the cardboard box of dollar paperbacks outside Moe's Bookshop. A woman says she's looking for a book with "Turbulence" in the title. Her male companion laughs. Everything is happening around her; she's in the world, but it feels like it's withdrawn from her, turned its back on her. Her irrelevance is astonishing. It sends a shiver over her scalp, into her bones. Her friend Sid lives close by, so in a last-ditch effort at buoyancy, she dials his number and invites him for coffee.

"Thank god you called," he says. "I need a break from my painting. It's not working at all, and god knows where Miriam went."

She tells him to come out of his turpentine-scented flat.

"You're fabulous," he says. "I love you."

She is relieved because she doesn't want to head home to their lovely Victorian on Green Street, a home she and Arthur bought in the 1970s when things were still affordable in San Francisco. Some days, like today and yesterday and the day before that, on and on, it feels like an empty old box.

After her mother died, her father never remarried. Instead, he adopted, of all things, a zebra. They lived in an old house in Gig Harbor, Washington, with twenty-five acres and a cavernous red barn. Her dad, a financial adviser, somehow heard that the Woodland Park Zoo didn't want the zebra anymore, so without telling Eleanor or her sister, he drove the pickup truck to Seattle and returned with the zebra named William. Eleanor thought nothing of it as a girl. One day, there was a zebra in the barn when she went out to feed her pony, Daisy. On subsequent days, she'd go to the barn and there would be her father, brushing William. When she looks back on it, she marvels at this; her father was a reasonable, rational man, immersed in the world of stocks and bonds, interest rates and asset allocation. Adopting a zebra was so out of character. How did he know to do this? How did he know that stepping out of himself, out of his way, was the exact right thing to do?

At the coffee shop Sid talks about his ugly painting, how he thought he was painting the ocean, full of blues and whites and silver, but at the last second he found he was holding a brush full of red paint, and now there's a big red streak through it all.

He is flamboyant compared to her, with his purple velvet blazer, a red kerchief around his neck, and his great pompadour of silvery hair. Though older than she is, he is vibrant with his big gestures that take up significant space. To her, he seems to be made of a different substance, more alive and intuitive and spontaneous and effusive. He reminds her of Arthur's father, who was French and wept at movies, wept at the end of a good book, wept when he hadn't seen Arthur for months. He called Eleanor an intelligent, beautiful woman, and his son was eminently fortunate to have such a companion for life. He lived in Fontainebleau, a small town outside of Paris. When he died, Eleanor felt as if the possibilities for humankind became that much poorer.

Like Arthur, Sid is not concerned about decorum or social norms. She's known him for fifteen years and has always been attracted to him, though not sexually, because he is so different from her. And today, he is a respite from her worries about the Goldman prize and the ruinous state of the world.

"What do you think it means?" Eleanor says.

"Oh, who the hell knows. It's a crack," he says, smiling playfully. "I've cracked up. I'm headed for the looney bin. Look out."

"I'll join you," she says.

They laugh and the ripples fill the air.

"Really, I hate my painting now," he says. "Ugly as shit."

She tells him the red streak makes her think of a gash and that it absolutely should be there because it will make people see what it would be like if it all vanished.

"Oh god," he says. He no longer reads the newspaper because it's too much. At seventy-nine, all he wants to do is paint. "It makes me want to cry."

"Me too," she says, her eyes watering.

"We're softhearted."

"I am only around you," she says. For everyone else, she's steady and sturdy, weathering whatever comes her way, the one to keep a calm mind and forge a solution. Even Arthur saw her this way, in part because she kept him out of her inner tumult until she could put it into well-formed sentences. He had enough going on with his troubled patients.

On the walls are a series of watercolors of nude women. The women are stretched out on couches and rugs, or standing, half turned, leaving little for the imagination, utterly exposed. Pink skin, brown skin, olive, Eleanor imagines them all wearing golden slippers.

When she tells him about the award, he claps his hands, and his face brightens and widens; he is truly happy for her. For a moment she feels pleasure in seeing his pleasure. "Oh, sweetie, that's wonderful!" His expression quickly rearranges into concern. "But," he says, "what?"

"My entire life—look where we are."

Last week, she found out that all the work she did with the Bardone Corporation in Brazil to stop the deforestation of the Amazon has been wiped out. Bardone was bought by another company that refuses to meet with her, with anyone, and is busy chopping down the palms—the *Euterpe precatoria*—at an obscene rate in order to plant single cash crops—coffee, tea, cacao, soybeans, and bananas. At least five other companies in Brazil are also cutting down the trees. And so the water from the rainforest will no longer be enough, which means the people and businesses in São Paulo are seeing their reservoirs dry up. "The Amazon rainforest was once the flying river," she says. "Now it's a listless dribble."

She picks up her coffee, her hand trembling. "And the gorillas. The work I did with my colleagues in the Congo to set up eco-tourism." She stops, tries to gather herself. "With the war, the endless war, the gorillas and the park rangers who protect them...two more gorillas were shot last week."

"It's awful."

She stares at her empty coffee cup, with glued-on coffee grounds at the bottom. "Awfulness clumps together. One awful thing stirs awake another and another. Only when that energy runs out does the good stir awake and clump together. I've always seen that pattern. An expansion, a contraction. It's a rhythm. Right now, it's awfulness, a contraction. This award is coming during a string of awful events. It's not happening at the right time, it's not a good thing, at least that's what my gut tells me."

Sid tells her he went through eleven months in the state she's in now when one painting after another no longer fed him. It was like eating dirt. He was dried up inside, but he couldn't find anything that made him feel alive. He ate too much, drank too much. Drank a lot, in fact. Slept. When he looks back on it, he sees it as severe depression. At the ugly rock bottom of it, he thought about taking his life. He couldn't have planned how he climbed out of the awful clump. It was so stunningly unexpected. He saw a tiny painting, about the size of his palm, the barest outline of a nude female, almost like a drawing done by a child. "I stood there for the longest time, thinking the lines captured everything, the curves, the softness, the strength, just enough to invite the imagination without being overbearing. There, but not all there, like looking at the remnants of an old broken sculpture. I felt the intense urge to rush home and draw. Oh, it was so beautiful! To want to create again. An expansion, as you say. I wanted to make something like that little painting, a suggestion, a hint, with a wide opening for the viewer to step in.

I understood my paintings had gotten too loud, and I needed to quiet down, to leave space."

The waiter refills their cups. She can't remember when she was too loud or overbearing. If anything, she's been too restrained, too silent, so damn polite. The reasonable, rational, level-headed Eleanor, Arthur would jokingly call her.

"Maybe you accept the award, and it stirs the good clump awake," he says.

"It never works that way."

"It's worth a try." He turns serious. "I think Arthur would say the same thing. Don't go too far down the hole. I had Miriam nagging me all the time. Come on, put the bottle away. Get up, take out the garbage. I hated her for that and loved her for it, but you—"

"I'm stumbling around with Blue following me, wondering what the hell is going on. I don't know where I'd be if I didn't have Blue."

"I wish Arthur were still here." He holds both her hands. "I'll be there as much as I can." He looks intensely into her eyes. "Have you had those awful thoughts?"

She knows what he's asking and what he can't bring himself to say, what she can't say. She won't tell him that six months ago, a well-known environmentalist jumped off the Golden Gate Bridge. A man in his fifties, he drowned in his immense grief. His suicide note said his early death exemplified what humans were doing to the earth.

"At times, I feel I'm just taking up space on this exhausted planet," she says.

"You have to call me."

"In the middle of the night?"

"Yes. I'll come over."

"And Miriam?"

"She loves you, I love you, and we don't want anything bad to happen to you."

She pulls her hands into her lap, and he studies her as if

trying to think of the right thing to say, but it's impossible.

"There's something new about you," he says. "I don't know. Frail maybe. Shaky. Please call me."

She consents, but she can't imagine calling him at four in the morning when all thoughts spin around dread.

When she gets home, she finds the Goldman Environmental Foundation has left four messages: Did she get the letter? Can she please call? They are so happy to honor her work. Could she please call soon? Each time the tone becomes more desperate, urgent, bewildered. A couple of newspaper reporters left messages, wanting a quote. Two calls from Ava, chiding her to accept the prize, and Eleanor can hear the angry words rumbling underneath: act like an adult, for god's sake.

Why the hell is she doing this? She doesn't want to draw attention to herself like this; she has no interest in upsetting the foundation's mission or good intentions. Not by choice was she one of only two women in her economics class at Harvard, and the only woman in her PhD program who combined economics and environmental science, a combination that at the time was viewed with so much suspicion, incomprehension, and ridicule. It took months to find a professor to sponsor her. Professor Madeline Burns. Eleanor is forever grateful for Madeline's courage and tenacity, standing up to her colleagues to support Eleanor's unusual PhD.

She steps outside. The lavender sways lazily. She moves deeper into her garden and smells basil. All the greens are bright in the soft sun. The white table under the tree glows. She watches a squirrel make an extraordinary leap from one branch to another, then the squirrel stops and looks at her to see if she saw the amazing feat. "I saw it," she says. As a scientist, she was counseled against anthropomorphizing nature. She followed the rules, until she couldn't any longer. She felt it promoted human exceptionalism, and she was done with that. She sits in the wicker chair, the squirrel chatters, and the oak tree sings with the wind. The idea seems to come from the tree, fully formed. She calls her friend Greg at Greenpeace. "What would you do with $200,000?"

He laughs his big belly laugh, though he's as skinny as a sapling, all bony architecture. "Oh, Eleanor, you know us, we'd have a hell of a party."

Something lightens inside. She picks up the letter. "Are you in an awful time or a good time?"

Blue is stretched out on his side in a patch of sun, snoring. He's always been a sun seeker.

"We always know how to have a good time. In the best of times, in the worst of times, we have a good time."

She puts the letter down. "I like you, Greg. Have I ever told you that?"

"Yep, and the feeling is mutual. Whatever you got going on, I'm all for it. We're game, aways game. Keep me in the loop."

For a long time, she listens to the sounds of the neighborhood, a motorcycle's engine like a pulse in her body, the moan of a siren, the wind fingering branches. If she could hide in the garden, withdraw into these pleasures. Look at the ancient oak tree, bursting the two planks of the back fence, its will to live expansively.

When the phone rings again and she sees it's the Goldman Environmental Foundation, she answers and tells the board president that she received the letter, yes, the phone calls, and she's honored to be a recipient.

"We're so pleased," says the president. "You've had a huge impact."

She bites her tongue. "Thank you." There will be an awards ceremony, and she'll give a speech, says the board president. Everyone is excited to hear what she has to say.

She looks for the squirrel, but it's gone. A car door slams shut, the growl of an engine. She pinches the hem of her shirt and says nothing, though she feels she's conceded something that she may regret.

He asks for a list of guests whom she'd like to invite, and

Eleanor includes, in addition to her children, Sid and his wife, because she'll need the support. As soon as she hangs up, she wants to call back and say she's made the wrong decision. It seems in a moment, the doorbell rings, and a young man is at the front door, holding a bouquet of twelve red roses. From the Goldman Environmental Board. "Congratulations!" says the card.

When Ava calls again, Eleanor tells her the news, and her daughter says, "I'm thrilled for you." She'll drive Eleanor to the event, then to the celebratory dinner. "And, I have a surprise," she says. "I invited your sister."

"Hazel?" says Eleanor. She looks at the roses on the kitchen table, and for a moment her vision blurs, and they look like an ominous red blob. "You did? You invited her before you knew I'd agree to this?"

Eleanor begins to pace the room, fuming; how could she? How could Ava do that? Hazel, who lives in Tanzania and gave herself to God years ago. Hazel, who is now called Sister Maria. Her sister took their father's refrain and ran with it, that's one way to look at it—"you can be anything, do anything"—though their father hardly meant become a missionary. When Hazel renounced the material world, she included him and his advice that she was making a big mistake. He told her she'd never know the joy of marriage, a rich, deep connection with another human, the immense joy of children. "Hazel, think of life as a big table filled with food from around the world, and you," said her father, "you're choosing the small table in the corner, with a slice of dry toast and a bowl of weak broth. I'm trying to give you a different perspective, from my fifty-nine years." That was when Hazel told him he didn't understand her, not one iota, and she refused to discuss her decision with him anymore. When she left, she cut off all contact. Over the years, she's barely kept in touch with Eleanor, and Eleanor guessed it was because she was inextricably linked to their father and the life Hazel left behind, the one she discarded.

The missionary life must have become too arduous because

a decade ago, Hazel joined a church in Tanzania, which runs a small school, a pharmacy, and church services. The last letter Eleanor received from Hazel included a description of her life. Up at five a.m. for prayers and then kitchen work and then to the garden and then to the classroom to teach kindergarten, then more prayers, more work, cleaning, scrubbing, preparing, then prayers at night. The church opens its doors on Sunday for a service for the locals, and Saturday is spent preparing for that.

"It's a once-in-a-lifetime award," says Ava. "I wasn't going to stand by and let you refuse it. And Hazel wants to attend. It's been far too long since she saw you."

Ava probably said these exact words to Hazel to get her on a plane. Her daughter, her PR manager, promoting Eleanor to her sister to rally her to travel halfway around the world. Her daughter, who, for whatever reason, thinks she knows what's best for Eleanor. Mothering her, but a suffocating mother.

Poor Hazel, who surely didn't want to come, who told Eleanor that she shouldn't bother contacting her, who recited Biblical verses liberally and often, who didn't even fly home for their father's funeral. Their father died regretting the tumultuous nature of his relationship with Hazel. How distraught he was in the hospital; their father kept looking at the entrance to his room, hoping Hazel would show up because, he told Eleanor, one wants to die with a peaceful heart. He wanted to apologize. Eleanor did call Hazel, but the nun who took the call said Hazel, Sister Marie, was out in the field, and she'd convey the message.

Eleanor is still angry about this. She read one short novel, *Mariette in Ecstasy* by Ron Hansen, which helped her imagine Hazel's life—a passionate love for Jesus, bordering on eroticism, the material world be damned.

She can't imagine playing host to her sister in the state she's in. What about those hours when she is so drained of energy she just sits in a chair, staring out the window? Ensnared in a suffocating gloom? Or those states where she can't sit still, trying to ward off despair?

She stares out the living room window, looking at the shadows as the day trickles away. Maybe Hazel will understand her situation. Maybe she's gone through a similar time. Eleanor reminds herself to stay open, to let whatever her sister has become fill it. Still, Eleanor senses she'll have to swallow so many words—at the awards ceremony and now with her sister.

Night knows how to swallow things too. I'm envious of night, how it seeps in like a leaky black pen bleeding on a white shirt, snatching the edges, smearing where one thing begins and another thing ends. Night and I, we are the oldest of friends, all the way back to the beginning. It moves up from the ground, fusing trees, bushes, and bodies. As it inks the sky, night reveals a great truth. Edges, boundaries, separation, they exist, but the fragmentation is contained in something bigger and that is wholeness. Like Sid's painting—there's the crack of red, but it's held in the bigger painting.

How night makes the Pacific Ocean boundless, mirroring the boundless sky. How the moon comes out, brushing the ocean with silvery white. With daylight out of the way—and don't think for a second that those two don't need each other—night licks the forest and acres of fields and the little houses on hills and the pot of pansies on the porch. Night's dew dripping down green stems.

During the night the plants get busy doing math, dividing their storage of starch by the hours of the night, so they keep growing because life is for living before there is dying. Look at the evening primrose and the casa blanca lily in the dark, spreading their petals like white and yellow fingers. The night-blooming jasmine opens herself up and gives the air a pretty scent.

What I'm really jealous about is night's voice. Wake now, whispers night, its lips pressed to the big ears of bats clinging upside down under bridges and eaves. Wake now, and the bats blink open their eyes and fly webbed-winged into the dark platter of sky. The owl heard night's whisper the first time; the sound is the color of dark that ruffles feathers. Before the hunt, the owl makes silent parabolas because pleasure is a sort of prayer, and it knows how much night enjoys the way it silently soars.

The earth spins; night becomes denser, black on black; and a hush falls over one side of the earth. Words festering in the corners, shoved aside for another time, night says tenderly, it's all right, don't be afraid, let me hold them. Night coaxes and consoles, gathering up the shoved-aside words because it can take it. What have you denied? What losses have you suffered? In a dream, or with their guard down and vulnerable, people begin to speak from the deep cave of themselves: I'm so sad, so lonely, so frightened. Go on, night urges. I love you, I hate you, how could you, how could you not? Please, another chance, one more.

The terrifying rawness of words is what I wait to hear because that's where it begins, because fear, if never spoken, festers, and hardens into denial. It paralyzes or turns to violence. Nothing gets done and faces turn to the wall and we get nowhere.

Bargain

The tall wall of baby pictures has cast a weird magical spell over Ava, and she can't stop staring at it. She tries to look at the doctor, but the babies, over 300 babies, babies sleeping, babies smiling, alert, drowsy, babies with faces like grouchy old men, red and wrinkled, mouths open. Babies calm and composed, with perfectly shaped round heads, bald and glistening like cups of cream. Babies dressed in soft pink, in soft blue, babies with ink-black hair at least an inch long—all that energy and cell division allocated to create magnificent hair.

What yanks Ava away from the babies and to the fertility doctor are the words "Really, you're ideal candidates."

Dr. Harrington's voice is reassuring, a chipper voice that says they have two options: One—the hormonal path to induce Ava to ovulate multiple eggs, which would be used in an IVF cycle. Two—donor eggs. For both options, the technology is highly advanced. In the twenty years she's been working in this field, she's seen incredible leaps in precision and efficacy. In the past, they implanted four fertilized eggs and hoped only one would take, if you can imagine that. So many twins were born during that era, and, thinks Ava, so many frazzled parents stumbling out of the dark, deep mine of home and pushing double strollers like a lawn mower, mowing down people in their path. Now they implant only one fertilized egg, the best egg. Yes, they can determine that, the one most likely to thrive. Isn't that amazing? Ava rigorously nods. Dr. Harrington pushes her blond hair behind her ears. Remarkable, cutting edge, couples who gave up hope now have a real chance at making a family.

"You, as a doctor, Nelson, and you, Ava, as a scientist, can appreciate the advances of technology. We've come so far."

"It's fascinating," says Ava.

Ava won't mention that she spent an entire hour watching

and re-watching a two-minute video of intracytoplasmic sperm injection and another hour glued to the first hundred hours of an embryo's development to the blastocyst stage. One cell becoming two, the nucleus dividing into new nuclei, the newly formed cells bubbling and wriggling to separate from each other and begin the process over and over. Then, more and more cells dividing and churning like boiling water. Ava envied the powerful microscope.

Nelson reaches for Ava's hand and squeezes. She looks at him and smiles. His high rosy coloring, his big voice and big expressive eyes, he's such a good man; he adores her, loves her; and with his playfulness, he has a way of putting her and the rest of the world at ease. But after two years of trying to get pregnant, of agony and frustration, their only concrete achievement—let's be honest—is demolishing the pleasure of sex and reducing it to a reproductive act, with charts and temperature checks and urgent phone calls—hurry home, now!

They took a break from the craziness and settled into their work, and it was working for a good five months, a stretch of calm, but the desire for a baby ambushed them again, tearing down whatever they'd managed to build. So last week, they went to the doctor for blood work, which confirmed what they suspected but didn't want to face. Nelson has a low sperm count, and she has poor egg quality and quantity. A double whammy, but Ava was ebullient it wasn't all her fault. Not unusual at all, Dr. Harrington assured them, one in eight couples have trouble getting pregnant. But for Ava, the doctor's reassurances didn't assuage or normalize their situation. In their thirties, they're both healthy; the reasons for their "hostile reproductive environments" are idiopathic, as are so many things in the world.

"I'm feeling good," says Nelson, smiling big, showing his teeth, which means it's not a performance smile but a real one.

Ava feels it, too, for a moment. "We have solid options."

"I can't guarantee anything," says Dr. Harrington, "but, yes, there are options." The doctor looks at her for another beat as if searching her face to gauge her emotions, but Ava, like her mother, knows how to keep those under wraps. "You probably know this, but poor egg quality means that if the egg is fertilized, there's a higher chance the embryo won't implant, or it might implant, but the embryo doesn't develop properly." The doctor smiles warmly as if trying to soften the news. A cloud of strong perfume wafts over Ava, and she coughs. "Take a look at our egg donor database. We have an extensive screening process and have had great success."

The doctor says she'll order the tests, FSH screening, estradiol screening, and other tests that Ava barely hears because she's in shock, or maybe that's too strong of a word, that she and Nelson are suddenly in this world. They've known it existed, it's been running parallel to their lives, but now they are in it, crouched at the starting block.

They agree to get back to her within the week. Before they leave, the wall of babies casts its magnetic spell again. Staggering—all this life would not exist without the aid of Dr. Harrington, along with research and technology. For so many people, making a baby is the most ordinary act, done thoughtlessly, the result from a night of pleasure, drunkenness, intimacy, and a one-night stand. But for Ava and Nelson, it's become extraordinary, like climbing Mt. Everest. Are they closer to the top? Will they slide down the snowy side? Become buried by an avalanche? She feels like weeping.

They sit in the car in the parking lot.

"How are you feeling?" says Nelson.

"Okay," she says, releasing her ponytail. The car smells of coffee, the dregs in their cups in the cupholders. "No, not okay. I'm frightened to feel hopeful. What if it doesn't work? And I feel like screaming, *Why us*? More work, that's what I'm thinking, and she said there's no guarantee. None. And what does she mean, 'higher chance' the embryo won't implant? We need to find out what chance because 'higher chance' is vague." She feels the scientist that she is kicking into high gear. "You can't make decisions based on incomplete or faulty evidence."

She's heard the tragic stories—couples trying IVF four or

five times, months of injections, even years, gobs of money spent, and the marriage limps along, gasping until it keels over.

"Do we even have enough money to consider an egg donor?" she says. "I mean, $30,000 to $40,000 is a lot."

"We'd have to make sacrifices. We have enough money for one roll of the dice, but we stand a good chance because," he says smiling, "we're lucky."

Lucky? Is he kidding? Sometimes she hates his optimism. She could ask her mother for some of the prize money. How ironic would that be: using that money to add another human to an already depleted, weary earth, an irony she quickly brushes aside because of the furious baby-fever dream that's consumed her brain.

Nelson's eyes are soft, searching. They've been on a wild roller coaster ride, with dramatic ups and stomach-curdling downs, and sometimes the roller coaster leaves the tracks altogether, and they hurl through space.

But options number one and number two may be different sorts of rides, smoother, with an end in a desirable spot. Of course, there's even more irony that they're in this position. Nelson is a pediatric doctor and his days are baby-filled, pudgy, milk-scented babies; he holds them, burps them, and consoles them after a shot. He loves babies. When he comes home, she hugs him and secretly puts her nose to his shirt and breathes in baby.

Dark circles lie under his eyes; his skin has a gray tint. It's easy to think of him as solid, dependable, and capable, but he's as vulnerable as she is. She's overcome with tenderness for him and kisses his cheek.

"I love you, whether we do this or don't do this," he says. "You know that, don't you?"

"I do."

He smiles and winks at her. "Did you just agree to marry me?"

She laughs.

He takes her hand and kisses each knuckle. "I do, I do, I

do." When he's done, he looks at her again. "Should we put adoption back on the table to make things even more agonizing and complicated?"

The last round of adoption discussions ended when their therapist friend told them about a couple he was treating. They adopted a child from Mexico, and the boy, now seventeen, has been diagnosed with severe schizophrenia. The couple doesn't know what to do—he needs full-time care, they don't have the money, etc. Nelson has a sister who is bipolar, and the family crumbled under the weight of it, his parents divorcing when he was a teen.

"No," she says.

It's 8:30 a.m., and they no longer have time to discuss this. They both have to get to work, so they agree to talk tonight. Throughout, Nelson has kept his sense of humor, and for that, as well as many other reasons, she loves him and marvels at his skill at popping the pressure balloon, the exhale of agitated air. He has a buoyance utterly alien to her nature. She imagines him at the office, cracking a joke, and the anxious parent with the sick baby smiles, takes a deep breath, whisking away tight shoulders and neck. Wherever he is, he can widen the container of the moment, so it holds the shock or tragedy, and also humor and sometimes happiness.

She doesn't have this skill. Stress obliterates levity and clarity of thought. And trying and failing to make a baby has made her stressed and gloomy, her mind turning to the negative, the worst that can happen, that is likely to happen—she can see it unfolding so clearly. Married six years, trying to conceive for two, they're exhausted to the bone. What if the IVF doesn't work? Or the egg donor? How much more can they bear before the marriage splits in two?

By 10:30 a.m., thoughts of sperm and eggs and the wall of babies are visiting a faraway country, and Ava is firmly and happily ensconced in the world of the miniature. The lab has no scent,

no mustiness or dust. With a clean slide, she drips a drop of distilled water on the slide, and from a test tube, she adds the bacteria. The magic begins when she slips it under the electron microscope, and the veil hiding the unseen lifts. Though she's seen this thousands of times—eight years of research—a thrill and shiver run through her because she'll never be immune to the shiny miraculous—bacteria chomping on a six-millimeter disc of plastic.

The beauty decenters her. Dr. Harrington thinks she's cornered the market on fascinating, but right here, right on this slide, Ava has her own fascinating. Her mother would love this, at least before her judgment adheres like a hard resin and she says something biting: Why do we keep turning to technology to fix what technology messed up in the first place? How does that make sense? Her mother let that comment slip out when Ava first told her about her research. Nelson was impressed but not blown away like her. He needs humanity, he needs a kid's heartbeat and warm skin.

The oscillating fan fiddles with the photos pinned to the bulletin board, pictures of a mountain of plastic in Thailand—water bottles, soda bottles, containers, diapers, the problem staring right at her. Another photo from Indonesia. New Delhi. A menagerie of the grotesque. Ava found the images and stuck them there for inspiration.

A window is open, letting in an interplay of laughter and voices, along with a loud yet fragmented argument about Shakespeare and his most tragic play. "I want real tragedy," says a male voice. Tragic and astonishing, she thinks, looking at the bacteria. How rapidly it adapted to the garbage dump of plastic, devouring a substance that typically takes 400 to 500 years to decompose. The rhythm of the life cycle: growth, decomposition, rebuild, growth, decomposition, rebuild, on and on.

She runs her other hand along the smooth black epoxy resin countertop, cool to the touch. Everything is clean and orderly. In the wood drawers, she'll find the same: sterile test tubes, wire, slides, and pH testing tape. Every object in the lab is here for a reason, and it calms her. She recognizes the paradox because, despite the order, the experiments are crap shoots. When she was an undergraduate, the experiments were eloquent and worked perfectly, leading to the desired outcome. In graduate school, she entered the unknown, with experiments teasing her, making promises, then grinding to a halt. And now, it's like working at night with no light. But through it all, she's loved science because, unlike many other disciplines, it deals with real problems that need real solutions. And it rewards maniacal curiosity. Curiosity made her pull over, stop at the recycling center on Bayshore Boulevard, and leap out of the car. While Nelson shouted, "What the hell are you doing?" she scooped up a test tube full of sludge. Turned out the stinky mud housed plastic-eating bacteria.

She pins her eye to the microscope again. They're eating, but not fast enough, and that is the next problem. Problem-solution, problem-solution, another rhythm of life. Six weeks to eat a sample PET sheet. There won't be one solution, but many, and hers might be one of them. That's her retort to her mother's objection to using technology to solve a problem created by technology.

The lab door opens and in comes Stan, one of the graduate research assistants. He's slim, boyish looking, with short dark hair. "You're here early," says Ava.

"I changed the temperature and need to check," he says, heading to the storage area.

He's in charge of monitoring and changing the temperature to see if he can coax the bacteria to eat faster; she isolates the ones that eat fastest and from those, cultivates a new batch. A directed evolution.

"Well, 25 degrees Celsius is lousy," says Stan.

Trial and error. She watches the bacteria demolish the plastic. Problem: What is the best way to make a baby? Rule out: the missionary position, the side position, on all fours, so-drunk-barely-able-to-stand, pressed up against a wall, in the shower, at the beach, sand glued to her back. Possible answer: on her back, feet in stirrups, a fertilized egg carefully inserted via a catheter through her vaginal canal into her uterus.

"I'm going to try 24.5," says Stan.

She comes out of her reverie. "Good. No, wait. I think you already ran that temperature."

"You're right," he says.

She'd like to consult her mom, tap into her mother's level-headedness, her intelligence that is a hot streak, about the best way to increase the rate of the bacteria's consumption. She and Ed used to call their mother Ice Queen, her white-blond hair, her voice steady and stripped of emotion, her imperturbable face. She always had a yellow legal pad nearby, if not under her arm, on the table next to her. An image is burned in Ava's brain of her mother diligently jotting down notes while her father sang in the kitchen while cooking dinner. Ed would scream about something, and their mother wouldn't flinch. It drove him crazy. Only when she was older did Ava admire her mother's ability to stay reasonable and calm under immense pressure. Despite her protest, her mother did win significant battles; for years, she stopped the burning and destruction of big swaths of the Amazon rainforest. Her mother was always flying to Brazil and returning with a win. It hits Ava again: her mother won one of the most prestigious environmental awards.

But her mother has been swallowed up by extravagant emotion. The anguish in her voice, an almost devastating nihilistic tone. Ava is surprised how angry it makes her.

"Run two tests," she says to Sam. "24.3 and 24.2."

"Okay," he says.

Maybe she should invite her mother to go hiking. As a family, they'd walk the dirt trails for hours, her mother greeting each tree like a long-time friend. "Ava, look at the buckeye! The fuzzy white flowers filled with nectar are feeding all these butterflies." "Oh, the California bay laurel loves this spot. She's thriving."

"Did you know the Pomo Indians used the lance-shaped leaves to cure headaches?" Ava, too, found that nature gave her handfuls of beauty and the coveted feeling of awe and asked nothing in return except to exist. It was a bargain she couldn't resist. Whenever she's asked how she became interested in science, she credits these hikes, her mother's effusiveness about nature.

She stares out the window and has the urge to have a big lunch today. Stuff herself with a sandwich and cake and strawberries. The sky is clear but the blue seems too blue. Other microbiologists are frantically working on how to speed up the bacteria's consumption, a team in Japan, Germany, and Switzerland. It doesn't help to put pressure on herself, and yet, if she were the one to figure it out, doors would open, more funding, more opportunities. She's identified two enzymes in the bacteria that devour the plastic, a two-step process, like the two sisters who used to whisk into her childhood house and clean it, one sister charging into a room and doing the big stuff—floors, counters, bathtub or sink or stove—and the second sister coming in and tackling the smaller stuff, the molding, the grout, the grime around the sink. Finding these two enzymes was a breakthrough, but everyone working on this has had the same breakthrough, so it's not a breakthrough at all.

At dinner Nelson is full of stories. He glued glow-in-the-dark stars on the ceilings of the exam rooms. A three-year-old girl asked him to turn off the lights, and when he did, she stood, put her hand on her heart, and sang twinkle twinkle little star at the top of her lungs. A boy showed up in a fireman's costume, complete with a plastic fireman's hat, his hair so sweaty it was plastered to his skull like a monk. He kept asking if Nelson had any fires he could put out.

Nelson thinks humans are at their best when they're young—two, three, five, seven, nine years old—not only their innocence but the eager, unmediated desire to connect. The instant smile, the unsolicited story. Of course, there are shy children, but under that shyness, they're trying to figure out how to be with you. They watch Nelson intently as he explains everything he's going to do—this is a stethoscope, and I'm going to listen to your heart. Do you want to listen to your heart? He'll put the stethoscope on the child, and their eyes widen with excitement as the hidden world of the heart is made audible, thud, thud. No one taught him this at medical school; there was never a class on how to relate to children. Her mythic sense of him is that he prefers children to adults and becomes his best self around small humans.

It reminds Ava of the one philosophy class she took as an undergraduate, Introduction to European Philosophy. The professor ended nearly every class with a lament about the modern subject, an invention from The Age of Enlightenment, thanks to Descartes. The "I" in "I think therefore I am," and since the only certain thing was the subject "I," everything else became uncertain, including nature, and, consequently, insignificant. How lonely we've become, her professor would say, how alienated and disconnected from each other and nature.

She deals with the consequence of Descartes's modern subject, the human who has become the most destructive species ever to have evolved in the history of the planet. The human who stingily values the non-human by what it can give the human.

Outside they can hear the bulldozer. Across the street the one-story house is being torn down by the new owners, to be replaced by a two-story house.

"So," says Nelson, spearing his lettuce. "Have you given any thought to our options?"

"I was pretty busy today," she says. "I did get some fast-eating bacteria."

"You gotta love bacteria."

"Not fast enough, but faster." She's stalling, though she can't say why. "Did you?"

"One patient after another." He finishes his beer. "We could always talk to her about a sperm donor."

"Why?" She puts down her fork. "Your sperm isn't the problem. They're just slow."

He pouts. "I bet you say that to all the guys."

She laughs, and he runs his fingers through his mop of black curly hair. His hair grows so fast; he shaves in the morning, but by the end of the day, he has stubble. "But if it would feel fair."

"It's not an issue of fair or unfair. It's a matter of solving the problem." Her mind starts spinning with the problem. "Do you think I should ask my mother for money? I mean, if we go the egg donor route?"

He slowly chews. "We might not need it if all goes well the first time."

She feels like there are fundamental questions they aren't asking, as if they've stepped on a fast-moving escalator, rushing at a steep incline, and the destination is the store's top floor, which is filled with babies. Swept up, swept along. The questions are on the bottom floor, far away.

Late at night, with Nelson sleeping, Ava logs on to the egg donor database.

Suzie, twenty-three years old, four pregnancies. Graduate school, studying political science, Italian and Greek descent. GPA: 3.9

Melody, twenty, three pregnancies. Undergraduate, studying international finance and math, Scandinavian and German descent. GPA 4.0

Gigi, twenty-one, one pregnancy. Undergraduate, studying kinesiology, South Korean and British descent. GPA 3.7

Tina, twenty-two, two pregnancies. Undergraduate, nursing. Scottish and Welsh descent. GPA 3.5

Josephine, twenty-four, three pregnancies. Undergraduate, nursing. French and Italian and Russian descent. GPA: 4.0

Beth, nineteen, one pregnancy. Undergraduate, economics. English and Dutch descent. GPA: 3.4

Sophia, twenty-four, two pregnancies. Graduate school, biology and math. Spanish, Italian, and English descent. GPA 4.0

She imagines Sophia, late at night, injecting hormones into her thigh, becoming plump, plumper, turning herself into a vessel for healthy eggs. She does it for money or for the goodness of it or both—who knows why. The list of donors goes on for another three pages, but a hooting sob rises in Ava's chest. She can't explain it. Self-pity that she can't do the most basic thing? For the women who are volunteering to grow healthy eggs? Something else? There are more donors, but Ava can't look anymore.

☙

They forgot about the dinner party at Dimitri's, a friend of Nelson's from medical school, who is a thoracic surgeon and a wonderful cook. Begrudgingly they went, but now, sitting around a table with good friends and the room bathed in candlelight, Ava feels remarkably buoyant. Their conversation skips from politics and the strand of stupidity and fear gripping the country, the climate, and the refugees flooding into Europe. Despite the tragedies piling up, Ava is immune.

"Okay," says Nelson, "now let's really get into it. What do we think of Nike's new shoe, VaporMax?"

Everyone laughs, and Dimitri says he has already bought a pair. "It's the next evolution of speed."

Nelson squeezes Ava's thigh, and she puts her hand on top of his. He feels it, too, she knows. A lightness, an unburdening. Something has sloughed off, and here they are again. She reaches into her purse and pulls out a pack of Marlboro cigarettes, and keeping them below the table, out of sight, she taps his leg. When he sees them, he raises his eyebrows. They rarely smoke, only to celebrate something, but after dinner, they take their wine and step out on the balcony, and she hands him a cigarette.

"Do we dare?" he says.

She smiles. "We dare because we are daredevils."

He inhales and blows smoke in the air. He's kind to participate. They have achieved nothing, she knows, done nothing, only breathed in rich possibilities. The future is an open field again.

That night, they find pre-trying-to-get-pregnant sex. Sex that isn't a chore, isn't dictated by her temperature, sex that's laughing and groping and unable to get enough of each other. Wonderful sex, happy sex, sexy sex. After, they lie side by side, sweaty and physically spent.

"What a relief it's still there," she says.

He kisses her neck. "All there, and more."

The next day Ava teaches her microbiology class, and though she's taught it for five years, she flares up with new enthusiasm because each year, there are new studies, new findings, new things to think about that electrify her brain, spinning it in many different directions. She spends the hour talking passionately about a process developed by MIT researchers to protect seeds from the stress of water shortage. A gel-like coating that holds moisture, a cheap, easy fix.

A student approaches her after class, her eyes shiny and alert. "This is so great," she says. "I love this class. I love how you tell us about cutting-edge stuff."

Ava nods and smiles, thinking this is the manna of teaching. To light a spark in someone, to ignite excitement about learning. Maybe her mother should return to teaching. She did it for a while, and Ava thinks she enjoyed it, this lifeline to enthusiasm. The student says she'll come by tomorrow during office hours, and Ava says she's looking forward to it.

When Nelson comes home that night, he barely eats.

"What happened?" she says.

Nelson puts his hand over his mouth, a stricken look on his face. A bad day is when a child is so sick that he or she must be admitted to the hospital, and today a four-year-old boy's cough suddenly turned into double pneumonia with a strange roving rash all over his body. Nelson is only half present because the other half, or maybe three-fourths, is preoccupied with the child, wondering what's happening. What can be done? And the most painful question—what did he fail to see? How did it get this bad?

His phone rests next to his plate as he waits for a text with an update, glancing at it every few seconds. Outside they hear the rumble of the bulldozer engine, followed by glass shattering. Though she hoped they could go for a walk after dinner and talk about the options, that's out. Not tonight, maybe not tomorrow or the next day, not while the boy is in the hospital.

"Nelson, just go," she says, hoping she doesn't sound resentful because she isn't.

He leaps from his chair, kisses her cheek, and heads for the front door. "I'll be an hour at most."

More like two or three. After the front door closes, she gets up and washes the dirty dishes. The water is warm, and for a long time she lets it run on her hands. The open kitchen window delivers a breeze of warmth, and her mind drifts to the summer before medical school and marriage, when she and Nelson went to British Columbia and stayed in a cabin on Shuswap Lake. The Summer Days, she calls them. They caught fish, cooked them on the grill, picked blackberries, and made pies. One month of waking up with the sun, making love, and drinking wine late into the warm, starry night, their conversation roaming everywhere. He played the violin for her—he'd brought it, he admitted, to show off and woo her. If they had a child, they could take him or her...she stops.

Out the window, the big oak sways its green leaves, its spiraling branches spanning the backyard, making a lace of shadow on the ground. The apple and peach trees hand her incredible shades of green, and her nose fills with the fragrance of resin and deep moss. She hears quiet, which means the bulldozer is done for the day.

After she showers, she climbs into bed and reads a short

story about a woman who wakes up with a tail. She has to buy new clothes designed for her new body, and scientists hound her because they want to study her. But she refuses; she likes the tail and has no desire to understand it. It exists, and that is enough. When Ava finishes the story, she tosses the book on the floor. She rarely understands stories like these, as if they withhold their meaning on purpose, reminding her that there is far more to life than she could possibly understand.

Nelson is already gone in the morning—at the hospital, she knows. As she drives into the Stanford parking lot, Ava calls her mother, who says she regrets her decision to accept the Goldman Environmental Prize. A moment of weakness, she calls it, and hubris, and, god, the world doesn't need more of that. She knows she sounds ungrateful, but it feels as if her body was moving one way, and she took it by the shoulders and dragged it the opposite way.

Ava is not sure what to say. Her mother sounds overwhelmed, as if teetering on the edge in a pair of wobbly high heels, though her mother owns no such thing.

"I'm glad you won it," says Ava. "You deserve it."

"No. That's not true."

It's a relief to hear her mother's usual blunt retort.

"And what am I going to do with Hazel?"

"Just ask her what she wants to do," says Ava.

"And if she wants to visit all the churches?"

"I'll go with you," says Ava.

"You will?"

Ava watches the sun pour down on the students. They look so young, talking freely and expansively. Innocents, all of them, with no real problems. "I like the high ceilings. And the echo."

"Ah yes. You were always a strange child."

"Thanks, Mom. What a compliment."

"Don't get me wrong. I loved that about you. It made you so interesting, and you didn't turn out so bad."

Ava announced that her sixth-grade project would be to measure the echo at Grace Cathedral. She forgot why they had gone to the church, with its maximum height of 174 feet, but she was intrigued by the sound. She used a microphone and a data logger to record the echo and spent five hours moving around the space, saying "hello, hello" and taking measurements.

"I forgot to ask," says her mother. "How are you?"

"Busy," she says, "but a good busy." And it's true. She thinks of the bacteria as *her* bacteria. She can't wait to get to the lab and grow more, even better bacteria. It's a calling and a challenge that she welcomes.

"You'll have to show me what you're up to," says Eleanor.

"Really? I'd love to," says Ava, getting out of the car. "Mom, if I ever needed to borrow some money—"

"Do you need money?"

Ava turns her head side to side to relax the orb of tension buried at the back of her neck. "No. I'm not sure."

"What aren't you telling me? You like to carry on as if all is well, but I'm your mother."

"Don't worry. I probably won't need it," says Ava. "I have to go."

When she hangs up, there's a message from Nelson that he'll be at the hospital all day. She texts him: *Thinking of you. Love you.*

Three days have passed, and the boy is still in the hospital. Throughout the day, Nelson texts her: *oxygen improving, oxygen dropping, stable.* In a half-asleep daze, she glimpses the shadowy form of Nelson when he slips into bed late at night and slips out early in the morning. Last night they had dinner at home together, but he was so tired, his head resting on his hand, he could barely speak.

"Any more thoughts about all this?" she said.

It takes him a second to understand what she's asking him about. "I've been so distracted."

"My mother said she'd give us money," said Ava.

"Did you tell her what for?"

"No," said Ava. "I'm not ready to get into it."

Nelson nodded, poked at his roasted chicken, then pushed the plate away. "We might not need it, you know."

"But we might," she said.

She wanted him to say again that they were lucky and give her one of his fabulous, optimistic smiles that burn away her pessimism like low-lying fog. Instead, he said, "You're right."

He pushed his chair back and said he had to get to the hospital. "My patients, I carry them around with me everywhere. I've got to be better at this."

You will, she thought, when we have a baby of our own. He was gone before she picked up his plate and carried it to the sink. She walked around the block then stopped and stood for a long while looking at the demolition site. A pile of boards, a garbage bin full of broken glass and drywall, but the original house is gone. There was nothing wrong with that house with its big front windows like benevolent eyes staring out at the world.

Today she teaches her fertility class. Last spring, when the dean asked her to teach it, she eagerly agreed. Back then, she still believed she'd become pregnant on her own, and she viewed the class as an intellectual undertaking. But now, seated at her desk in her office, reviewing her lecture notes, she's overcome with a sense she's ransacking herself, flinging off pieces, a sort of decomposition.

At the appointed time she heads down the hallway and opens the door to the auditorium. A handful of students are already there, notebooks open. She makes her way to the podium and pulls out her lecture notes. More students come in, and she glances at the clock, the exit.

For the next hour, she discusses diminished ovarian reserve and how to measure the health of the ovaries, the quantity and quality of eggs, the blood tests needed to determine if a woman has this condition, and the possible treatments.

At the break she steps into her office and grips the back of her chair. It feels as if she's stripped naked in front of her students, and everyone now knows the most intimate details. The mole on her hip bone, her left breast is slightly smaller than her right, and she has an outie belly button. She sips water and eats an apple. A pounding thrums at her left temple and her shirt collar chafes. Two more hours to go—how will she make it? A text from Nelson: *Oxygen levels are in the 80s*. She sinks into her chair and closes her eyes. When the break is over, she rouses and heads back into the auditorium and lectures about polycystic ovary syndrome, her words falling in pieces on the floor.

Another break and she is so exhausted she goes to the faculty lounge for a coffee and dumps in four sugars, though her stomach feels like a lead ball, and when she sips the concoction, it tenses and tightens. Her thoughts move as if traveling through syrup. Her phone pings. *Parents are breaking down and bolstering themselves up. Heroic, tragic.* She pictures the boy, coughing, labored breathing, pale, weak. The poor parents, pacing, watching, fretting, and Nelson doing the same. She, too, feels as if she's walking the long halls of worry. She writes, *Take care of yourself.* But he won't. He'll do whatever is needed, even if it destroys him.

She lasts another forty minutes, then, like a car out of gas, she abruptly stops. If she had to repeat what she'd lectured about, she couldn't. A mishmash, a rambling, because her thoughts are jumping from the boy to Nelson to her lousy eggs.

"Any questions?" she says. Please say no so they can end early.

A raised hand, a young woman with a serious yet apologetic expression. Ava feels a thread of cold slip down her neck.

"This isn't necessarily a straightforward science question, and maybe this isn't the place to ask it, but I'm wondering about a bigger question: I mean, if a couple can't have a baby, maybe they shouldn't. Maybe technology shouldn't be developed to allow them to have a baby. That may sound cruel, but, I mean, overpopulation is a major issue, and maybe it's nature's way of trying to restrain us somehow since we can't seem to. I know that isn't scientific, but it's just a thought."

The room fills with stiff silence. The woman is nineteen, twenty, long black hair, slender, no makeup, but she doesn't need it, a natural beauty, though she doesn't rely on her looks to navigate the world. Ava doesn't know this for certain but senses it because the young woman reminds her of herself—the pointed question asked earnestly, not because she wants attention, but because she sincerely wants to know.

Of course Ava has had this thought, and from that, an explanation why she and Nelson are unable to have a baby. The earth has had enough of the human species. It's done. But hearing it spoken out loud, in public, has dusted it off and given it renewed power. It overwhelms Ava's justification that allowed her to step over it, like a rock on her path. And that justification was: what's one more baby on the planet? What does it matter? Besides, their plan is not to have two children, so they aren't even replacing themselves; they're reducing. And maybe their child will have answers to the most critical world problems.

The young woman is looking at Ava intently, waiting for a response.

Maybe the reason is not that nature has put up the stop sign, Ava thinks, but humankind itself—humans polluting the environment with chemicals and plastic and endocrine-disrupting chemicals that harm reproductive systems and cause infertility. Humans inadvertently annihilating themselves. Of all people, she can't claim ignorance about the environmental devastation. So if they proceed, if she, who is well informed about the earth's dire condition, wants what she wants, what does that say about the chances for the earth? For human survival? About her?

The stillness in the class stretches beyond uncomfortable. She must say something. "It's a fair question." She didn't mean to be curt, but the words come out sharp edged. She takes a deep breath and continues, hoping to soften her response. "It's true, we must grapple with the ethical considerations and the consequences of our discoveries. It's a good question. Ethics, morality, responsibility, these should enter the discussion. If we can leap over our limits, not heed them..." What's she saying? "It's a good question, a very good question."

She looks down at her lecture notes, which are a blur. Ten more minutes until class ends, but she dismisses everyone early.

She hurries to her lab and retreats behind a closed door. Silence wraps around her, and she hears the blood thudding in her ears. The latest batch of bacteria is devouring plastic at a slightly faster rate. A good development, but more is needed. She'll have to pursue another track, abandon the natural approach and begin researching how to bioengineer bacteria that eats plastic faster.

She welcomes a concrete task that will absorb her. She takes one of the enzymes and begins mapping it on the computer, analyzing its structure. Hours go by. The light shifts, purple shadows color the room, and the deeper she goes into the structural analysis, the more she finds herself in a pool of calm and clearheadedness. Graduate research assistants come and go and remain in her periphery, beyond the scope of things.

She loves this, she's held by this; it is enough. And Nelson has his fill of children through his patients. His patients *are* his children. The boy in the hospital, it's as if he's Nelson's child, hers too. They are lucky. They've found work that engages them, that they're so willing to make an absolute commitment to. They'll probably learn something profound if they don't try to leap over their limitations. She goes deeper into her analysis of bacteria and feels the desire for a baby lessen, loosen, and drift beside her.

All afternoon her movements are skillful and perfect. She's floating in a pool of calm, past pain, past desire and longing. No longer on a roller coaster, she's sailing on a boat on a glassy lake. No need for a baby, no sleeping baby, smiling baby, crying baby. No baby to cramp their style, their work. No baby that will ruin their sleep, their social lives. No baby that becomes feverish and drives them into the ground with worry. No baby, because what exists is enough.

Toward the end of the day, Nelson texts her: *The boy* is *going home. Thank god for antibiotics! I'm heading to the clinic. Be home early.* It's a sign she's made the right decision. She drives straight to the clinic. The receptionist says he's with a patient, so Ava sits in the waiting room. A mother is there, her arm around her young daughter who, with her red cheeks and glazed eyes, looks feverish. Ava pages through *National Geographic*, looking at a photo of a season of blooming and then a photo of a man with the saddest eyes. She hears the receptionist making dinner plans, something about Italian and garlic. She leafs through a magazine and the world seems foreign: sleek clothes, shoes, coifed hair, faces with smoky eyes. Ava is too lazy for all that, or too indifferent.

When Ava hears Nelson's deep laugh, she heads to the hallway that leads to the examination rooms and sees him before he sees her. She can feel warm air on her skin, an electricity in the air. Nelson is in his white doctor's lab coat, holding a baby wrapped in a blue blanket, a young mother looking lovingly at the baby. But the mother doesn't exist for Nelson and the baby, who have locked eyes as if their bodies have fused and slipped into another world. Something melts inside of Ava as she watches her husband lovingly hold the baby.

"Oh, aren't you lovely, little Bo," says Nelson in the kindest, gentlest, sweetest voice. "Look at you, look how wonderful and healthy you are."

The baby coos and grabs Nelson's nose.

"Now you have me, Bo," he says. "Now you've got me."

The air feels hotter, as if there is friction in it, and she wants to move closer to Nelson and the baby so her skin touches the two of them. The mother laughs, and Nelson takes Bo's small hand, which wraps around his finger. Now Ava feels as if she's holding the baby, breathing in the baby, looking deep into Bo's blue eyes. Love and longing for each other, a falling into the depths of each other. The baby's pale, flawless skin, so soft and delicate. The baby yawns and Nelson laughs, and a hot, almost electrifying feeling shoots through Ava, razing whatever she'd managed to build up.

Nelson sees her, his face full of light. She comes over to him, into their world of baby lotion and Nelson's scent of eucalyptus. An incomprehensible inner compulsion grips her, a magical and magnetic pull, the same thing that has Nelson in its grip.

Nelson turns to the young mother, introduces Ava, and asks if Ava can hold the baby.

For a moment, Ava can't swallow.

"Of course," says the mother.

Nelson carefully hands the baby to Ava, and Ava cradles Bo, and it's so natural, holding him against her chest, so natural to rock him gently, his surprisingly heavy head propped on her arm, cheeks of pink. She smells curdled milk and his lotion, and from his blanket, a whiff of laundry detergent. He is gazing at her with round blue eyes, and she is gazing at him, and now she's making soft baby talk. "Oh, Bo, wonderful little Bo," she says, and she begins to bargain: if only if they can have a baby, if she and Nelson, a baby, she'll do whatever—no more flying on planes, no more meat, no more plastic or wasting water with baths; she'll plant a garden, grow vegetables, work for politicians who fight against climate change, never fall into despair like her mother, figure out how to speed up the bacteria, work day and night. If only, she thinks, with tears streaking down her cheeks as she fondles the baby's fat, soft, perfect, beautiful arm.

The human heart is a mysterious force. Did you see it? How it strong-armed reason, flipped it on its back, Ava's desire for a baby obliterating everything?

When she was a girl, Ava would analyze and scrutinize, making lists, one column labeled "pro" and the other "con," to decide whether to try out for soccer, run for class president, or date Joe or Phil. She turned the practice on herself, listing her assets and her liabilities. (Assets: intelligent, hardworking, tenacious, resilient. Liabilities: perfectionist, don't know when to stop working, chocolate.) But underneath or residing parallel to reason is emotion. If it's strong enough, emotion prevails and reason scurries behind it, then in front of it, masquerading as the fundamental force.

All these years of humans touting reason as their crown jewel, the thing that differentiated them from all other life and made them exceptional. Better than the smart and playful chimps and brainy dolphins and brilliant octopuses. An entire era named for Reason that reasoned I was wild, chaotic, and needed to be mastered and controlled, that decided I was mechanistic, along with all the non-human beings.

Eleanor, with her charts and data about CO2 and ozone, couldn't possibly succeed. Her reasonable, measured voice must have been too thin and far away to be heard. Human hearts don't beat fast for a reason. Nearly eight billion people on the planet, desires flinging everywhere.

I've heard some people say I'm indifferent to humans. How could I be? You're made of the same material as the stars, and most of your body is water. Here's reasoning for you: The idea that humans are ephemeral is no longer accurate. You have become a force, reorganizing the world forevermore. Where's my evidence, asks your so-called reasonable brain.

Slide 1: Your redistribution of fresh water has slowed the earth's rotation.

Slide 2: Almost every piece of plastic—Ava's obsession—which was first mass produced in the middle of the twentieth century, is still present in some form on earth.

Slide 3: The nuclear fallout from your testing of weapons will take 4.5 billion years to disintegrate, which is the age of the earth itself. By the way, everyone born since 1951 has man-made radioactive matter in their teeth.

Slide 4: Your activity has permanently changed the earth's carbon and nitrogen cycles.

The slides go on and on.

I watched a man and his son step out on their porch with their drone. They wanted to fly it but weren't sure what they were doing. (I'm giving them the benefit of the doubt to find the good.) Reason would have counseled them to read the instruction manual and test the drone elsewhere. But they wanted what they wanted, and the drone soared, sputtered, and crashed in the Bolsa Chica Ecological Reserve, frightening 3,000 elegant terns. In an instant, the sky clotted with long white wings, abandoning a sandy shore of nests full of eggs.

To fly a drone or protect the unborn elegant terns.

The elegant terns embody elegance, with their sleek white bodies and sharp, angular wings like triangles, black-capped heads, and long orange beaks for catching anchovies, and now thousands of eggs are scattered like a broken necklace of black-speckled pearls.

It's a small thing, I tell myself in order to calm down, the loss of 1,500 new birds. Each year 60 billion chickens are killed for human consumption, so what's 1,500? I'm scrambling to find shreds of hope, but sometimes the pain is unbearable.

At least the fog is rolling in. At least I have that, the fog whisking across the bay, spreading like white icing on a cake. In an instant it has gotten into everything, filching colors one by one—green, blue, red, purple, orange—greedily slurping them down as if they are sweet substances.

It runs down the city sidewalk, pocketing cars and trucks, joggers, and vendors selling hot coffee and hot dogs. Wrapping around a woman like a thick gauze, it pilfers her curls, her warmth. Buildings disappear, along with trolley cars, eucalyptus, cypress; a blind boat bleats like a lonely lost soul.

It's a masterpiece, this ghostly landscape. I love it, I can't stop admiring it. It's more potent than a list of devastating facts about temperatures rising and glaciers melting, because fog whisks the world away. Gone. Disappeared. Maybe people will feel the loss before the loss becomes absolute. Maybe this powerful feeling can stir something awake. Maybe they will see the limits of their world view. That's my desire.

Free

Lincoln is full of desire. He's sprinting up Divisadero, jagging right on Broadway, left on Webster. He's got on running shorts and a white T-shirt because his dad says to be careful in this neighborhood, though he doesn't know Lincoln is here. Joe knows, so do I.

Lincoln can't help it, he can't stay away. His whole body needs to see that deep green up on the hill and color splashed everywhere. That was always the first reason. The trees and the tall green bushes in front of the houses, houses that want to stay hidden, as if they are too special for eyes like his. He can't explain it, but he wants to see the green and what the green conceals, see everything, take it all in. He peers through the bars of a front gate or a small hole in a big hedge. Sees the BMW M5s, Mercedes AMG E 63S, Porches GT4, and Tesla Roadsters. He knows the names. Thirteen years old, he has a thing for cars. At that mansion on Greenwich Street with the peaked roof like something out of Hansel and Gretel, he saw a Lamborghini. Saw it when the garage door opened like a big mouth and burped out that jewel of a car. "You're a beautiful jewel," his mom tells him, fluttering her dead bird hands, "so don't get into trouble."

Only at night can he run like this. He sucks at basketball, kickball, soccer, almost every sport, but he can run. Even Nyla said so at PE. "Whoa! How fast can you go?" she said. "Dunno," he said. Even Kevin thinks he's fast. Lincoln can't run like this during the day because they'll think he's done something bad. Stole something, robbed someone, up to no good. He probably shouldn't even run at night because they'll say the same thing. But see, he has to run, and he wishes Nyla could see him right now.

He sprints by the old church, heels kicking up to his butt,

arms pumping, lungs sucking down air, and it feels so good to go full speed. There's another reason he's out at night. He feels something. Felt it for three hours now. Something is waiting. He knows it the way you get that feeling when a person walks in the room, and you either want to meet them or get the hell away. Lincoln has a sixth sense or maybe a seventh. He hasn't told anyone about it, not even Joe, but it's there deep inside, like a second heartbeat under his ribs, and he feels it in his fingertips, vibrating. He runs up Jackson and down Van Ness, crosses Filbert. So quiet, no cars, most houses are sleeping or sleepy, only one or two lights glowing milkily.

His limbs are loose, his breathing deep and steady, and the night is with him. Up ahead. On the right. He spots it. When he gets there, winded and panting, he circles it. A wood chair with a teal cushion, and four long bars on the back. He crouches down and runs his hand along each carved leg. Checks the cushion. Nothing wrong with it. Not a scratch or a stain or a tear, not one damn thing. FREE waving in the breeze. He picks it up. This is what called to him and told him to come and take it away—the owners had enough of it. The familiar charge runs through him, filled with gleeful possibility. He holds the chair by the back and carries it as if he went out walking with a chair because the two of them need to breathe the cool night air.

When Lincoln gets down the hill to his neighborhood, the janky apartments and not a speck of green, there are five of them on the corner. He swallows the lump in his throat. They weren't there when he slipped out his bedroom window, but they're there now, and there's no way around them. Streetlight pours down on them as if they're on stage.

"Hey, what you got there," says Jamel, who has glistening hair.

They're two or three years older than him, already in high school—the age difference might as well be a galaxy.

"What's it look like?" says LeRoy to Jamel.

"What you need with a chair, bro?" says Jamel.

Jamel shoves Lucky, Lucky pushes back.

"Where you going with it?" says Cody.

"You so skinny you look like a stick," Lucky says to Lincoln.

Lincoln makes sure he's an arm's length away so they don't grab him or the chair. He keeps his face empty. If he has to, he'll drop the chair and run. They'll beat him just for the fun of it to see if he'll cry. They've done it before. Joe says that happens if you've too much time on your hands. If you don't have a dream. Look for trouble and it's easy to find.

"Your mama needs a chair? Huh? Give your mama a present? Is she the one who named you Lincoln? What kind of name is that? Why did she do that to you?"

They all laugh like it's the funniest thing in the whole goddamn world, and Lincoln keeps going, a forced swagger, right by them, as if he doesn't give a shit, as if he's not shaking inside, goes right on by as if he's chill.

He's down the block, past the overflowing trash can smelling of rotten meat and putrid eggs, and he can hear them still laughing, a shitty chair.

The farther he gets from them, the more his breath deepens, settles. "Okay, okay, okay," he murmurs. Lincoln heads to Joe's and lets himself through the side gate to his backyard, which isn't much of anything. Weeds, tall grasses, dog shit from Joe's old mutt. Joe lets him use the shed. He knows what's up; he says Lincoln can use that old shed whenever he likes. Joe's birthday was last week. Turned eighty-two. "That's eighty-two years young," Joe said, laughing. "I'm a spritely thing who has seen it all and still has a sense of humor." Used to be a mailman, walking five, six miles a day, until he wasn't walking but plodding, then shuffling. Joe, with his wiry gray hair and deep laugh that ripples through his skinny body. When he laughs, his whole body gets into it. Thinking about that laugh makes Lincoln smile.

He wishes he could make Joe laugh every day, wishes he could make his father laugh, but he's all serious all the time, a man with a college education and a room full of books and a vocabulary that makes people squirm. Whenever he can, whenever the spirit moves him or the opportunity arises, his father lectures. Equality. Justice. Integrity. Freedom—freedom of the body, the spirit, the soul—and when he gets going, he doesn't stop, telling Lincoln he must walk the straight and narrow path and read the classics, MLK and Booker and De Bois, every single one of them, and study hard, and speak well and make eye contact and read Douglass and Baldwin and write his essays early and revise them. "Nothing in all the world is more dangerous than sincere ignorance and conscientious stupidity," says his dad, quoting their good friend MLK. Lincoln must sit there and listen and say yes sir, yes sir, though he wants to say, Dad, things are a lot more complex these days. None of his friends get lectured like this. They play video games and basketball, talk smack to each other and talk about girls.

"That man loves to orate," says his mom, her hands hidden under the table. "Should have been a professor, all those books he has in his brain. A whole library in his head."

Lincoln loves his father but hates his voice rolling over him like a boulder, as if there's some bad inside him that must be smashed, because after a while his father gets louder, and he starts pounding his fist on the table. All those damn lectures as if trying to beat something wild and bad out of Lincoln.

Joe's voice is calm as if he's got a deep river running inside him. And he's got that rumbling laugh, and he asks Lincoln questions, and he listens. "Why do you ask me so many questions?" said Lincoln. Joe laughed and laughed. "Because I don't know all the answers, and I like it when you think because you're a good thinker." Joe asks, "Now tell me, what's on your mind today? From the expression on your face seems like a lot." "How are you feeling today, Lincoln?" "What should we do about all that garbage on our street?"

Now that's something: to be asked and listened to.

Lincoln opens the door of the old shed slowly, so it doesn't creak like the broken thing that it is. Doesn't want to wake Joe, Joe who says he needs his beauty rest, so he's in bed by nine p.m. He puts the chair in the shed next to the nightstand he found last week on Union Street. He's also got a lamp with a long silver neck, a rocking chair, three white coffee cups, four glass vases in different sizes, a black-framed painting of a sail-boat, and a poem by John Dryden, but the writing is so small you can't read it without a magnifying glass, and he hasn't found one of those yet. He likes that about the poem; you have to want to read it, which means you'll pay attention. And a shitload of books. If he went hunting every day, he'd come back with books for sure.

He's going to clean up that chair and give it to Mrs. Fielding, who lives on the second floor of his apartment building. Just put it in front of her door with a handwritten sign, "For Mrs. F." He never signs the note, he doesn't want the attention. Doesn't need it because he can imagine her expression; he lets it bloom in his mind, her happiness, her renewed belief that the world is a good place. The other day, Mrs. Fielding came to their apartment and complained to Lincoln's mom that one of her chairs broke. "I got too fat," she said. "Damn thing nearly killed me when its leg split in two, and I went sprawling backward." They both laughed, and his mom said she was sure glad she didn't get hurt, and Mrs. Fielding said she's too fat to get hurt, all that cushioning, and that made them laugh for a long time.

He closes the shed door, and then he's out—sprinting up the hill again because the tingling in his fingers is still there, but he knows he shouldn't. It's one of his rules: only one thing per night. So he tells himself he's going to run down the street with the giant sycamores, and that's it.

His fingers are zinging, his breathing light, quick. Yep, something out here calling to him, singing to him.

He doesn't keep any of it. He gave a blender to his mom as a birthday present. She didn't ask any questions, maybe because it was in a box, like new, and maybe because he told her he saved his money, two dollars a week for taking out Mrs. Fielding's garbage, bringing in her mail, and carrying her grocery bags up the stairs. His mother's pleasure overwhelmed her curiosity.

A dog barking somewhere, a lonely sound. A car, but far away, at least five blocks.

"Hello."

He stops. Heart pounds.

"Nice evening, isn't it? Night makes you feel alone in the world."

She's standing right in front of him. An older white woman. Tall, her face bony, full of sharp angles, wearing a camel-colored coat. Black boots with square toes. She reminds him of a streetlamp because she's so tall. Make her feel safe, he hears a voice in his head say. Joe's voice, his father's.

"Yes, ma'am," he says. Politeness syrups his words. Her eyes are soft and sad. A sag to her shoulders, maybe that's age, maybe not.

"I come out here and walk when I can't sleep. Me and the night air and the stars and the moon, though you can't see the moon." She looks up at the sky. "Where are you, moon? I've come to prefer a world without much humanity in it. You probably don't feel that way, but I've landed on a dismal view of *Homo sapiens*."

Is she drunk? She talks sort of weird. He takes a step back. "Yes, ma'am."

Now her eyes look watery as if she might cry and her lower lip trembles. "I'm sorry, I'm in a sour mood."

He likes old people; there's something soft about them, well, not all of them, but this woman and Joe, as if the world has walked a lot on their souls, softening them, putting holes in them, so they say what's on their mind, even if it's sad or shows how helpless they are.

He nods.

"My name is Eleanor. What's yours?"

He introduces himself.

"I tried hikes, but the hills around here are crowded with people, and they are so damn intent on a destination. I know it shouldn't bother me, but they aren't seeing what's in front of them and that's part of the problem. So, the hike that was supposed to console ends up making me angry. I come home pissed off."

He's still assessing her. Harmless or harmful? Maybe he should dash now. But if he runs, won't she get suspicious? She seems nice enough, if a little crazy. Maybe she's lost her mind and, when no one was looking, she slipped right out of her house. That happened to his aunt Myra. Maybe her people will come looking for her.

"But really," she says, looking around her, "these houses are monstrosities."

His eyes widen. "You don't like them?"

"Oh, I love the magnolia trees and sycamore, the poppies and gladiolas."

He wants to tell her he knows all those names and others too. When he sees something he doesn't know, he searches for it on the internet and learns its name because it makes him feel they're on a more intimate basis.

The woman named Eleanor wipes her cheek with the back of her hand, but the shimmer is still on her face. She's crying. Now he's sure she's suffering like his aunt Myra, who cried at the strangest things, a napkin falling to the floor, a drooping flower. He wants to help her, and at the same time, he wants to run away.

"My father quotes Booker T. Washington," says Lincoln. "'I shall allow no man to belittle my soul by making me hate him.'" He can hear Kevin's voice in his head—*Don't be quoting stuff like that to people. It's not cool. People think you're weird or something.*

She puts her fingers to her throat. "Ah, now."

"But to tell you the truth," he murmurs, "there's a lot of things I hate."

"It's natural to hate," she says. "If you can think, you can hate."

He nods, not sure what it means. He wraps it up and stores it for later.

She smiles. "Well, Lincoln, and that's a fine name, a very fine name, a name destined for greatness. Have a good evening in this lovely night air. It's rather late, you should probably head home."

She turns, gives him a little wave, and heads down the sidewalk, and though he thought she'd stumble or stagger, she walks in a straight line. As he watches her go in a tall straight line, he wonders if she's going to be okay. When he gets old, he doesn't want to be like that, to hate so much it makes you sad and angry, and you have to walk the streets at night alone and call to the moon. But she didn't have hate in her eyes—he's seen hate; it turns eyes into blazing hard marbles and then the hate he sees is his own.

The tingle is still in his fingers, but he tells himself it's enough. The chair is a good find. Mrs. Fielding will be happy. Don't get greedy. Go home.

He turns right on Divisadero and the tingle sharpens, making his fingers move as if they're playing the piano. That's when he sees it. A glow of lavender. That's what's been calling to him all night. The streetlight shines on a pot of lavender flowers. He doesn't know their names. Joe loves lavender. Joe's mother always wore lavender—lavender scarf, blouse, and shoes. It's the color of royalty, Joe told him. It also came to mean holiness, since royalty were considered gods or descendants of God. Lincoln looked that up. In those long-ago days, the dye was expensive because it came from thousands of mollusks. Lincoln could take that pot of purple and put it right on his porch, and Joe would have lavender every single day. A late birthday present or an early one, depending on how you look at it. His fingers are on fire for those flowers. To have Joe's face open up like a flower blooming with happiness. Joe doesn't have any children, and his wife died a decade ago, so there's no one to give him a gift of flowers.

But there's no FREE sign on it. He's never taken something that doesn't have a FREE sign. That's another one of his rules:

he needs a FREE sign. He's got to have a compass in life, or he'll end up somewhere he doesn't want to be, that's Joe talking. Leave it, he tells himself.

But that old woman didn't call the cops, and two weeks ago, he broke one of his rules, and it worked out fine. He's standing in the dark, gazing at the flowers. Like enormous dandelion puffs painted purple on a long green stem. They bewitch, pull him close. No one on the street—he checks again and again, then lets his eyes rest again on lavender. They seem from another world, a better world. Like his favorite map that he drew, with beautiful black trees and a purple sky, pink streets, and orange horses and yellow pigs. The sun, scarlet. He loves that map. Pinned on the wall right by his bed.

The moon appears from behind the clouds—does that woman see it now?—and the flowers look like the purple stained glass at St. Luther's Church. He squats to get a better look. The petals have swallowed the moonlight and have a little light inside. Sublime. He read that word in a book, and it describes what's happening to him, changing from a solid into a vapor, turning him into something else, something as light as one of these petals. He hears his father's voice boom in his head—a man needs to be tough, strong, don't bend with all that rough wind. Stand as if you were an oak tree. Stand up to the harsh world. But he's bending all over the place right now, folding himself in half, disappearing in the beauty of lavender.

These people don't care about these flowers. Stuck out beyond the hedge where they can't even see them. Look at them bursting with beauty, and during the day, he bets they walk right on by—not even a side glance. You need to love these flowers. Joe will love them, he'll look at them every day and his face will soften the way it does when he sees something beautiful or when he plays the piano and the wrinkles on his forehead soften, his brown eyes soften.

But no FREE sign, so it's theft and he's no thief. But who says the world is running the best way right now? This place, this whole neighborhood is drowning in natural beauty. So much beauty, they don't even see it. Makes his eyes tear up thinking about it, and then thinking of his street with the garbage and graffiti, not the pretty graffiti with swooping colorful lines, but the FUCK on the walls of the apartment buildings and EAT SHIT, and even if you take a spray can and block it out, it comes back the next day, so what's the point? His father says it's the rage of the Black man, but it seems to Lincoln the rage of the Black man is screaming not at the world but at Black people who live in the neighborhood.

Down the street, headlights come right at him, slice him. He quickly stands and starts walking away, thinking I belong here, I belong here until he comes to a tall hedge and hides behind it. He shouldn't have come back to the hill. Shouldn't have broken his rule. He waits, but waiting is the shape of fear, making his heart race. His mind flings open locked doors, unleashing a flashlight in his face, blinding light, what are you doing in this neighborhood, what you got in your pockets, a smack to the side of the head, a fist in the eye, he tumbles back, falls on the hard ground, but he knows better and gets up, so a boot doesn't slam into his head. His friend Kamel stood too long in front of Macy's downtown. Cops shoved him up against a wall, said he was loitering, his head smacked brick. A big lump on the back of his head, a spike of pain in his brain. He couldn't rise from a chair without the world jerking to the left. He up-chucked his lunch. Days went by like this.

In his mind, Lincoln scrambles up, but the handcuffs are on—but I didn't do anything wrong, no back talk, be polite, do what they say, don't put your hands in your pockets, but Dad, hands yanked behind his back, his shoulders stretching out of their sockets, police walkie-talkie static, young Black male loitering on Broadway, bring him downtown, and the call home—he'll get to make one call, he has rights—his mom's voice in his head now, you have rights, if they stop you, you have rights.

The car headlights turn right, then the incoming fog gobbles them gone. Lincoln's racing heart knocks in his chest. The air is full of chill now. He blows air out and sounds like the wind.

Climbs out from behind the bush, trembling. The lady sneaking up on him, the car lights, him thinking about taking something with no FREE sign. Go home before you get snagged on trouble. He sprints home, climbs through the window, lies in bed, and pulls the sheet up, his heart still thumping. He vows to stop—stop running at night, stop looking for FREE things.

The day is a long stretch of school with all the boredom and shenanigans, then home, homework. After he finishes algebra, he heads to Kevin's house and they play Dread Ship, killing zombies on the ship and trying to save the humans. When Kevin's mother says to shut it down, they grab basketballs and walk the five blocks to school to shoot hoops. No one's there; the court is all theirs, though the court is crap, full of bumps and cracks.

Kevin is lean and tall and muscular, and he looks sixteen already. He's got a solid shot outside the key. Lincoln tries to block him, but Kevin zigzags, pivots, ball between the legs, and always finds a way.

"You even trying?" says Kevin, laughing. It's a joke between them, how good Kevin is, how Lincoln can't do much of anything.

"You keep doing tricks on me," says Lincoln.

"No tricks. Talent." Kevin has a big smile.

Not true. Kevin practices all the time. Endless hours. They used to play Legos or ride their scooters around the block. Not anymore. Lincoln wishes he were as good as Kevin at something. Feels like Kevin can bend the world to his desires.

The sun dips lower in the sky, and Tray and Jack emerge from the blue of the afternoon.

"I'm gonna kick your ass, Kev," says Tray, who isn't as tall as Kevin, but he's feisty, sometimes too feisty, and it turns hot-tempered, mean. Jack is chill, or maybe shy. Lincoln knows that type because he's that type. They're all heading for high school next year, and as eighth graders they're at the top of the heap, but next year they'll be at the bottom again. No one wants to think about it.

Lincoln passes to Kevin over and over, and it's tight, with Tray swearing and acting cocky. "Gonna get you this time," he taunts. "I'm a badass and you a punk." Tray's long arm shoots a high-arcing ball, but it misses. Back and forth like this, racing from one end of the court to the other. Kevin gets the ball and heads to the basket. Jack, trying to stop him, steps on one of the cracks, turns his ankle.

"Fuckin' hell," shouts Jack. He hops over to the side of the court.

"These courts are shit," says Tray.

They stand around Jack as he clutches his ankle, his face pinched.

"Sucks," says Kevin.

The hill behind the school is still covered with patches of tall green grass. Mostly, though, it's red dirt. Lincoln has the urge to run up that hill.

"How am I gonna get home?" says Jack.

Tray looks at Lincoln. "You never talk much, do you?"

Lincoln doesn't say anything, doesn't want to rile him because he already looks heated.

Tray gets his bike. Jack hops on the seat, and Tray pedals him home.

The crows caw, and a car full of high schoolers drives by, rap blasting. Their future is breathing down their T-shirts. Kevin dribbles until the car drives away, then he practices his free throw, and Lincoln sits on the concrete and throws stones at the metal pole. He likes the ping of rock against metal. Kevin's going to be six feet five, maybe six. Lincoln's lucky to make it to six feet. He pulls in his stomach and looks at his ugly, scrawny legs.

Kevin comes over, all sweaty. "Gonna try out next year for the freshman basketball team."

"You'll make it for sure," says Lincoln. "You still dreaming of the NBA?"

"Yeah, if I live that long and the world lasts that long."

Lincoln nods. Kevin has a Plan B: if he doesn't make the NBA, he's going to be a doctor or lawyer and make some serious money.

Kevin sips his water. "What about you?"

"Don't know," says Lincoln.

"You should try out for track."

"Maybe."

"You're fast. Maybe even faster than me."

Lincoln throws a stone at Kevin's shoe.

"Hey!" says Kevin.

"What if I don't make the cut?"

Kevin starts dribbling the ball. "Then you don't make the cut. Won't know unless you try."

Easy for Kevin to say—whatever he sets out to do, he does it. Basketball team, softball, soccer. Feels like he has a magic touch. You look at him, it's like looking at the sun.

Kevin says some girl in their class likes him, but he doesn't like her. She keeps calling him. Pain in the ass.

"Who?" says Lincoln.

Kevin shoots. The ball rolls on the rim and goes in. "You can't tell anyone."

"I won't."

"Nyla," he says. "You know the tall girl with those green eyes. She's hot, but man, she talks too loud and way too much. She's like my mom's radio, you know?"

Lincoln loves his mother's old radio. Made of dark oak, about the size of a small refrigerator, it has knobs, and if you fiddle with them, you can find the world—voices from France, Switzerland, Germany, Russia, and languages he doesn't know. When they were younger, he and Kevin spent hours listening to these voices. They haven't done that for three years, though Lincoln would like to. He throws another stone. He likes Nyla, likes how much she talks because it fills in the quiet, awkward spaces. But she's too pretty, and Lincoln's nose takes up too much of his face. It stresses him out just thinking of her, what he'd say to her.

"Get anything good?" says Kevin.

Lincoln instinctively cringes. That was the rule he broke two weeks ago; he told Kevin what he does at night, but he shouldn't have because when he sees it through Kevin's eyes, it looks stupid. Sneaking out to find other people's leftovers, what they think of as junk. Joe calls it Lincoln's recycling company and says he's helping people out, but Lincoln didn't say that to Kevin because it makes it sound like it's more than it is, like he's trying to be a big shot.

"A chair," says Lincoln.

Now he wishes he hadn't told Kevin because Kevin's eyebrows shoot up as if to say: that's it? A flash across Kevin's face, and Lincoln knows he's deciding if Lincoln is too much a loser to hang out with.

"Just a stupid chair," says Lincoln.

Kevin stops dribbling. "You really should train for track. It would give you something. You gotta have something. High school is when the real pressure kicks in. Girls, college apps. You got to find a way to stand out. And get rid of that slouch."

"I slouch?"

"Yeah, dude, all the time like an old man, and you got that serious, old-man look all the time. That's got to go."

Lincoln tries to sit up, but it feels so weird, like he's sticking his chest out, like he's really something.

When lavender worms its way back into Lincoln's thoughts, he shoves it away. He stays after school and runs the cinder oval track around the football field. He times himself for one lap, a quarter mile, and the number seems good, but he doesn't really know. He runs around again, again, it's boring as hell, sweat dripping down his face and back. An older boy is running too, and he's running effortlessly as if he could go forever. When he leaves, Lincoln copies what that boy did—jog-trot with high knees for half the track, then sprint the rest of the way. Nyla walks by, talking to another girl. He hopes she sees him running this fast.

He starts doing this after school, running the red-orange track, and using a stopwatch. Kevin stops by.

"Don't hold back," says Kevin. "You're thinking too much. That's your problem!"

"I know!" says Lincoln, breathing heavily.

He jogs over to Kevin.

"Give it your all," says Kevin.

"Okay."

"Imagine if you don't go faster you're going to die," says Kevin.

"Is that what you do?"

"Sure, all the time."

On the football field the soccer players are stretching their calves. Lincoln watches the bees zip around the showy milkweed. He gulps water and wipes sweat off his forehead with his T-shirt. "Do you ever wonder if the Greeks were right?" says Lincoln. "That humans are only entertainment for the gods?"

"No," says Kevin, frowning.

Something retreats inside. It feels like he doesn't understand the ways of the world anymore. In elementary school he did, but not any longer.

On the fifth day Lincoln's legs are so tired he can't run, so he walks home slowly. Millions of crows fill the sky, and the sky is the color of sand. Fires somewhere again, the smell of smoke blowing into the city. He wonders if the lavender flowers can breathe.

When he gets home, his mother is working on his sister's hair. "Lincoln, take out the trash," she calls out to him.

He throws his backpack on his bed. "I've got homework!"

He knows it's his chore. His mama can't do it—her ugly hands, her fingers glued together, knuckles pointed to the sky. Twenty years as a court reporter, her arthritic hands look like dead birds, their wings folded tight to their sides. Nothing she can do about it; their health insurance won't cover a cent. Every time he looks at her hands he feels a pain in his throat.

"I look beautiful," he hears his sister say.

What's beautiful, thinks Lincoln, are those lavender flowers. And Nyla.

After he takes out the trash and does his homework, he asks if he can go to Kevin's. Only an hour, his mother says. School night. Nyla lives two blocks from Kevin. He tucks the radio in his backpack. He'll walk by her house. If she's outside, he'll say hello. Maybe she'll come out and talk to him, and he'll let her talk as much as she wants.

Lincoln plunges out the front door into the changing light. Soon the streetlights will turn on, and the sky will turn murky and dark blue. He walks in the opposite direction, away from the older boys on the corner. From the higher apartments children's voices pour out. "Don't do that! I got to do it!" Music streams from a low window, a song he should know. It's something popular that kids his age know, and he makes a mental note to find out the name of the song.

Nyla's not out in front of her house. He won't knock on her door or anything. He'll leave the little radio in her mailbox. He rips a piece of paper from his notebook and writes, *Thought you'd like this. From Lincoln.* He found it in a cardboard box three weeks ago on Arguello near the Presidio. An old-fashioned thing, but it works and fits right in your palm. Dark blue, like the sky at the end of a summer's day.

He heads to Kevin's, and the leaves are rustling and two streetlights flick on. He passes by the sewer grate where he once lost his bouncy ball—called a moon ball because when you threw it hard on the concrete, it leaped as high as the telephone pole. Except it rolled through the grate.

Kevin is in his front yard, but he's with someone, and, as Lincoln gets closer, he sees it's Nyla, and they're both laughing. She lightly pushes Kevin's shoulder, and he pretends to fall backward, saying, "Whoa, girl, you are strong," and she laughs harder.

Lincoln slows.

"Hey," says Kevin to Lincoln.

Nyla gives him a little wave.

"We're just hangin'," says Kevin.

"Yeah, this guy's a fool," says Nyla, pushing him on the shoulder again, and Kevin does the whole act again, falling backward, farther this time, and she laughs and laughs. Lincoln can't stop looking at the two of them. Kevin's face is so happy, happier than Nyla's. Or maybe the same. He forces himself to look away. A breeze is setting all the leaves of the sycamore tree in motion.

Nyla turns her glittery green eyes to him. "What's your name again?"

Lincoln doesn't know what to say.

"Lincoln's his name," says Kevin. "Just walking around?"

"Yeah," Lincoln manages to say.

He turns, heads back the way he came, and puts the radio back in his backpack.

At the dinner table that night, he can't sit still. He picks up his knife, sets it down, picks up his fork, and taps it against his spoon matching the frantic rhythm in his body.

"What's wrong with you?" says his mother. Her dead-bird hands trying to hold her fork. "Eat your dinner."

Toes tapping.

"Finish your peas," says his father, who starts in on being grateful and not wasting, but Lincoln can't hear much of it.

He goes to his room and finishes his homework. On the internet he learns the name of the flowers. Allium. They attract butterflies and like the sun. Lavender is still on his mind at 10:00 p.m. Feverish energy. He hears his dad snoring. Mom falls asleep before his dad. The older boys are not hanging on the corner. He puts on his black hoodie, his worn-out sneakers, his shorts. Slips out the window. The night air is a cold slap on his cheeks. Feels good, feels alive, lively. He runs fast, a singular focus.

Up the hill, lots of houses are still wide awake, lights blaring as if they're watching him. He's not usually here this early. Maybe he shouldn't. Too much action. Things whirring, stirring. A siren cracks open the night.

He turns on Webster, then heads to Green Street. Be quick. Snatch them, head to the shed. He slows, looks around, and stops. This isn't right. There was a big white Victorian like an ice cream cone—wasn't there? His heart thumps with fear as he looks to try to recognize his surroundings. Where are they? Maybe he's on the wrong street. Maybe it was on Lombard or Greenwich. He turns and stares at the brown house with the black shutters, all the windows lit up. He's not on the right street, he's sure now.

He takes off, sprints to Fillmore, then tells himself to slow the hell down, to look like he's out for a jog. He heads up to Jackson, and as he runs he begins to worry. What if they're gone? What if someone else took them? Or the people moved them? Maybe they threw them out and bought something else. That happened at a house on Chestnut—it seemed every month there was a new plant in a white pot. What did they do with the yellow daisies and the blue hydrangeas? He burps, tasting his mama's roasted chicken. Running too hard, too fast.

More cars over here. A blue Civic zooms by, music blaring a heavy downbeat. Mean, wild laughter floats by. It's okay, he'll be so quick. Up ahead, a woman is walking a little white dog. He cuts to the other side, jags over to Washington Street, a street of empty. He's a knife slicing through the night. There they are. Hello, Allium. The lavender glows as if it's beaming, happy to see him. He crouches down. Feels as if he's saving them, freeing them. Those people don't deserve them. He tilts the pot and scoots his arms underneath, and lifts. It's like he's got a big baby in his arms. He imagines Joe's big smile, that deep laugh that always catches him like a net. "Oh my," he'll say, his big hand on his chest.

He can't run; the pot and dirt are too heavy. He's walking with purpose, as if they belong to him, out for a stroll together, and he's halfway down the sidewalk when he sees a man up ahead on the sidewalk. No dog. Smoking. Fear runs through

Lincoln's fingers, his body quivers. The man is on the same side of the street as Lincoln.

There's nowhere to go—the next street is still seven, eight houses away. Should he turn around? Head the other way?

The man throws his cigarette on the ground. "Hey."

The man starts walking toward him. A series of revelations—dark hair, streaked with gray, or maybe that's the streetlight, looks older than thirty, maybe forties, he's never sure of white people's ages.

"What are you doing?" says the man.

About six feet tall, white button-down shirt, a tie, but it's loose, the knot hanging there as if he tried to yank it off but couldn't.

"Now I've seen everything," says the man.

Lincoln feels a thread of cold creep up his neck. Drop them?

Long dark eyelashes, his eyes are big, not flat, not hard, they look like he's telling himself a joke. Maybe he's okay, like that older woman. Out for a stroll, can't sleep, like that woman.

Lincoln tries to make his mouth smile. The man is shifting from foot to foot as if the world is rocking like a boat. Drunk, he's drunk. Smells him now. Lincoln could drop the flowers and run. But what if the man chases him? Catches him? He's got long legs.

The man pulls out his phone, and Lincoln's breath catches. Calling the police? The screen lights up the man's face, turning it bluish. Lincoln's legs tremble, arms turning weak.

"Don't," says Lincoln.

"Oh, you can speak."

"I'll put them back."

The man is holding his phone. Lincoln is paralyzed.

"Quite a night," says the man.

"I'll put them back, sir."

"Sir? It's sir now." He laughs. "Where'd you get them?"

"Garbage can. Someone tossed them."

"Really?"

Lincoln blinks. "I'll put them back."

The man slides his phone into his pocket, lights a cigarette, and blows smoke out of his mouth like a gangster. "I don't give a fuck about the flowers."

The word "fuck" comes out angry, like a punch. Lincoln doesn't know what this man wants. Can he leave? Take the flowers with him?

"I've had a hell of a night. One bad thing after another, but you've come along, stealing a pot of flowers. That's fantastic. Makes things better, a little Thursday night absurdity. I gave her a kitten, and she didn't want it. She said it would scratch her hands and cats are selfish. Called me selfish for thinking a kitten would solve everything. Said it was pretty fucking arrogant to think I could make it work like that. If that's what she wants, that's what she'll get. But it was a kitten, gray, and it didn't have a home, just wandering around, and now it still doesn't have a home. She's an ungrateful bitch."

Lincoln doesn't know what he's talking about.

The man stares at Lincoln—or maybe not. Lincoln can't tell if the man is seeing him or not, his eyes seem glazed over.

The man starts snapping his fingers. "She likes music. Jazz. Loves jazz all that jazzy stuff. Can't sing worth crap." The man swivels his head left and right, then looks right at Lincoln. "How about you dance for me?"

Lincoln hears Joe's voice in his head: a man with too much alcohol in him, anything could happen. Lincoln takes a step back.

"Show me your moves, man."

"I don't got moves."

"Sure you do. You're all movement, the way you're shifting right now, can't stand still. Put the flowers down and show me your moves."

Do what he says, his father's voice in his head. But another voice—don't, if you do, you'll break and never be put back together again. Lincoln hears his father's voice again—yes, sir, no, sir. Now Joe's voice, Listen, Lincoln, I don't want anything to happen to you. If it did, I'd die. Do you hear me? Hears his mother sobbing.

Lincoln puts down the flowers.

"There we go."

He feels stiff, like concrete. Fear jagging through him. He shuffles his feet.

"Shit, you can do better than that."

Lincoln moves his arms. It feels like he's flapping broken wings. The man claps his hands to some music in his head. "That's it. You got it now. Looking good. She'd like this shit."

Lincoln slows down. Bile in his mouth. He should bolt, but he wants the flowers. He wants to see Joe's old face happy.

"Hey, how about you sing? Sing me something."

Lincoln stops moving. No, he will not. He will not do it. The man leans over and with cool fingers brushes Lincoln's cheek. "Forget it. Pick up those flowers and take them to your girl. Make her smile. Maybe you got better luck than me."

Heart beating in his throat. Lincoln lifts the flowers, and as he heads away he hears the man chuckle as if they are in on some joke together, as if the night has joined them at the hip. Lincoln's whole body is jittery. He whips his head around to see if the man is following him. Only the night. Still, his heart is beating fast, even though he's walking. He pores over what just happened, what could have happened.

He goes down the hill and doesn't stop shaking until he makes it to the shed, where he sits for a long time, feeling the anger rise in him as he stares at the flowers and their little buds that look like teardrops.

In the morning before school, he heads to Joe's. He can hear Joe playing the piano in his living room. Lincoln found the piano keyboard on Filbert in front of a big house with a red door. Worth at least $400, that's what he found out. A heavy thing, he carried it in front of him, glued to his chest, and brought it straight to Joe's house, a man who loves music, whose mama once taught him how to play the piano, a boy who would sit in his living room for hours and play, the sunlight floating in, settling on the piano, on Joe's long, nimble fingers.

Lincoln goes around back to check on the flowers. They're there, but he's not really looking at them. He feels his face heat up, no goddamn right.

Lincoln heads into Joe's apartment through the back door, sits glumly in the cushiony chair. Joe gives him a little nod, and Lincoln leans his head back and lets the music pour over him, and it feels like little fingers tapping his skin. Nice, this tapping, sometimes pressing a little harder, like someone getting his muscles to loosen up. A pat-pat now, little light drops on his forehead and temple, he starts tapping his right foot to the music, the pace is picking up. He opens his eyes and sees Joe's fingers flying on the keys, his head rolling side to side, and he knows Joe is deep inside the music, and so he closes his eyes and joins him there, letting the music sweep him up like a wave and take him along into a big ocean of sound. Floating along in this big body of music, he drifts and feels the tension in his neck and shoulders disappear.

When it stops he opens his eyes, and it takes a moment to enter the room again, Joe's living room, Joe at the piano keyboard, sweating, his shoulders still rippling to some residue of the music.

"How are you?" says Joe.

"Got something for you," says Lincoln.

Joe studies him for a long time. "School soon?"

"Got something."

Joe nods. "Where did you get it?"

He doesn't say anything. The man from last night flashes in his mind. A sudden seething inside, a hot boil in his stomach, his chest.

"FREE sign?" says Joe.

"What the hell does it matter."

Joe's eyes bore into him. "It's the most important thing," Joe says softly, so softly it slips right in.

Joe slides his fingers up and down the keyboard, not pressing them enough to make a loud sound. Lincoln crosses his arms in front of him, prepared to argue any point, anything at all.

"Today I'm feeling heavy," says Joe. "Mrs. Johnson, the woman in apartment B, her tremors are worse. She can barely hold her cup without spilling tea on her skirt. She needs her daughter to move in with her, but her daughter is wild and won't have it. And then Mr. Baxter in apartment C across the street, his son died."

Lincoln sits up. When death gets someone young, it jerks him to alertness. Youth doesn't get a free pass and so watch yourself; you think you know, but you know nothing. That man last night, threatening him as if it were a joke. Fear is still lodged like a clot in his throat. How much fear can a body hold?

"Shot in the back," says Joe.

"Where was he?"

"Hunter's Point. Got caught up in something. Nineteen years old. I went over there this morning to see what I could do. Mr. Baxter in his old ratty chair, not saying a word, tears streaming down his face."

"I'm careful."

Joe runs his fingers along the keyboard, this time playing all the notes, then moves into a song, something low and slow and sad, and Lincoln feels his heart sink into his back as if it crawled into a cave. Many times, his heart has found this cave, many, many times, when he comes back from the hill with the pretty houses and nice yards and trees, so many trees, when he comes back to the gray cement and black asphalt, sometimes his heart curls, tucks in that cave. Huddled there, alone, lonely, sad. Takes a long time to coax it back out again—a real long time.

When he finishes playing, Lincoln stands. "Come take a look."

Joe slowly pushes himself to stand. Lincoln takes him outside, where he's put the lavender flowers on the porch.

"Oh, now," he says, his hand to his mouth. "Lavender, you know me and lavender, we have a thing."

Lincoln smiles.

Joe bends down and tenderly touches one of the petals.

"I could dig up this weed patch," says Lincoln. "We could plant those flowers."

"I'm too old for digging."

"I said I could do it," says Lincoln.

"Listen to you." He sighs. "You know, you're going to have to take those flowers back."

Lincoln folds his arms across his chest. "You should have what you want."

"You're waking up. There's justice in your blood."

"Already got it."

"You do, but now it's mixing with anger. And that's some thing powerful."

Lincoln smiles. "I know."

"No, you don't. You're a young man, and that anger can bubble up at the wrong time, that's for sure. In front of the wrong person, and I don't mean just the white folk, and then you got a fist coming at your face or a gun stuck in your gut, you hear what I'm saying? You got to know when to let it out and when to keep it down."

He nods, uncertainly. "Okay."

The lavender flowers are still glowing, but something has changed. The roar of a car fills the air. A bus groans, sighs. The world rolls over.

"I've seen it spark in you, I have, and I've been watching for it. For it to rise up and take over, and before it does, I want you to take a look at it, hold that anger in your two hands and decide if it's the right place, the right time." Joe puts his hand on Lincoln's shoulder.

"You take deep breaths, son, when you feel that anger rise. Take long, deep breaths before you act on it. No more taking stuff because you feel righteous. You use that intelligence you have in your head; otherwise, that dream of justice you got isn't going anywhere."

❧

He's out, the sun warm and bright, and he's heading up the big hill, not hunting, not this time, but looking for ideas of what else he can plant in Joe's new garden. Got some of the weeds and the junk out. Someone threw a tire back there, a handful of smashed plastic water bottles, plastic containers, milk jugs, and chunks of concrete. That little patch of the planet was treated like a personal garbage can.

Joe bought eight bags of good dirt. When Lincoln opened one of the bags, he thrust his hands into the deep, dark dirt. Soothing to run your hands in it. Smelled good, too, the smell of growing. A scent that changes from mineral to wet to pungent. The smell stayed on his fingers, and he was happy about that.

He passes by the Big Blue Lilyturf, waving its purple at him, and smiles at the Double Knock Out Roses, so many red petals spilling out beauty. Look at the blue-and-white dahlias; Joe would love those to remind him that the world delivers good surprises.

He almost trips over it. Because he wasn't prepared, no tingling in his hands. But now that he sees it, his fingers feel on fire. A bike that looks his size, with a FREE sign. Ocean blue, Cannondale Treadwell. Tires are still good, the brakes work, a little rust on the chain, nothing he can't scrub off with a wool pad and lime juice. Make that chain shine silver again. He climbs on—it fits him, suits him. He's never given himself anything before, but this bike…he could ride during the day and feel those deep breaths, his legs burning, could feel like he's running in daylight.

He takes off the FREE sign, folds it, and puts it in his jeans back pocket. When he was seven years old he had a bike, but someone stole it. Cut the lock and took it from their porch. He cried big tears. He gets on and begins to pedal down the street, and the memory of riding is in his legs. This is good, real good;

he starts heading up a hill, deep inhales of air, and he stands up and pedals harder. He's riding up Webster, pumping hard, passing parked cars, people. At the top he stops and looks out to the bay. How easy to soar down this hill, how easy to soar like a bird to the water. He could even ride to the De Young, and, hell, he could ride to Ocean Beach. It's been years since he's been to the ocean. He and Joe once took the bus. He could ride this bike to the beach and hear the big crash of waves, and watch the seagulls knitted into blue sky. He could even ride to the Golden Gate Bridge! He's never been on it, but he thinks bikes are allowed. He's allowed. A boy on a bike: he can fly as fast and free as the wind.

Lincoln was a beautiful baby, all smiles and coos and big alert eyes. He was a good sleeper, which always warms parents' hearts. An early walker at nine months, he was pattering around, wanting to get on with it. Even then, he had something, a keen curiosity, a need to look at the world closely, intensely. The glimmer of a key, a whine of a dog, a wood floor creaking grabbed his attention as if he felt the world come closer and swell with significance. Flowers, those joyful expressions of beauty, of rapture, stunned him into stillness. I don't know if it was the color or shape or smell or all of it together, but they dismantled him as if they held an inner meaning for him.

He's got a dream. He's keeping it to himself because he doesn't want anyone's opinion and doesn't need anyone to tell him his dream is foolish or wrong or childish. I'm glad he's taking care because people can be careless and cruel. Harsh, jagged words pop out of their mouths like a whip or a knife. I've seen them stomp on marvelous dreams like swatting flies or mosquitoes, killing without thought. But whatever that dream is, he's going to make it a reality, and I'm pretty sure it means not only the rich and the white have green to look at, along with purple and red and pink that crackle, and Japanese maples and oak trees, but everyone does.

In his notebook under his bed, he's got long lists of names of plants, flowers, and trees—how much sun, water, shade—because he needs to know the specifics, every detail to not only imagine it but make it happen.

He's in Joe's backyard, digging up the last of the weeds with a shovel, sweat dripping off his nose, and the sweet smell of dirt in the air. He stops for a moment to catch his breath. Joe bought a packet of wildflower seeds. No need to pick and choose flowers, just toss the seeds everywhere and love whatever comes up, that's what Joe told him. Don't say one flower is better than the other, that's what's got this place in trouble in the first place.

Astonishing, the human imagination. I'm happy to hear Lincoln's voice because I forgot how the human imagination can leap five, ten, fifty years not to an apocalyptic future, but a beautiful one, seeing the granular, down to the lilac planted next to the oleander until the one who imagines with such passion is compelled to make the thing exist.

Day cooperates, making Lincoln's vision bright, lifting the fog from the city, and all is once more decked out. The eye can see more clearly; the nonexistent thing takes on more contour and texture. Get busy, says day. Everything is moving, hustling, hurrying—people, cars, plans, day infusing a purpose in the air, beaming its light on time, something to do early morning, late morning, a meeting before lunch. The pulse picks up; day ramps up the speed, and at some point, it feels as if the world is running so fast it will burst into flames. The thing must exist!

It's a magic trick, this human imagination. The beauty that comes from it: the magnificent sculpture, *The Force of Nature*, by Lorenzo Quinn; *The Starry Night*, by Vincent van Gogh; *The Thinker*, by Rodin; *The Caring Hand*, by Eva Oertli and Beat Huber, an enormous human hand cupping a tree so carefully as if it is a precious thing, which it is.

But, I remind myself, also the immense horror: the atomic bomb unspeakably aging the world; plastic seeping into everything, the sea, the fish, the human lungs; cars and trucks spewing carbon monoxide, chewing away the atmosphere; meat processing plants, or what I call death camps.

In San Rafael, California, above a parking lot 50,000 starlings have congregated. An enormous, dazzling, dark cloud, swirling, pulsating, contracting, and expanding, like a wave, like a lung. Not a single starling smashes into another because they play a gigantic game of telephone, one starling telling the closest seven starlings to change speed or direction, and those birds tell the next ones, and the next, the message rippling, and incredibly, the message is transmitted ungarbled. What's behind this magnificent cohesion? What caused this beautiful sight? A hungry falcon is circling, looking to eat a starling. Danger brings beauty and unity.

Can humans do this? Cohere against disaster?

I can imagine Lincoln telling seven others his dream, those who will hold his dream gently in their palms, and they tell seven more, on and on, until the momentum is for action. The thought of this excites me, and I want to celebrate the recognition of the possible.

The crows are calling. They're having a birthday party in the Moreton Bay Fig tree in Valencia. The tree's 186 years old today. Don't wait up.

Belonging

Here comes Hazel, stepping into the airport, her thoughts not on the earthly but on the heavenly. When Eleanor sees her, she's toppled over by an unexpected wave of emotion. It's been so long, how could they have let so many years go by. Eleanor has not seen her sister for ten years, a brief visit to Tanzania when Eleanor had talks with Delmar Company about limiting its CO^2 emissions. Nothing has prepared her for this. Eleanor's early thoughts of her sister made Hazel small, an afterthought, but she is anything but that. She looms large in Eleanor's heart, and the image of Hazel here stirs so many memories of the two of them as girls, as teens, growing beyond the envelope of home. And here is Hazel, in her dark blue skirt, matching blazer, and a starched white blouse, a prominent gold cross necklace laid openly on her chest, looking around for Eleanor.

Hazel seems glued to her spot, like a log in a stream of people, so Eleanor comes to her. As she approaches, she sees that Hazel has deep grainy stains of black on the thin skin under her tired eyes. Such a long flight, twenty hours traversing the globe for Eleanor.

When Hazel sees Eleanor, she brightens or startles, Eleanor isn't sure. Eleanor embraces Hazel and senses a holding back as if Hazel's body is a wooden board. "Was the flight terrible? It's so nice of you to come all this way."

"It's been a long while," says Hazel.

"I'm touched, I really am."

Hazel waves her off as if the trip was nothing, like she jumped on planes all the time, a real globe-trotter. "You're receiving a high honor, Ava explained to me. A once-in-a-lifetime occasion."

Ava's words, thinks Eleanor.

"And there happens to be a conference I want to attend," says Hazel.

There's her sister, practical, self-contained. Hazel's gaze darts around the crowded, noisy airport, voices blaring over the intercom in search of lost people or delayed flights. Eleanor guesses Hazel is overwhelmed by the San Francisco International Airport, where it seems representatives from every country have congregated. They start walking to get Hazel's luggage, and as they move from the gate, Hazel tells her about the conference, a gathering of Catholic leaders to talk about programs that address poverty.

They were once both attractive, maybe even beautiful, though Eleanor was the one with the big charismatic smile and what Arthur called a finely chiseled face as if made of rose marble. Exaggerating, thought Eleanor, but she soaked it in nevertheless. In her mid-sixties, Eleanor's face caved in on itself as if it grew weary of the upkeep, the scrutiny, and probing. Age sucked her skin dry. Still, remnants remain, as they do on Hazel, the high cheekbones, the unflinching, intense look in her eyes, especially when she's keen on something, as she is now, looking at Eleanor. Perhaps that isn't what most people call beautiful, but Eleanor does. Looking things in the eye, turning the cool white light on the truth before it slips out of sight.

After meeting with the Tanzania-based company, Eleanor took a taxi to the nunnery. She arrived unannounced, it's true, but Hazel refused to stop her duties, so Eleanor was left alone to wander the grounds and eat a scant meal with the other sisters, who were silent types, prone to side glances at her, the one who was not in a long robe.

"I'm sorry," said Hazel, who was folding sheets. "The work doesn't stop."

Eleanor told Hazel it was fine, she'd explore on her own, but she had, in fact, hoped Hazel would spend time with her, at least a few hours. Hazel explained that they were doing God's work, and everyone suffered if one person in the community didn't pull her weight. Community, service, and God's work peppered

Hazel's speech. Chastised, Eleanor nodded sheepishly, though she wanted to say, I just want to be with you.

On the drive back from the airport to San Francisco, Hazel fills her in on the convent, the church's work, and a recent grant that allows them to open a kitchen and serve meals. The convent is located down a dusty road, with nothing around it for at least two miles. The village nearby is a cluster of small shops—a shoe shop, a shop for meat and fish and fabric, and a post office. No rush of traffic, no shiny new cars, no tall, shiny buildings in the distance, and everyone moving at what must feel like the speed of light. It must be overwhelming and exhausting because twenty minutes into the drive, Hazel falls asleep.

When they reach Eleanor's house, Hazel jars awake and peers out. "I didn't realize you were rich. This house, the neighborhood, it's expensive."

Her directness is refreshing, though Eleanor doesn't recall this trait when they were growing up. Her sister feels sturdier and more substantially present in the world. Eleanor explains they got in when the prices were much lower. "We did all right, though."

"Do you miss him?" says Hazel.

Eleanor holds herself very still. She had written to her about Arthur's passing, and Hazel sent a note quoting Ecclesiastes 12:7, "And the dust returns to the earth as it was, and the spirit returns to God who gave it." If Eleanor remembers correctly, Hazel had one boyfriend in high school and a couple of months of dating. That was the end of her romantic days because she was accepted and then enrolled in The Seattle School of Theology. Did that high school romance involve kissing? Touching? Love?

"All the time," says Eleanor. "Every single day."

Hazel nods and tells her she'll pray for her. Eleanor feels the vein at her temple throb.

"Do you mind if I lie down?" says Hazel as she opens the car door. "It was a long flight."

"Not at all."

Blue greets them at the door, and Hazel barely acknowledges him. Eleanor wants to conclude something about her sister, something not very nice. Hazel never liked their father's animals and hated spending time in the old barn, complaining it stank of animal poop. Then again, Hazel's indifference to Blue may mean that she is tired.

Eleanor shows her to the guest bedroom and the bathroom and hurries to the kitchen to get her sister a glass of water and a plate of sliced apples and cheese. Hazel thanks her and closes the door.

Eleanor goes into her study, where she pulls out a chair and sits in front of her computer, trying to think of what to write for her speech. Blue comes in and lies near her chair. She knows what the Goldman people want to hear—the work she did in Mexico, negotiating with DeLittle Lumber to slow the cutting of old-growth trees (stalled for a while, then it went back to its previous ways of clear-cutting); endless meetings with Connell Metal to stop dumping toxins in the Tijuana River (two years of cleaner water, now one of the most polluted rivers in Mexico); her work in Indonesia to stop the building of a hydropower plant in Batang Toru, home of orangutans (it was stopped, but now the project is back). Same story—some successes that collapsed into failures—in Botswana, New Delhi, Ecuador, Afghanistan, Bhutan. The big leap was the creation of her nonprofit, The Environmental Economics Institute, in 1995 when she publicly brought the economy and the environment together. Heady days, working with Home Depot, Walmart, Intel, McKesson, Chevron, and others, proselytizing that to address environmental needs would lead to more—not less—profits. Not either/or, my friends; it's *and*—corporate enterprise *and* the environment. Flying everywhere, trying to fend off what she saw coming, Arthur urging her on—go, go, go, I'll take care of Ava and Ed, go, this is your time. She became a consultant to the big companies—the ones blatantly exploiting, the ones who could make a difference if they wanted to. Her job was to coax that desire into the world.

She taps away on the keys, writing this. When she finishes, she looks at it. It's what they want, what they expect. It makes her sick to her stomach.

In the morning, Hazel looks about the same, exhausted to the bone, as if no amount of sleep will revive her. Her complexion is slightly grayish, though she announces she slept well, and the quiet is lovely. Earlier, Eleanor went into the garden, cut reddish fuchsia from the garden, and put them in a glass vase on the table. The leaves were covered in dew, and now there is a puddle of water on the table as if the flowers are releasing an essential, mysterious substance.

Hazel's wrists remind Eleanor of a delicate teacup, and she worries her sister isn't eating enough. Not that Eleanor eats much anymore; her appetite seems to have vanished. Eleanor brings Hazel tea and suggests a big breakfast.

Hazel laughs girlishly, and in rushes the memory of young Hazel's quiet, almost swallowed, laugh. "I can't remember the last time I had a big breakfast."

Their father loved to cook, and on the weekends breakfast was a huge spread of food. Eleanor makes scrambled eggs, toast, hash browns, and cut grapefruit, and, happily, Hazel devours a full plate, though she keeps patting her stomach and complaining she must stop, she's going to burst, though it's delicious.

"When did you learn to cook?" says Hazel.

"I'm two years older than you," says Eleanor. "I've had more time on this earth to learn such things."

They laugh, and Eleanor feels warmth for her sister, who holds the most intimate details about her. The morning feels nearly buoyant.

"Remember when I collected all those bugs and put them in Mason jars in our bedroom," says Eleanor.

"You kept them on the shelf above your bed. They gave me the creeps. I'd dream they got out and were crawling in my bed."

They are sitting across from each other, and if Eleanor wanted to, she could reach across and touch her sister's hand. "They were so beautiful."

"At least you eventually let them go."

"Dad and his zebra," says Eleanor, smiling.

Hazel purses her thin lips. She has their mother's mouth, prim and tidy, while Eleanor has their father's, full-lipped and slightly red. "I always thought he loved William more than us."

Eleanor sets down her coffee cup. "Really? I never thought that."

"He was always out there. And then he kept getting more and more animals, and they took up all his time. The llama and the three greyhounds, the lamb, I lost track. A regular Noah's ark. I kept waiting for a Bengal tiger to show up."

Eleanor laughs, but Hazel doesn't.

"I loved that he had such generosity," says Eleanor. "It wasn't there before Mom died."

Hazel rests her chin on her palm. "I suppose that's one way to look at it."

"What's your way?" says Eleanor.

"He retreated from us, he entered into another reality, almost surreal. Those little goats running around everywhere, eating Mom's flowers. He couldn't face Mom's death. Dad and his precious animals. If you wanted to have some semblance of a relationship, you had to enter his menagerie. You could do that, and you did. I couldn't, nor did I want to."

She's never heard Hazel say this before and wants to ask if that's why Hazel didn't show up for their father's funeral. Surely she got Eleanor's message that he was in the hospital, and it didn't look good. But Eleanor stops herself because she doesn't want to strain their short time together. And she won't mention the zebra she adopted and keeps at a barn in Woodacre. Eleanor refills her sister's teacup and asks if she can make anything else for her. She has a desire to keep feeding her sister. Hazel says she's fine, but undeterred, Eleanor gets up and makes more toast.

Hazel neatly folds her napkin into a square. "After Mom died, we all buried ourselves in something," she says, smoothing the creases of her square. "First, you and Dad huddled in the barn with the animals. I didn't know what to do with myself, so there were my books and then, ultimately, the Bible. I started attending Bible studies class at St. Marks and met many good friends, people I'm still in touch with all these years later. And you, you like our father, became enraptured by nature. Your scientific, almost cool observations of the world, the way you could look at a dead animal was amazing and unnerving."

Eleanor has always viewed that time as idyllic, the perfect childhood, but Hazel's expression looks pained, as if reliving a bad memory.

"We found our way," says Eleanor.

"When we lost Mom, we lost the glue," says Hazel, her tone solemn and firm. "She was the center, the axis, and we were spokes. When we lost her, we all spun out in different directions and lost our way back to each other. I really missed her." She puts her napkin on the table and smiles stiffly at Eleanor. "But all that was long ago, water under the bridge. We've had many experiences since then, so we've revised our sense of ourselves."

"What's your sense of yourself?" says Eleanor.

Without hesitation, she says, "A woman of God."

Eleanor nods. Again, she's amazed at how solid her sister feels, so unlike her memories of Hazel as barely present, as if made of the lightest substance. She has to say that she's envious of this solidity.

"Have you read any work by Simone Weil?" says Hazel.

"I haven't."

Hazel sips her tea. "Well, I suppose I'm like her. My life and my whole attention are attuned to God."

Again, her certainty is enviable and also slightly suffocating. Eleanor refills Hazel's cup.

"And you? What's your sense of self?" says Hazel.

Eleanor feels her cheeks burn as if an embarrassing fire has been lit inside. She stares at a scratch on the wood floor. She has no idea how it got there and doesn't recall it being there two days ago. "I don't have one. I did, but it's gone." She laughs incredulously. Other losses, which she won't mention. "Someone my age with no self? A self-effacement."

Eleanor imagines all the things Hazel might say to her: without the anchor of God or the belief in Jesus, Eleanor will forever be adrift, there will be no salvation; she is lost without God, her spirit tormented, in anguish. But she says none of these things. "Self-effacement is a step closer to God." Her voice is light.

"Not if it's a helpless self-effacement," says Eleanor.

Hazel looks into her teacup as if the answer might be there. "If you can cultivate patience and not frantically seek a solution, I think the truth will arrive."

What a kind thing to say. Eleanor feels a swell of love for her sister and wants to tell her how much she's missed her, how it's been far too long, this coming together, how come they didn't reach out to each other sooner? Eleanor puts her hand on top of Hazel's, and Hazel sits there looking a little stunned.

The next day, late morning, Ava arrives to drive them to the awards ceremony at the San Francisco War Memorial Opera House. Ava looks like she's the one who should give the speech. Gorgeous, her daughter is in her youth, her sensual white silky blouse and gray pencil skirt hugging her curvaceous hips. Her face is pink-cheeked, and her bright-red lipstick draws attention to her plump lips, though the color is too loud for Eleanor's taste, too anxiously demanding attention. Compared to her, she and Hazel are cracked relics from another time, best kept on a side table with a low-lit lamp.

Hazel is wearing the same suit she wore on the airplane, hopefully with a clean white blouse, but maybe not. Eleanor didn't think to offer her sister something to wear, and she won't do so now because she doesn't want to offend Hazel.

Ava scrutinizes her mother. "Are you sure you want to wear that?"

Eleanor looks down at her black skirt and her charcoal gray blouse. She even managed to put on black stockings without ripping them. She thought she looked stylish, modern. "What's wrong?"

"It's so… austere," says Ava. "Like you're going to a funeral. Can you add a colorful scarf?"

Hazel has a passive expression as if she's withdrawn to another realm. Eleanor remembers this about Hazel, how adept she is at retreating, tunneling so far inward, unreachable like a cat tucked under a couch, refusing to come out. Eleanor would call her sister for dinner, and there would be no response. She'd find Hazel in her bedroom, in bed, swallowed up by a book.

Does she look too severe? She doesn't feel very celebratory, and she doesn't want to go searching in her bedroom. A strange spark of rebellion takes residence in Eleanor. "I don't think a colorful scarf is necessary."

Ava nods, but her mouth signals her disapproval. "Did you hear from Ed? Is he coming?"

"He's deep in rehearsal," says Eleanor. "A big performance coming up."

"Of course he can't make it," says Ava. "He's such a baby, and you baby him."

Eleanor imagines Hazel rolling her eyes at the petty family squabbles.

"Don't make this into such a big deal," says Eleanor.

"I've done no such thing," says Ava, "because it is, in its own right, a big deal."

❧

The opera house is packed. Eleanor has been told about 4,000 attendees are here. It's what she expected and why she didn't want to do this. There is the stage, and the podium, and there is the glass of water, and the ficus plant, and a microphone, and everyone has an assigned task—the audience, the recipients, the foundation that is giving the awards. It is the root of the problem, she thinks. That the ritual is carried along, as it's been done for over thirty years, but the times are extraordinary and dire, and by no means should the standard affair continue like a steady drumbeat.

She looks at the sea of people, and then, standing in front of her, are Sid and Miriam. She hugs them both. Miriam gives Eleanor a quick kiss on the cheek.

"I'm so happy you could make it," says Eleanor.

"We're here for whatever you need," says Sid.

Miriam, lovely with her curly, red-colored hair and pale skin like milk. "Absolutely," she says, looking searchingly at Eleanor as if to decipher what it is, exactly, that Eleanor needs. Miriam, like Sid, is a good friend, ready to surround her with care.

A young woman with soft, pale hair comes up to Eleanor and introduces herself as the program assistant for the foundation. She's supposed to take Eleanor backstage with the other Goldman prize recipients.

Eleanor looks at the people filling the auditorium. A tremor runs through her, quaking her core, and she suddenly doesn't want to be apart from Sid and Miriam or Hazel and Ava. It's as if once she loses sight of them, she'll lose them forever. An irrational thought, but she can't shake it.

"I can sit out here with the audience," says Eleanor.

The woman glances around as if seeking help, but there is no one.

"Mom, just go," says Ava.

"Really, this is good," says Eleanor.

"The others are backstage."

"I'd like to sit with my family and friends," Eleanor says more firmly.

The young woman hesitates, glances at her watch, then says she'll let the folks backstage know what's happening.

Eleanor doesn't look at Ava because she knows she'll see an expression of annoyance. Hazel is studying Eleanor, but Eleanor can't decipher what she's thinking. Eleanor leads the way and finds a row of seats about halfway to the stage. Hazel takes the seat next to her, and Sid and Miriam scoot to the other side of Hazel. Ava sits in the row in front of her as if trying to distance herself from Eleanor. Eleanor takes it all in, the dazzling dresses and sharp, dark suits, the dark-red carpet running down the aisles, and the loud, excited voices bouncing off the walls. The aristocracy is here; San Francisco prefers to think of itself as progressive and tolerant, but behind that, old money runs the show. She's been in enough corporate offices to know the way old money pulls the levers and turns the knobs.

"Remember when Mom took us to the opera?" says Hazel.

"How old were we?" says Eleanor.

"I think you were nine, and I was seven. She wanted us to be cultured," says Hazel, laughing. "She certainly would disapprove of me. Not a museum or opera house where I live. Not even an art gallery."

"I hated the opera," says Eleanor.

"Me too."

"What did Mom love about it?" says Eleanor.

"No idea. She used to play those records and sing along."

Eleanor laughs. "She couldn't hit the right notes, but that didn't stop her."

"She had courage, that's for sure."

A gray-haired man approaches the podium, most likely the president of the Goldman Foundation. He's glancing around, waiting for the voices to quiet. Hazel has that passive, detached expression again, and when Eleanor makes eye contact with Sid, he winks and gives her a thumbs-up. Miriam nods to her reassuringly. Ava is alert, perched on the edge of her chair, darting her gaze here and there as if on the lookout, ready to smile, to greet, to stand, and to shake hands. She'll grease the wheels, if need be, to make sure her severe, funereal mother doesn't further offend.

But then again, Ava might be paving her path here for some time in the future. She's doing exciting things in the realm of biology, working on a bacterium that eats plastic. That's one way to address an enormous problem plaguing the world. Well, good for Ava. To someday find her way right here, to this auditorium, to give a speech of her own. If that's what she wants, then Eleanor hopes she gets it.

The lights dim, and the opera house settles. More of what is always done at events like these ensues: the exuberant talk about what has been achieved to help the planet, the chance to pat themselves on the back. She glances at the program. The prizewinners are young and bright and brimming with a fighting spirit, grassroots environmental warriors, everyone except her. She's met Carlos Hernandez from Guatemala, who founded an organization to stop illegal clear-cutting. They were at a meeting seven years ago with government officials, trying to elicit help to stop drug dealers from cutting swaths of the rainforest for clandestine airplane landing strips and roads. In the program she's listed as the last speaker, Eleanor Gergen.

The opera house is dark. Broadcast on a screen that stretches across the big stage are images of vibrant green, healthy forests, clear blue lakes, streams, white snowy mountains, and faces of people smiling, all of which make Eleanor terribly sad. She closes her eyes and listens to one recipient's speech after another, full of hope and fiery passion and optimism. How do they do it? How can they breathe in the tight space of illusion? Eleanor is amazed and envious, and her mouth is full of so much grief it's hard to swallow.

"We could leave," whispers Hazel. "Just slip out that side door." She gestures her head to the right. Eleanor spotted it too.

Eleanor rubs her eyes, and an image is dredged up from her murky memory, one she hasn't thought of in years. Those summers spent at the rented beach house at Bewilster Lake, jumping off the dock together, holding hands, and screaming in anticipation of the cold water. Muscle tight to bone. Underwater, she'd open her eyes and search for Hazel's pale legs and arms thrashing, her long hair swaying like its own entity. They'd swim furiously to the surface and pop up into the world of air. She'd look at her sister, how beautiful her sister's shiny wet face, so alive. In a flash, they'd swim hard and fast to the white buoy, and by the time they reached it, their bodies were warm, and they'd swim back to the dock, leisurely, sometimes floating on their backs to look at the blue sky with the puffy white clouds. Eleanor was always aware of where Hazel was in the water, how close, how far, and if she got too far, she'd swim toward Hazel. Hazel was a strong swimmer, but as her older sister, Eleanor felt protective and wanted to ensure her safety. It was also fun to hold hands underwater and peer at the tiny silverfish swimming beneath them among the big gray rocks.

They'd climb up the ladder and spread out their beach towels at the dock, so they didn't get splinters. Hazel would lie down with Eleanor beside her, Hazel in her green one-piece bathing suit, Eleanor in her blue-and-white polka-dot suit, the summer sun warming their cold skin. Looking back on it, she can't remember another time when she felt so close to Hazel, and the sound of water gently licking the dock has to be one of the loveliest sounds in the world.

The room fills with spirited applause, and Carlos Hernandez from Guatemala is speaking with forceful passion punctuating the room like a drum. "We will fight. We won't stop fighting. We will prevail because we must. There's no other option."

The tsunami of applause hits Eleanor. She opens her bag to see if her speech is still there, pushing aside her glasses, wallet, and bottle of Tums. When she can't find it—Hazel murmurs something—her pulse picks up another notch. She dumps the contents of her bag onto her lap and in a frenzy, her heart racing as she searches through her things—her wallet, peppermint gum, grocery receipts, a speckled rock from a beach, a folded program from the symphony, Brahms' *The Alto Rhapsody.*

Tucked in the program, she finds her speech in a tight, folded square. She doesn't remember folding it like that.

The auditorium fills with applause. The board's president is at the podium again, and Eleanor is swept up by the sensation of seeing herself from the ceiling as if she is accompanied by a second self, an observer watching with curiosity as the self in the seat struggles to find the energy to do what she has been asked to do. With her knees pressed tight together and her arms wrapped around herself, her hands look cut off. At that moment, another memory surfaces, a time when Hazel had gotten mad at her for something and when they'd gone swimming and reached the buoy, as Eleanor's head came out of the water, Hazel pushed her head back under. And she kept it there for what seemed like minutes, though it probably was only a handful of seconds, but enough to make Eleanor's lungs tighten and panic to grip her.

A jab of an elbow against her ribs. "You're up," says Hazel.

Eleanor slowly stands and smooths her skirt. Ava smiles up at her, a hint of panic in her eyes and upper lip. Eleanor heads up the stairs and crosses the stage, listening to her heels click against the wood, feeling the bright lights blast her. When she reaches the podium, she puts on her glasses. She looks out at the audience in front of her, then the people in the higher balcony seats, then beyond them at the back beige wall, and the two exit signs glowing hot red.

She unfolds her speech, tries to flatten the creases. When she glances at the opening, her stomach roils. Sweat pops on her forehead because it sounds so false, so wrong, because she can't find an ounce of celebratory joy, and if she pretends it's there, she's ignoring the chaotic mix of despair and rage and regret; if she pretends, something vital will be sacrificed, something she can't afford to lose.

"I"—and even that isn't what she wants to say, and now she sees her life bared in front of her, a life of restraint, of holding back the harsher words, as if those words have been placed in a cage, the anger at the mindless destruction, at the refusal to think beyond one's desires, the heartless killing of the plants and trees and animals, all of it locked up, humans placing themselves at the center of the world, and the key to the cage is hidden—even from herself, because she always told herself, to be heard, she can't come across as strident or angry or heartbroken, and even if she has the key in her hand as she does now, she can't bring herself to unlock the door—"I thank you."

In the silence, a sneeze, the rustle of papers, the squeak of a chair. She thinks she sees Hazel's gray head of hair, Ava's face full of attentiveness and worry. She heads back to her seat. The applause is hesitant and dies out quickly.

"Well, you showed them," says Hazel.

Eleanor stares straight ahead, not sure what she just did. Ava turns around and looks at Eleanor, eyes wide, aghast. The board president is at the podium, thanking the guests and the recipients, and he's talking rapidly, praising the excellent work of the awardees, and Eleanor senses he's trying to move quickly from what just happened, from what Eleanor just did. Her doing. When he stops, the room erupts with movement, as if it can't contain itself, and everyone must flee from Eleanor. Eleanor hurries to the exit, not bothering to check if Sid or Miriam or Hazel or Ava is following because she, too, feels she must escape. What did she do? Near the door to her freedom, a tall man with a beard and dark eyes blocks her way out.

"Eleanor," he says, his voice smooth, calm.

She stops and tries to place him. He says he and Arthur went to college together, but she still can't place him, but then again, she's out of sorts.

By now, Ava and Hazel have caught up to her.

"There's a reception at city hall," says Ava, her tone chastising. "You have to go to that."

Hazel has a quiet, knowing smile, as if she and Eleanor are aligned, sharing a secret; but what could that possibly be? Ava corrals Eleanor and walks shoulder to shoulder with her out the front door and into the night as if she fears Eleanor might dart away like a rebellious child. The air is cold, smudged by car exhaust, and the city lights blot out the stars. Hazel is behind her, and Eleanor hears her telling Sid and Miriam about the convent. She's working on a book—Eleanor didn't know that—something about Christian agape. "It's not a feeling," says Hazel, "it's a motivation for action. A sacrificial love that voluntarily suffers for the benefit of others."

Inside city hall, Eleanor is dazed by the already sizable crowd gathered around the long tables with white tablecloths, where there is an assembly of wine bottles and hundreds of sparkling wine glasses. Waiters are lined up like soldiers in black trousers and skirts and white aprons, holding silver platters of hors d'oeuvres. In her mind, Eleanor made the reception optional and banished it from the night. Ava is eyeing her as if to stop her from walking out or doing something outrageous again.

For a moment, Eleanor marvels at herself—that she could do such a rebellious thing! How wondrous! But that feeling is avalanched by shame. What came over her? She shouldn't have come, shouldn't have accepted the award. Her first impulse to refuse the award was right. She should have urged them to choose someone who could get in line and celebrate the small victories. People are in little clusters, holding drinks, talking, and keeping their distance from Eleanor, who feels the tension in the room—her doing; she is the one who summoned the storm cloud.

Carlos comes over. A muscular, lean man with beautiful white teeth. "That took courage."

"It took something," she says.

He laughs loudly, and Eleanor feels her twisted stomach ease slightly. Ava is about ten feet away, talking to a woman who is gesturing wildly. Eleanor is afraid she left Ava to pick up the shattered pieces.

Carlos's smile quickly disappears. "What's going on in my country is terrible." He shakes his head. "The government is no help, and we're constantly putting ourselves in danger. I try to stop doing this work, but can't, I can't accept the situation.

And so, I keep going and keep working and fighting. I'll probably die doing this. We've formed a new group to stop a waste facility near Flores. It's too close to the drinking water supply." His lower jaw juts out as if ready to fight right now. "The government will do anything that provides jobs, and the facility is promising 200 jobs. We don't have many people on our side because they want the work. Except," he says, smiling softly, "the Madres. The Madres fight hard. They have vision."

"Yes, the mothers."

"They feel the weak pulse of the planet. They are life. God bless them."

"And everyone else?"

"Ah, Eleanor," he says, shaking his head, smiling. "You should have spoken up there."

She finishes her wine and feels it rush to her head. "I've been talking and talking my entire life and look what's happened."

"We are moving boulders. Maybe in another lifetime, they will budge."

"We don't have another lifetime, you know that," says Eleanor.

When a waiter hands her a new glass of wine, she sees that she and Carlos are surrounded by a small gathering of people, including Ava and Hazel, who are listening to their exchange.

"So, is that why you said nothing?" says a man with a sharp face and sharper eyes. He introduces himself, Bernard Schatzire, a member of the Goldman board. "Surely we should celebrate the accomplishments."

"I'm sorry, you're right," says Eleanor. "I truly am sorry, but I can't celebrate, you see, because it glosses over the awful truth."

One bushy eyebrow raises. "The truth?"

"That it isn't enough, none of what we're doing is enough. Even with the actions of these courageous, passionate environmentalists honored today. We can't get beyond self-interest, which is one of the most destructive forces."

Ava, tight-lipped, shakes her head. "You've always said that."

"Visit any economics class, any business class," says Eleanor.

"Meet with the CEOs of the Fortune 500."

"But in the environmental studies, you don't hear that," says Ava. "We hear about Darwinian evolution and cooperation and the public good. Or listen to the anthropologists who tell us as a species, we're neither strong nor fast, but because of our ability to create and cooperate, we've survived. Yours isn't the only narrative."

Eleanor doesn't want to have this argument in public with her daughter, but she's caught up in it and can't stop herself. "I think the only thing that will wake people is disaster."

"But then it's too late," says Carlos.

She feels her face burn. "It's already too late."

Hazel steps forward. "It's never too late."

Eleanor stumbles out of her shock at her sister's voice and introduces her.

"What's your view, Sister Maria?" says Bernard.

"Let me remind you, there's a benevolent Being," says Hazel. "An omniscient, benevolent Being. I know San Francisco isn't a bastion of religious types or churchgoers—"

"Please, I'm interested in your view," says Bernard.

"We're part of God's plan," says Hazel. "With our humble and minimal knowledge, we can't possibly know what the plan is, but there is one."

Eleanor feels a quickening in her chest, a detonation of hot anger as Hazel quotes St. Augustine, saying how God is ineffable, unspeakable, and transcends even the human mind. It's God's world, His creation, and He wouldn't let it be destroyed. Hazel's tone is full of authority as if she were the one who won the award and now has stepped up to a podium to give a speech.

How easily the key fits into the cage's lock, how easily it opens the door. "God must be looking elsewhere because the earth is being decimated," says Eleanor.

"Maybe we must lose something to value it," says Hazel coolly. "But I come back to the truth: God has a plan, even if it involves destruction."

"How can you say that?" says Eleanor, her tone veering toward a screech. "There will be immense suffering. There *is* immense suffering right now."

"God's plan," murmurs Hazel.

Is that all she can say? Over and over? "Religion introduced a terrible bias in Western thought," says Eleanor, seething, "namely anthropocentrism, namely that humans are the most significant thing in the universe. I gave a speech back in 1960—that long ago—tracing the Christian influence in the Middle Ages to the ecological crisis in the twentieth century. And what's that influence? That the earth is for human consumption, for human exploitation."

Hazel frowns. "You're wrong. You're conflating anthropocentrism with the destruction of the—"

"That terrible word 'dominion' in Genesis," interrupts Eleanor. Words she kept caged seem suddenly just and right. "We're still living with this: 'And God said, Let us make man in our image, after our likeness: and let them have dominion over the fish of the sea, and over the fowl of the air, and over the cattle, and over all the earth, and over every creeping thing that creepeth upon the earth.'"

"I'm surprised you even know that verse," says Hazel coolly.

A hush falls over the crowd. The world feels stripped down to one woman, the woman in front of her, Sister Maria.

"We now say 'stewardship,'" says Sister Maria.

"A little late."

Sister Maria's face tightens. "You're being simpleminded, putting the blame on religion's shoulders. What about capitalism, which you supported and never tried to reform? That economic system is based on exploiting people and the earth. So I'd say you bear some of the blame. Maybe that's why you had such trouble accepting this award. Your guilt stifling you."

Eleanor is balanced between anger and sadness because her sister's words cut too deeply to brush aside. That man, who earlier said he knew Arthur in college—is staring at her, looking at her with concern and pity. She wishes Arthur were here, and now she tips into a well of grief and fights to modulate her breath, but the cage door is still wide open. "I regret so many things, I regret I didn't do more or didn't go about things a different way. Maybe because I'm seventy and death is loudly jabbering in my ear, it's all become too much. I wish I could close my eyes to it all, and sometimes I can, when I read a novel and slip out of reality. It's such a relief to leave this world, and then I'm alarmed and devastated because I love this world." She quickly pinches the bridge of her nose to stop the tears. What is happening to her? "The trees and birds, the mountain lions and ducks. The flowers, my god, don't get me started on the flowers. You call young women beautiful, but have you truly looked at a flower?" Now tears are coming. "What did the birds do to deserve this?" She turns to Sister Maria, sincerely wanting an answer. "How does that figure in God's plan?"

Sister Maria stiffens and heads for the door. It's clear she's had enough. So has Eleanor.

In the car, no one says a word. Eleanor sits in the passenger seat, astonished and ashamed of herself; it feels as if she were swept up in a current, thrashing in the wild rapids. She still feels she's being tossed in turbulence. It's never been so easy to cry, but tears continue to gather again and again, as she wipes them away with her hand. Even at Arthur's funeral she did not fall apart but stood there, dressed in black, feeling like a block of ice. She stares out the window, watching the world blur by.

Finally, Ava breaks the silence. "Mom?"

"I'm sorry," says Eleanor. "I'm exhausted, my nerves in shreds. Hazel, I'm sorry."

Hazel, who is in the back seat, says nothing. The rest of the car ride is stony silence until they turn on Divisadero.

"We put on quite a show," says Hazel.

Eleanor startles. "A show? You weren't serious? It was a performance for you?"

"I was very serious," she says. "But it became a performance.

I suppose it's what you wanted all along. To give some sort of speech, to show them. You've always found a way."

Eleanor isn't sure what Hazel is speaking about because it goes beyond this moment, burrowing back into their history.

"You should have spoken at the podium," says Hazel. "Instead, you pulled me into it."

"I didn't pull you into anything. You stepped right in."

"My bright, brilliant sister," says Hazel.

There is it, the old history between them, their father's affection for Eleanor, his disappointment with Hazel. Is that what this is about? Her father wanted someone to argue ideas with him at the dinner table, he wanted robustness, and it wasn't going to be Hazel, who was so quiet, so withdrawn in her world, who found what she needed in the pages of the Bible. What attraction did it hold for her? Rules? Guidance? A clear path? What she didn't get from their father?

"You didn't even bother to come to Dad's funeral," says Eleanor.

"I found out too late. It would have been over by the time I found a flight."

How convenient, Eleanor wants to say. She stares out the window, wanting Hazel to confess to her regret about missing the funeral and her feelings of guilt, but Hazel doesn't say anything.

Ava drops them off, and in silence they stride into Eleanor's house, both to their respective rooms, doors shut. Eleanor takes a long, hot shower, climbs into bed, and feels the fogbank roll over her mind. She falls asleep, and when she wakes, she's disoriented and then feels terrible, as if the world has tilted on its axis precariously.

She hears the click of a glass against a plate coming from the kitchen. She looks around her room, almost as if she is a visitor: the dresser with the small figurine of a glass elephant, her row of earrings dangling from a rack, and the photo of her and Arthur at a windswept beach. The row with her sister—in front of everyone—is a pain in her ribs. Almost at once she relinquishes any justification for what she did. It was a show, as Hazel said. As she pulls on a pair of jeans and an old sweater, she feels a pang at her behavior, at herself.

Hazel is eating a bowl of tomato soup.

Eleanor stands on the threshold. "I want to apologize again."

Hazel looks her up and down as if trying to gauge what Eleanor might do next. Blue comes over, and Eleanor opens the back door. He heads out and pees on a post.

"I've put it behind me," says Hazel, and before Eleanor can say anything more, Hazel holds up her hand, signaling no need to talk about it.

Eleanor offers to make her a salad, olive bread with goat cheese, or a vegetable stew—she hears the pleading in her voice to make amends, somehow—but Hazel says she's happy with what she has. Eleanor isn't sure what to do or say until Blue scratches at the door. When she lets him back in, she tells Hazel how she and Arthur found him at the shelter, thin with patchy hair and kennel cough, and she prattles on, hoping to fill the air with something calmer.

Surprisingly, Hazel whistles and Blue goes over, wagging his tail. Hazel caresses his head. Hazel used to bring home strays, not dogs, but girls. That's what their father called them, stray girls who got kicked out of their houses. That one girl whose parents were deeply religious and refused to let their daughter wear jeans or sneakers or go out with friends on a Friday night until she couldn't stand it any longer. She left and moved in, sleeping in the twin bed in Hazel's room. At night, listening to the sound of their muffled voices and occasional bursts of laughter, Eleanor marveled at how alive Hazel was, how vibrant, so different from how she acted around Eleanor and their father. How much she wanted to go to Hazel's room and join them, but Eleanor knew she'd feel left out, the two of them already so close. In her memory, Eleanor's pony was her best friend, along with William the zebra, and, of course, their father.

Hazel's hand trembles, and she spills soup on the placemat.

Hazel must have had at least one close friend of hers pass away, she must hear death whispering to her too. Eleanor is suddenly struck that she doesn't know her sister at all, this woman who seems to have found all the answers.

"Tell me about your life," says Eleanor. "What do you like about it?"

Hazel puts her spoon down. "Are you asking me honestly or to find some way to put me in my place?"

Eleanor leans her back against the counter. "I'm asking honestly."

"My beliefs are aligned with my actions. It's a very serene and joyful way to live."

"You don't wish for more?"

"You probably don't believe me, but I have all I want. In fact, this might surprise you, and it would certainly surprise our father; I feel a sense of abundance." Hazel smiles softly. "There is the sisterhood, with very good, generous, kind women in the convent. Women who would do anything for me."

A jab at Eleanor, at least that's how it feels.

"It's joyous," says Hazel. "The Word, the study, the prayer, the community, work as another form of prayer and worship." She looks around. "I don't belong here. The noise of the city, the roar of traffic, the trucks, the clatter, the abundance of material possessions—my life is quiet by choice. We serve each other and the community, and God. I'm woven into the fabric of care."

"I'm glad to hear that." Though Eleanor can't believe that's the whole story. There's never loneliness? Never doubt? Doubt that God even exists. Eleanor roots around her stash of memories, trying to recall when Hazel turned her back on the world. Did it start when their mother died? Or her love affair with books, which stretched as far back as Eleanor can remember?

"You can't be serious, placing all the blame on religion," says Hazel. "That was hyperbolic, I hope. In the heat of the moment, as they say."

Eleanor doesn't want to argue; she's too tired for that. Her old self seems to have returned, the one that is conciliatory, that hates conflict, and seeks the middle ground. "Again, I apologize."

"If it wasn't hyperbolic, then you're wrong." She suggests Eleanor do some more serious reading into the matter. "I can send you some suggestions."

Eleanor is struck again by Hazel's authority, her gravitas, and her power. It's not only in her voice but in her posture, with her shoulders back and her spine straight. The girl who floated along, barely voicing her opinions, is gone.

It is the opposite for Eleanor, who now seems to doubt everything. But she does know her attack on religion isn't wrong. As she fixes herself a salad, she thinks it's not only the word "dominion," but also the problem of sin. If humankind lives in a fallen state, lesser than God, what better way to feel good about yourself than to find something more inferior still? And is there any better thing to make lesser than nature, which is unable to defend itself? Though some interesting things are going on in that area, lawsuits on behalf of animals, giving them a voice. New Zealand has passed a law that declares animals as sentient beings. Bolivia and Ecuador adopted laws, the Rights of Mother Earth, giving legal standing to nature. The high court in Uttarakhand, India, declared the Ganga and Yamuna Rivers legal persons. And nature is finding its voice and defending itself in big loud ways that will destroy many parts of the world and humans too.

Hazel tilts her head, studying Eleanor. "You should be placing the blame at the feet of Descartes. Nature is soulless. I think we can both agree on that."

Eleanor readily concurs, happy to find a small patch of common ground. "Can I make you some tea?"

"Sure," says Hazel. "That would be nice."

Hazel spends the next day at her conference, and Eleanor heads outside with a broom, sweeping her front path and sidewalk.

She keeps going, tending to Ilana's patch of sidewalk, path, and front porch. Ilana opens the front door and thanks Eleanor, telling her she's feeling better. Would Eleanor like to come inside? Eleanor knows Ilana gets lonely because her children live far away and rarely visit.

In Ilana's kitchen Eleanor offers to make her an omelet, and while she eats, Eleanor cleans her kitchen counters and wood floors. She can feel herself warding off the depression.

"You're a whirlwind, Eleanor," says Ilana. "I wish I had your energy, but you're making me exhausted just watching you."

After she vacuums and dusts the front living room, Eleanor heads home, leashes up Blue, and meets Sid for a walk in Golden Gate Park. He is still grappling with his painting, still at war with himself, and she, too, is stuck in her own muck. But there's solace in that—two souls struggling and commiserating.

Fortunately, today she works with her neighbor's daughter, helping her with reading. Claire comes by after school, and they sit side by side at the kitchen table. Claire pulls out her book, *The Raccoon That Ran Away.* She has a homemade bookmark, a picture of what looks like a lightning bolt—white on a dark blue background—and in small letters, she's written, *I Love Marshmallows.* Eleanor sits beside Claire, listening to her small voice grapple with the consonants and vowels, her tongue maneuvering this way and that. S comes out as sh, and b gets mixed with p.

She stops. Eleanor glances at the page. Claire is pointing to a word: *situation.*

"Tricky, isn't it?" says Eleanor.

Eleanor helps her sound out each letter, and from Claire's mouth the word emerges. Claire beams and continues unraveling the words. Eleanor closes her eyes, listening to the story of the raccoon that ran away and has lost its way in the world and is now sitting underneath a blue Buick.

At the end, Claire closes the book. "I liked the story. How about you?"

"I did too. What did you like about it?"

"That the raccoon ran away because it was sad."

"Interesting. I liked when it rained, and the raccoon pulled out an umbrella and enjoyed it."

"Yeah, that's good."

Eleanor walks her to the front door.

"You're a lot more patient than my mom," says Claire.

"I'm glad I can help. Moms are busy. Lots of things to get done."

When Hazel returns at dinnertime, she is drained. "There are no easy answers to the complex problem of poverty."

"That seems to be the conclusion of every modern problem," says Eleanor. "It makes me wonder if we've evolved enough as a species to address all the things we've ruined."

Hazel takes a deep breath as if prepared to launch into a lecture, but she doesn't. They both seem to be censoring themselves, tiptoeing. It's exhausting. Hazel eats her vegetables with a deliberateness that suggests she's counting how many times she chews before swallowing.

Eleanor climbs on the stepping stool to reach a wine glass, hoping to entice her sister, but the plastic stool cracks. Luckily, she doesn't fall, but the sharp plastic cuts the bottom of her foot. She hobbles over to a chair. A bright line of red blood is drawn across her arch.

"Sit," says Hazel. "Lift your foot on the chair."

Eleanor does as Hazel suggests, and Hazel heads to the bathroom, returning with a wet cloth and a Band-Aid. She presses the cloth on Eleanor's foot, and slowly the bleeding stops. Carefully she dries off Eleanor's foot and puts on a Band-Aid.

"Thank you," says Eleanor.

"It'll be sore for a while," says Hazel.

After dinner, Eleanor suggests watching a movie, but Hazel says she's too tired and should go to bed, a long flight ahead of her tomorrow. Hazel does the dishes so Eleanor can keep her weight off her foot. Eleanor watches from the kitchen table, noting her sister's singular focus as if a clean plate is all that matters in the world. It's how she used to be, thinks Eleanor, wholly enveloped in whatever her work demanded. A beautiful sight. When she's done Hazel wipes her hand on the tea towel and says she's heading to bed.

Eleanor is surprised that she feels a sense of rejection. She sits for a moment after Hazel has left for her room, trying to think about what she should do. Knock on her sister's door? Ask if she needs anything? When she hears the shower, Eleanor hobbles to her bedroom and reads in her bed, half listening for Hazel, half hoping for a knock on her door, with Hazel standing there, confessing that a movie sounds like a good idea after all. When an hour goes by, and she hears nothing, Eleanor turns off her light.

In the morning Eleanor drives Hazel to the airport. She doubts she'll see her sister again. It's a long flight to Tanzania, and she can't imagine what will bring Hazel here again except perhaps Eleanor's funeral, if that.

"I'll walk you in," says Eleanor.

"There's no need," says Hazel. "You can drop me off at the curb."

Eleanor is about to argue but hears something final in Hazel's voice as if she's had enough of this world, of Eleanor. Hazel must spend most of her days in solitude, not unlike how Eleanor spends her time now that Arthur is gone.

In the passenger seat Hazel looks directly at Eleanor, her dark, steady eyes. "I hope you find some peace in your life." Hazel opens her stiff black bag and pulls out a small Bible. "For you."

Eleanor laughs, and Hazel smiles.

"You were always into books," says Eleanor, taking the book.

"To the very end," says Hazel. "I'm sorry I didn't get to see Ed."

"Ed lives in his own world."

"Ava is a smart girl. You're lucky she's in your life."

"For that, I'm grateful."

Hazel looks at her with kind eyes as if something deep inside has been moved by the presence of Eleanor. Or maybe she's assuming that what is happening to her is also happening to Hazel.

"Okay, then," says Hazel, her hands properly folded in front of her. "I know you don't want to hear this, but God will provide."

"I'll take whatever he can give me," says Eleanor.

Hazel gets out of the car, and Eleanor follows and comes over to the curb. It is Eleanor who steps toward her and hugs Hazel, Eleanor who hugs her tight.

"Thank you for coming," says Eleanor.

Hazel says, "From Romans, 'May the God of hope fill you with all joy and peace in believing, so that by the power of the Holy Spirit you may abound in hope.'"

In return, Eleanor quotes Emily Dickinson, "Hope is the thing with feathers that perches in the soul." Hazel smiles, and Eleanor asks Hazel to call when she lands so she knows Hazel made it there all right.

"I know I sound like I'm mothering you," says Eleanor.

"I don't mind," says Hazel.

"Okay, then you need to eat more."

Hazel picks up her suitcase. "One more thing: you can find God almost anywhere," says Hazel. "And heaven on earth can be found right here."

Eleanor widens her eyes. "That sounds pretty unorthodox."

Hazel smiles. "I think that's what Dad did with all those animals. He made his own heaven."

It is Eleanor who gives Hazel a soft kiss on the cheek, which makes Hazel step back. She quickly recovers, hugs Eleanor tightly, then turns and heads on her way. Eleanor stands on the curb, suddenly feeling bereft and forsaken. She wants to chase after Hazel, to say wait, stay longer, stay here. She watches Hazel enter the airport, and the darkness inside swallows her up.

Eleanor used to be up before the first pale light sneaked through the gap in her curtain. As a girl she would scamper outside as if she must plunge herself into 5:30 a.m.'s frigid air and be the first one to the barn, the first one the waking animals would see. Sometimes the stars would still be out, but more often a heavy gray cloud layer swollen with future rain. I remember that: she'd look up at the sky, maybe to feel a moment of vastness or only to check the weather. She'd feed William and the llamas, but not the sheep who liked to sleep late. She'd hum as she worked in the barn, something lyrical and light. Her father would find her brushing Daisy the pony or cleaning the silver buckets.

As a grown woman, her habit continued, and she would rise before the sun, her bare feet on the wood floor, the house dark and quiet, and she'd step outside when the day was full of anticipation. She'd go for a walk. When Arthur was alive they went together, and after he died she continued her ritual, at least for a couple of years. The morning was her church, her prayer, her meditation. Arthur wanted the exercise before he sat all day in his therapist's chair and listened to the tumult of the human condition. Eleanor wanted to see the darkness dim like a door opening. She tried to explain it to Arthur, but the words failed her. The light changed something in her, renewed or reawakened or revived something, she couldn't decide. Maybe awakened hope, rugged and gritty and steely. They'd walk through the tree-lined Presidio or head to the bay along the marina, with the docked sailboats, the water gently murmuring, the streets not yet growling, and the first light would come, always quicker than expected like a golden substance poured from a pitcher. First the shadow of trees appeared, then the bushes, and suddenly the wildflowers rushed in with bright color and the birds sang, the sky an open auditorium for them to fill, and she'd grab Arthur's hand in awe—such radiance reigned! It was as if she'd never seen this moment, the beginning of a new day.

But now she's glued to the bed. Slow sinking, waterlogged, a vital organ has been crushed or the order or rightness of things. It's 11:00 a.m., her dog is whining, and she's still in bed, a pillow over her head. Her garden is dying, and the kale has keeled over. It feels as though she could sleep all day, drifting back in her mind to the barn in Gig Harbor, to the animals and the pristine clean lake and young Hazel and swimming and her father and the wood table he built from a barn door, where they ate their meals on white plates. Back to the garden behind the barn where she grew green beans and lettuce and kale, sometimes for them, but more often for the gray rabbits that slipped through the fence. To the time before she knew too much, and the knowledge became heavy rocks sitting on her chest, relentlessly flinging and beating her brain.

In all honesty, it sounds magnificent, the before time. I'd like to go, too, to the before time when the water in the rivers and lakes and streams was fresh and the fires few. When the temperature of the earth hadn't risen by two degrees Fahrenheit, and the alarm of extinction was not constantly blaring. Her despair, I feel it; it's suffocating, a gray cotton wrapping, warping, numbing. I'd like to crawl like a hermit crab into the smooth, polished inside of a nautilus shell and sleep and sleep, waking only if the world were returned to me as it once was, which now feels like a beautiful dream.

The Object of Dancing

It's true that Ed inhabits his own world, but right now he's trying to leave that world and enter another. He takes a delicate sip from his water bottle and crosses his thin, elegant legs like an aristocrat. He stretches his hamstring on the barre and watches Henry. The fog casts a strange light, and Henry's blond hair looks illuminated. Ed's always loved his legs until he met Henry, who has legs that reach up to his armpits, and his quads bulge in the most beautiful, sculpted way, like they are now, as he lifts one female ballet dancer after another, high into the air; Henry's legs are chiseled to perfection, like a Rodin sculpture.

Colleen claps her hands. "Okay, Ed and Henry."

Colleen is directing this performance, and that's what he should be thinking about, how much he wants the performance to succeed, how much it matters to him; he is putting his heart and soul and body and every molecule of himself into this because, for the first time, it makes sense. Him, dance, the dance itself, a lead role. And it doesn't require long legs or leaps or tossing lithe, nearly vaporous females into the air. He is to become something other, something outside of human. What is required is movement, but also the mind, the mind of an artist that knows how to get out of the way, to step outside the tragically limited confines of human and become other. Henry is to become a cat, and Ed, a rat.

Henry gracefully slips down on all fours, moving silently, as if traveling through liquid air, with feet and hands now padded paws, and he is a mere eight pounds. He's wearing his costume. Yesterday Henry showed up with a stretch of black fur stitched like a tube around his midsection. Colleen objected. "I want you to inhabit the cat before we get to props. Props are a crutch." But Henry was the lead dancer in *La Sylphide*. Henry, petulant Henry, pouted and whined and sulked; he needed the costume, he told her, it would help him, you'll see, just watch. Colleen caved. A hard, clean line drawn from Henry to the world that he wanted. Ed felt a collusion of envy and admiration for the man who gets what he wants, who can so easily become a cat.

Henry is more cat-like than he was two days ago, almost outside the oeuvre that is human. Not quite cat, but closer, and Colleen, Ed can tell by the way she's watching Henry with a warm smile, is delighted. Henry and his allure like a seductive perfume, smoothly moving across the floor, the sensuous shape of his back.

Ed gets down on all fours, his belly low to the ground. It's not a secret he's fallen out of Colleen's favor. For two weeks now Ed has not performed well. He keeps thinking he is a man acting like a rat, which is the problem. He needs to eliminate the word "man" from his thoughts and leapfrog straight to rat; to shed the human body and mind, to step out of it, beyond it, and experience the world in a radically different way—but how?

Ed lowers his head to the ground. He's never been so aware of the dirt and dust, the scuff marks and scratches on the wood floor. The floor has a history; the floor has a lived experience, all the ballet shoes, the sweat, bodies, dreams, and desires. If a rat has a consciousness, does the floor have one too? What about the piano? Henry is across the room, eyeing him. God, Henry is so beautiful, his shock of blond hair, flushed cheeks, full pink lips, and eyes startlingly china blue. Eyes that change color; the other day, Ed could have sworn they were cornflower blue.

"Okay, stop," says Colleen. "Ed. Ed. What's happening, Ed?"

Ed sits on his ass.

"You've lost it again. Where's your focus?" says Colleen frowning, her tweezed eyebrows inching together.

Henry stands and audibly sighs. He heads to the ballet barre and stretches his calves.

"There's a cat in the room," says Colleen. "Life and death, survival. You should be feeling the tension, living the tension."

Ed nods, watching Henry practice his grand pliés.

"The right tension," says Colleen. "Let's try it again."

Henry doesn't wait. He's on the ground, and as soon as Ed is down on all fours again, Henry leisurely circles the room. Ed practiced for hours in his tiny apartment, but there were rugs and lamps and human voices leaking through the walls, and he was too aware of a human pretending to be a rat. He's here now, he tells himself, and Henry, the embodiment of cat, but those long legs of his. Does he love Henry?

Ed expects Collen to stop him again, but she doesn't, and Henry circles, eyeing Ed, and Ed begins to feel actual fear. His jaws ache. He hunts for a place to hide. But when Henry licks his lips, Ed imagines that tongue on his chest, shoulder, and dick.

"Okay," says Colleen. "Enough. Take a break."

Henry stands, turns his head left and right, picks up his water bottle, and sips. Every movement seems to swell with awareness, as if Henry has found an opportunity to create art through the act of living. What Henry does, I will do, thinks Ed. Ed moves his head the same way and imagines that the air has substance, and he must proceed with intention to shape it into a beautiful space.

"Okay. Ed, remember, the cat is hungry, the cat presents danger," says Colleen, her tone stern.

Henry's eyes are closed as if he's nestling deep in the body of a cat, and he will not be found, not by a human who is looking at him, lusting after him, not by anything. Ed tries not to think of Henry as Henry but as a hungry cat. But he has lusted for Henry for five months, ever since Henry moved from New York and joined the San Francisco Ballet. Henry, born in Russia, or so Ed heard, trained at the Kirov Ballet. Tired of the competition and the cruelty in New York, Henry told Ed that he was looking for camaraderie, for friends. New York wants to grind you down, New York burns through dancers at a frenetic pace because there's a whole goddamn line of them waiting in the wings to replace you. I'm not giving up, he told Ed. I'm trying it a different way. No more one-night stands with fellow ballet dancers and the destructive jealousy and all that comes with it. He didn't want to get involved sexually with anyone here. All his energy would go into his work. "I have grand ambitions, and I'm not going to blow it this time." Henry wants no regrets when he looks back at his life.

But that was five months ago, and surely emotions shift, surely the body, Henry's strong, lovely body and heart grow lonely. He must get horny.

The music has started, old Mrs. Miles at the piano. Become the rat, for Christ's sake, be the rat. They're waiting. Henry is in the corner, dozing—like a cat stretched out on his side, his arms and legs in front of him, his right ear on the ground, but both eyes are open, tracking Ed.

Ed begins frantically to scurry around the room, zigzagging one way, another way—a cat is after him, a cat, but it isn't enough, so he adds a hawk, an owl, an eagle, a weasel. Fierce, hungry, sharp talons digging into his flesh. He remembers summers as a boy in their Sebastopol house, roaming the woods and the cow pastures, red-tailed hawks soaring overhead, dive-bombing rabbits and rats. Bodies torn open, guts, blood. The hush of the tall grass, the heat of the sun in the open field by the little pond with silver minnows. Henry is rising, stretching, arching his lovely long back, looking hungrily at Ed, and Ed somehow becomes more real, not as a rat, but as Ed, more certain of his substance, more solid, alive. He is suffocating in desire.

"Okay, stop, just stop," says Colleen. "Ed, can I talk to you?"

Henry looks at him, his expression unreadable, and heads to the bathroom. Ed tries not to watch him go, his sculpted shoulders, his tapered fingers.

"What's going on?" says Colleen. "You were so excited for this part, and I thought you'd be ideal, but now…now—"

"I'm sorry, I'm having trouble getting into it," he says. "I need more time. I need to figure out how to lose myself, dissolve myself."

She stares at him. "You need to wrap your head around this. Find your focus, because you don't have it. You're done for the day. Go figure it out."

Fear sprints through his spine—it's a big part, it's avant-garde, a transgression that will either succeed or fail, but if it succeeds, the dance world will be radically altered. He's twenty-nine, old for a dancer. This could be his last chance to leave a mark on the world. He got that one small mention in the press for his previous performance: *Ed Gergen's unearthly rhythmic sensibility, his strength and stamina are astounding, he moves effortlessly, silently.* His mother's voice from long ago lodged deep inside from his boyhood, her voice haunting, reverberating, encouraging: "You're a fabulous dancer, my love. Those little boys who make fun of you will recede in the distance. Specks, dots, as you rise." He'll get a big write-up, the attention he's always wanted, and the interviews, and Henry will too. Henry, who wants to make it big, who has put all his energy into dance. The two of them will be mentioned in the same breath.

"I'll get it," says Ed. "I will."

Colleen looks at him skeptically, then heads over to Tabita, who is standing in front of the wall of mirrors, watching herself brush her long dark hair, stroking it with such affection as if her image is a different person altogether. Colleen talks to Tabita's reflection. Henry is gone, probably hating Ed. He imagines Henry thinking that Ed is determined to sabotage everything and ruin Henry.

Ed props his leg on the high barre and leans his long trunk over his thigh to stretch his tight hamstring because if he doesn't do this now, he'll have trouble walking later. As he exhales, bringing his nose down to his knee, he thinks it's all a bunch of fucking bullshit—impossible for him to be a rat because he's trapped in a human body, a human brain, human consciousness formed by human experiences. Henry is an imposter putting on a good show with his cat-like moves. He is a man thinking about cat-like behavior, how a cat sees, moves, and smells. Impossible to rid oneself of the container that is human. He remembers his mother talking about how it was a waste of her time to argue the intrinsic value of nature. "The human mind isn't designed to get out of its own way," she'd say. "It isn't a judgment. It's a fact of human nature. We haven't evolved enough. There's more to the human story if we manage not to kill everything." Christ, she just won the Goldman Environmental Prize, so she must know something.

But, he argues with himself, he's an artist. He has an imagination, and if he wants to keep this part, he has to dismantle his humanness and become the rat. And what if he does it? Could he blaze the trail to another way of thinking? Rejecting anthropocentrism, going beyond the human as the center of it all? It could really be something.

His buddy Jose told him to tap into his inner sucio. Mi amigo, we all have sucio. Though Ed laughed, he felt his intense resistance to this sucio because he's had enough of thinking of himself as dirty, years and years of that when he was young, hiding his desire for boys. Buried it for fear of being bullied and beaten like Luke in sixth grade, out back behind the school by a group of eighth-grade boys. Luke, with his swollen face and black eye, and nothing ever happened to those bullies. So, it happened again—and again and again. Luke lost his front tooth, and suffered a scar on his arm from a knife, a kick to the knee that left him limping. Ed cowering, cowardly, always expecting he would be next, but assuring himself it couldn't happen because he liked both boys and girls. It never made sense to him to prefer one over the other. A body is a body with its velvety stretch of skin and nerve endings and scents and movements. Seeing a slender female hand reaching into a backpack could make him swoon, but so could a boy smacking a ball with a bat.

Henry reappears in the studio and stands in the middle of the room, feet in first position, perfectly still, a perfect statue. His eyes are not seeking out anyone but himself, but it doesn't seem like he's looking at himself in the mirror. He bends his knees slightly and pushes off with his right foot into a perfect pirouette, spinning, spinning gloriously, his blond hair flying like a pinwheel, glowing now as if the motion has caused him to burn brighter. When he stops, his cheeks are a brighter red, and Ed turns away and looks at Mrs. Miles, the doughy piano player, to stop his erection, and when that doesn't work, he thinks about the rat. When that fails, he heads into the lobby, digs in his backpack, and finds a chocolate bar. Akiko comes over and grabs his arm.

"What's happening, love?" she says.

She's a beautiful woman, long lines, long coal-black hair when it's released from its bun, skin so soft, so pale like the inside of an orange peel. She grew up in Japan, where the sun is an adversary blocked by a black umbrella. To think that a couple of days ago his hands clasped her beautiful naked ass.

He tells her that this whole undertaking is a fraud, a sham.

She taps the tip of her tongue on his cheek. "Pierre is dying to have your role."

"Fuck Pierre."

She laughs. "Have you?"

He smiles and rubs his lips together. She knows he's not going to give up. She and he, and everyone in the dance troupe, pulse with raw ambition; if you lack that, you're not going to make it. You train and train and practice and push your body to exhaustion and pain, and you keep doing it, facing rejection, enduring the aching muscles, the five-, six-hour practices, day after day, until maybe a door opens. And the door did open, and Colleen chose him to be the rat.

"I don't love you," she says, nibbling his earlobe.

"I don't love you either."

She grabs his dick. "I like you, though."

He kisses her cheek. "I like you too."

"And you like Henry."

He opens his mouth, preparing to protest.

She laughs and puts a finger on his lips. "But Henry is not Henry. He's a cat, a crafty little cat full of himself and only himself. Remember, dear Ed, cats aren't social creatures. Cats take what they want and have no problem giving nothing back."

She squeezes his balls, and he grabs her tight ass. Akiko feels as if under her skin, she has threaded thick wires. When she leaps in the air, she looks like she will never land, as if gravity has no purchase.

She stops and steps back, a beautiful distraction. "You want to head to my place?"

He's surprised to find black-and-white photos of him on her bedroom walls, unframed, held up by tacks. She took them the last time he was here. In some photos he's clothed; in others, half naked; and in others, buck naked. He tries not to be too critical of them.

"Aren't they beautiful?" she says, admiring them. "But," she says, taking him by the shoulders, digging in her fingernails, "the question is, the most pressing question of all is, can you make love to me like a rat?"

"No, absolutely not."

"Sorry, wrong answer. You have to," she says.

"I don't want to think about all that," he says.

"Or," she says, kissing his eyelids, "you fuck me, I fuck you."

He gives her an exaggerated expression of alarm. "Aki-ko-san, where did you learn such naughty language?"

She laughs and shakes off her white blouse. Small, pert breasts point at him as if he is the one, the only one. Outside a car horn bleats long and low. He kisses her neck and releases her hair from its high bun, and it becomes lines of black ink running down her pearly shoulders, her breasts, and her back. Akiko tilts her head back as if she is an offering of vanilla pudding, and his hands travel the stretch of her, his tongue roaming the flat terrain of her stomach. She lives on coffee and chocolate; her skin carries their scent. She doesn't drink or smoke because, she says, she doesn't want the impurities. Coffee, she told him, comes from coffee beans, which are natural, and chocolate from cocoa beans. She's left the window open, and a breeze plays with the white shade, tapping it against the sill. Everything is white: white walls, white comforter, a white wicker chair. The car horn stops, and now comes the repetitive beep of a truck backing up. He holds her at arm's length to drink her in with his eyes, her hair fluttering from the breeze as if it has wings.

Akiko landed the lead female role as the wind. Collen got a sizable grant for performances that blend art and nature. The goal is to reach people on a deeper, more emotional level and engage them in the climate narrative. He has watched Akiko, everyone has, when Colleen turns on the fans, and with her gauzy costume, her hair down, she looks as if she is moving, though she's not. With the stirring of her clothes and hair, she is the embodiment of wind. When the music begins, when she does move she seems to fly, hovering inches off the ground, and no one, absolutely no one, can look away.

He turns her over, and she moans with pleasure, and he moves slowly to make it last.

"Ed," she says.

He runs his hand down her back, and he pulls out, and in a flash, she is on top, taking what she wants from him, the deepest pleasure. He holds her by her hips, but she removes his hands and pins them to the bed. Splayed, he lets himself be swallowed up by her.

After, they lie side by side. The sun strokes the sheets. It's noon or maybe three o'clock.

"You're a generous lover," she says. Her eyes are soft and full of emotion. In her chin is a slight indentation, as if in the making of her, someone gently pressed.

"It's easy with you," he says. "You're so lovely."

"Doesn't it seem that everything lovely just pours through our hands?"

He caresses her cheek. "You'll always be lovely."

"I did have sex with Henry."

He leans away and studies her. She has a spark of mischief in her eyes.

She laughs and pulls her hair in front of her, covering her breasts. "You should see your face. You're not very good at hiding your emotions."

"When he moved to San Francisco?"

"Henry and I were in the Paris Opera Ballet together. He became very French. He wore a black beret." She reaches over and traces the outline of his ear and tugs on his earlobe. "But he wasn't a very French lover. He's not generous, not at all. You'll be very disappointed."

"Are you trying to warn me?"

"Maybe I'm telling you something so you will see him or a part of him you haven't seen. We live our life in fragments, don't you think? We never see the whole of anything. We can sense it, so we long for it. But we can never have it. It's so sad."

He hands her a glass of water from her nightstand. She drinks, dips her fingers in it, and dribbles water on his chest. The light is shining on the glass and he sees the color blue.

"He's a cat inside and out," she says. "That's what I'm telling you."

He is overcome with the feeling that he must leave, he must practice and become a rat, or his world will collapse. He must do it for himself and for Henry. He wants to look at his watch, but it would be too rude.

She sits up and swings her head side to side, her hair flying as if she's on a mad, wild ride at the fair. Abruptly she stops and speaks to the dresser across the room. "I'd like to go somewhere with you in the snow. We could live in a cabin and brush the snow out of our hair."

"And what would we do for a living?" he says.

"Dance for each other, naked," she says, kissing his hair.

"Ah, I see."

"In the Chinese Zodiac, people born in the year of the rat are curious, witty, and imaginative. Did you know that?"

"I didn't."

"You have only a piece of the rat. There's much more to it," she says.

"And?"

"Cats eat rats."

"Even a curious, witty, imaginative rat?" He touches his forehead to hers. "He'll chew me up and spit me out, is that what you're telling me? Or is that what he did to you?"

She turns her face away, and he looks at a photo of himself on the wall, a white sheet covering his torso, his eyes closed, asleep. The last time they had sex, he collapsed into the deepest of sleep as if he'd sunk to the bottom of the sea.

"If we lived in the snow, we could sit at the window and watch it fall," she says.

He lets himself imagine her coffee and chocolate and his tea and toast with strawberry jam, and they'd walk together, this woman with a knowing face who drinks too much coffee to sabotage her appetite. She said she cannot let herself weigh more than 107. She's five foot seven, tall for a Japanese woman. Her face would be soft in the light from the snow like a child's. He'd be bearlike in his languor. He imagines them in bed together, naked, reading books, the days unfolding in blueness and snow and bright light. They'd lose their ballet bodies. Grow fat. Maybe he'd fall madly in love with her. His scalp is beginning to show through his hair. Soon, he will be too old to dance. When does that happen? The body's natural decline, but one must remain blind to it to do what one must, which is throw oneself headfirst into life. He's suddenly filled with sadness. He loves his body, it has given him immense, deep pleasure. He's so sad it has to die.

"We could cook dinner together," she says. "I'll teach you how to make katsu chicken."

He looks at the dark hairs on her arm. "That would be nice." His voice sounds hollow as if it lurched out of him with no tone. He tries to crawl back into the dream of them.

She takes his chin and peers into him as if searching for something.

"Yes, let's go to the snow," he says. "Let's leave all this and build a snow castle. I'll run you a bath every night."

She laughs. "I'm serious, sort of, and you're not." She touches his nose. "A rat can't love a cat."

The light changes. The city is becoming dark. Soon the streetlights will flicker on and fill her apartment. There is a time in the day when her room, so white, glows. He wraps a strand of her long hair around his finger. It looks like someone drew on him. The photos are tacked on the wall, gently flapping from the breeze through the window. With a strong wind, they'll fall. He's not serious because what would he do with his desire for Henry?

In the morning before rehearsal, he walks from his apartment down Bush Street, takes a right on Divisadero, up the big hill through the well-kept houses of Pacific Heights, then down to Union Street with the little shops, flower shops, shoe shops, and cafes infusing the air with coffee and sweet pastries. He walks all the way to the bay, and on a dock he stares at the water, because someone told him that looking at an expanse would change his brain waves. For a long time he stands there, listening to the lapping waves, watching the little sailboats with puffed-out sails, the water the color of his gray, knitted leg warmers.

On his way back to his apartment, he stops at the public library and checks out a stack of books about rats. They are old books, many times viewed, and he likes that. As he pages through one of the books, he remembers his mother's Meyer lemon tree, how she'd step outside and scream, a scream that made his entire body seize in terror, his mind rifling through possibilities—a dead man in the garden, a man with a gun, his mother injured, a gash on her hand; he wished his father were home so he could rush out and defend his mother, until he realized what he knew it to be—a rat in the tree, devouring one of her precious lemons.

"Ed!" she'd call out, her voice high, strained, insistent. "Hurry!

He was not brave. He was a skinny, cautious kid frightened

to death of a rat in a tree that might fall on his head, scamper down his shirt, sharp claws scratching him, and crawl into his pants. What if it ate his penis? His balls? Where was his damn father? Why couldn't *he* do it? Most likely at work with a patient, unraveling the dark tangles of the mind. He pictures his father at the end of the kitchen table, his black-framed glasses perched on his nose, listening to Ed in such a way it felt as though he was crawling underneath Ed's words. His father, a therapist; it was like living naked, Ed told his friends. He learned to be private, to turn inward. It would be Ed who would fight the dirty rat, beating it down with a broom.

Does he need to find the good in a rat to become a rat? He's never cared much for being good or polite. When boys—clever boys, sleuthing boys, cruel boys—figured out he was a ballet dancer, they called him a sissy, a fag or a fairy, or gay or cocksucker or buttfucker. Years of that and he decided all bets were off—he'd be who he was, and the rest of the world could go to hell. His mother encouraged him to ignore the world—to listen to his calling—bless her. He loves his mother. The only goodness he's ever cared about was to be a good dancer.

After another lousy rehearsal, Colleen sends Ed home because she wants to give Pierre a chance to rehearse with Henry. Humiliated and sad, Ed heads to the changing room, takes off his tights, leotard, and ballet shoes, and jams them in his bag. He leaves quickly, not wanting to speak to anyone.

He soaks in the bathtub, feeling punished for his ineptitude; he's been expelled from the only world he wants to be in. He won't eat, only a banana to further his punishment. After sulking, he spends the afternoon holed up in his apartment, reading about rats, hoping to find some detail that lights the ember of inspiration. When Ed packed up his ballet bag, Henry wouldn't even look at him.

Ed hears the high-pitched whine of a car outside. Must be the old woman who lives next door; her old Cadillac, the color of red wine, makes that sound as if it were crying. From the South, she reminds Ed of Blanche in *A Streetcar Named Desire.* Everyone is in exile, thinks Ed. Outside the window the sky is the color of beer, and the wind is knocking everything down. A shiver runs through him, and he goes back to reading. The rat's teeth are harder than iron or steel and can gnaw through cinder-block. Ed grinds his teeth, trying to imagine chewing through asphalt, the graininess coating his soft pillowy cheeks, collecting in the gaps and grooves of his teeth, turning his tongue into sandpaper. Before Ed left, Henry, not looking at Ed, hissed at him, "Get a fucking grip."

Rats can go longer without water than a camel and fall five stories without injury. Ed heads over to the big bay window and peers out. Across the way there's the small restaurant that serves waffles with maple syrup. He's often worried about what he'd do if there were a fire in the hallway. No fire escape—he'd have to jump three stories, and maybe he'd make it across the street to the apartment where the young woman with bleached hair walks around in her bra and underwear, talking on her phone.

But maybe he wouldn't, and his dancer's body would be crushed. If he lived, what would he do? He's only ever wanted to dance, to be a premiere ballet dancer. In his mind, his leaps and splits and leg raises are always farther, higher, and better than they are in real life, and he tells himself that means there is still potential. How else could the ideal exist? Though some part of him realizes this is fantastical thinking, since he can also imagine himself flying like a bird, a simple flapping of his arms and up he goes into puffy clouds, peering down at everyone.

The phone rings, and he sees it's his sister. For hours he has said nothing to anyone, and now he has the urge to speak. "Hello, Ava. What brings you to my world?"

"Just called to see if you're alive."

He won't tell her about the rehearsal and how the world has been plunged into terribleness. Her compassion is a dried nut.

"You couldn't even come to Mom's award ceremony?" she says. "I mean, you live in the same city."

He stares at a drawing of a rat. "My dear Ava, she didn't care one whit about that award. Those are her exact words."

"It's about you always, Ed. You're a selfish prick."

He smiles, remembering how she spent her tenth birthday party tucked away in her bedroom, ignoring all her guests because she'd figured out how to use a laser pointer and a slide with a drop of water to see tiny, squirming life. "How are you, Ava?"

"I think Mom's in a really bad way. I'm worried about her. I called her, and her voice was so weak I could barely hear her. It's like she's vanishing."

He heads to the kitchen for more tea and a slice of apple. He didn't have bananas, so he allows himself only apples and lettuce, not even dressing. Bare lettuce. With the window closed he can't hear the city. "She knows too much about the raping of the earth. Knowledge can be a terrible thing. Most of us live in denial. I know I do."

"Don't give me platitudes. I want you to feel something for once."

"I feel all the time," he says. "I'm a walking wound, which is another name for an artist."

"Don't give me that artist shit. I think she might kill herself."

His heart does a strange roll. He reminds himself that despite her training as a scientist, his sister can veer off the logical edge into the hyperbolic. But Ed hasn't talked to their mother in a while, so maybe Ava is right. Their mother's dark moods. Her passion has always been her work; it was never tied to her children. When he was young he resented how he seemed to float in her periphery. But what happens when the work has come to nothing? The thought hits too close for comfort, and now his arms itch.

"I'll call her," he says.

"You're the one who can make her laugh. Try to do that. Or if you can, go see her. That would be better. Can you manage that?"

He will, he promises her. But really, she has no understanding of his life. She, on her high horse of science, looks down at him as if he's goofing off. How does he explain to her about rehearsals and exhaustion and mental preparation and how he needs to enter the mind of a rat? She doesn't hold art, at least dance, in high regard. You get to leap and twirl all day, she's said more than once, as if it were play. It was once play when he was a boy. He remembers falling in love with dance when his ballet teacher, a short woman with long auburn hair who smoked at every break and had yellowish teeth, told them to dance as if they were leaves falling to the ground. In his mind, he easily slipped into the form of a green leaf from a laurel tree, a leaf plucked from the tree by a strong wind, and as it floated to the ground it twirled like a propeller; and before it hit, the wind swept it up again and tossed it up high. That was the day he knew he loved to dance, how big his life could be, how many things he could inhabit. Not one life, but many. He'd live a hundred lives. His old life felt anemic. He wanted the expansiveness, the wide-open field of it. No other choice made sense to him.

Ava tells him about the awards ceremony, how their mother gave no speech—nothing. An anti-speech, a flip-them-the-bird spectacle. The audience was flabbergasted. She had to apologize to the director and the board, on and on. She felt like their mother's handler, trying to smooth over everything after a petulant child threw herself on the floor and had a temper tantrum.

Ed smiles. He inherited not his mother's analytical mind or need to change the world but her rebelliousness. She always used to tell him, "The world needs a lot of work—remember that, Ed—don't buy into it blindly."

"You should have seen Mother's performance at the lunch afterward," says Ava. "She and her sister got into it. A public fight."

"Hazel? She showed up?"

"Yes, even *she* managed to make it, all the way from Africa."

The Gambian pouched rat, which he just read about, can grow up to fifteen pounds and is used to detect land mines in

Africa. It can also detect tuberculosis in humans. Not infecting humans, not polluting the world, or carrying diseases that bring death, this mega-rat saves humans. And what good is a damn cat?

"Mom gave the money away. She didn't even take it," says Ava.

"Good for her. She's got an artist's heart."

"Oh God. Don't pretend you dance for the sake of dancing."

He stops and stares at an ant crawling on the white kitchen counter. "You don't understand a thing about me."

"So, if they said, sorry, no salary for you, you'd stay with the dance company?"

"I don't dance because I'm getting paid, and I think I speak for most people who have passion. They don't do it for the money or even necessarily for the possibility of fame, of being at the top of their profession. They do it because they love to be absorbed in it. Life lived wholeheartedly."

"You should hear yourself," says Ava. "Just call her."

After he hangs up, he looks for the ant, but it's disappeared. He eats a saltine, then eats the entire row of them. He'll call Eleanor, but not right now. Something has sparked inside. He put the rat in a tight little box, labeled it *sucio*, and wanted nothing to do with it. But now he understands he used a small category. If he'd been raised in Africa, he'd have encountered the Gambian pouched rat and held a different view of rats. He'd be astonished by them, indebted to them, and feel excruciating gratitude and benevolence toward them.

He goes back to the couch, feeling the little flames of excitement. *Dear Colleen*, he writes in his head, *be patient with me; my mind has gotten in the way of my body. Dear Henry, watch out! Your little cat act will pale next to my performance. Dear Mother, bravo to you, your refusal to bend to the rules. Dear Ava, you're going to age rapidly with all the fretting.*

He's restless as if those little inspiration flames are singeing his muscles. It's always been this way. He has a body that needs to move; he could never sit still at school. He was the boy who was always scolded. Sit still. Stop squirming, stop moving your feet, stop tapping your pencil. Another little boy, Rolfe, couldn't sit still either. Rolfe, with his pretty, full lips and wide mouth. He taught Rolfe his trick; ask to go to the bathroom, run there, and in the bathroom, do jumping jacks, one hundred of them. Ed gets on the floor, legs in front of him, and reaches for his toes; his chest touches his thighs, and the backs of his legs slowly relinquish their tightness.

He reads on the floor, his heart thumps faster, and his eyes widen. He breathes deeply as if every bit of him must inhale this new knowledge and make it his: the biggest, feistiest sewer rats can send the average house cat running for the hills.

"I've got you, Henry. I've got you now."

In the morning the dance studio is empty. The sunlight daintily drifts in, and when Ed opens the big windows, little airs saunter into the room. Colleen gave him a key and told him to come early and practice. Ed stands in the middle of the room and breathes; his heart steadies and softens. This big empty space with sunlight and wood floors and a wood barre, it's all he's ever needed. Here, he can unfurl.

The mirrors, he is everywhere, he is multitudes. He slips on his headphones, turns on U2's "Pride," and jogs in place. When the chorus whines, *what more in the name of love*, he sprints, sending his heart whacking against his ribs, then slows, as the music quiets, back and forth—sprint and jog—until he's sweating. On the floor, he stretches on his Styrofoam roller, ironing out the aches in his low back, then brings his feet together, flares out his knees, and stretches his hips. At the barre, he goes through pliés and elevés and battements and ronds de jambe until his muscles are warm, loose, long; he swivels his head side to side, then bends at the waist and touches his toes, grabbing the back of his legs, pulling his forehead to his shins, his hamstrings refusing to yield, until they do and he presses his head between his legs.

He stands, gyrates his hips, and with the music crescendoing, he moves around the room, leaping and spinning; he is the little air fluttering in the empty room, scurrying here and there, rushing to the mirror, sweeping to the window, brushing against the piano bench, gliding along the shiny wood floor; and soon, very soon, he will be bodiless and everywhere, and swept up in grace—

Pierre is standing at the studio entrance, hands on his slender hips, watching. Ed stops, takes off his headphones, sweat pouring down his face. Pierre and his dark eyes.

"Hey," says Ed.

"She made me your understudy," says Pierre. "But really, there's nothing to study."

"Fuck you too."

Pierre, only eighteen years old, snapping gum, cocky as shit. Ed watches his jaw work under the flesh of his cheeks.

"Don't be a sensitive twat. I've been a fucking rat all my life," says Pierre. "Been treated like one, too, so there's nothing to study, bro." Pierre grins nastily. "It's in my blood, rat blood."

"You're the bad boy," says Ed.

"Yup. I own it. You should have seen me at the party last night. The girls couldn't keep their hands off me. Testing the heat."

Ed heads to his bag, grabs a towel, and wipes down his face. "How did you know I'd be here?"

"I didn't. I came to practice. You know, just in case you get tossed to the sidelines. I could use a lucky break."

"We all could." What he felt earlier, alone here, dancing—salted and expanded and swirled into another life—is destroyed.

"Henry says you've got a self-destructive streak," says Pierre.

Ed stiffens. "He did? When did he say that?"

"The biggest part you've ever landed, I mean, you got it, Colleen gave it to you, and now you're falling apart."

What Ed would give to subtract ten years and be Pierre's age again, an age when he had immense energy coursing through him, his body responsive to every move, every command, never reluctant, never shouting out with pain, and doubt seemed to belong to a foreign land.

"Henry, he's the perfect cat," says Ed.

"That's cap," says Pierre, shaking his head in disagreement. "He works his ass off."

Ed looks around, arms spread wide. "Where? I don't see him."

"You a fool," says Pierre. "He goes to the studio on Mission and Twenty-first. Small place but he likes the natural light. He's there every day before we rehearse. He's there all the time. He's like the Kobe Bryant of ballet, bro. Now me, it comes naturally."

Why wouldn't Henry have said something to him? Why would he go to a different studio? Did he want to hide how much he was working at it? Why? Bad thoughts come hurtling at Ed, mostly about himself—why hasn't he pushed himself harder? What's wrong with him? Does he have a self-destructive streak?

Pierre has taken off his coat and is going through his own warm-up. Ed's concentration is shattered; Pierre in the room, Pierre, who will watch his every move with a critical eye, telling himself he can do hella better than Ed.

Two days later, Ed is alone in the studio. He arrived at six a.m. to make sure Pierre wouldn't be there. Pierre is going after Ed's part like an ambitious douchebag, and he's so blithe about it. "Yeah, Ed, watch out," he said the last time he was at the studio. "I'm good. I'm really good." He gave Ed a bad-boy grin. Colleen has set them up for a dog fight, and though Ed sees right through her plan, he can't stop himself from going head-to-head.

Ed is dancing, headphones on, clearing his head to make room for the rat—not the dirty rat that courses through Pierre's veins, but a complicated rat, one with good and bad, with ferocity and compassion, one that holds mystery and will never neatly make sense.

He read Thomas Nagel's "What is it Like to be a Bat?" in which Nagel argues that humans can never imagine what it is to be a bat because humans don't echolocate. But Nagel's real intent was to eviscerate physicalism—that everything in the universe is physical and nothing more: lightning is two electrically charged regions equalizing themselves, causing an instantaneous release of energy. All the poetry is stripped out, all meaning and myth and metaphor.

Ed doubts Nagel tried to become a bat. It was an intellectual exercise only. And a bat isn't like a rat. Besides, Nagel was a philosopher, not an artist. An artist is an open heart. An artist is vast.

He's dancing as he once did as a boy, imagining he is a fly zooming through the air, touching every corner, greedily, hungrily, wanting to know the texture of every single thing, the wood floor, the barre, the piano keys, the slick mirrors; he puts his hand on the mirror but doesn't look at his face, afraid he'll break the spell. The hope is to no longer exist, to make room for the rat. He moves faster around the room, a huge gust of wind hurtling him through space, and it's marvelous, this freedom of movement, this freedom to become other. He hears the front door open and the spell is broken. Goddamn Pierre, a true sucio.

Ed rushes to the restroom and throws water on his face. He is sweating and red-cheeked, but he doesn't want Pierre to know how hard he is training, afraid it will spur on Pierre. He gulps water, rubs his lips together, and takes deep breaths, pushing the air into the bottom of his lungs.

When he is gathered, he steps into the studio.

Henry, with his black ballet bag on his shoulder. "Hey."

Ed feels sweat trickle down the center of his chest. "Hey."

"You're here early," says Henry.

Henry looks windswept, his hair tousled, as if he hiked over hills and streams to get here, a ruddy color to his cheeks, his lips tantalizing, his upper lip pillowy. For several days Ed hasn't really looked at Henry, not wanting to tease himself, to agonize himself, tempt himself, but now he takes him in. Gulps him down.

"Yep," says Ed.

Henry steps toward Ed and the sun lights up half of Henry's face, and he looks like an art piece, a marvelous, stunning sculpture.

He nods. "That's good." He sets his bag down. "I like San Francisco."

Ed forgot that the city is new to him, that he has lived in many different cities. Paris, with Akiko. Russia, Austria, Canada, who knows where else. Born in Russia, that's what Ed heard.

"It's a crazy place, you know," says Henry. "I was out last night at the DNA Lounge, and a bunch of queens came in and turned up the music, and we danced until the place closed down. It reminded me of Paris, that joie de vivre."

In all his imaginings, not once has Ed pictured Henry—full of rectitude and concentration, striving for the elusive goal of perfection, disciplined and restrained—going out at night. From their last conversation eons ago, Ed made a picture in his mind and ossified Henry into an ascetic. Now he feels himself busy altering the picture. It includes a bar, dancing, a bunch of queens. What else has he left out?

"I love that place," says Ed.

Henry rubs his quads vigorously with his hands.

"If you go again, let me know," says Ed.

"A band that's supposed to be good is playing on Friday."

Ed nods vigorously. "Let's go."

"If my energy is good, then sure."

Ed tries not to show his disappointment. "Yeah, me too."

He looks at Henry and wonders if Henry is truly beautiful or if he's conjuring up images of beauty from all the magazines and art books he's looked at over the years, all the photos of famous dancers he's gazed at, comparing Henry to those images and finding he matches them perfectly.

"You ready for today?" says Henry.

That's the closest Henry will get to the truth of what he wants to say.

"You bet."

"At least we have another two weeks to practice."

"That's right."

"We can get it right in that time. I mean, we have to."

Ed almost cringes because he hears not "we" but "you"—you have to.

"If you don't think you can do it, Pierre wants it bad," says Henry, stretching his calves. "He's doing pretty well. I mean, we've rehearsed four or five times and it's going well."

Oh, fuck you, Henry.

"But he's cocky," says Henry. "He shouldn't have such a big role at such a young age. It's not good for him."

Ed feels awash with relief.

"But I must say, he's good," says Henry. "Really good."

Ed says he has to go to the changing room, and he stays there until he hears the front door open and close again and again, the studio filling up with voices. Mrs. Miles begins to warm up, playing the scales. Mrs. Miles, with her big lap and pale fat legs, her puff of dyed brown hair; but what pours out of her fingers is marvelous, transcendent. Like me, thinks Ed. He might not be a classic beauty like Henry; Ed's nose is too big, and his eyes are a little too close together—but when he dances, he can become astonishing, no matter what Henry says. He's done with Henry.

Ed hears Colleen's laugh, something low and sexy, not because she's that, but because she smokes too much. Ed heads out to the floor. It is a pool of autumnal light, golden. The sky hides the stars. Colleen claps her hands, and Ed stands taller and doesn't search out Henry. The light bounces off the soft wood floors, the mirrors, and the dancer's bodies, and a soft breeze ripples the hair on his arms. The music glides through the room, and Ed feels it in his limbs, his joints, and his muscles twitch and tighten. One does not understand music; one feels it. Ed takes his place at the barre, Jenny in front of him, Jenny with her leg that flies effortlessly up to her head, he almost weeps at how beautiful she is, and, for a moment, he feels overwhelmed by how lovely everyone is, and this room and this light and the music and Colleen, who is watching them with a blank face, who refuses to give words of praise because this is high art and there is much to learn and she does not reward easily.

When he hears Henry clear his throat, a crackle of energy runs up his spine, and before he can stop himself, he turns and looks down the line of dancers at Henry, who is looking directly at him. Henry smiles. Before the smile penetrates, Colleen claps—the music changes, and it's time; Ed is down on the ground, grinding his teeth, which squeak and scratch, enamel against enamel, and Henry silently moves on the other side of the room. Ed scurries the length of the mirror, muscles tightening, flexing. Henry stops, a moment of motionlessness, looks at Ed, looks away, meanders to a patch of sun and licks his paw. Ed scampers toward Henry, turns, rushes back. In an instant, Henry arches his back like he's swallowed a balloon, and Ed feels something slough off. Terror is a tight wire around his throat. He scampers to the corner and watches the cat with its belly low to the ground, dark eyes on him, moving slowly, one paw after another, so slowly, moving closer. Run? Stay still? Heart thumping madly. The cat moving silently closer, he sucks the inside of his cheeks. The cat leaps, and before it lands, something takes over, something primordial and incomprehensible, and the rat races across the room, huddles behind the chairs. Peering out, the rat sees that the cat has stopped; doubt flickers in its eyes, and Henry bursts into the moment, Henry looking at him bewildered, brows knitted in astonishment, as if he rehearsed everything but this.

Colleen is gushing: Ed, fantastic, Ed, the best you've done so far, whatever you're doing, keep doing it. "I was transfixed," she says. Akiko blows him a kiss and begins to prance around the room, warming up to become the wind. Pierre pouts and says, "You a bad boy after all, dude."

Ed heads over to Henry, who's on the floor by the barre, stretching. Henry nods, barely.

Ed was expecting exuberance, accolades, and high praise.

"You were great." Henry's dull tone betrays him. He's not even looking at Ed but across the room as if trying to catch a reflection of himself in the mirror. Ed is having trouble making sense of it. They need each other for the performance; if Henry shines and Ed does not, the performance fails. If Ed shines and Henry does not, they fail. What is Ed missing? All the times he's disappointed Henry, but not today. Why isn't Henry elated? Ed has the urge to comfort Henry, to put his arm around him and assure him—but of what?

"I need to up my game," says Henry. "I fell out of it at the end."

The piano starts. Akiko is becoming the wind.

"You did really well," says Henry. "I knew you would." Henry massages his toes and sighs. "I'm sorry," says Henry. "I broke that scene wide open. Ruined it. You were spot on, and I was awful. Bad."

Ed sits on the floor beside him. Breathes him in, his sweat, the smell of Henry, something musky and pungent and orangey. Before and after practice Henry sucks on orange slices.

"Hey," says Ed. "What I saw across the room was a cat. I was convinced; not only that, I felt a cat, I was responding to a cat. You were a cat. I could be a rat because you were a cat."

"Until I wasn't."

"God, Henry. You're a brilliant dancer."

Henry looks directly at Ed, and Ed senses he's craving more, he needs Ed to keep talking, to resuscitate whatever has been immolated, so he does, he gives Henry what he needs, and fills him up, resurrecting him. Henry puts his hand on Ed's shoulder, then lightly, ever so lightly, brushes his fingertips along Ed's cheek.

Henry is already at the DNA Lounge, standing on the edge of the dancing crowd, the music blaring from the four musicians on stage, four young men dressed in black, finding the groove and mining it.

Ed comes up beside Henry. "They're good," says Ed. "Throwing themselves in it."

Henry is nodding his head to the beat, a slight movement in his hips. He has on tight jeans and a tight white T-shirt, and his blond hair shimmers. A new scent, eucalyptus, maybe from aftershave, is throwing Ed off because it's not Henry's smell. A woman dances in front of them in a short black skirt and a red tank top in the thralls of something intense. Dancing alone, eyes closed, she's waving her arms around to some mystery beat.

A waiter comes by. "Whatcha want to drink?"

Henry shakes his head no. Henry isn't drinking, so Ed won't. Two men are dancing together, their hands swarming all over each other, with sweaty faces and shirts glued to their backs. Ed gives Henry a side glance to see if he's watching them.

Henry leans close to Ed's ear. "My father was a famous dancer in Berlin."

"Berlin?" says Ed. "I thought you were Russian."

"No, no, born in Berlin. We hate the Russians. My father danced with the West Berlin Ballet and had the most beautiful kinetic intuition. His jumps? Astounding, time stopped when he was at the top of his leap. He was also a mean son of a bitch. Ballet was everything to him, and he despised anyone who took him away from a moment of dance. That included his wife and children."

"My mother could be ruthless," says Ed. "Her concern for the big world—she wanted to save it. We were gnats, my sister and I, brushed aside."

Ed is exaggerating; his mother loved them with her whole being, but she traveled so often that it was easy to feel sorry for himself. But Ed wants to align himself with Henry, to say whatever Henry says.

Henry nods solemnly. The music pulses frenetically, and the two men dancing together are no longer in sight.

"Your father gave you the gift of dance," says Ed.

"True," he says. "But it doesn't redeem him. He had many lovers who would call our home. When he was home, we wished him away. I wanted my mother to leave him to find happiness, but she had old-fashioned values and refused to divorce him. When I became a dancer, she was so sad. You'll end up like your father, she told me, a man who gives his heart to no one. I gave her more misery. She calls me selfish, and I am."

Is Henry warning him that he's his father's son, his heart kept in a tight box? With a faint smile, Henry is watching a woman who seems to be flying high on drugs, her arms above her head seemingly of their own volition.

"Excuse me," says Henry.

Ed watches him head for the tripped-out woman. The music crashes down on him. Ed looks around for someone or somewhere to go. Henry is dancing with the woman, who has opened her eyes and looks delighted to have found Henry in front of her. The air is hot, sticky, thick. Henry is moving in a way Ed has never seen before—almost like a robot. With straight arms in front of him, pivoting on his heel to the right and left. The woman is enchanted. Ed thinks Henry looks idiotic, all his grace and elegance erased. A bad mood is rolling in like a rain cloud.

A woman comes over with a drink. "You just standing, or do you want to dance?"

She has wild curly brown hair and bright green eyes, thick black eyeliner as if she's peering out from a cave. Her tight pink dress looks painted on. He motions to her drink. "Can you dance with a drink in your hand?"

She laughs coyly. "Watch me."

He laughs. "Okay."

She's attractive in her own way with a Cheshire-like smile, as if she's certain she's working her magic, that he won't refuse whatever she's offering. Did he say the wrong thing to Henry? He looks for Henry on the dance floor but can't spot him.

The woman in the pink dress leads the way, and they carve a little spot on the crowded dance floor. The music has a heavy beat, and the woman dances by jabbing the air with her elbows. He finds the beat in his hips and toes.

"You're a good dancer," she says in his ear. "Most men can't move. They're like fish flailing around, you know?"

He knows he should reciprocate, but he doesn't feel like talking. He's already sweating because the air is so hot. Darkness covers the walls and the corners; it smells old, old beer, sweat, and floorboards. He sees Henry with the woman about six feet away and presses his back into the crowd, parting the way to make it over to him, the woman in tow.

"My name is Dorte," she says, leaning into Ed's ear.

"Ed," he says.

"You from here?" she says.

For some reason, he doesn't want to give anything away. "Berlin."

Her face brightens as if she's pleased he is from somewhere far away. "I've never been, but I'd love to go."

She puts her hand on Ed's shoulder and slams her hip into his. He stumbles, catches himself, and wonders how he can leave. When she dances behind him, Henry is suddenly right in front of him, and he begins to gracefully gyrate his hips. Ed mimics him, wishing the crowd would give them more room. At the same time, there is intimacy, with the people pushing them together, two feet apart. Ed meets Henry's gaze, and although they've looked at each other a thousand times at ballet practice, Ed feels himself deliquesce, and what was once holding back rushes forward, and he almost touches Henry, grabs his strong arms, and kisses his lips.

The women are dancing with each other, the drugged one rolling her head around as if it might topple off. The crowd gives Henry and Ed more room, and though they are connected, unlike Henry, Ed has a big smile on his face. The music pulses a steady eight counts, and he circles Henry, brushing his ass against his, then back around. The song spirals and turns, heads to high notes, and the pace picks up, and they move as if the musicians are inside them, and they are right with the musicians when the beat changes and Ed is Henry and Henry is Ed, and Ed doesn't want it ever to end.

Abruptly, the music cuts out. The musicians announce they're taking a break.

"You two—whoa, you are dancers," says Dorte.

"Ballet dancers," says Henry.

"Ah, that explains it," says Dorte.

Ed watches her face rearrange itself as all the associations with male ballet dancers proliferate and reconstitute whatever she thinks of them.

"You boys look good together," she says. "Cute."

The tripped-out woman is staring at Henry's muscular pecs.

"You'll have to come to our performance," says Henry.

He tells her about it.

"Let me guess," says Dorte. "You're the cat," she says, and pointing to Ed, "you're the rat."

Henry claps his hands. "You're right. How did you know?"

She smiles slyly. "I have a sixth sense. You move more like a cat," she says to Henry.

"And how does a rat move?" says Ed.

She laughs and shakes her head.

"I'd say the other way around," says the other woman.

But no one pays any attention to her.

"Acting like a rat and cat?" says Dorte.

"No, no, my friend, not acting," says Henry, smiling, showing his beautiful teeth. "We are a cat and rat. There is no acting. You're not an artist, no?" Henry looks at her with pitying eyes.

The other girl seems to have come out of her fugue. "I make crazy bead jewelry."

"We're always creating," says Ed, to keep the story going.

Henry bats away the comment with a flick of his wrist. "No, no, no. We make games. We're playing right now."

Dorte leans closer to him, her eyes spark. "Cat and rat?"

Henry laughs. "But who is who? I think tonight I'll be the rat."

Ed is about to say he'll be the cat, but Dorte claims it.

"What should I be?" says the woman who finally says her name is Margaret.

"Anything you want," says Henry.

"And what about him?" says Margaret, looking at Ed.

Henry looks at Ed and smiles. "He's the world. He can be anything. The man is magic."

Ed's face burns hot and bright. Henry laughs and takes Ed in his arms and kisses him on the mouth.

Outside, Ed and Henry head down the sidewalk. A cat wanders out from under a parked Volvo. It comes right up to them as if prepared to weave in and out of their legs, brushing their pants. Henry doesn't bend down to pet it but watches it intently as if memorizing its movements. Time stretches as he stands there, watching.

Ed shifts on his feet. "You got it?"

"I don't have a cat," says Henry, still watching, "but my neighbor does, and she lets me have it now and then."

"Why don't you get a cat?"

Henry turns and looks at Ed and smiles how a cat might smile while eviscerating a bird for pleasure. "I don't believe in ownership."

"You could say you're just taking care of it."

"Everything takes mental space. You think about the cat at home, lonely, waiting for you. It pulls you from the present, from full engagement. You must decide what to commit to and commit fully."

Ed ignores the comment. He is overcome with desire, and the consequence of whatever transpires tonight doesn't matter to him.

"Want to come over?" says Ed.

"Sure."

When Ed unlocks his front door, he rushes around, picking things up, folding the blanket on the couch, and putting the pillows where they belong. Henry silently strolls around the living room, tilting his head to read the titles of books, slipping books out, leafing through them, putting them back. A shiver runs over Ed as if Henry is touching him. Henry stands in front of the black and white photos of Ed's family: Eleanor holding Ed's hand when he was five; Ava holding a bouquet of daisies; and Ed dancing, at least twenty of those. He imagines what Henry is thinking—how vain, how solipsistic—and Ed explains that a friend who is a photographer shot them. They were a birthday present, and even as he's talking, he knows his explanation doesn't erase the stink of narcissism. Ed hung them up, didn't he—but he could never tell Henry he did so not to gaze at himself in admiration but to bolster his confidence. That trite phrase, believe in yourself.

Henry stops in front of the one in which Ed's right leg is extended behind him, bent at the knee, and he's arching back, holding his foot with his right hand. Ed's scalp tingles. He tries to imagine what Henry is thinking, seeing. The lines? The negative space? The muscles bulging in his leg? Henry's face is blank. Ed can't wait any longer. He comes up behind Henry and wraps his arms around his, pressing his chest to Henry's back.

"I like this one," says Henry, still looking at the photo. "You're released from earthly things. I don't like to be bound by the earth."

Henry turns and kisses Ed generously, unrestrainedly, his eyes closed, and Ed tastes his tongue, peppermint. Ed slips his hand under Henry's tight shirt and roams his back; how many times he's wished to do what he is doing now, how many times he imagined this moment, his hand gripping Henry's shoulder, his tongue encircling Henry's tongue, as if trying to make a braid, never to be undone. His heart beats a fast rhythm, and he knows he should slow down, luxuriate in the smooth expanse of Henry's back, the steely strength running parallel on each side of his spine, his bulging, taut shoulders; but at the same time, it's impossible. He undoes Henry's belt buckle, the top button of his jeans, and his zipper as Henry runs his fingers through Ed's hair.

"The perfect rat," says Henry, pressing his hands to Ed's cheeks.

Henry removes his shirt and his underwear with ease, a comfort that suggests he loves his body and wants to show it to Ed and has perhaps shown it to hundreds of lovers. Right now, Ed doesn't care. There is Henry's nudity, like the statues of the Greek gods, a beauty that surpasses all other human bodies' beauty, man or woman. His skin gleams.

Ed takes off his clothes, and they stand in front of each other, two naked bodies. Ed steps toward Henry.

"Wait," says Henry, holding out his hand.

Ed stops. Not sure what Henry wants or what's happening, a new game?

Henry smiles. "Look at me."

Ed stares into Henry's eyes, midnight blue, and Henry stares into his and the moment is like a new form of nakedness. He looks away.

"No," says Henry. "Look at me."

Ed has never done this before, never stood staring into someone else's eyes this long, and as the seconds tick by it feels as if he's sinking into a deeper form of nakedness, being taken inside of Henry, swallowed whole; and as more seconds go by, he feels Henry tunneling into him, touching everything, accepting everything, and he's burrowing into Henry, Henry's eyes are softening, and now Ed is weeping. He's never felt something so intimate, so honest, so vulnerable, and for a moment, before he falls under the sword of his passion, he fears this is not what he should be doing, not if he wants the performance to go well.

Henry reaches for his hand.

The night of the performance. Henry and Ed are backstage stretching. For one week they've rehearsed in costumes, but it still feels strange, like an extra layer of skin. Ed isn't used to it, especially the mask with holes cut out for his eyes. Yesterday, he wore the costume all day, even in his apartment, to try to make it merge into him. Still, it sits on top of his skin awkwardly.

The other dancers flit in and out of the small space that Henry and Ed have carved out as their own. Akiko comes by, kisses Ed on the cheek, and waves to Henry.

"Be the wind," says Ed.

She smiles. Dances around both of them, whisks away, and heads to makeup.

"You slept with her," says Ed.

"A long time ago," says Henry. "And you slept with her."

"Friends, always just friends."

"Let's not do this right now," says Henry.

In between the buzz of frenetic activity behind stage, Ed can hear the seats filling up, the low rumble of voices punctuated by the occasional screech of laughter. People gathering, the anticipation, the electric charge in the air, they're here for the new, the different, the dance at the outer limits of experience, so they can have that experience and tell their friends about it. The most unusual thing, you have to see it.

Eleanor's in the audience, and so is Ava, probably reluctantly.

"I wish this were over already," says Ed.

"That's not the right approach," says Henry. His eyes are dark and large and intense. "You must live for this night. You must make love to this night. This is the culmination of everything, the orgasm; when we shine and become more of ourselves, bigger than ourselves, we take the parts and put them together and have a whole. We are little pearls, and we make the necklace tonight."

"You aren't nervous?"

"Hell, I'm nervous. And it will either help me or destroy me."

Ed frowns. "Don't talk like that. It sounds like you're performing."

"We are. We're performers on a stage, you and I. We are playing the game of performing."

Ed hates when Henry starts talking like this, performance and art, as if art isn't real, as if there is something deeper and beyond what they're doing. It's all very real to Ed, and it may be a performance, but it doesn't mean it's fake or less than reality. They are in it; it is the world.

"My calves are tight," says Henry.

"Want me to work on them?"

"Please. Press here. Hard."

As he digs his thumbs into the taut muscle, Ed wonders what his mother will think of tonight. His sister won't understand it, baffling, all of it is baffling and absurd. She'll lump it in the category of Dada or nonsense and that will be the end of it.

"Ouch," says Henry.

"Sorry."

Akiko comes back. She is transformed completely, utterly, with makeup, her hair pulled up in a high ponytail flowing down her back, a white leotard and white tights, and a white gauzy-like cape that flows all the way down her legs to just above her heels. She bows low, not saying a word, then moves to the barre at the back of the room and goes through her warm-up.

They've reached the most delicate time; a wrong word, a wrong gesture will rearrange everything, tilting it toward disaster. The worst thought comes to Ed, and when it does, he knows it's true. They shouldn't have slept together—not before the performance. It was the wrong thing to do because now they are connected in a way that a cat and rat would never be. It's as if each cell, each molecule of Ed's being is tuned to Henry's being, aware of Henry cracking his knuckle, the click of his tongue on the roof of his mouth, the saliva swishing in and out of Henry's teeth. Too attuned, too intermingled.

The auditorium quiets and the music starts, and the light shifts. They are the first act. Ed's heart leaps. What if it flops? How will he come back from it? He's too old to resuscitate himself.

"Okay, you're on," says Colleen.

They move to the front wing of the stage. Henry is in front

of Ed, and Ed touches his finger to the back of Henry's neck. Henry flinches, pulls away. Ed feels a pinch of rejection.

The music crescendos, the blue-white light blares on stage, and Henry crouches on all fours and silently saunters into the brightness. No, Ed corrects himself, not Henry, the cat is on stage, the cat is licking its fur, the cat is standing still, its tail twitching. Ed's heart is thumping hard—his big premiere, a lead role, after all this time. Henry is doing beautifully—he is a cat.

Ed dashes onto the stage, races through the light, scampers to the shadow, the light spilling just a little short of him. Nose twitching, watching Henry, he hears the murmur in his mind, Henry, his beloved Henry, his lovely body, his back arches almost into a U when he orgasms. But no—the cat.

The air feels tight, tense, the audience on edge as if waiting for something to happen or someone to make a mistake. Ed scrambles through the light to the next patch of dark, and Henry is still moving slowly, leisurely in the light, as if the sun is shining and it's a beautiful blue day. It's not flowing, Ed's muscles are too tight, his hamstring seizing and releasing. Trapped in this costume, this human body. And Henry—the cat—is barely doing anything, as if waiting for Ed to do something. Henry should be stalking him. What's Henry doing? He seems self-contained as if he's alone on stage, and Ed is nowhere, nothing, he means nothing to Henry. Akiko's words haunt: he is not a generous lover.

We aren't in it, thinks Ed. We are far from it. Fear floods him. He wants Henry to look at him the way he did when they had sex, that deep looking, tunneling into him, stripping him, pulling him inside this moment, opening all the doors inside him, so he becomes everything. But Henry is curled up, his eyes closed as if he's perfectly content in his solitude.

Ed has to step out of the way, let the rat take over, but Henry is lying there, stretched out on its side like a lazy fool. He hears someone cough in the audience and imagines someone yawning. It's failing. Everyone is falling asleep. What is Henry doing? Henry rolls on his back and flutters his legs in the air as if batting a ball of yarn. The audience laughs. Henry's playing it for the audience, he wants the attention, he wants the fucking glory. Goddamn you, Henry, lure me in. Don't forget about me.

Ed circles, backs away, scampers into the corner, only his face is in the light. Still, Henry is goofing around, chasing his tail. The crowd is eating it up. Minutes tick by. There was never a set choreography. Let it flow, Collen would say. Henry flops on his side in the bright light. Ed creeps out of the shadow. Henry opens one eye and looks straight at Ed. Their eyes lock. It's not a human eye but a cold, alert eye of wildness that Ed stumbles into. He cannot look away as if they are two lovers or two deadly enemies. The cat rises and begins to move, one paw after the other, silently, stealthily, not once taking its wild eyes off Ed. Its face is small and pointed like an arrow. Ed smells the stench of pungent fear, his fear, and the cat picks it up. Both eyes, eyes of death, trained on Ed.

Come on, come on, Ed urges himself, let go, give into this. The cat flattens itself, belly on the ground, and Ed feels some of his humanness fall away. The cat steps closer. Alongside his fear is something new, a fierceness Ed has never known, sharp as steel. Something smacks his brain, and obediently, he hisses and bares his long sharp teeth. The cat stops. Raises its belly off the ground, eyeing, studying, only two leaps to pounce on the rat. The cat strolls away to the right, not taking its glowing death eyes off rat. Rat's pulse pounds with terror and ferocity. His upper lip rolls up higher. A flash of doubt like a new color washes through cat's eyes. A new smell—cat's sour fear. A surge of supremacy, rat hisses. Cat halts, swivels its head away, unlocking their eyes. Rat charges. Cat scampers into the shadows, but rat keeps coming, chasing cat into the light and bites down, tooth to leg. Cat swats at rat with a front paw, claws extended, squealing, but rat does not let go. Teeth in deeper. A swipe of claw to rat's back. Cat rolls, rat rolls with it. Deeper, split the Achilles tendon. Squeals turning to high-pitched screams of agony, the cat writhing in pain.

The curtain falls. Ed releases Henry. They let out their

breath, both soaking with sweat. Applause swells, whistles, bravo. The curtain lifts. In a trance, they walk to the front of the stage and bow. They run to the wings. Still applause—Colleen pushes them out there again. Bow again.

Then backstage. A pause, a catching of breath; Ed is in limbo, somewhere between. He can't look at Henry. The music is playing, and Akiko is on stage; she is the wind.

It is the aftermath. They sit in it, the release, the catharsis, it is over. Neither one of them speaks. For a long time they say nothing. Someone brings them water and they lap it up. They sit in the wings, watching the wind. Ed is only partly watching now, reliving what happened on stage, the fear, the fearlessness. Something cracked open, wide open, something whooshed in. What to make of it? What happened out there? Henry is beside him. They say nothing as if words would break the spell because the spell is still there, like vapor in the air.

❧

Afterward, Eleanor finds Ed backstage. "Marvelous," she says, hugging him. "I was with you the entire way. You felt like a rat to me. I believed you utterly."

Ed is euphoric; he hugs her and introduces her to Henry.

Ava stands off to the side. "Nice job."

Ed bows.

"So, the point was," says Ava. "What? To cross boundaries? To say we are more alike than not? To say we can enter the mind of an animal?"

"Does there need to be a point?" says Ed.

"Our species likes to interpret," says Ava. "I mean, it was interesting."

"Oh, Ava," says Eleanor. "Leave it alone. Please."

Henry laughs, and Ed hears he is laughing at Ava.

Ava crosses her arms, and her face reddens along with the rims of her ears. Not anger, Ed knows, but embarrassment.

"Really, fantastic," says Eleanor. "I loved it, absolutely loved it. I saw the rat had its own experience, its own reality."

Ed is too elated to respond.

"It's hubris, don't you think?" says Ava. "That we can know what an animal—or for that matter, a tree—thinks. An anthropocentric distorted view."

Henry smiles brightly, and Ed senses he wants to say something caustic but is holding off.

Eleanor commends them again. A real artistic achievement, she says. Others are hovering nearby, smiling, wanting to congratulate them. Eleanor takes Ava by the arm and leads her away. Colleen introduces Ed and Henry to the art critics from the *New York Times* and the *Washington Post*.

It's only later at the after-party when they find themselves on the red leather sofa at the Black Diamond Bar, drinks in front of them, only one drink each and in small glasses because there is rehearsal tomorrow morning and another performance in two days, sitting in the murky light, the atmosphere smooth with the others dancing to some madness, Akiko gliding by in her white gauzy cape, sitting thigh to thigh; only then does Ed ask, "So did you really slip all the way into the skin of the cat? I mean, were you a cat?"

Henry smiles, his teeth gleaming like a beacon.

Ed laughs, a little tentatively. What will become of them? He senses that what happened on stage, that deep connection, that intense engagement twining them together, is something that will occur only on stage. Already Henry feels separate from Ed, a distinct being with his own desires and whims and trajectory that may include Ed or may not.

"I felt something," says Ed. "I felt something different, other."

Henry says nothing.

"But we did it," says Ed.

Henry sips his drink. "Your mother is a very smart woman. You are lucky."

"She felt something too," says Ed. "She's not one to give false praise. She really liked it."

Henry has the slightest grin around the edges of his lovely

mouth. "The artist Henry Moore said the secret of life is to have something you devote your entire life to, something you bring everything to, every minute of the day for the rest of your life. And the most important thing is, it must be something you cannot possibly do."

Is that right? Ed doesn't know if he agrees. He wants to feel the inflation of completion, the warm blush of success. Will there never be a moment of arrival? But if he isn't striving for something, what would he be doing?

"Tell me, though, we did okay, right?" says Ed. "We did it?"

Henry looks at Ed tenderly, and tenderly Ed kisses him on the lips.

❧

Tender is the breeze through the oak leaves and the open window. Touching the whisker of a mouse, the cheek of a man, an overflowing garbage can. Tenderly I move in the night and in the day as I watch for signs of something good. Hope may be the thing with feathers, but it's a necessary thing for me. I've lived eras of restless nights. Everything and everyone sleeping, except me. I'm up, roaming, meandering, pacing, full of worry. Even if I had a chair that was soft and well padded, I couldn't sit still. You, me, we are part of the world. A sunny day tosses into happiness and wide-openness; a wrong word and we're closed down.

Did they do it? Henry and Ed crossing over to another consciousness? If a human can think like a cow, become a cow… or a rabbit, a coyote, a cat, a rat—

No, they didn't. They didn't cross anything. To do that, they have to decenter themselves. Ed loves himself too much; so does Henry, both of them staring at themselves in the mirror, lovingly, adoringly, obsessively.

Or maybe. Maybe their desire to succeed on stage demanded they unhusk themselves from their idea of self and cross. They heeded the call, at least for a moment, a flicker, and maybe the audience, at least for a moment, felt it and saw the world through a nonhuman lens. Tried on, like a new coat, a new way of thinking. Or, at the very least, became aware that a rat and a cat are not extensions of the human mind but beings in their own right. That they have an inexhaustible reality beyond human thinking. I can feel my excitement spark because if they did, I mean, how much harder to kill a rat, slaughter a cow, or indifferently respond to a wildfire raging or a flood ravaging.

I'm aware I'm grasping, but I don't care. I need to conjure possibilities to keep up my spirit. Isn't it hope the thing with feathers perched in the soul? Ed and Henry love each other, Ed's hand on Henry's thigh and Henry's hand on Ed's, a whisper, a laugh, and a smile, loving and intimate. A kiss on the lips, on the cheek. It may not last, it probably won't, but it's something to have loved at all. And it's something to have something other than the usual in a story; not humans on center stage, but a rat and a cat. For once, animals got to shine.

I'm going to the bay because it's a favorite place of mine, and you need happy moments with the water lapping the rocks, water running in, running out, smoothing and polishing the grains of sand, back and forth, like the poetic sweep of a line, accompanied by the rattle and click of stones.

It's lovely, the steel blue, the flicker of light on the waves, the waves licking the feet of the sandpipers scurrying along the shore. People are here, wanting to be nurtured and loved by the sand and water and waves. They're taking off their socks and shoes and walking barefoot in the waves, and their faces lightening because something deep and ancient inside has stirred.

The meaning of pleasure is settling in, and complete immersion becomes the only answer. The cold shocks, wakes. We need a moment of release from the terror and panic, the world crying out for help. Beauty, some of it is still here. I'm soaking it in to replenish. I, and everyone and everything, crossing over, inhabited by the rhythm of the water flowing up and down a spine, feeling the rhythmic tides in the body.

Paradise

Hugh knows what he needs, what his family needs, and what is coming. New Zealand is the answer. Isolated, self-sufficient, clean water, clean air. Hugh pictures his family swimming in the blue ocean and birds in a blue sky. His son loves birds. Lush green hills, white sand. It has to be New Zealand. He keeps returning to water: clean drinking water will be an issue. So will heat. Drought. Fires. Smoke. Lack of food, Jesus, food will be a big issue. They could build a greenhouse and grow their food.

Hugh gazes out his big bay window at a bright San Francisco and a sky with tattered white clouds. Thoughts of what's coming are like a pack of ravenous wild wolves nipping at his heels. He can feel their hot breath on his neck, hear their panting and growls, their paws pounding the pavement, the stringy saliva splattering, one solid leap to bite his neck, that's how close they are.

Sailboats race across the water, and someone speeds on a windsurfer. And part of what's coming is a stark divide, even more pronounced than it is now, between the Haves and the Have-nots. Have-nots—put that in the liability column for remaining in the United States because today's rumble of civil unrest will seem tame, like a little roughhousing between boys. If you're hanging on by your fingernails, morality is out and violence in. A gun to the back, to the head; a knife to the throat, at night, day—daylight won't protect against abject desperation.

It's got to be New Zealand, with its wealth heaped on the senses. Dick bought twenty acres and paid only four million, but he got in early. Roy bought land in Canada, but now he thinks it's New Zealand, and Ben, good ol' Ben, one of the biggest stoners at Columbia, now worth hundreds of millions, made the move to New Zealand permanent. His last Christmas card was a picture of him and his family of six, all smiles and tan with sun-kissed hair.

The wind is blowing, and the windows have taken on a chill. Below, cars crawl along stretches of shadow, and the bay looks like a sheet of hard metal. He respects metal, how durable it is, how versatile and resilient, and so many things made out of metal, though his entire adult life has had nothing to do with metal or the material world. Founder of MD CONNECT, he has more than five million of the ten to fifteen million doctors worldwide on his site, and the advertising revenue is mind-boggling. At Stanford Graduate School of Business he had to write a business plan, and his vision was MD CONNECT, though his professors warned, "Not likely. Get ready for a string of failures before you hit one out of the ballpark." But this one hit, soaring into the big sky, and it's still hanging up there like the blinding sun.

On his computer he pulls up one of the houses the real estate agent showed him half an hour ago. Five bedrooms, four baths on the north shore, a pool, tennis court, and basketball court, very modern, clean lines, minimalist look. A steal at five million; in California, it would be at least fifteen mil. The nearest neighbors—they don't exist. Inside, lots of natural light, white walls, and wood floors.

There's the one even farther up the north shore, but it's got too much gold, though they could tear that out. A huge pool, a fitness and movie room in the basement, and a putting green by the driveway. He could teach his son how to play golf. Gabe likes anything repetitive. In his bedroom he has on his shelf at least 200 miniature Pokémon figures that he made out of clay, each with incredible detail, including Venusaur with six sharp white teeth and claws. Gabe could sell them if he could bear to part with them. The doctor said to keep him off screens because they're a stimulant, like caffeine or amphetamines or cocaine—he needs physical activity and nature to calm him.

He clicks to the next house, newly built, everything state-of-the-art, energy efficient, fifty solar panels soaking up the sun, and four Tesla batteries that power the entire place. As he roams through the house with his mouse, he heads to the jacuzzi in the master bedroom. Franny will love it. When you head to the beach, you go down—he zeroes in on the screen—this little path here. White sand, water, and seagulls snapping up orange crabs.

Hugh uses Google Maps and flies up high and then zooms down to the house, three sides of a rectangle, the pool off to the right, the basketball court closer to the garage, and not a soul on the beach. Sun, sand, wind, and water are not sullied by humans. Humans need the rhythm of nature. The irony isn't lost on him, he who spends hours in front of his computer screen.

Hugh asked the agent for any other recommendations—any other country, state—and the agent brought up the luxury nuclear bunkers in Kansas—that former Atlas Missile silo—but Hugh said no to that, they aren't heading underground.

It's New Zealand because he needs to put a hell of a lot of distance between himself and the wolves with their snapping jaws and meaty breath, which he occasionally smells. Maybe he'll fly over and look at this house. Or they can all go—call it a vacation. Hugh looks at the house on the screen. The obstacle is Fran. If he can get Fran to listen to him, see his vision. He can picture Fran on the sunny porch, her long beautiful legs, her elegance, her hazel eyes. Her face open with happiness. His children swimming in the ocean. Only the waves and sea birds. He'll swim with his children, and the fatigue beneath his eyes will vanish. At night they'll sleep so deeply after rearranging themselves in the waves.

He looks up from his computer, busy formulating arguments in his head because he's picturing Fran's expression—her eyes, stern, hard, steady. She's not a screamer. She steels herself, revs up her intelligence, her logic, cold and calculating. In a former life, she must have been a prosecutor.

❧

He's on the phone for several hours with legal and product, handling privacy issues. With doctors exchanging patient information, it must be 100 percent secure, but the product team is always enthusiastic about some new idea to use the info. The money is tantalizing, but he's not stupid; he knows the core product can't be compromised.

In between calls, he clicks on the New Zealand house. He didn't see it the first time, but off to the right, down by the ocean, there is a greenhouse. Fran will love that. This is the house. He can't stop looking at the sun pouring on the house and the beach. The ocean is bluish and brackish, and the sand is gleaming white.

He's bursting with the news; it's the answer he's been searching for. He feels imprisoned by it; his obsessiveness makes New Zealand whistle in his ear. He calls home, and the phone rings and rings. A couple of minutes later, Fran calls back. "I saw you called. How's your day?"

He wants to blurt it out. He's not good at secrets. When his parents told the family at dinner they were going to have a new baby sister and let's keep this news in the family, he excused himself to go to the bathroom and instead ran next door to tell the neighbors. Excitement and enthusiasm burned down the walls of the secret. But he can't; it needs to be the right time. He needs to see her face to determine her mood.

"Good, just checking in," he says.

"Everything's good here. I spent the morning writing my way into a deep, dark corner of despair, but it's the truth, so it's good."

"I'm glad."

In a world of her own making, she can enter the most awful things.

"Miss you," she says. "Are you sure everything is okay?"

Her intelligence is wide and probing, not only brain power but emotional intelligence. The way she picks up on the most minute discordant vibration, even over the phone. "Yep. Just called to hear your voice."

A pause. "Okay. Will you be late tonight?"

"Nope." A sailboat is heading toward Angel Island. The seagulls are black curved lines. "Gabe good today?"

"He's so cute. He picked out his clothes this morning. His blue pants and red shirt with the big green dinosaur on it."

A custom-made shirt. Most fourteen-year-olds have outgrown their obsession with dinosaurs. "He loves that shirt."

"I can barely get it off him to wash it."

"We'll have to buy a second one, maybe a third."

She laughs. Twenty years married, and he loves this woman. How patient she is with Gabe, how loving, how kind. Half the time he wants to throttle his son. A boy with so many challenges, Hugh can barely think about them all without being clobbered by sadness. Whatever gods there are, they turned their back on his son. His struggle to read, to write, to understand math, to relate to people, but man, he's a fabulous artist. When he thinks of Gabe, his protective hackles go up like hair on an animal's back.

"And Louise," says Fran, "is Louise."

"Fran," he says.

"Are you sure something didn't happen? Your voice is full of energy like something happened. Or you're really excited."

He feels a particular loneliness. The secret of New Zealand is a wall between them. "Love you. See you soon."

"Love you too. See you tonight."

Hugh opens the front door to garlic, tomato, and onion, which means Fran worked all day, which means she's in a good mood—the writing flowing, the story moving—leaving little time for anything but spaghetti. It's the perfect time to bring up New Zealand. Days like these, she disappears in her play, and when she emerges, she's dazed, half there, as if she disintegrated, becoming each character, fragmenting herself into three, four, or more people, depending on the play. To Hugh, it is terrifying. He could never do it; it took him too long to build a self.

She's writing a play about two Black boys in the inner city, loosely based on James Baldwin's short story "The Rockpile." And that's all she's told him. She'll let him read the script at some point, but not yet, not when it's inchoate.

He should leave New Zealand alone and let them glide on this mood. He still looks forward to making love to his wife. How many spouses can say that after all these years? She is a silhouette in her black sleeveless dress against the sheer expanse of the white kitchen. She turns to him, and her face brightens.

"You're home early," she says.

He kisses the smooth skin of her neck, breathes her shampoo of honey and garlic from cooking, and under that is her scent, hers alone, sandalwood and the air after a hard rain. He's read the science behind pheromones, and usually, when he understands something better, it loses its hold on him. But not this, never this. Her scent reshuffles him.

"Where is everyone?" he says.

She tells him Louise is doing homework and Gabe's outside. "You can't get that basketball out of his hands. He's getting so good."

She rests her head on his chest, and he fingers her dark curly hair. All the things he knows about her, all the things he doesn't know. He can't say, exactly, how she'll react. Maybe she's been reading the same reports and newspaper articles. Maybe she's got a pack of wolves chasing her too.

"I'll change out of these clothes and help with dinner," he says.

He won't bring it up. Everything is so nice right now. These moments are a world of their own, he's learned to roll them around in his hand. Louise isn't in a teen turmoil, Gabe's in a rhythm—those awful days when he sat in his room alone for hours, not speaking to anyone.

He goes upstairs. Through the wooden floorboards, he hears Fran singing to the radio, Aretha Franklin's "Rolling in the Deep," and Fran's voice is rich, riding a deep vein. Too many of their friends' marriages have run themselves into the ground or are limping along, one leg severely injured. Will and his wife, what a calcified nightmare that is. Always fighting, bickering, saying horrible things about each other in front of each other. The last time they had them over for dinner, he and Fran said never again.

As he changes into shorts and a T-shirt, he hears his daughter on the phone. He stops, knocks, opens her door, and waves hello. She frowns, waves him away. Louise looks like Fran, Francesca, the same coloring, long-necked and lean, the same black hair, though Louise relaxes hers. Fran has tried to understand, concerned that Louise is rejecting, or worse, loathing, her Dominican heritage; but it ended in a fight that culminated in Louise's tense silence for too many tense days.

He tosses his shirt in the hamper and takes off his socks. His feet are long-toed, and as a kid, he always thought of his feet as ugly. Still does, but he likes to walk around barefoot because of the texture of the wood floor. He hears the steady beat of the basketball. A bird sings, and another one starts, louder, blotting out the first one. It's not like he's asking Fran to move to Houston or Toledo. It's a good thing, New Zealand, and they aren't moving there; it's Plan B. If he had more time, he'd formulate a Plan C too.

In the kitchen, he slices red onions and tomatoes for a salad. "So, I've been thinking," he says before he can stop himself.

She's stirring the pasta in the pot.

"Maybe it's time for a vacation."

"That would be nice. You've been so busy. Me too. Where?"

Louise wanders into the kitchen, and he kisses the top of her head and smells the hair relaxant. "Wheez, how are things?"

"What do you think? Gobs of homework. They're killing me."

Sixteen and predictably hyperbolic.

"You've been in your room for hours," says Fran. "What are you working on?"

AP Comp, she's studying logical fallacies. "You know, ad hominem attacks, the false dilemma fallacy," she says.

"What's that last one?" says Hugh.

"Basically, either-or reasoning. An oversimplification that states something in only two ways." She puts her hand on her hip, one foot in front of the other slightly turned out—a stance of Fran's when she's sassy. "*You* do it all the time."

"I do? Me?" he says, his eyes wide with exaggeration.

Fran laughs.

Louise lowers her voice, smashes her heavy dark eyebrows together. "'Either you study hard, or you won't get anywhere.'"

"I look like that?" he says.

Her big green eyes—they are from him—twinkle with amusement. "You also use equivocation big time."

"What are you talking about?" he says. "I'm just a simple guy, prone to the false dilemma fallacy."

"The way you come into my room and say, 'Just checking to see if you need anything,' when you're really checking to see what I'm doing." The conniving smile of someone who knows a secret she'll never let you in on.

Fran laughs harder. "She's on to you."

"I think you're going to be a lawyer," he says. "Your argumentative skills are superb, along with your cross-examination."

"Or something artistic," says Fran.

Louise picks up a stalk of celery and takes a bite. "No," she says to Fran.

"Why not?" says Fran.

Louise waves her celery around at them. "I don't have to do what you do."

"Of course not, but you don't want to underestimate yourself, or you'll limit yourself," says Fran.

"Why does everything have to be about my future?"

"It isn't," says Fran.

"See? Equivocation," says Louise. "You always do it."

Louise is moving her hips to the music. One moment she's happy; the next, she's picking a fight. Everything is subject to debate. She has a meter reader, checking how much energy they have left in the tank; if she finds an extra ounce, she proceeds to use it all up so he and Fran collapse in bed at night. A cynical view, but there's a lump of truth to it.

He heads outside. The trees are holding the light in their leaves. Birds unfurl the last of their songs. He lets his good fortune fill him, a sense of accomplishment that he can provide for his family. Down the gentle slope to the basketball court he goes, admiring the stretch of cheery green lawn. The air is woven with the day's last warmth, and Fran's garden revels in the last of the light. New Zealand has good soil for gardening, he thinks.

His tall, lanky son is standing at the free-throw line, the ball raised, preparing to shoot. He is stunning in his concentration. At fourteen he's grown three inches in one year, and his feet are large. His voice has changed; he sounds like a man. When he makes the shot, Hugh says, "Nice."

Gabe looks at him, noticing him for the first time. He races to the ball, claiming it before Hugh as if Hugh is a thief.

"Gabe," says Hugh. "Let's play. Toss me the ball."

Gabe looks at him, intensity in his dark eyes, which means he's been out here for hours. Not for anything will he give his father the ball. He looks away and makes five shots in a row.

"The new Curry," says Hugh.

Gabe crouches down and begins dribbling between the legs, rapid side to side.

"Man, look at you. Can I try?"

Gabe doesn't even look up, as if the ball is glued to his fingers. He is locked in his own world. Last year, it was Pokémon clay figures; the year before that, origami; the year before that, twisting wire into sculptures. Hundreds and hundreds of these. At least he's active this time, not hunched in his room on the floor, making another thing that will drown his bookshelf.

A blue jay squawks and the sun dips lower. The kitchen window is open and Hugh can hear the water running and the clink of glasses. Five acres in Los Altos, they are sitting ducks. No security code at the black metal gate—Fran vetoed that—the gate is easy to hop over. When Gabe heads over to his water bottle, Hugh picks up the ball, dribbles, shoots, misses.

"That's a bad shot," says Gabe. "You need more wrist."

Hugh knows coders like Gabe, burrowing into the minutiae, sitting for hours and hours, forgetting to eat, shower, talk, the world winnowed down to numbers. There would be a job for Gabe at a tech company if the work held his interest. Hugh takes a few more shots, Gabe barking advice as if Hugh were an incorrigible child: bend your knees, more jump, point your elbow at the basket.

He tosses the ball to Gabe, who methodically and with great discipline begins shooting from specific spots on the court, making most of his shots. He is godlike.

"Do you want to play horse?" says Hugh.

"No."

Always honest, Hugh can count on that. Hugh gets on the ground and does push-ups and planks. He spots another basketball by the bench. He leaps up, grabs the ball, and plays on the other half of the court, until Louise comes down and tells them dinner is ready, then heads back up.

"Let's go, Gabe," says Hugh.

"Not hungry."

Gabe is standing to the right of the basket, shooting.

"Come on, son."

"I don't want to. Leave me alone. You're always making me do stuff I don't want to do."

Fourteen years old, but he might as well be two.

"We're a family. We want you at the table."

"I don't care."

"Son."

"No."

"Come on."

"No. I want to play basketball."

As Hugh steps toward Gabe, Gabe throws the ball at Hugh. It slams his ear, his brain jostles. Hugh grabs the ball. A time-out? Take his basketball away—no ball for a week? What he really wants to do is throw the ball at Gabe's head. The kid is six foot two inches, 150 pounds, already taller than Hugh. Hugh remembers when Gabe, as a toddler, threw violent tantrums—didn't matter where they were, grocery store, toy shop, shoe shop—thrashing, throwing things, hitting, biting like a vicious animal. Hugh would have to tackle him and pin him to the ground until Gabe wore himself out.

There won't be an apology. Hugh's tired, a long day at work, another long day tomorrow. Hugh clutches the ball to his chest, his son eyeing it as if scheming to get it from him. "You'll come to dinner now."

The muscles in his son's face clench. Another fight is brewing. Hugh imagines all that might happen. Gabe ran away once, and they found him in the vacant lot a mile away, curled under a bush asleep. Or he refuses to come inside, sleeps outside in a sleeping bag on the lawn—he's done that, too—Hugh and Fran lying awake all night, wondering if he's all right. Hugh doesn't want any of this, a long night of turmoil.

"You can play after dinner," says Hugh, cringing inside. A concession, a reward to him.

The last of the day's light strikes Gabe's dark hair, and it sparkles as if he's been doused in glitter. Gabe smiles gloriously as if he won, which he did.

At dinner, Louise brings everyone up to date on current events since her history and environmental science teacher requires her to read the daily newspaper and a news-related magazine. She reads *Time*, *Newsweek*, *U.S. News and World Report*, and the *New York Times*. Her voracious appetite for social media adds another heavy dose of news. Protests in Hong Kong, corruption in Russia, China's suppression of political dissent, and the environmental/political refugees from the Middle East flooding Europe, all said in a surprisingly chipper tone as if she's discussing what's on a restaurant menu.

Hugh marvels at her ability to consume tsunami-sized waves of hideous news without letting it extinguish her optimism.

Perhaps growing up in turmoil, where nearly every book and every documentary on the natural world ends in a warning—another species endangered, another environmental disaster to address now—she's used to it.

Hugh lights candles. Everyone looks more beautiful in the golden light. Fran bought daffodils, trimmed the stems, and put them in a glass vase. He wishes he could always have this moment. Fran smiles at him, her dark eyebrows framing her triangular face.

Louise says she has to do community service for school, and she's thinking about Greenpeace.

"They're fire," says Louise.

"Don't they do radical things?" says Hugh.

"They did this totally amazing protest against Samsung," says Louise. "They climbed up the walls of the Berlin Palace and hung this banner 'Go 100% renewable energy now!' And they got the company to agree!"

Gabe is balling up pieces of his napkin and shooting them into his water cup.

"What do you think of that, Gabe?" says Hugh.

Gabe says nothing and continues his game, along with a low humming.

"Some woman just gave them a lot of money, like hundreds of thousands," says Louise. "That's privilege, to be able to just hand over money like that."

Laughable for her to bring up privilege, given all that he and Fran have provided. Private education, piano lessons, ballet, lacrosse, tennis, sailing, SAT prep, and tutor. Endless.

"You have a lot to be grateful for," says Hugh.

"I didn't say I wasn't grateful."

"I'm glad she gave it to such a great group," says Fran.

"I disagree," says Louise.

"Of course you do," says Hugh, laughing.

Louise folds her arms, her lower lip pouting. "What's that supposed to mean?"

Hugh knows to shut up but can't help himself. "Whatever we say, you disagree and—"

"Okay, I'm out," says Louise.

"We're listening," says Fran.

"Yeah, well, I'm not. I have homework," says Louise. She throws her napkin on the table and leaves. That stirs Gabe, who darts for the door, and in an instant, the basketball court lights come on, and they hear the beat of a ball.

"Sort of takes the wind out of my sails," he says.

She smiles faintly. "It's developmental, remember that. Think of her as a work in progress. You wait, in a minute she'll be back, and it'll be as if nothing happened." Fran raises her water glass. "Cheers to us."

He raises his glass. The house breathes and sighs. A feeling of great warmth comes over him, affection for her calm, her patience, her love of their children. He lets himself be swept up in his good fortune to have met her. She tells him a bit more about her play; she's in the final act and it's going well, things are connecting, characters are alive, full of surprises, of depth. "It's a relief to step out of my own way and let the story unfold—all that I wanted to control, well, that's out the window, and thank god," she says.

He loves when she talks about her writing because her face becomes illuminated as if she's in this world and another of her own making. Her last play ran for three months at the Orpheum Theater, and when it received high praise, it felt as if she and the rest of the family were floating. It fed her, it made her more courageous, more daring. She is lovely and brave. He moves from the end of the table, pulls up a chair beside her, and kisses her.

"Say," says Hugh. "What if we went to New Zealand for vacation?"

"For spring break?"

He holds her hand and twirls her wedding ring. "Or earlier. I've got some time next week."

"Next week? That's fast. The kids have school."

"They can miss a week."

"But you had mentioned Berlin."

"I've never been to New Zealand," he says. "And I think we need beaches and water more than urban."

She's looking at him closely as if sleuthing between the lines.

Louise comes into the kitchen and pours herself a glass of water. She is now a different human being, self-contained, confident, happy. Her right cheek has an indentation, a lone dimple. He knows he should wait until Louise leaves the room to say more. Long ago, he and Fran agreed to present a united front. Fran grew up in a family where her father and mother were always divided, her mother the disciplinarian, her father less so: let her go out, she's a teen and wants to be with friends; no, she has homework and a curfew. A divided family, so divided it fell apart.

Outside, the lights on the basketball court create an eerie glow. A dog barks and now the coyotes are howling. Louise looks at him, tilting her head slightly to the left, the way women do as if sensing something in the air.

"There's a lot to do in New Zealand," says Hugh.

"New Zealand?" says Louise. "I want to go! Julia went on the trilogy tour and said it was fire! *The Lord of the Rings* was shot there. The Hobbiton Movie Set, Middle Earth, where Frodo and Bilbo began, the Green Dragon Inn, over 150 locations."

"Gabe loves those books," says Fran.

Fran's words trill through him, spark his impulsive enthusiasm. "Maybe while we're there we can look at a house."

"Yeah!" says Louise.

She is his ally, but Fran is not. Fran puts down her fork and narrows her eyes. Her face tightens, making lines on her forehead, and he can see how she'll look when she's sixty, seventy. He feels himself notching into a quicker gear, preparing for whatever path she's about to head down. At the same time he wants to turn back. Where is the pool of contentment?

"Let's have this discussion later," says Fran. Her tone cool, full of warning. The mood in the room curdles.

"We could learn to scuba dive, Dad," says Louise. "Not where the sharks are, but somewhere else. Let's get a place right on the ocean."

He wants to wholeheartedly agree.

"Louise, can you leave us alone for a minute," says Fran.

A grating edge to her voice, the anger rumbling behind the words like a saw, buzzing away, waiting to say what she really wants to say to him.

Louise says, "Sure. Whatever. Dad knows how to have fun, just to let you know. You don't. You always have your face in a book. Dad actually does stuff."

Louise leaves, and he gets up and starts clearing the dishes.

"A house?" says Fran.

He suddenly feels the effusiveness rocket out of him, and the prospect of a lovely evening in bed with his wife is gone.

"I'm sorry, I was thinking out loud," he says. "I get going with something."

"Come on, Hugh. A house?"

"Just an idea, we can talk about it."

"You're too effusive, you don't think things through. And in front of Louise? Come on."

He opens his mouth to defend himself, but she puts up her hand. "I don't want to do this right now." She pushes back her chair and says she wants to finish a scene in her play. She has about an hour of solid writing left in her, and then they can talk.

"Do you want to tell me about your play?" he says.

She frowns. "No, I don't."

He put his hand to his brow, feeling a moment of panic. This is what he's up against. A woman who is fierce, smart, direct. After she leaves, he sits in the aftermath of her perfume. But he can't sit still. He starts washing the dishes and loading them in the dishwasher. He takes a tea towel, cleans the counters and the table, and listens to the pounding of the basketball, which is no longer reassuring but like the approach of a storm.

❧

Hugh's in his study, sending out emails at ten p.m., waiting for Fran to finish. His friend Tom wants to run the fifteen-mile loop in the hills this weekend. *If you got it in you*, writes Tom. They go all the way back to college, where they ran track together, the 800 meter, the 1500 meter. *Sure, I got it in me*, writes Hugh. *Ha! We'll see*, writes Tom. *Last time I whipped your ass, but you're always up for a challenge, so let's do this!*

The house feels chilled, as if all warmth has fled. He throws on a hoodie and finds himself in a survivalism chat room. His friend Tom mentioned there's a shitload of info. He starts paging through the Disaster Preparedness General Discussion. Lists of edible foods in the wild: crickets, grasshoppers, bugs with a crunchy exoskeleton, also slugs, and worms. Hugh feels his stomach turn. *Stay away from anything bright and colorful!!* writes someone named Achilles. A discussion on how to sew a suture without causing deadly infection. The best gas masks, best bunkers, and ammunition. A guy whose handle is Amped bought a helicopter and keeps it gassed up AT ALL TIMES. Learned to fly it so he didn't have to rely on a pilot to get him the hell out. A discussion about air filtration systems—Hugh makes a note to look into that.

Compared to these guys, Hugh is a whimper in an exploding scream of frenetic survivalist activity. He should tell that to Fran, but she isn't going to want to know about this chat room or that he visited it and will continue to. Some guy named Rhino bought a Honda Rebel 300 motorcycle because of the gas mileage—*70 miles to the f-ing gallon!* Hugh owns two Teslas, but Rhino is right: if a tornado or earthquake wipes out the electrical or PG&E shuts it all down like they did with the last wildfires, he's screwed. But a motorcycle with 70 mpg. But where would he put the kids? Fran could ride on the back. Maybe he gets the kids dirt bikes.

Yes, to an air filtration system. Yes, to a Rebel 300. Maybe an indoor basketball court in the New Zealand house; if they have to stay inside because of air quality, they'll have something to do. An indoor pool?

Some guy named Cryptozoo is loading up on gold coins. Hugh jots it down. If the currency goes sideways, all value lost, the stock market crashes, what does he have? Property, so yes, to gold coins. Maybe he should buy property in Canada too. Real estate is a passive income and an escape haven. He's thinking too small, socked away in denial. What else has he forgotten?

He feels his heart racing, the wolves howling. All these guys must hear the wolves. Hugh takes deep breaths and shuts down the chat room, but his heart is still pounding. Weeks ago, he vowed to read that Baldwin story, so he heads into their bedroom and finds the book and pages through it to "The Rockpile." The allure to a child not to a park or woods or waterslide, but a pile of rocks. Urban setting, poverty, Black boys sitting on the apartment fire escape, staring longingly at the rock pile. Mother says no way they're joining the neighborhood boys who climb and clamor and inevitably fall off the rocks. But the temptation. Mom distracted, one of the boys sneaks over, joins the boys, a fight ensues, a king-of-the-rock-pile game. The boy is pushed off, hurt, bleeding, comes home crying. Mom was right. Parents fight—father blames overworked mom for failing to watch the boy, Mom lashes back.

Which bolsters his argument. Nature gone, decimated—they're playing on a pile of goddamn rocks. Though you got to love kids, they can turn anything into play. The power of imagination—can he get Fran to imagine life in New Zealand? Safe, beautiful, a normality where everyone can thrive. Thrive is one of her favorite words. In the story, there's the inevitable violence, the pushing, shoving, and blood. Who knows the level of violence that will come? Tim at Yahoo is hiring security guards—armed—to guard his estate on Long Island. Yes, Fran, we're in the 1 percent. Probably the .01 percent. The masses versus us—do you know how easily we'll be pushed off the rock pile?

❧

At 10:30 they are finally in the bedroom alone. It's a terrible time to start this. They are both spent, fumes of their selves. The night is dense, heavy. She has washed her face, removed her makeup. The house feels ready for the rhythms of sleep, but Fran stands in the middle of the room, arms crossed, frowning at him as if she's already decided something about him that she doesn't like.

"It's not just a vacation," she says.

He's sitting on the edge of the bed. Her accusatory tone of voice amps up something, the fast beat of being shoved against a wall, a hand on his chest, and now he must defend himself. Is there any way to postpone this? Plead that they are too tired? But if not now, when? Most likely, they'll find themselves in the same situation tomorrow—late at night, exhausted.

Gabe is asleep. He can hear Louise in her room talking to friends on the phone or maybe playing a videogame. High screeching laughter. Hugh or Fran will have to go in and tell her to shut it down. The gloomy face, and the tone that she never gets to do what she wants, they are cruel, awful, terrible, she can't wait to go to college. Parenting is endless.

"Say something," says Fran.

"I know some people buying places in New Zealand, that's all," he says. "I've heard fantastic things."

The frown deepens. "Don't bullshit me."

It's late. He has to cut right to it. He tells her New Zealand seems like the best place, because everywhere else is a keg and is ready to explode, it is exploding, god there are so many problems—so if the whole thing blows up, and he's not saying it's never happened before in the history of the United States; there was the Civil War, the rounding up of Japanese sent to internment camps, the McCarthy era, the civil rights movement, and racism—but these are unprecedented times and they've got to get away—

"Away from what?"

Her eyes are full of harsh judgment.

"From it."

"What?"

"Whatever happens here. If it happens."

The crease between her eyebrows is a big dent of anger, and mingled with that anger is a bafflement, a questioning—of him. He can see it in the way she's looking at him, tilting her head to the right. As if asking: Who is he? Because she doesn't recognize this man who is talking to her, this Hugh who's proposing what she thinks he's proposing, which is to flee. Run. Escape from the civil unrest—is that what he's saying? As if she's witnessing his true self that, under pressure, emerges from the depths of his being but is usually kept hidden. Mistrust is settling over them like ash. When did he become a man who would think moving to New Zealand is the answer?

He remembers when they first met, that glance across the room at a lecture at NYU about postmodern art. He went with his friend Alan, who was looking to hook up with a smart broad—language of another era. Alan, who would probably be diagnosed with attention deficit disorder today, bouncing from one woman to another, from one job to another; but he had charisma and lit up the New York night whatever they did.

Hugh didn't know a thing about postmodern art, and he could barely understand what the lecture was about, though the man who kept swiping his hand through his scant hair was a spectacle and provided enough entertainment. Afterward, Alan was chatting up a woman who was tall and elegant, a sort of 1920s anachronistic beauty. Behind them was a woman with a sheen to her face, and a neat ladylike afro bloomed from her head. In her sleeveless white top, she showed off muscular arms. She was talking to a man, laughing, when her eyes met Hugh's. He was staring at her, mesmerized. It was so movie-esque, so cliché, the eye-locking thing, but it was also real and intense. He walked right over and introduced himself. Later, when they made their way to McSorley's, she said, "You're someone who goes after what he wants, aren't you?" And her glowing, happy eyes said to him that she approved, and later, she said she fell in love with him that night, quickly, happily, he was a passionate, alive man. He fit her belief that life was not handed to you but must be made.

"Let's back up," he says. "Let's go and see New Zealand. A family trip."

Hands on hips, one hip jutting forward slightly. "But you clearly have another motive, and I want to hear it. I want you to say it out loud."

"I'll set motive aside."

"No, I want you to say it."

"You sound like you want to bite my head off. We're not having a discussion, not even close."

She sighs, exasperated with him. "Listen, if you're thinking what I think you're thinking—shit, what's wrong with you?"

Ad hominem attack, was that on Louise's list? Or should it be filed under post hoc fallacy? He stands; the hope of her sitting next to him on the bed, having an easy conversation, is gone. A stretch of wood floor between them. The house creaks and shifts.

"You can't even say it out loud," she says. "Doesn't that tell you something? That what you're thinking is wrong? Morally wrong?"

Anger flushes through him. "I want the best for our family. That's what I'm thinking, and there's nothing immoral about that."

"And I don't?"

He puts his hand up as if to stop her, the barrage of words ready to knock him down. "I keep reading the data, the dire predictions, and I want us to be okay. And my friends—"

"What friends?"

"Doesn't matter. Some of them are taking great precautions, and New Zealand keeps coming up. Not Australia, with its fire danger, too arid. Maybe it's Canada, though I haven't read enough about it. Could be Alaska, though I'd prefer Canada. There are silos now in Kansas, old silos that are being converted into luxury apartments, but that would be too—"

"Too elitist?"

"I'm not saying leave everyone behind and let them suffer."

He won't bring up Paul, who bought an entire island in the Pacific Northwest. He went the whole nine yards. Generators, solar panels, guns, rounds of ammunition. He says society has lost its founding myth, and it's only a matter of time before we descend into anarchy. "Hugh, you got to get on this now," he said. "You're usually such a planner, strategizing, analyzing, but you're living in a dream world if you aren't taking action." Hugh won't mention Ted, who had laser surgery, so he's no longer dependent on glasses or contact lenses—just in case everything collapses.

Over ham sandwiches, he told Hugh in a hurried, hushed tone that he refused to be dependent on an unsustainable external aid for perfect vision.

Fran's hands are on her hips, her chin is jutted out. "You're not? Because that's what I'm hearing. Hey, we're out of here. Good luck, everyone. You're doing what your friends are doing. That Aristotle quote—man differs from other animals in that he is the one most given to mimicry."

"Give me a break."

She takes a step back as if preparing to leave the room. He comes over to her, so close he sees the streaks of amber in her eyes, but right now they look like sparks.

"I want a backup plan," he says. "I'll still give to all our favorite causes—the Sierra Club, NRDC, Environment California—and I'm not going to stop doing that."

"Well, that's good to hear."

Her sarcastic tone strikes him in the chest.

"I'm not running away," she says. "That's for damn sure. I'm not going to an island while everyone else goes down. How fucking selfish can you be?"

He crosses his arms. "You're calling me selfish? I'm not selfish. This is about us, my family. It's what I care about the most."

She jabs her finger at him. "How about you call your rich friends and have them call the senators and advocate for alternative energy. Tax credits to those who go solar or wind. Tax credits to the companies that make the panels." More finger jabbing and waving. "And while you're at it, invest billions in planting trees. They suck up carbon dioxide. And how about local energy grids—people gather energy from solar panels and share it with their neighbors. We get off this fix of oil and gas."

"You make it sound easy."

Her chin is jutting out. "You want to know my plan? I'm going to help out. I'm going to be part of the community—my community—and help with food, supplies, whatever anyone needs, and I'm staying here to work on this and stop it."

"There's no stopping it."

"What's wrong with you?" she says.

"The tipping point was long ago."

"Says *you*?"

"Say the experts."

"If we always listen to the experts, we'd be dead by now."

They've reached a dangerous spot. Something turns inside him quietly, like a blade. Cruel words lining up in his throat, ready to charge out of his mouth—how naïve, how goddamn naïve you are, and you're willing to put your family, your children at risk—for what? So you can call yourself a good person? Let me tell you, that won't matter when we're in survival mode. Whom do you want to be here for? Your friend who works as a checkout clerk at Safeway and makes that chimichurri burger you love so much? For your other friend who teaches Spanish at the local public elementary school? The one who got you to host that big fundraiser for her school? He sees the bank account, sees Fran slip them money—$100, $500, $1000 now and then, and he never complains, never asks about it, never asks about the thousands she sends to Asociación de Ayuda a la Familia.

He's got to back things up, calm down, calm her down. The house feels like it's tilting. Gabe has left the court lights on, and it looks like the moon has fallen in the backyard. "Look, we're helping as much as we can right now," he says. "And that's the right thing to do."

"We can do more," she says. "Let's figure out how we can help more. If people pull together—"

Is she really this naïve? What has she been reading? Or hasn't she been reading—tucked away in her rock-pile play? She lives in her imagination, and he has been her accomplice. He sees her feet are bare, and they are as ugly as his. Flat, squarish toes. Does she really think one great community will form and everyone will help each other? It's dog-eat-dog, a zero-sum game. Darwinism at its best. If she wants community, go elsewhere. Go to Asia, go to Europe, to New Zealand where they have real community, where socialism isn't a bad word. In America, everyone is out for himself, climbing to the top of the damn rock pile and staking a claim, and you do it on your own. The hero, the rugged individual foraging for himself, survival of the fittest, can't tell him what to do; even if you did get some lucky breaks along the way, no one admits it.

"Now, Fran."

"Stop. Don't patronize me."

"I don't mean—"

"When I need help with the kids, I call one of my friends. We're there for each other. The moms, the working moms, we've always helped each other out. Someone's sick, we step in. When someone needs a little help, we reach out. The women are there for each other. We were the ones who got that park for the neighborhood. Remember?"

Her version of reality is becoming clearer to him. She sees the future as a bit of rain now and then, maybe a flood down the street. At worst, a hurricane. Despite her robust imagination, she hasn't envisioned mass migration, nativist panic, resource depletion, rising sea levels, and civil unrest. She's in a bubble, an innocent bubble—oh, how he wishes he were there too. It's beautiful there. Everything has a solution. If he lets her, she'll stay in the bubble until her hair turns pure white. This is Fran. Does he want her to join him in his panic? Who would she be then? Certainly not his bright star, full of hope and optimism.

Now he has the urge to protect her, not to burst that bubble. Even now, her belief in community, and people pulling together, it's a lovely, idealistic, utopian vision. He can't bring her down with him. It's like insisting—mandating—that everyone be an atheist. If he destroys her belief, who would be there to balance it out? To tell the kids there is a bright future? He's never believed in that Nietzsche bullshit that whatever doesn't kill you makes you stronger. Sometimes it weakens or debilitates, or leaves a life punctured irreparably. He wants her to have the impossible, not the unachievable, but the pure.

"Okay," he says. "I hear you, I do."

She drops her hands from her hips.

"We won't abandon ship. We'll fight the good fight. That's who we are."

"We have values," she says.

He thinks about Matt, the former Google exec, with his caches of water and food and his latest—weaponry. He's taking classes in archery, so he's ready when the masses come. Matt, a pudge who once had a gigantic laugh and a booming voice that sang with good cheer, a naturally kind and generous man. Matt, who pulls out all the stops for a dinner party—seven, eight courses. Who loaned Hugh $10,000 when he first launched his business, and when Hugh tried to pay him back, Matt said, No, sir. Friends, we're friends. Hugh gave him stock, though he didn't ask for it. Now, every week Matt is doing target practice.

He sees Fran turn inward, her gaze softening, the intensity fading as if she's trying to decide if he means it. She's far more intelligent than he is—he's been lucky, that's all. Timing and luck.

Though there are days when he is full of himself, when he gives an interview to a magazine or newspaper or TV reporter talking about high tech or AI, they call him for everything because he rarely says no. Sure, he likes the attention. He was one of six children; of course he likes the attention. So starved for it, his mother spread too thin, he was number three in the lineup, kicking and spitting and pulling hair while his mother told them to take it outside. "Work it out, I'm busy." Because she was busy. Those fights between his brothers and sisters over food, the bathroom, sports stuff, no, that's my baseball glove, it's mine, asshole. His older brother was militant and had a hard fist, knew where his soft spots were—i.e., stomach, head. There was never enough food, never enough anything. "Work it out!" his mother shouted at them from the kitchen. His father, bedraggled, never doing much at home except read the newspaper after dinner on the couch.

But he made it out of there, made it big. And, yes, he helps his brothers and sisters who didn't make it very far. His older brother owns a tire shop in Black Butte, Oregon. Knows all about cars and tires and engines and nothing else. It's as if he read only one book his entire life. Two sisters became elementary school teachers and barely make it on their salaries. Another brother is a store manager at Petco.

Some days he gets full of himself and believes in his genius when a newspaper raves about him or his ingenuity or foresight. But in the privacy of the night, he knows the truth. Sure, he had the idea, but lots of smart people have great ideas. You need timing and luck and to surround yourself with really smart people. So, when he gets too full of himself, he remembers he was once a ski bum, a scant $100 in his savings account, spending his every waking moment in the snow, carving up Sugar Bowl, until his knees screamed. Flat-out roared every time he skied down anything. The doc said he had the knees of an eighty-year-old. Obsessive, that's been his greatest strength and his greatest weakness. After he quit, it took six months to walk without pain shooting through his legs. And then, in business school, he came up with his idea for connecting doctors worldwide. He latched on to that and hasn't let go, working day and night, thirteen-, sixteen-hour days for so long he can't remember another way of life.

How he and Fran have made it through those long days, with him constantly on a plane, pitching his idea, flying everywhere to get the venture money. He and Fran are a marvel, a miracle. And here they are in a grandiose bedroom, a king-sized bed, his and her bathrooms, changing rooms; she has three closets full of fine clothes. In his head he can hear his deceased mother ask, how much money does Fran spend on shoes?

He strokes her arm. He cares more about his family than anything else. He's not Gandhi, doesn't want to be. He has a heart, but not a huge one—he's never been one for public love, that great big amorphous pulsing thing that comes with fame.

Fran's dark, intelligent eyes are soft and loving. She wraps her arms around him. He unhooks her bra and haunts her breasts, his mouth finds her mouth, and they move to the bed, stripping off clothes as they go. He knows her body so well. She is glorious. But his mind is already thinking about when the sex is over and he can fall asleep.

"Shit," he says.

"It's okay," she says. "I'm tired too."

"Let's try a little longer."

His hands are on her buttocks. She finds a rhythm, but nothing. She tells him it's fine.

"God," he says.

They lie there in the silence. Either Louise has gone to bed or she's listening as one of her friends tells her a very long story. One of them will have to check.

Fran's big eyes are studying him.

"What?" he says.

For a long time, they don't speak. The silence has the texture of sandpaper rubbing on his skin.

"You've always been someone who fights," she says. "A good man, a strong moral core."

His deep exhaustion cuts into his thinking. He's forty-three years old and can't have sex with his wife. It's been a month. Come on, longer than that.

"Oh, honey." She runs her fingers along his cheek. "You must be really scared of the future."

Just like that, she's exposed him. Stripped him bare. His innerness exposed. Only she can do that to him. It's what he needs, and it's terrible.

She kisses him. "Maybe we'll all figure it out."

We won't, he thinks. The moisture from her kiss is cooling his skin. It's too late. "I hope so."

In the early morning, before the light, he wakes. He no longer needs an alarm clock. Fran is curled on her side, one foot wiggled out of the covers, her toenails painted rose. Her face is calm, relaxed, beautiful. She is in a dream.

He heads over to the bedroom window, quietly lifts the shade so as not to wake her, and looks out as if he needs reassurance that it is still all there. Hugh feels the cold air seeping through the gaps in the window. Across the street, Hamilton's house is cloaked in darkness, but the porch light is on, and Hugh can see the shimmer of the dew on their green grass. The white blossoms of the azaleas glow, reflecting the moon. The wrought-iron bench sits stoically on their lawn. A lone car rolls by, and then it's an empty street, and it's so lovely, everything so lovely. A masterpiece. How can such a thing happen? How can this not exist in the future, the near future? He was raised on idyllic days; what will his children have? A sadness as vast and powerful as a tidal wave sweeps him up and tosses him down hard, flattening him. He wants his children to have a future that resembles his past. Birds chattering, rain falling on evergreens, bees visiting flowers, air that you can breathe, water that you can drink. He closes his eyes, but it doesn't stop the tears from coming. It's him they depend on, to give them the story that it will all be fine, no need to worry. Progress, an onward movement, an advancement, a gradual betterment—it's on him. It depends on him, like how he keeps this entire system running—the mortgage, the utilities, the kids' private schools and activities and vacations, clothes, and toys.

Even Fran needs him to be steady, stalwart. Sometimes her voice is a refined version of his children's: What do you think? Should we do this? A weight so heavy—yes, he willingly signed up, but perhaps not knowing the full contours of it.

He's downstairs, drinking coffee, dressed for the gym in his gray sweats, when Fran steps into the kitchen in her nightgown. There's a crease on the side of her face, her hair is wild.

"Was I too loud?" he says.

"I wanted to see you before you left," she says, her eyes soft, warm. "I'm sorry. I overreacted. I know you want the best for us, for our family. I'm so grateful for that."

He takes her hand in his, still warm from sleep.

"I just don't want to become assholes, I don't want that."

"I don't either," he says.

"It's obscene to me, the idea that we're special, above it all. I can't stand it."

"I understand," he says.

"But," she says, taking a deep breath, smiling, "I love you. We can go to New Zealand for a family vacation."

Something lifts from his chest.

"But not to buy a house."

He nods. "I think we'll have a good time." He feels the wolves back off, back away. He presses his face into her hair. "Let's just have a nice vacation."

He'll have his assistant book the flights. They'll do all the tourist things and have some extra time. And there, the nugget of an answer that is New Zealand is glowing again.

Everyone is packed, and suitcases are in the car. They stand in the front hallway in a bubble of excitement.

"Do you have the tickets and passports?" says Hugh.

Fran double-checks her purse. "Yes."

"Wait," says Louise, and she runs upstairs.

Gabe asks when he can watch something on the iPad.

"Forgot my other book," says Fran, and she runs upstairs.

"Come on! We're going to be late," says Hugh.

"Dad," says Gabe.

"Not now."

Louise runs down the stairs, then Fran, and Hugh raises

his arms overhead in triumph. "New Zealand, here we come!"

Louise rolls her eyes, but she's smiling. She's so lovely when she's happy. Even Gabe makes eye contact and seems interested, though it might be because he'll have at least ten hours of video games on the plane because neither Fran nor he will have the energy to get him to read a book. Hugh might read to him for a half hour, and Fran will do another half hour. Maybe they'll enlist Louise, but that amounts to only a fraction of the time. The goal is to make it across the Pacific Ocean without Gabe throwing a fit.

They load into the car and head down the road, and Fran triple-checks tickets and passports. Hugh imagines pure days. They'll swim in the sea. Their skin will turn darker, their hair lighter. He is overwhelmed with a feeling of contentment. His travel agent booked tickets to the *Lord of the Rings* tour, and he and Louise are scheduled for scuba diving lessons. They'll kayak, take an ATV off-road tour, and ride mountain bikes. The salt water will turn Fran's hair even curlier. At the last minute he called the real estate agent and told him they were heading to New Zealand, and maybe—who knew—if things worked out, if the moment felt right, maybe, they might look at that house. Nick gave him the phone number of his colleague.

"Did you bring something to read?" she says.

"A big stack," he says.

"No work, okay?"

"Got it," he says.

Louise has her earbuds in, listening to something with a steady beat. Gabe is staring out the window. The tall trees greet them. All the stoplights are green. It's a sign, he thinks. New Zealand is the answer. They sail on the black asphalt. They've made it onto the freeway in good time, though Hugh wishes they'd left twenty minutes earlier, because if they hit traffic—

"Oh no," says Fran.

Hugh slows down, slams to a hard stop. Cars and trucks all the way up the hill, as far as he can see. No one is moving, and they're only at the Corte Madera shopping mall, far from the Golden Gate Bridge, miles from the San Francisco airport.

"An accident?" says Fran.

They're in the far left lane. Cars on all sides, boxing them in.

Louise pulls out her earbuds. "What's going on?"

He checks his phone—red all the way to the bridge. "Damn it!"

Gabe leans forward, putting his head between Hugh and Fran, and jabs the radio button. "Precious" by The Pretenders blares. Hugh punches it off.

Fran rubs her collarbone, her nervous habit. "We didn't know about this."

Everyone is silent as the situation sinks in, the mood shifts, falls into a hole. Gabe pushes the radio button again. Fran gently tells him no, later, maybe. Hugh calls his assistant and asks her to look for another flight. Cost doesn't matter—he wants his family to go, and so they'll go. His assistant says she'll get back to him.

He puts his blinker on and gestures to the young woman in the car next to theirs. The woman has a long, lean face and fierce dark eyes, and she shrugs her bony shoulders and mouths, *I can't.*

"How are we going to get out of here?" says Fran.

Hugh flares his nostrils. In rushes the memory of how his older brother would get so angry at him, he'd push him to the ground, pile pillows on his face, and try to smother him. Then his other brother would dive on top of his back, and Hugh, pinned to the floor on his stomach, would thrash and kick and scream, the air getting hotter, harder to breathe, and he'd call for help, hoping his mother would come. If his sister was around, she'd dive on the pile, further flattening his body to the carpet. He could smell the chemicals in the rug, old dirt, odor like eggs. His arms were trapped, so he couldn't push them off. All he could do was kick his legs like a sea creature that had washed ashore and was flopping on land, gasping for air, gills opening and closing. At the last second, when he felt there was no more air to breathe, when he was down to the last lungful, they'd get off. He lay there, sucking down cool fresh air. Dizzily, he'd get up, and they'd run, laughing, scattering, but he was so weak he couldn't chase them. He felt like crying, but that would only make it worse because they'd laugh harder and feel more triumphant that they'd brought him to tears.

Hugh whips open the car door and gets out, wheezing. Car fumes swarm him. The open sky is no reprieve.

"A protest," says Louise, staring at her phone. "A big one."

He looks around. Hundreds of cars and trucks, and they seem to be multiplying on both sides of the freeway, as if there's a magnetic pull attracting everyone, making one big clump. A mass exodus, except it's going nowhere. A man in the car ahead of them throws out his cigarette butt. It smolders, gray smoke swirling. They don't belong here. This doesn't happen to them. He should have done better. A strange smell in the air, the gaminess of wild animal. "Shit."

Gabe laughs. He loves profanity. "Shit," says Gabe. "Shit, shit, shit."

Louisa guffaws. Gabe keeps repeating the word, Louise's giggles egging him on. Hugh stays outside, breathing in fumes and other odors. His phone rings: his assistant—everything is booked for a month. They're on a waitlist.

"Why don't you get back in the car, honey?" says Fran.

"No one's getting out of this alive," says Louise. Her tone is chipper, as if this is the adventure.

The man in the gray Datsun is howling to his blaring music. The young man in a beat-up Chevy is looking in his rearview mirror, picking at his long, sharp teeth. A woman, her hair slicked back tight against her skull, is hunched over as if ready to pounce.

Hugh's left cheek starts to twitch. The air is thick, thickening.

"What are we going to do?" says Fran.

The question is directed at him, and its weight is as heavy as a boulder, made heavier by the lack of an answer. He can't say he doesn't know, he can't give up, can't just stand here doing nothing. All that he does to spare his family from harm, all that cannot be stopped. The world is made of an inexorable substance for suffering, and there's nothing he can do about it. That awful smell, pungent, sharp, like animals out for the kill. He feels a thickening of his limbs, a slow feeling of things not as they should be. A sickening sense that they will never get out of here alive, they will be pulled down with everyone else.

He starts walking.

"Where are you going?" Fran calls out.

The sun falls across the cars with high benevolent indifference. The gulls overhead call out, and he is overwhelmed with terrifying insignificance. He will become significant again when there is white sand, blue water, birds, and fresh air, and his wife and children are in the sea.

He picks up his pace and starts to jog. He runs along the meridian, littered with beer cans, cigarette butts, plastic bags, and rocks. When the wind picks up, it throws dust in his face.

He hears Fran call out, "Hugh? Where are you going?"

It's pointless, what he's doing, irrational, but he doesn't say anything, and he doesn't stop because the urge to climb the hill is overwhelming, as if the hill existed for him to climb, as if reaching the top is the answer. His shoes are crunching the gravel, his head is tilted up, and the wind is screaming through his hair. He looks at the big pile-up of cars.

I understand Hugh's desire to escape, and I'll sorrow over this for ages. Hugh and the other powerful, dangerous men—yes, men, shouting and scaring themselves to sleep—looking to abandon others, abandon the earth as if no one gave them anything, no one helped, as if they weren't given trees and air and the sea that nurtured them and cradled them, from a toddler to a man.

The story of the rugged, lone individual conquering what needs to be conquered. A manly myth. Sometimes I like to pretend I'm that powerful, letting myself run roughshod over everything, knocking over buildings, hurling boulders into the sea. I get the allure, the appeal of the illusion of invincibility. The idea is like honey.

But there's a truer story, and I'm not sure *story* is the right word: everyone is held in a soft mesh of step, swing, shuffle, nurture, care, and love. Without this, it would be dangerous to live even one day. Besides, in the hero story, would you truly want to be that alone?

Don't you want to fall in love? Care for someone or something? The other day I watched the infinite gap between two people disappear over a cup of coffee and a biscuit.

What's happening now is the heaviest of burdens. It's awful and scary, but to plan an escape is like saying you refuse the sunset, the touch of the wind. It's pure folly but bitterly human. Wherever they flee, New Zealand, Canada, Alaska, the wind is there, scampering up the trees, fluttering feathers, flinging birds high into cottony air; the wind, pushing and pulling the clouds, turning them into the shape of a ship, a chandelier; the wind whistling through wires, rattling windows, scraping tree branches against the bluish glass until it finds a gap and charges in, billowing the curtains, swirling dust balls from corners and under the couch. It balloons a girl's short white skirt, shimmies up the sleeve of a man's shirt, and creeps along his broad back and out the other sleeve. Up one trouser leg, airing out his privates, down the other.

Rushing outside again, wily and mischievous, the wind hurries to the Golden Gate Bridge, where it saunters, sways, strolls, fingering and flinging long hair, weaving a fine net through people, cars, and trucks. It smacks Hugh's face, cold and colder, Hugh, with his inward-focused eyes and tattered blanket of panic. The wind picks up a hamburger wrapper, rolls it along like a ball, skids over to a woman, and flutters her scarf, wafting it behind her as if unraveling her. It snatches a man's hat and tosses it over the bridge rail. You breathe the wind, the wind is the air of everything.

Lately, the wind has a monstrous roar. Long ago, when the pavement was grass and the land was swamp, through the age of dinosaurs and mammoth, I never heard it so loud. You hear it, I know you do, the way you stand at the darkened window and peer out, worrying your fidgety fingers on your coat zipper. How easily it knocks down power lines and trees and telephone poles, how easily it shoves cars off the road into brick walls. Trees fall on houses, the sea smashes on shore. People are killed. Up in the mountains, it tosses eighteen-wheelers over cliffs like they are children's toys. So much wreckage, the state of the world; there's no escaping that.

Hugh is running up the hill to the bridge, his long lanky body taking great strides, seized by the urgency of escape. The wind is furiously flapping his jacket, he's in an altered state, telling himself he's doing this to save his family. Not once has he looked back to see; in fact, they are following him, calling for him. Dots in the distance. He believes in plans, goals, lists, creating order out of chaos, yet he has no plan to save them. If he stopped, he'd realize this. He won't, though. As I watch him, he looks strong, as if nothing will stop him, and now in my mind, he's running so fast, he makes it to the bridge in a matter of seconds like a jaguar, and the bridge is packed with people, and he's so fast, so strong, he's running on top of people's heads so he doesn't have to slow his speed, and people are shouting, "Hey!" and he's sprinting faster and faster. approaching the speed of light, and he can't stop, and he hurls over the bridge railing, falling fast to the water, like a hat flung from someone's head.

Shh. Listen to the wind gusting through the bridge's safety slats, playing a song, what some people call a nuisance or just plain awful. It's a sad, ominous song, the warbling of the notes A, B, G, and high C, like a dirge, a eulogy, a lament; the lyrics, I am in danger, you are in danger. A terribly beautiful dissonant moan, perfectly fitting for the reeling landscape.

Muscular Activity

Two months ago, Jake worked on the twenty-eight-member paint crew for the Golden Gate Bridge. Not a bad job, he's had worse. Probably the fishery up in Alaska was the worst, couldn't get the fish smell out of his clothes, his skin, his mouth. Once he found a shiny silver fish scale in his ear. But listen, the color of the bridge isn't golden. It's reddish orange, a hue that Jake stared at so long—eight hours a day—it made his eyes burn as if he stared at the sun. He lost count of how many times he walked the 1.7-mile-long bridge with a five-gallon bucket of International Orange paint. And it wasn't how he thought: You don't start at one end of the bridge and paint your way to the other, then turn around and go back the other way like a fucking machine. Thousands of rivets glue the bridge together; you paint those first because if they rust, the whole thing comes tumbling down, London Bridge style.

After he got the lay of the land, he quit, as was the plan. Recon task force, membership of one. Now he's walking on the bridge as if he's a tourist, two people between him and Melinda at the .2-mile marker. Members are already on the bridge, blocking traffic for the past half hour. Jake and his team, they're the surprise. Bridge security doesn't drive across for another three hours. Pretty lax actually. He thought they'd patrol more, given the jumpers every year. He glances up, sees the foghorn mounted at the south tower, and another one on the other tower; the horns emit different tones to guide the ships through dense fog. He has fond memories of those cold, foggy days. Two main cables cross along the top, 7,669 feet long and 36 3/8 inches in diameter. The cables, which look like sewer pipes, can bend twenty-seven feet laterally to sway with the wind. Airway beacons top each tower to keep the planes from crashing into them. He's grown intimate with the bridge and has a deep affection for it.

Jake has never held a job for long—by choice. When he starts to feel numb, he fires himself. If you stay too long, you fall into the habitus of that world, the language, the assumptions, the gestures, the value systems; and after a fairly short period—five, six months—you're no longer aware of what you're thinking or doing. He refuses to become dead while he's still alive. Moves on when the humming aliveness fades. His daily check system: do you even know why you're doing what you're doing?

On the bridge the wind is blowing 20 to 25 miles per hour, and he and the team wade through German, French, Chinese, Australian, Japanese, and languages Jake doesn't recognize. The French makes him tilt his head, so it funnels in smoothly, the music that it is, and in his mind he hears his mother. Sees her pretty oval face, her motherly, loving dark eyes. Ethiopian does the same thing because he hears his father. Rest in peace, dear parents.

Ropes around their shoulders, leather belts around their waists, hoods up, thin-soled shoes, jeans, layers of clothing, backpacks full of food, and army-green vests stuffed with more food. Over the years, he's worked as a carpenter, a dishwasher, a tile layer, a pool cleaner, a legal assistant, a fish cleaner, a bridge painter, and a notetaker at UC Berkeley. That job lasted the longest, three years because it was inherently changing; no day the same, and the massive amounts of knowledge—and wisdom, yes, he'd call it that—expanded his mind. Introduction to Business, Intro to Philosophy, Macroeconomics, Micro, Banking, Greek Mythology, Intro to Biology, Shakespeare's Comedies and Tragedies, Heidegger's *Being and Time*, anything the college kids didn't want to get their asses out of bed for, and who were willing to pay for the notes.

Word got out. His notes were the best. He was meticulous, the notes were clear and detailed, you never had to go to class, and you could still get an A. Little pussies, missing out. He communed with some of the best minds in the world while they slept away their lives.

He rented a studio apartment on Telegraph Avenue and found a desk and chair abandoned on the sidewalk, along with a desk lamp, a small table, two wooden chairs, and a mattress. When the college kids head home in June, all this shit is dumped on the sidewalks. His apartment walls are thick with white paint, and the scratched wood floors creak and whine. One room, a little bathroom, a linoleum counter for a hot plate, and a mini fridge. Rent: $300 per month. Jake, twenty-six years old, a college dropout because he ran out of money, can now hold his own on the esoteric topic of nineteenth-century English literature and the Japanese poet Matsuo Bashō.

He thought he could do the notetaking job for a long time, but one class got under his skin like a bad rash that turned into an incessant itch that changed into a fever and upended everything. Professor Richard Whitman, who would pace the front of the lecture hall, his face blooming rose-red from the heat of his lectures. He was passionate, a lover of what he taught, and endlessly fascinated with his subject matter. It was like watching a train wreck, and Jake couldn't turn away. Whitman took a stick and poked and probed the remains and called everyone over to take a closer look at the gutted mess.

Whitman's class was Environmental Science, and he went on and on in a cheery tone about the collapse of the ecosystems, water, air, agriculture, food supply, oceans, forests, and biodiversity systems, i.e., animals. Jake sat there spellbound, terrified. Why did he keep coming back to this horror show? Every other subject was trivial compared to what he was ingesting every Monday, Wednesday, and Friday morning from 10:00 to 10:50 a.m.; everything else was a distraction, diverting his gaze from the massive destruction going on.

After class, in a daze Jake would stumble out. Like going from one world to another. From horror to comedy, from devastation to pseudo-order, he couldn't shake the terror. It clung to him. He'd head to the library and, in the periodical room, obsessively read the newspapers, hunting for news of the earth's collapse—rarely on the front page, but tucked away, A5, A12, B2. Sometimes, outrageously, nothing at all. The world, he decided, found endless ways to look away. He, too, was guilty of it. If you have a mind that likes to think, you're one of the worst culprits. Guilty as charged: look at him, gobbling up all this subject matter.

Now he looks down at his broad hands and prays that his hand-grip exercises will pay off, along with the squats and balance-beam work. He yanks on his harness to make sure it's secure.

The fifth week of the semester, Professor Whitman had a guest speaker, Eleanor Gergen. An elegance to her—tall, thin, with a bony angular face and piercing eyes. Like a sculpture in a museum that has become animated, she captivated the room, all eyes on her. Jake imagined if his mother had lived, she would look like that in her old age, though she wouldn't have Eleanor's voice, which was deep and laced with anger and disbelief. Eleanor told them about her work, how she spent her life trying to persuade the big US companies to internalize externalized costs—air and water pollution, cutting down trees, contaminating rivers.

"Some wins, sometimes a big win," she said. "Those were glorious! Getting Brazil to stop burning down the Amazon by forming a coalition of international investors who said they'd no longer invest if the country continued. Do you want the good news first or the bad?

"Let's start with the bad. The world is breaking down. It is dying. Now some of you are going to stop listening to me. Denial is part of human nature, sometimes it helps, but in this case, it does not. Physics and chemistry don't care about denial. Billions of people will soon be migrating—it's happening right now—across borders as the land they call home becomes barely habitable because of extreme weather. Today 1 percent of the world is a hot zone. By 2070, it will be 19 percent. Have you been to Guatemala's Alta Verapaz? It used to be so lovely, so verdant, with crops of maize and coffee. Anything could be grown there in that dark, rich soil and temperate climate. Now, with the alternating droughts and sudden floods, barely anything can grow. Corn as dried out as Halloween decorations. Rainfall in this area is expected to decrease by 60 percent, so there will be no more corn—or beans or rice. Half the children are already chronically hungry, with bellies of air," she said. "And the same thing is happening in Southeast Asia, with the increase in monsoon rainfall and drought, which have made farming nearly impossible. More than eight million people have moved to the Middle East, Europe, and North America. This will only get worse if nothing is done. I have not even touched on displacement from rising sea levels."

She smiled softly, shook her head. "Frankly, you should be enraged at the older generation, at me, who knew and didn't do enough to solve it. And we didn't because we're too invested, too much skin in the game, as your generation says. Do you know how much the oil and gas lobby spends to sway politicians? Do you know that industry is subsidized to the outrageous sum of billions of dollars?

"But here's more sad news. You're not angels. It would be so much easier if you were, wouldn't it? To blame and point your finger at me, my generation. Unfortunately, you're complicit too—our combustible engines, our heating systems, and the manner in which we grow food. Of course, your defense is that you didn't build these systems; you inherited them. But you have no defense when it comes to changing things. I'm sorry. Denial is no longer an option. Really, I'm surprised you haven't started a revolution to tear it all down and build something sustainable. I mean all of it, including the antiquated educational institutions—sorry, Richard. Especially the energy system. Oil and gas, we should have weaned ourselves off this awful stuff years ago."

She went on battering him with awful facts and data as if she'd thrown him in an ambulance and taken a bat to his head to make sure he arrived at the hospital utterly incapacitated.

After she was done, Professor Whitman thanked her—thanked her!—and said she'd given them a lot to think about. The students who did go to class to dutifully take their notes closed their notebooks, put on their backpacks, and headed to the cafes or gossip with friends outside Stanley Hall as if Eleanor Gergen was talking about another planet.

Numb, shaken, the tectonic plates inside permanently shifted, Jake grabbed his backpack and waited for her. The moon was out in the blue sky. His body shuddered, a pit as large as a peach at the base of his throat. When she came out with Professor Whitman, he cleared his throat and said, "Excuse me."

They stopped.

He had the urge to shove this woman, push her to the ground. He didn't know what he wanted to do or say.

"I'm sorry," she said. "You look pale. Are you all right?"

"You said there was bad news and good news. So what's the good news?"

She put her hand on her clavicle. "Oh, you're right."

He waited.

"I don't have any."

They went on their way, and he stood there, stunned, trying to think what to say, to yell at her. Go to hell? Fuck you? He looked at the students swarming around the plaza with bewilderment, awe, rage, and loneliness. Some students from the Environmental Science class huddled together, staring at a girl's phone. Their laughter boxed his ears. Loneliness took shape, a lump under his ribs, making it hard to breathe.

He doesn't make eye contact with anyone on the bridge but uses a soft gaze to look around. When he served on the bridge crew, they had one jumper. Before they could get to the skinny guy, he climbed the guardrail and leaped, feet first. At the time, Jake was under the bridge, inside the latticework, so he didn't see the guy jump, only heard the stories, and maybe, out of the corner of his eye, a flash of feet going by. The paint crew was shaken, and some men asked for the day off, but Jake was fine. Which meant he wasn't—a sign, he knew, that he was in trouble, that he viewed jumping off a bridge as an acceptable, understandable act because we are doomed.

After Ms. Gergen's lecture, he couldn't stop thinking about the end of the world. He'd experienced, in the philosopher Alain Badiou's terms (thanks to Professor Scholund's course, French Philosophers of the Twentieth Century), an Event—a Rupture in Being. After the rupture, according to Badiou, Jake was supposed to find realization and reconciliation with the truth. But the only truth he found was that he couldn't sleep and barely ate, and some days couldn't get out of bed. He tried to stop thinking about it and threw himself into Greek Mythology and Phonology. When that didn't work, he signed up to take notes for Recombinant DNA, but that didn't work. He quit the notetaking gig and got a job at a nursery.

Plants, trees, shrubs, dirt. Perennials and annuals. How to prune a lemon tree. Pollinator plants. It was something, he told himself, caring for the plants and flowers.

A woman came to the nursery looking for a plum tree. She wore a sleeveless shirt, and her arms were ripped as if Rodin had had a field day, chiseling her biceps, triceps, and shoulders. As if every day she lifted heavy boards and steel pipes, like his construction worker buddies. Her ginger hair was pulled back in a ponytail, and she had dirt on her hiking boots, jeans, and T-shirt. Her face was lightly tanned, with a sprinkle of freckles and wrinkles at the corners of her eyes. He imagined quads and calves that popped.

After he showed her the row of plum trees, he said, "Why do you want a plum tree?"

She smiled, and her face arranged around her smile as if her entire being existed to make that smile. "I love plums."

"I do too."

She seemed to come from another world, outside the dominant strictures, as if she'd peeled back the veil, saw what was what, and decided she'd define her own way. He stroked the leaf of a plum tree. "Do you want to go out with me?"

"No," she said.

He stopped touching the leaf. His hand stuffed in his pocket.

"But you can come to a meeting tonight." Melinda was her name. She said the meeting was at a house on the corner of Shattuck and Blake, seven p.m.

On the bridge, the wind is blowing so hard the seagulls are having trouble flying. One gull hovers right in front of Jake, an arm's reach away as if suspended on a string, wings not flapping, the bird not moving, just hanging in space, the space being a four-by-four-foot square. People pull out their cameras and click at the bird. Melinda has trained them in all sorts of weather, but only two days with wind, and it was slight, about 12 miles per hour. This feels like 30 mph. He knew about the wind. It was in his Recon Report.

Long meetings of Do's and Don'ts. Don't make eye contact with strangers. Don't answer questions. Don't stop walking. Don't let anyone touch your equipment. Do go straight to your spot. Do be agile, quick. Do wear layers, the weather is erratic. Do wear a diaper—we don't know how long you'll be up there. Do stuff every pocket with food.

They have one focus, a singular concentration: stop the pipeline from Canada to the Bay Area; stop the pipeline delivering millions of gallons of oil; if there is one crack, one leak, the bay will be flooded with oil, killing unspeakable numbers of birds and sea creatures. Keep your focus.

The bay is shimmery blue; compared to it, they are minuscule, pressed against the deep blue infinite and all the life in the water, the seals and dolphins, the sharks and sting rays, the crabs and copepods. Bunch of crap to call humans supreme, to put them at the top of the heap. How is man superior to a whale that knows to blow bubbles, encircling its prey, which won't cross the bubbles, so they're trapped; to a dolphin that can use tools, fitting a marine sponge on its nose to protect itself from sharp rocks as it hunts for fish; to a shark with its snout that can sense electric fields emitted by animals in the water; to the kestrel that can see ultraviolet light, enabling it to make out trails of urine left by moles. Like neon diner signs, these bright paths light the way to a meal.

Jake feels alive, at the edge, where he likes to be, but he's also trembling. They are at the spot where the cable leads up to the tower. There's a door made of wire, and it's locked, standing between them and the cable. On recon, he learned the code. Melinda reties her shoelaces. Jake does the same, and so do the two others. On the other side of the bridge directly across from them, Jake sees the group mirroring what they are doing. It's part of the ritual of preparation. Melinda checks her ropes, then Jake's, then the two others. Through the crowd of tourists, he sees six members carrying what looks like a white sail. That will go in Melinda's pack. Hundreds of members behind them, more on their way. Word was sent twenty-four hours ago. It's a Go.

In a flash, Melinda is standing on the cable, her rope attached to one of the wires that runs parallel to the cable. Five hundred-plus feet above the glimmering bay. Jake doesn't take his eyes off her, watching her exact foothold and handhold, because he will do as she does, climb as she climbs. He tries to memorize her ease, her grace, her unbelievable mastery. She looks so fucking comfortable. They will ascend to 746 feet above the water to the top of the tower where there is a little platform, like a basket on a hot-air balloon ride. Without looking, he knows that on the other side of the bridge Arjun is making his way up at the same pace as Melinda, and behind Arjun is Camilla, then Quinn and Alejo.

On Jake's side, it's Melinda, Baker, Katya, then him. He didn't expect it to be so cold or wet or windy. The sun isn't warm. Last night he drove to the headlands and parked on the hill, imagining the climb to the top. The fog rolled in, but he could see the bridge lights like a necklace, 128 lights running horizontal, and another twelve-string running up each of the towers. In the fog, the lights looked like ghostly moons.

Right before Melinda went up, her face glowed, euphoric. What makes her unusual, he learned at the first meeting and later, is that she is mostly monkey. It's in her DNA, her blood, whatever you want to call it. She spent hours in the warehouse in Novato, teaching them to climb the wall and a rope, talking to them, assuring them that they, too, have monkey woven into their fabric; they inherently know how to swing from limb to limb, to scramble up a tree trunk, rise above the dirt. They've just forgotten. "Jake, get out of your head," she said repeatedly.

Jake goes up the stairs that lead to the cable when he hears a French woman say, "My hair is whipping my face." He turns, looks at her (don't look down—Melinda's voice in his head—your goal is up; clear your head, focus on *up*). The young woman grabs the arm of the man she's with and holds on. Her brown hair is thrashing, whipping her face, and the man is brushing it out of her eyes. Jake's pulse is not where it should be. Not steady, not beating loud and strong, but quick, like a man who is fucking scared. Afraid of heights.

Melinda, Baker, and Katya are now on the cable. As he sat there last night, he imagined this moment, imagined being Melinda, born to go vertical, her feet designed with different sensory devices, little nodes on them, giving feedback so you find the slightest indentation for your big toe. Jake saw her climb freestyle halfway up Yosemite's El Capitan. A beautiful, terrifying sight. She's not human, or more human than most, more angel or more animal, hard to say. One night after a meeting, she told him that she started climbing when she was three years old: kitchen counters, ladders, bookshelves, as if she belonged off the ground. At age five, she climbed their ten-foot apple tree. At age eleven, she and her father climbed Half Dome.

Every substance speaks, she told him. Feel it, listen to your fingers and toes. Let them find the bends and nooks, it's there for you, but you have to put your mind in your hands and feet.

"Let's go, Jake," Baker calls out.

Melinda isn't moving; he knows she's waiting for him.

It's okay, he tells himself, it's okay, okay, okay. He volunteered to be on this team in a moment of hubris. Or maybe to be close to Melinda. Or maybe because he'd spent too much time in his head, reflecting, brooding; he needed action. Emerson's advice: "Intellectual tasting of life will not supersede muscular activity."

He climbs on the cable, clips his rope onto one of the wires that run on both sides of the cable. Handholds, Melinda told him, grip the wire to steady yourself, but not too tight, or you'll cramp.

They trained in Yosemite. Melinda pointed to a sheer rock face and saw what none could see. Like magic, an invisible map, she saw the path to the top. Here and then there, and there, and cross there—she drew a line with her finger in the air, and like a photograph slowly developing, it emerged. At that moment Jake trusted her completely.

Melinda looks at Jake. One eyebrow arched, half of a circle as if saying, Okay? We are prepared, a murmur in Jake's brain—Melinda's voice, Baker's, all the others, we're ready. But the murmur doesn't help. He's not the best climber, never was. All that training, he never really took to it. He has to shake it, this fear, it won't work. Got to release it because a tense body can't glide, it missteps. A tight body panics, slips, falls.

He inches forward on the cable; the wind blows harder. The hood of his jacket flaps madly like a wounded bird. The wind scrambles the screech of a seagull, the roar and coughs of car engines. Then, suddenly slicing through the noise, the French woman says, "Look! Look at the people climbing the bridge!"

He looks down. A silent scream in his head ricochets, throwing him off balance. He yanks on the wire. She's pointing right at him, her mouth open, eyes wide.

❧

"Jake!" says Melinda.

"I'm okay," he says. But he's not.

"Okay," she says, smiling, her face calm as a still lake, an expression that says she's exactly where she wants to be; there is no other place.

She looked like that after they had sex. His face, he was sure, reflected hers. They had trained all day at the warehouse, propelling high above the ground, holding on to a rope, his feet learning the language of a smooth wall. They'd walked out of the warehouse together, sweaty, muscles tired in a good way, and she said, "Want to come to my place?"

She stripped off her clothes so casually, so easily, as if she felt more comfortable without them, and he followed, quickly unzipping his dirty jeans, pulling his sweaty T-shirt over his head, yanking off his socks, his underwear. She led him to the shower, he took the soap to her beautiful muscles, and he called her astonishing; he blurted it out, "My God, you're astonishing," and she laughed, and she kissed him as the water pelted on their heads. "You're not so bad either," she said. He entered her from behind, and when she screamed her pleasure, he roared with her, and they laughed and laughed. They tumbled out of the shower and onto the bed, and soon they were all over each other, and she was glistening as though she had just risen from the sea or come down from a mountain covered in mist. The bottoms of her feet—in her apartment, in the warehouse, even after the shower—were still dirty. As if her feet must at all times be in contact with something.

They didn't see each other for four days, and when they did, they didn't talk about it. Then more days went by, and it seemed like a dream that might not have happened. But after a meeting, the same thing happened, though they didn't bother to shower. Again, they didn't speak of it. She didn't avoid him; he didn't avoid her. They talked about climbing and footholds and bumps in rocks that can serve as handholds, but not their naked bodies folded into each other. It was a secret life, buried under the planning and preparation for today.

Today his face is the opposite of hers. The skirling wind roaring in his ear is determined to pry him off the bridge as if it thinks he doesn't belong here, standing on a cable high above the water. And he doesn't. He wasn't the child climbing everything vertical. He was a land baby and didn't walk for eighteen months. When he finally stood, he was ready and walked as if he'd been doing it his entire life. His mother told him later he's someone who closely studies things.

But where does he belong? Back at the nursery talking to the plants? In the classroom listening to a professor pontificate on ontology? He did love the Heidegger course and the shimmering prose of Shakespeare. His mother was a sculptor, working in metal, marble, and concrete. Articulate and composed she was; in his teens, he thought her beautiful, like a movie star. She never pressured him to become one particular thing; she never pressured him at all, and sometimes he felt as if he didn't exist for her. His father was a financier; numbers spoke to him, and he spent most of his time on airplanes, flying to places to talk to people who wanted to hear the language of money. A loving figure, a daunting, distant figure. When he was seventeen, their plane crashed in the Sea of Cortez, the sea taking both of them. His mother did say to him once, almost as if she thought she should give something, "Do something that enlivens you, my love." And: "We never wanted to get in the way of what is innate in you. If we suggested or pressured or directed, it would get twisted." "Twisted?" he said. She smiled. "Into a reflection of us. The originality of you would be distorted. Be an original man."

So, he's become a man standing on a cable; each step will take him higher. But how much of this is truly original, and how much is it guided by unconscious forces? The force to be original? To do something enlivening, per his mother's request? To follow the woman walking on the cable as if it's a sidewalk, in an ecstasy he finds unattainable? His motives are overdetermined, too many to single out one and create a singular line of causation. *What is he doing up here?* is a refrain, a Greek chorus screeching in his head.

He only knows he's the weak link in this chain of climbers. His fingers feel tight, clutching the cold metal, and he's only managed five steps. When he was on the paint crew, Jake often stared at the little platform at the top of the tower. I'll be sitting there someday, but he never really believed it. Not once did he think that would happen. More like a fantasy, something tucked into the corner of his mind so he could imagine himself closer to Melinda, and he, someone else, a man who could climb to great heights. He thinks about Melinda's strong fingers, remembers folding his lips around them. She told him she liked how his mind worked, not confined to one discipline but weaving them together, biology, language, mythology, and physics. A free-roaming mind, she said. "But it trips on itself a lot, doesn't it?" she said. "Doubt can be deadly."

Slicing through the wind yelling in his ear, for the first time he hears people shouting below.

"Block fossil fuel projects! Clean energy only!"

A quick look down. Hundreds of people with signs crowd the middle of the bridge, in between cars. Traffic piling up in both directions. Suddenly sharp, jubilant energy charges through him. He takes five more steps, moving higher. What was a mere idea has materialized. Those long meetings, the arguments, the best way, the method, the message, the risk, and the benefit, have led to a new reality. Interrupt the habitual action, unglue society, rip apart the habitus, that's what's happening, open up potential outcomes. There is always the part of yesterday in us; yesterday's man predominates since the present amounts to little compared with the long past, in the course of which

The wind pummels him. He looks down. A violent shiver lacerates him, and the wind climbs under his collar. He can hear Melinda's voice in his head: Relax, stay loose; if your mind seizes, your muscles follow and then you're using twice as much energy. You'll lose your grip, your hands turn into claws, can't move. Legs quiver, shake uncontrollably, fatigue. Whatever it takes, calm the mind. Sing a song, a lullaby, chant a mantra, ohm na ma ha, do mental math problems: 5+7–3=? He's always liked math. 7+9–4=12, 13+6=19-5=14+2=16-9=7+5=12-5=7+11=18-7=11.

But his arms are still violently shaky, and the muscles in his body have seized like a frightened animal. Sticky dread like a wound oozing. "Melinda?" he shouts. A gust of wind tears the words from his mouth.

"Melinda!"

"Yeah, Jake."

He can't get the words out. Jaw locked.

"What's going on?"

"Little shaky," he rasped.

"Deep breaths, Jake. We're fine. It's beautiful up here."

He focuses on breathing, trying to soften his body to settle into the natural contours of himself. The wind flails him.

"You're roped in," she says. "You're good."

"I hear sirens."

"Sure. They're coming."

"Then what?"

"We sit tight like we practiced."

"My arms are shaking."

"You're holding too tight. Using your arms too much. The rope has you."

A seagull blows by.

"The wind."

"Yeah, the wind's strong," she says. "But we've got the rope."

"Okay."

"Take one hand off the wire. Shake it out."

"Okay."

"Did you do it?"

"No."

"Do it."

He looks at his hand and wills his fingers to let go of the metal. Nothing happens. He probably should have admitted he's terrified of heights. He thought all that training they did in the warehouse would help. Desensitize. Baker had complimented him, telling him he was a natural at climbing. "You took to it, man," said Baker. "Ate it up." But it's not true. This relentless wind—and it's so far down. He doesn't want to die. He has to release his hand, but what if he falls? What if the rope doesn't hold? What if he falls and yanks the wire so hard that the others fall with him? He'd have to live with that. A murderer. If he killed the others, he'd have to kill himself. The guilt would be too much. He knows if he doesn't let go, eventually his hand will be so tired it will release on its own, and maybe at the wrong time.

"Did you do it?" she calls out.

One finger loosens, another—they are quivering, a life of their own. He's never been part of a group; he avoided them because he wanted to think for himself. Think only about himself. Not selfishly, but his own way of going about things. An original man.

His hand is off the cold metal wire. He stares at it, an entity standing free in the air. It looks miraculous.

"I did it," he says.

"Good. Do that every so often."

Her soothing voice melts him inside.

"Hey, look out at the water," she says. "See how beautiful it is."

His mouth is dry as if he'd eaten chalk. "Yeah."

"No, Jake, really look," she says.

He looks up at her.

She's gazing out to the water, a big grin as if she's high. "God, it's stunning."

"Yeah," he says, still looking at her. She's smiling like mad, as if the madness below them, the shouting, the cars honking now, people gunning their engines, as if preparing to ram through the protestors, isn't happening—or she's transfigured all the madness into some sort of glory.

"Wow! I think I saw a whale," she says. "Look northwest."

Something floats down from the sky and lands on his coat. A pigeon feather. He stares at it, the perfect pattern of filaments, each one precisely spaced, letting enough air pass through for flight. White with a hint of metallic blue. From a bird considered a pest, a rat bird, shooed away or kicked by people, the target of rocks, such beauty. His father's voice comes to him now: "You're a dreamer, my son, living in your head." He remembers his parents arguing, how his mother said, "Let him be. He has a rich interior." And his father countered, "How will he live? How will he ever make a living?"

"The traffic is backed up for miles and miles," says Melinda. "We've got people's attention. We've got them. They're awake. They're angry. Good! Time to get angry." She laughs. "Listen to that howling, angry wind."

He's getting used to the wind. He's not going to fall unless they—the angry mob down there—pelt them with rocks or arrows or shoot them.

With his heart thumping less viciously, he finally sees the Pacific Ocean, the stretch of blue for as far as the eye can see, a blue watery drape wrapping around the curve of the earth. His mother loved the color blue. He remembers Gustave Flaubert: "To make anything interesting, you simply have to look at it long enough." A pattern of ripples, of waves, a small sailboat in the distance, a white sail. Farther out, a gray ship the length of a football field. The water glistens endlessly.

A fragment of music floats from a car window and finds him perched here like a bird. "You'll find it in the strangest places," sings a female voice.

He looks out to the horizon and breathes in the view, though in the back of his mind, there is still a voice screaming—you're up so high, one swift kick of wind or the rope unravels or—he yanks his mind to the horizon, to the tiny sailboat. Puts himself on that lovely little boat and whisks along the surface of the sea at a tilt, the white sails puffed out like a big balloon, and he imagines the polished oak wood of the cabin inside, the small bathroom, two twin beds down below, each with dark blue blankets tucked around the mattress—thin, but thick enough not to feel the stiff board below—yes, he's on that boat—interesting, he's alone—and he's saved the world. To hear himself say that. Now, in marches words from Nietzsche, who wanted to—incite? create? spur?—an elite group of people, superhumans, with everyone else enslaved to these superior individuals. Jake feels a little of that, a superiority, a superhumanness because his deepest muscles have unlocked, and now he could stay up here forever, up in the bellows of the wind, the white circling seagulls, the miniature airplane flying high overhead.

They have stopped the world, halted it in its mindless tracks as it barrels toward destruction, stopping it so it can take a long deep breath and a look at itself. At the madness, at the inexorable obliteration—the dirty air, the dirty waters, the polluted dirt—

He lets himself slide into a dream, and the dream is everything that no longer works, the too-tight skin is shed like a snake's skin. What remains are the elements that let the world live. He can hear the trees, the wind, a hush, a swish, the scamper of a squirrel. Shed more by making the traffic sit for five, ten, twenty hours. No, make it a week, a month, months, a massive traffic jam, and in his mind, he sees long veins of traffic covering the entire Bay Area, the world, the unworkable at a standstill. People abandon their cars, and slowly their rhythm changes to the beat of the tree, the sea, and the wind, because the human heart is not digital or analog, but the shape of a cloud, a rolling hill, the shiny head of a seal, the flip of a whale's tail—he sees it!

Everything shuts down—the restaurants and cafes and hair salons, the gift shops and the massage parlors—shut it all down, pull down the metal grates and lock the doors, pull the curtains, turn off the car engines, the trucks, the trains, everyone shut it down. Get out of your fucking cars and houses and—whoa, it feels as if he's become everything, is everything; he's the wind brushing the leaves, the long grasses, nosing and nudging its way through the gaps and nooks and racing along the water, rippling it, making its own artful patterns.

He sees a red-tailed hawk above Crissy Field hunting, haunting. He's walked that pebbly shore, with its array of tiny rocks of rust, olive green, slate gray, light gray. Slow it all down, find the heartbeat, the one mimicking the waves rushing onto the shore, rushing back, and the sound of the pebbles rolling around down the slope, tinkling like tiny glass bottles.

In the headlands, the coyotes come out of hiding and patter down to the beach, their fur a blend of gold and gray, black and brown; he's doing it for nature and humanity because now he feels overwhelmed with emotion for people, a softness toward them, a love he hasn't felt in years, he's doing this for the people, for—

"Fuck you!" yells a woman from below.

His right foot slips. His rope tugs, pulls on the wire.

"Shit," shouts Baker.

Her voice cuts through the wind. "Fuck you and all of you!"

Jake grips the wire, looks down.

The screaming woman, her head tipped back as if screaming at the sky. She looks like a little baby bird, her mouth open, waiting for a worm. Her face is lined, her brown hair dried out from too many dye jobs. And with those bared teeth, she now looks like a vicious bear that wants to rip his head off.

"You asshole! I've got to get home, and you, you motherfucker!"

His body starts to shake. He looks to the horizon to calm down, but in his mind he sees her, and not only her, but other people who are out of their cars, yelling and shoving people holding signs. He glances at Melinda, who is staring peacefully at the sea. He follows her gaze to the stretch of deep blue, and he keeps going to where sea meets sky, the horizontal line; but he can't shut out the woman, and he glances down again.

"Yeah, you, I'm talking to you," she says, looking right at him.

He is the closest one to her. A deep tremble in his body. They talked about this at the meetings. The anger, the unleashed anger that will be directed at them—they are angry for millions of reasons, and they should be because of the destruction of the planet, but it will be projected onto us because we're an easy target, because we bring change, and we're an obstacle preventing them from continuing on their mindless ways. You got to weather it, man. Got to let it fly by you; imagine it's a punch coming right to your face. Step aside.

"You fucking moron! I've got to get to work," she says. "I've got my kids. I've got to get my kids. You lazy-ass piece of shit."

"Jake," Melinda calls out. "Don't listen to her."

Jake turns his ear to the rushing wind, and her jagged words bounce right off. He's lived long enough to see people crack—anger pouring out of them like hot lava. He feels sorry for her, in a way, so much rumbling anger inside. At the same time, he's getting a little pissed off. His muscles tense as if he's preparing to get hit or he's about to hit. He hears Melinda telling him not to listen to the woman, but this woman is yelling louder, this angry, black-T-shirted, wiry woman with her gravelly, baritone voice cutting through the car horns, shouting voices, sirens—this woman who has pinned all her problems on him. She can't see beyond her own sorry little life. Can't see if there isn't drinkable water, water for humans, for fish and birds, air to breathe, soil to grow things, nothing else matters. She thinks she's got it hard; just wait, it's going to get a hell of a lot harder. It's people like her who are the fucking problem.

"Go to hell!" says Jake.

"Jake," Melinda calls out.

"Losing my job because of you, asshole."

"That's all you can think about?" says Jake.

"Go screw yourself!"

"Take the high road, Jake. Take the high road," says Melinda.

Jake looks up at Melinda, who is looking down at him, her face knitted with concern, when he's hit with something hard, right on his temple.

He loses his balance, his right foot slips off the cable. He grips the wires hard, but the wire is now bouncing.

Baker screams, Katya yells. "Jesus!" says Melinda.

The rope stops him from falling, but he loses his water bottle from his pack. He turns, watching it fall, like a pinwheel turning over and over, all the way down to the water. The woman looks as if she's hunting for another rock. He scrambles onto the cable. Reaches up to his temple and his finger comes back bloody. He wants to smack her right on the jaw. He's never hit anyone in his life, but he'd like to punch her in the face or the gut, make her double over, so he doesn't have to look at her.

Melinda is talking to him, her voice full of reassurance. "Jake, we're okay, we're all okay, it's fine now, steady, hold steady." He won't look down, won't give her the satisfaction, won't even touch the bloody spot again. Melinda tells him to look at the far distance. He looks at the long stream of cars, idling in both directions, and sees more people coming with signs, hundreds of people from both directions streaming onto the sidewalks on both sides of the bridge, weaving in between the cars. A strange thing is happening, and he can't quite figure it out. There's the shouting of his fellow protestors and the woman, and angry drivers, and the wind, and the seagulls and the rustle of his coat. But something is gone. Something different. He tries to figure it out, the thing missing under the roar of humanity. That woman is shouting for him to get the hell down.

It's gone, the roar of engines, that's what's gone. They're turning off their cars. A thrill runs through him. At the meeting he asked, "How long will we be up there?" More engines go quiet. He has his answer: as long as it takes. He's up here for as long as it takes to change minds. Nearly impossible, said Professor Grassley, who teaches Contemporary Social Issues. Belief has long roots. We wouldn't have had centuries of religious conflict if it were easy to change minds. It's possible, said Professor Blasé, who teaches Psych 101. If you can inject doubt about the belief and how the belief was acquired.

He can't imagine having any sort of conversation with that raging woman. Can't imagine doing anything but taking her by the shoulders and shaking her and calling her a fucking idiot. She almost killed him. He wants to let her have his big hot roiling ball of rage. But it won't solve anything. The world is in a bad marriage, but there can be no divorce. He's stuck with her and her kind, and she with him.

Jake looks down. The woman is no longer shouting. She's

sitting on the sidewalk, weeping openly, tears streaking her face. He knows what she feels, though they might not be suffering over the same thing, he knows. He has the urge to sit beside her and weep too; he wouldn't say anything, there's nothing to say except sit side by side and wish the pain would end. Then she is up, pushing and shoving protestors, her wet face bright red. He has a flash of admiration for her—just a moment before it vanishes—her piss and more piss; to dust herself off and come up swinging, got to respect that. She pushes a woman holding a sign: STOP FOSSILIZED THINKING!

"You're a hot mess," he says, though with the noise, he knows she can't hear him. He takes five quick steps, moving closer to the top.

We don't need everyone, I tell myself. That woman who threw the rock, there's no changing her. I can't overthink her because if I do, in rushes the dread, and one thought leads to the next, that there are too many like her, and then the generalizations that humans are incapable of thinking beyond themselves; too selfish, too designed and intent on perpetuating suffering. So leave her behind, and Eleanor too, who has sunk too far.

Look at Jake, beautiful, beautiful Jake. He has no idea how beautiful he is. He's illuminated, his human flare like the sun. He's terrified of heights, and he's 500 feet off the ground. How astonishing a human is when he transcends the small cocoon of himself and his actions are imbued with not only the particular but the universal, letting his heart beat across the world.

The swarms of people, hundreds of thousands of people, signs and singing, the shouts of outrage and joy, it's uncannily like the cloud of starlings fending off the falcon.

I'll tell you this for free. Darwin's idea of survival of the fittest has become so loud, so exaggerated that it buried the most fundamental and vital thing. Only now, as we sit on the precipice of disaster, are humans picking through the pile of rocks to find it. Though the starlings never forgot this force; the ants who forage together to feed the entire colony didn't forget it, or the chimps who join forces to hunt and fend off hungry cheetahs; the three humpback whales below the bridge right now revel in this life-force energy, singing a song that is intricate and haunting and will be sung by the trio for the next year. Music to my ears. Banding together, collaborating, and conjoining, that is the most formidable force.

You once knew this, but it seems you forgot your history. I remember when the *Homo sapiens* first appeared on the scene about 250,000 years ago. I was sure the Neanderthal, already roaming the earth, would dominate this newcomer. The Neanderthals, with their larger muscles and larger brains, their use of tools and fire, and their adept hunting skills, seemed the clear winner. But the *Homo sapiens* surprised me with a superior strength: their imaginations. They wove stories and myths so seductive and so compelling that they united in huge numbers. Not just ten or fifteen, but hundreds, thousands. That is the birth of the Sapien, and it begins: once upon a time, there was cooperation in order to survive against hostile forces.

Here is an echo of that origin story right here on the bridge! Such a large gathering has a big, loud voice. As the moon exerts its influence on the earth, changing its orbital axis, the crowd's sound will... But hold on. Don't leap too far ahead. Many times I've seen this, many times I've watched people come together—the signs and shouts, the excitement, the cusp of change. The day contains nothing and everything.

So forget the woman who threw the rock and is screaming at the climbers. And forget Eleanor. When she finally got out of bed this very late morning, she polished the crystal glasses she had not used for five years, which she will not use for another five. When Blue began to whine too loudly to ignore, she took him outside, not seeing the dahlias or sweet peas or the smell of bay leaves. Even the blue jay, squawking and parading in front of her, failed to get her attention. She might as well shrivel up and blow away. At home she sat at the table drinking weak tea, picking at a piece of buttered toast, sensing the dank sensation around her.

A Living Soul

Eleanor drives out of the city, on her way to the Green Valley Stables in Woodacre. Once she passes through Corte Madera, the cars thin out and the trees thicken. The sun filters through the big leaves of the sycamore trees, with leaves the size of her hand, and the air turns green. Geography affords a different perspective. That's Arthur's voice, or maybe hers, because at this age her memory has a layer of dust. She had to get out of the house, the walls were moving closer and closer.

She drives slowly through Fairfax with its leftover hippies in their rundown shacks, nearly sliding off the steep hills. Gray beards and long stringy hair pulled back in ponytails, the '60s remnants occasionally saunter down from the hills to wander the streets. They've got guitars, and they sit on the outdoor benches, watching people go by, the expressions on their faces saying, My friends, sit back, take a load off, and watch the ridiculous circus show.

Or not. Eleanor knows plenty of them who are in the trenches trying to turn the world around. Her friends are civil rights and environmental lawyers; her good friend Greg at Greenpeace was giddy when she called to tell him she'd like to put the Goldman Award money to good use. "Oh, you just wait, Eleanor! We're going to do something spectacular! Whatever awful thing is going on for you, let's change that." Greg, who, along with other Greenpeacers, scaled an ExxonMobil oil refinery in Mexico and painted DIRTY in five-meter-high letters on storage tanks. Not satisfied, they climbed the anchor chain of a tanker ship transporting the oil from the Gulf of Mexico and stopped it from moving. Bad press everywhere brought ExxonMobil to its knees and back to the negotiating table.

She turns into the horse stables, and there is sturdy Barbara, removing her horse's saddle. She's in her jeans and red plaid shirt, a blue baseball cap on, her long blond hair pulled into a ponytail streaming down her long thin back.

"Didn't think I'd see you for another week or so," says Barbara, heaving the saddle onto the wall hook.

The air is chilly in the blue shade, and dew dampens Eleanor's sneakers. The smell of manure clogs the air, but after the car ride the odor is welcome. After Ed's performance, Eleanor wanted a big landscape, a big sky so she could think about what she experienced. She never thought a human could inhabit the consciousness of an animal, but Ed came close, or so it seemed. She'll have to discuss it with him: did he truly vacate the human mind? How different is a rat from a human? Whatever happened, he was glowing after the performance, so something was achieved. Ed mentioned that he felt vibrations, a different hum in his body.

What Eleanor feels are the reverberations of Hazel's visit, a fresh sense of longing and loss for her sister. Then there's Ava. She needed a break from her daughter, full of criticism and rebuke for Eleanor's performance at the awards ceremony. That snide comment on the phone the other day, "It was so immature."

"I needed to get away," Eleanor says.

From another stall, she hears the Guernsey cow lowing.

"I don't know how you do it. I can't take the city," says Barbara. "There's too much and too many wackos. Too much of everything." Barbara brushes her horse's back. "I just brought Joan in from the pasture. She ran like a looney this morning. I love watching her. She sure gets the horses fired up, better than any dog can do."

The wind blows and oak leaves flutter like little flags. A black squirrel runs along the top of the fence, and Barbara's horse exhales loudly. When she's out here, Eleanor can almost forget that the world is on fire, and that there are people like Barbara who are happily ensconced in a world of hay and horses and a schedule of feeding, watering, riding, and brushing. Arthur used to love to drive out here with all the windows open, the wind inside the car like a mini tornado. He loved the smell of laurel leaves, cut grass, and horses. Out here, nature is still healthy and thriving, though that's not exactly true—water has become increasingly problematic with stretches of one-hundred-degree days in the summer and land that has become parched and fire-prone. Thank god people are ripping out lawns. Regardless, when she's out here Eleanor finds bigger rhythms: the movement of the sun across the sky, the path of the moon, the tall grasses swaying, a horse's trot.

"Carrots are in the fridge," says Barbara.

"Thanks."

"Joan could eat a dozen of those," says Barbara.

"Wish I could live on them. I'd lose those stubborn five pounds."

"Wish that were my only problem," says Barbara. Her sun-tanned face becomes cracked with worry lines. "I had a big fight with my son. Old news, but this time he got in the car and took off. He has his driver's license now; that's a mistake." She laughs bitterly. "How do we let sixteen-year-old boys drive? God knows where he went. Haven't heard from him for three days. He's hot-headed—" She rubs her forehead. "He hates school. Says he doesn't see the point. He wants to own a farm and grow his own food."

"Farming is hard work," says Eleanor.

Barbara stops brushing the horse and looks at Eleanor. "I'll tell you what's hard work. Being a mother, even harder being a single mother. All the things you got to do to raise a good person, and even if you do them, there's no guarantee. Got a friend. She and her husband did everything right—loving, always there, attentive, the whole deal. Their kid overdosed and jumped off someone's deck and died. He was a good kid, just into the bad stuff. My son said that kid would go to school high as a kite, a regular thing, but he was nice, you know, always this goofy smile like he was happy. I knew him from my son's baseball days. You want an answer why, so you don't make that mistake, but there are no answers, or no simple answers. All the things I shouldn't have said to my son, and I said them anyway. Feels good to lash out, then I wish I could take it back. I feel like shit."

"I assure you, more than once I've lashed out," says Eleanor.

In whisks that long period of teen years, and Ava's vigorous sullenness like something rotten in the house; one-word responses, or nothing at all, or incessant bickering. Eleanor thought for sure she'd become a lawyer. Thank god Eleanor had her work and travel, something that enlarged her world, invigorated her, and created space between her and Ava. Ed, he was never a problem, but Ava always had one critical eye on Eleanor and was eager to point out the flaws. She still does that.

Barbara has gone back to brushing her horse but vigorously. "I have no idea where he is."

"Have you called his friends?"

She nods. "Nothing. Maybe he has a girlfriend I don't know about. He could be up to anything, and I wouldn't know." She stops brushing, and the horse turns around to see what's going on.

Eleanor feels Barbara's anguish, the torment of raising a child who has a mind and a will of his own. "Have you called the police?"

Barbara's eyebrows shoot up. "Should I? Do you think I should?"

Now she's done it. Barbara's heart must be racing overtime.

"I should have done that earlier," says Barbara. "I'm so stupid."

"No need to blame yourself," says Eleanor. "There's still time to call."

After Ava called Eleanor immature, Ava said, "Dad would have been so embarrassed." Eleanor hissed, "What do you know about anything? He loved me for who I am. For standing up for what I believe in. To believe your own thoughts, to believe what's true for you in your private heart, he'd call that genius." Ava said she was hanging up now, and it was best they didn't talk to each other for a few days.

Barbara is on the verge of tears, her son lost in the wild of the world, at the whim of every scratch and claw. A feeling of responsibility overwhelms, and Eleanor feels obligated to offer some morsel of wisdom, but the best she can do is say, "He'll turn up."

"I keep calling his phone. No answer. Such a selfish bastard."

"At that age, that's the way they're built. They're the sun. We revolve around them."

"I'm tired of it. So fucking tired."

"Mothers should unite and go on strike. We've had enough, damn it. Stop treading on us."

Barbara laughs and Eleanor feels a small triumph. She assures Barbara he'll appear, and they'll make amends, that it's a natural progression, the need to separate, to individuate, to leave mother. One's first home is mother, and after they trash that, they move out, and their home becomes the big wide world, and they go out and trash that. Who thinks to take care of mother? Blabbering now, Eleanor is, trying to abate her own feeling of helplessness. Platitudes to help Barbara, but Barbara isn't listening anyway. She's calling the police.

Eleanor heads to the fridge and grabs a carrot. Joan looks up from her pile of hay, a few stragglers hanging from her mouth. Joan never fails to astonish her with her black and white stripes and stark, dark eyes. When the Oakland Zoo wanted to put Joan out to pasture—their words, 'out to pasture,' weren't clarified, but Joan had developed a bad limp in her back leg, and the zoo didn't have the finances to care for her—they hunted for Eleanor's father and found Eleanor. How could Eleanor say no?

"Hello, Joan," says Eleanor.

Eleanor looks for Gwennie, the sweet little goat who is usually in Joan's stall, but she is nowhere. When Joan lies in the hay, Gwennie cuddles up to her soft pink belly but this isn't happening. Eleanor's phone rings. Ava. Eleanor isn't ready to talk right now because she needs to calm down.

Joan normally takes her time coming over to see Eleanor, but today she trots right over, and Eleanor watches with delight: four thousand dollars of vet bills, and Joan walks without a limp. Joan is smiling. She nudges Eleanor's hand. Though no one knows for sure, Joan is probably thirty years old and very social, reminding Eleanor of her human friend, Rosa, who plans parties for the silliest reason—tulips are blooming, the oak leaves are falling—Rosa flitting around, chatting with everyone. She's brilliant at it, making each person feel welcome, special, and loved. A talent that Eleanor doesn't have, nor does she want, but she is in awe of it.

"Where is your friend Gwennie?" says Eleanor, stroking Joan's nose.

Eleanor remembers waking in the middle of the night and calling for her dad. He wasn't in his bedroom or the living room, so she put on her rubber boots and headed out to the barn. She found him in the zebra's stall, with a bottle of red wine, reading *The Odyssey* to William. Her father, half drunk, patted the spot beside him. "William isn't feeling well," he told Eleanor. He was soothing William until the vet arrived.

When Eleanor's mother was alive, her father was never the nurturer. Tucked away in his study or buried in a book in the living room, the tall lamp peering over his shoulder, her father was in a private room of one. Or he'd be in the barn fixing something—an engine, a broken lamp, a faulty toaster; he liked to tinker.

But when her mother died, her father took over the mothering, at first tentatively and bumbling, but very quickly he was a natural, making elaborate breakfasts, lunches, and dinners. He loved learning and taught his girls how to play the piano and speak Latin and French. Though Hazel wasn't interested, he taught Eleanor how to read the *Wall Street Journal* and understand economics and stocks and bonds and see the invisible world with his 1000x LED compound microscope. His nature to nurture was like a dormant seed, waiting to blossom, though he was stubborn and didn't accommodate Hazel's need for something else; but what she needed Eleanor never understood, nor does she understand to this day.

In retrospect, he was exactly the right parent for Eleanor. Her mother had been intent on raising polite, good girls, teaching them to cook, sew, and clean. Mother was demure, full of smiles and loveliness, like a pink flower, but her father cared nothing for that. He wanted capable, competent, intelligent daughters. He always told Eleanor and Hazel they could do anything—and not to let anyone stop them.

Maybe she could find a house out here, some land, and start collecting rejects from the zoo, like her father. After William, he adopted Daniel, a lamb, and then Glen, a llama. Then the day Eleanor came home from school and found three greyhounds who could no longer run fast enough at the racetrack. Their house and barn were overbrimming with life. How could Hazel not see it like this?

Joan pokes her nose in Eleanor's pockets. Looking for carrots, thinks Eleanor. But when she nuzzles Eleanor's cheek and neck, something she's never done before, Eleanor senses it's more than that. She remembers how William used to seek out her father when he needed attention, butting his nose into him, wailing loudly like a grieving woman whose lover has left. Her father always hurried back.

"Are you lonely?" says Eleanor.

Eleanor brushes her back, and Joan puts her mouth to Eleanor's ear, seeming to whisper to her. There's a pit at the back of her throat, then suddenly Eleanor feels a loneliness so deep, so terrible, like an endless hole at the center of her being, as if someone has come along and cut out her reason for being. Tears spring to her eyes, and she swallows a moan of anguish. She misses Arthur, God, she wishes he were still alive; she misses work, her entanglement with the world.

She puts reins on Joan and leads her to the corral to let her run around, hoping to lift their spirits. Barbara comes over.

"What happened to Gwennie?" says Eleanor.

Barbara inhales sharply. "I think the coyotes got her. Or some creepy crawly."

"Creepy crawly?"

"People out here who hunt. Rabbit, quail, other animals. And then there are the freaks. I found a shot-up cat once behind the barn. Maybe it was kids, I don't know."

Before Eleanor can stop herself, she says, "People disgust me."

Barbara smiles sadly. "I haven't reached that yet. Probably because most of my time is out here with the animals. I haven't seen Gwennie in a week. Longer than my son." She laughs, desperation in her tone. "Feels like everything is going away."

When she returns home, Eleanor sits in her clean kitchen, and in the silence, the malaise grips her like a straitjacket. She's lived her life in a dream, trying to destroy the reality of devastation. The dream is gone, and there's no vacating reality. She picks up the *New York Times* and stares at the page, the headlines slamming into her. Blue trots in and stares expectantly at her. Usually, she'd get up and fill his food bowl. Usually, she'd head outside.

Minutes tick by, and she hears the house creaking and sighing as if it, too, is weary of existing. She feels as if she's behind a sheet of glass, and questions are busy dusting themselves off and invading. Who is she? What purpose does she have? Why does anything at all exist? They've found her again, these questions that once haunted her when she was young.

Blue licks her hand, and the act rearranges the sludge inside, enough that she gets up, fills his food bowl, and checks to make sure he has water. He'll want a walk soon. Life requires a future action to keep from devolving into a woman sitting in a room. He stares at her with sad, pitying eyes.

She doesn't want to leave the house, but the way he's looking at her, he needs to go out. She lacks a purpose, but he has one. Gathering her coat and Blue's leash, she'll stop by Ilana's to make sure she's okay and find out if she might need something, anything.

Outside, Claire's mother opens her front door as if she's been watching out the front window for Eleanor to appear. "You're here!" she says.

Diana's accent, Southern and full of musicality, has always been interesting to Eleanor's ear. "I thought you were gone."

Eleanor looks at the big sycamore tree in Diana's front yard and is horrified to find she sees not only the tree but the tree's future, dried up, dead, and stripped of leaves. It's as if the future is superimposed on the present.

Diana asks if it isn't too much trouble, could Eleanor pick up Claire from school?

Without hesitation, Eleanor says, "Sure." Because she's worse off than she knew, looking at the tree like that, a tree that has always filled her with wonder.

"Really! Thank you so much! You're a lifesaver. You know Claire just loves how patient you are. She says you're so kind, and you make good cookies. I'll phone the school and let them know you'll get her." Diana has a work call, and she can't reschedule it, so this is so helpful, so kind. "You'll probably need your ID."

Eleanor puts her hand in her pocket and touches her wallet. Presumably her ID is inside, and if she pulled it out, she'd find a bare-bones description of who she is, which is enough to pick up a child from school, enough to carry this body along, head down a sidewalk. She takes Blue around to her backyard and promises she'll walk him later.

She heads along the sidewalk, and the daylight swallows her whole. A relief to be held by something. It's true, she thinks, in life you travel through five, six, seven big changes, and the changes are born from the outside: a loss of a parent, a favorite teacher, a marriage, a birth, a divorce, a death of a loved one, an earth-shattering success. A symbiosis exists between a human and the outside world, and there is no dualism (then why does the mind like to sort things out that way?). You can't lock yourself in your house because the chances of change are minuscule. In a funk, always in a funk. And objects are far more than they appear at first glance, partly because of this symbiosis. Because you don't know the effect you'll have on another object or person and vice versa.

She keeps going over these thoughts, like running her fingers through her hair to find something, a twig, a leaf. In the distance, she hears the school bell ring, the voices of children like a million birds released at once, all that energy rushing to the sky. Eleanor passes by the chain-link fence and sees the chaos of children running across the blacktop, to the swings, the curvy slide, a ball, a friend, a mother. She remembers the feeling of freedom from the confinement of the classroom and into fresh air.

The questions from earlier are gone. She is immersed in what is around her, in front of her: the buzz of a lawn mower, the children's squeals and shouts. Morning glories twine around a telephone pole, their flowers like elegant sculpted purple cups.

She heads to the office, shows her ID, signs in as a visitor, and is told by the principal's assistant with a kind smile that Claire is in room 19. Making her way through the knot of ecstatic energy, Eleanor heads to the classroom. If this energy could be harnessed, the world would run cleanly, beautifully. Where is little Claire, with her straight coppery hair, her black framed glasses? She's probably loved by the teacher.

In grade school, Eleanor was an awful student. Before she went to kindergarten, her school was the great outside. The birth of a bird, the death of a bird, a claw mark on its side or a head eaten off by a cat. Animal tracks in the mud—who passed by this way—animal fur stuck in the rough tree bark—who passed by this way? The soil and sun and water, the green-bean plant pushing its bright green head through the dark dirt, shedding its hard shell. A marvel, a miracle. Pink worms in dirt. For hours she'd watch the black ants collect and carry their haul to their nest, the grain of wheat, the berry, the dead spider, and she was astonished by the organization, the order; all of it held her attention, in the backyard on a sunny day.

For Eleanor, the classroom was sterile, dull, deadly.

The girls hug their skinny arms around the teacher and around each other in a raw display of human affection, and the boys charge the wrong way up the slide. Eleanor can't help but think she's witnessing humans in their natural state. Before hurt and harm, before the heart is damaged and turns tentative or reluctant or scared, before everything flattens so the heart doesn't react at all. All around her she feels how alive the chil dren are, how unguarded, a human heart pulsing to the beat of another.

She sees a girl who reminds her of a young Ava: long dark hair, a round pale face, two skinned knees, and thin pole legs. She wishes Ava were young again. Despite their sometimes-tense relationship, she'd do it again, that raw, demanding purpose right in front of her. Ava, with her big dark eyes, unflinching, looking right at Eleanor, ready to devour whatever Eleanor handed her in terms of knowledge. She remembers finding Ava at the side of the road, studying a flattened sparrow.

Claire is waiting right by her classroom door, swiveling her head, looking for her mother, a good girl, patiently waiting. Eleanor forgot how frail she is, so slight, like a sun-deprived English schoolgirl with peachy freckles decorating her nose, her coppery hair pulled into a high messy ponytail. Blue tennis shoes and white ankle socks, a forest-green skirt above the knee, and a pink T-shirt that blares GIRL POWER. Her outfit is one of her own making, and Eleanor smiles at the incongruity. The resulting clash invites a myriad of interpretations, preventing any final conclusions. Eleanor approves.

"Claire," Eleanor calls out.

She looks over, a mixture of curiosity and bewilderment. When she doesn't budge, Eleanor heads over to explain that her mother is busy and she is here to walk her home.

"I don't go home right after school today," says Claire.

"What do you do?"

"I go to my meeting," says Claire.

"What meeting is that?" says Eleanor.

Eleanor looks at Claire's skinned knee, at her pale, intense face.

"You can come along," says Claire. "My mom always forgets about it."

Eleanor follows Claire into one of the classrooms. Unlike in a traditional class, the kids appear to have a great deal of luscious freedom. They are scattered around the room, in chairs, on the floor, sitting on tabletops, their limbs tossed over the backs of chairs, and they are eating, talking, and laughing. A group is huddled around a side table, intently drawing with markers. The chaos is thrilling for them, Eleanor supposes, because it's not typically allowed in the four walls of a class with whiteboards.

Eleanor folds herself into a small plastic chair, barely, with Claire sitting across from her. There's color in Claire's cheeks now, a shine to her as if something wonderful is about to happen. In the front of the class, a young woman with glossy brown hair appears, or maybe she was there all along. She is without gravitas, no real authority or command, but there is a sense that this is the way it's supposed to be. The girls keep coming up to her and hugging her around the waist, and the young woman pats heads and smiles like a female Pied Piper, though the children are clearly the ones in charge, and the young woman is a diminished creature, her purpose seemingly to urge them on.

Eleanor softens her gaze so she's not really looking at anything, only feeling the mood in the room—one of joy, animation, and freedom. She asks Claire what the meeting is about, and Claire puts a finger to her mouth, "Shh."

On the front movie screen, the young woman puts up an image: "What's the news? What did you see?"

Hands shoot up, and when Eleanor looks over at Claire, she's astonished. Claire is out of her chair, a burst of life, waving her hand in the air with gusto. Eleanor thinks of the audiences she used to face—the tucked down, solemn affairs, the men in suits, the women looking like the men in suits—the politeness, the restraint, the tense air. There is no restraint here; everyone wants a part of the action, hands waving wildly, with some of the children calling out that they have something, pick me.

A boy who looks to be nine years old is the first to be called on. In a tone threaded with excitement, he tells the group that he read that in Thailand they don't use plastic but banana leaves as wrappers. Forks and spoons are made of bamboo, not plastic.

Another boy with a baseball cap says he went to a science fair and saw a car that ran on algae. A girl on a hike in the headlands watched seven red-tailed hawks circle overhead; on Market Street in San Francisco, only bikes and buses are allowed, no more cars. A boy went to visit his grandparents in Greece. "Lots of trash on the beach," he says. "I filled a garbage bag with empty Coca-Cola bottles."

Claire, in a loud voice, says, "I saw a bamboo straw in a store."

Eleanor feels a tingle of excitement scurry up her spine.

A new image appears on the screen. A newspaper account of two sisters, ten and twelve years old, who started a petition to stop Kellogg's from cutting down palm trees to get palm oil. The tree cutting was devastating to the orangutan habitat. They collected 1,000 signatures and sent it to Kellogg's, but the company did nothing, so they collected 100,000 signatures, which prompted Kellogg's to invite the girls to their headquarters, where they took pictures of them and said they'd make changes in 2030. Not satisfied, the girls collected one million signatures and delivered them to the company, and Kellogg's invited them back, vowing to change their global palm oil program, not years later, but now.

"They didn't give up," says a tall girl with braids and knobby knees.

Eleanor feels profoundly chastised as if she's found a stick and is knocking her own head.

"We could do that for all cardboard boxes," says a girl who

has on tight black pants and a white top, her brown hair with a shimmery swimmer's patina. "We could start a petition and have Amazon collect the boxes and use them again."

The group concurs. Eleanor studies this girl whose voice pulses with authority. This girl can see the future, and it includes boxes that Amazon recycles.

"I know how to make a petition on the computer," says Claire.

A boy sitting across from Eleanor says to her, "Are you the speaker today?"

The boy is a beautiful child, slim and long-legged, a charm beyond loveliness with his smile.

"No."

"You're just here?"

"I am."

"We're trying to change things," he says, smiling, a mouth full of bright white teeth. The boy tells her about his idea for a sport mart; everyone brings their outgrown sports equipment and clothes to the gym and swaps them for things that fit. "Otherwise, most of it ends up in the landfill," he says.

"How old are you?" says Eleanor.

"I'm nine, and I'm Alexander."

"Nice to meet you, Alexander."

Eleanor introduces herself without mentioning her age. He would, she guesses, be dumbfounded. How can someone be so old?

"Nice to meet you," he says. "What's your idea?"

His eyes are green like spring clovers. His swatch of dark brown hair highlights his face full of sun. If she were a young girl, she'd have a crush on him. His energy pops and bounces; he needs to move in his chair a lot, the ricocheting energy bouncing off his insides. He might do great things; he might become the fastest runner in the world. He might have attention deficit disorder.

"I don't have any," she says.

He looks at her wide-eyed, as if he's discovered something

in the world he didn't know existed. "Is something wrong with you?"

Claire suddenly becomes intrigued and scrutinizes Eleanor as if wanting to be the first to find the fundamental flaw. What *is* wrong with her?

"My mom always has ideas," says Claire. She lists her mother's ideas: Claire should practice her multiplication tables, clean her room, practice the piano, play outside, and read for another ten minutes.

The weary task of mothering; the weary task of being a child under such heightened scrutiny. What about the lazy afternoons of seemingly unproductive play? Slipping into Eleanor's mind is her young self, a ladybug crawling on her arm, and she is counting the black dots, watching the beetle fly off, the nearly transparent red wings like stained glass. That one summer, she spent going to the lake every day, practicing how long she could hold her breath underwater.

"Did you ever have ideas?" says Alexander.

She's clearly an enigma. "Once, long ago."

"Thomas Edison failed 1,000 times before he invented the lightbulb," says Claire. "My mom says never give up."

But sometimes one must give up, thinks Eleanor, the act of beating one's head against a hard wall causes permanent brain damage. The problem then becomes, what should one do? We are not made to sit around and ruminate and brood, enough philosophers have come to that conclusion.

Something shifts in Alexander's face, a softening—compassion? "It's okay, we have lots of ideas."

Claire turns to a girl on her right and says something Eleanor can't hear, and when the girl glances at Eleanor, Eleanor sees that she, too, is beautiful, with long silky hair and fresh, alert eyes, as if she's just been scrubbed.

The young teacher announces it's time to choose teams. Claire leans toward Eleanor and tells her there are three teams: Kindness, Wisdom, and Earth. Now it's time to brainstorm and come up with ideas of how to make the world better. Claire heads to a table by the blackboard, though it's not clear which group she's chosen, and the room erupts with chatter.

Eleanor closes her eyes and listens. The children are brimming with ideas, so many ideas for the ravaged earth. Don't eat meat day, don't use plastic for a week, don't create any garbage day, go out and notice something good about the world. The Earth isn't the only recipient of their storming unleashed brains. At Team Kindness: Say hello to someone at school; sit with someone at lunch who is alone; keep a kindness journal; at the end of the day ask, What good thing did you do for someone? What good thing happened to you?

The young teacher is sidelined as the uninhibited, the idealistic, the untarnished run the room. Fresh, open, it all seems possible. Here is the value of youth and ignorance: the ability to forge ahead without the worry of Big Money, which fights to keep the status quo. And even when Big Money's ugliness rises up, it doesn't stand a chance against these young ones; those two girls standing up to Kellogg's, one million signatures. The boundless energy, the imagination for what can be, what must be. It's their future, and they're not worn-out shells of themselves, they're going to shape the world to their liking. If you don't like it, get out of the way. How did they figure out at such a young age that adults are not to be trusted? Is this what constitutes Claire? That sobriety and competence, because if she doesn't have it, her future is bleak?

Eleanor bathes in the perfect temperature of youth and it's a lovely bath.

It turns out Claire has chosen Team Wisdom, and occasionally Eleanor hears her say something about how to write their posters. They can't make people feel bad, Claire explains, they have to say it in a good way. Alexander went over to the table with markers and is busy making a poster. At Team Earth, a girl says, "What about the poisoned lakes? The fish are dying. What will the bears eat? What can we do about it?"

A million ways Eleanor can go, but every path in her mind whisks her to her former self: a young Eleanor outside in the field by the red barn, the tall grasses swishing around her, a sound she still searches for all these years later. It was June, and Hazel was in her room, playing with her dolls or reading. They'd both grown to prefer their solitude to each other's company. Hazel didn't like to get dirty, and Eleanor found the walls of the room suffocating.

The sun was out, the air cool. By the barn, Eleanor got there in the early morning because yesterday, right before dinner, she'd seen something. A single wasp on a log yesterday was now fifty, and as she stood nearby she saw that they opened their mouths and scraped off wood fiber and chewed, their lower jaws moving side to side, mixing the wood shavings with saliva. Off they flew to the oak branch, where a ball of silvery swirls was forming. They must have started weeks ago because it was the size of a tennis ball. Back and forth the wasps flew, and creeping closer, she saw that the swirls looked like icing on a birthday cake.

She ran back to the house, flung open the front door, yelling for Hazel to come see, hurry, and her words became bait, and Hazel leaped up, and they sprinted to the log, where they stood side by side, breathless, looking at the wasp's papery silver home. Hazel, who never wanted to go outside, who refused to dig in the dirt, who wanted nothing to do with climbing trees or streams or lifting rocks, said, "I hope no one ever tears it down."

She and Hazel made signs and tacked them to telephone poles. Save the Wasps! Don't Tear Down Their Nests! Eleanor wrote a letter to the local newspaper, explaining that people should like wasps because they ate the bugs that destroyed gardens—caterpillars, leaf beetle larva, aphids, whiteflies, crickets, on and on. She gave a presentation to her fourth-grade class. It was her first lesson in the intricate interconnections of the world and the burning desire—that desire she feels pulsing in the classroom—to change things and make a beautiful landscape.

They're little revolutionaries, Eleanor thinks, listening to the children turn their voices into musical instruments. Thank god they're here.

The teacher comes over. Eleanor hopes she's not shown the door. Eleanor tells her she's to bring Claire home. "It's a wonderful group."

"Unbridled energy and enthusiasm," says the teacher, smiling.

"Indeed."

Isn't part of the sorrow of modern societies derived from rarely giving oneself permission to dream for a better life—not for a few, but everyone? That ache in Eleanor's being, the primal desire for fairness. She loves this moat of innocence.

"I'd like to come back," says Eleanor.

The woman looks at her quizzically as if she wants to say, Who are you? Why should I grant you this?

Hazel's words come back to her: "Don't become dust before your time." As she got out of the car, Hazel quoted Genesis: "And the Lord God formed man of the dust of the ground and breathed into his nostrils the breath of life; and man became a living soul."

Because she's someone who wants to be a living soul again.

"I'd like to help," says Eleanor. Does she sound too desperate? What will this woman think of her? Whatever needs to be done, it seems a pure demand that she can meet and live up to. "Clean the boards, sweep, wipe the tables, anything, really."

The woman doesn't say anything. Eleanor finds herself murmuring a silent prayer, which becomes a plea that sprawls across the air. The bell rings and the class explodes with new energy: the packing of backpacks, the shrill of children's voices, girls' arms thrown around each other saying goodbye. They are so willing to love, so willing to open themselves up to each other, so willing to admit they need each other.

"If you'd like to clean the boards while I—"

"Yes," says Eleanor. "Yes, I'd love to."

I'd love to.

I never thought I'd see Eleanor smile like that again, wide and generous like a streak of sunlight. Her resignation shushed away, yielding to youthful energy—even if I don't think it will last. Her seared memory for a livable earth can't be extinguished. It's in her and as automatic as gravity. But enjoy this shimmer, I tell myself, it's got the feel of a day at the beach, the wind warm and soft, the seagulls darting, gliding, swooping; the sandpipers scurrying along the sand, scrambling; the dogs' ecstatic play, their joy in the freedom to run as far as their legs will take them. Nothing is static, everything is alive and moving like the churning ocean waves.

Like the children and their pulsing desire for a world they can live in, thrive in. The other day I watched a young boy tell a US senator that she needed to vote for climate change legislation for his future. She balked and lectured him that no one, certainly not him, would tell her what to do, she'd been an elected official for years—the young boy interrupted her and said, "You're my representative. You work for me."

A glorious triumph that quickly got squashed. The senator lashed out, "You're not old enough to vote. I don't have to listen to you."

The poor children. They're bossed around, belittled, disparaged, demeaned, neglected, and sidelined; they lack the most basic rights. So full of life yet denied so much life. I hear the platitudes, think of the children, for the children, the good of the children, but look at the earth they're inheriting; it's nothing like what the previous generations had. What kind of species fails to care for their young?

A huge wildfire is raging in California, menacing the air with smoke, gobbling dried-out trees and deer and bears and rabbits and raccoons. Apples are boiling on the trees. We're living in a moment of history-making, and I understand you want to turn away from the pain. I feel you doing that right now, turning your back, covering your ears. I wish I could, but I can't spackle on denial or delusion. Can't block out the crackling of fire or the screams of deer. The sound of the earth bubbling up, it's out of your range, but I hear it, faintly, weakly, incessantly, woo ah lo eee, the voice of the molten center, low and gravelly, a scrape against metal. Woo ah lo eeeeee, it follows me everywhere, it's in every corner, every cave. And it's remarkably like the sound of the Golden Gate Bridge as if the two are speaking to each other, an ancient voice of anger and sorrow.

The other night, I was staring at the bright moon, thinking about all the yesterdays in me, stretching to 4.5 billion years ago when the earth was formed, when I slowly, incrementally, began to fill the space of near emptiness. Empty, without oxygen and only pinpricks of water, so it was me, and night and day, and the winds and small airs stirring up dust. A quiet time, a time requiring immense, bottomless patience. I sang, I wept, I called out, I was so lonely.

The day finally came like a cool breeze after a season of scorching hot, 3.8 billion years ago: water was no longer flung into space but gathered, forming great glimmering bodies like prayers to the sky. That's when I really wept because I knew life would bloom soon. I didn't have to wait long; earth's first life was born 3.7 billion years ago, the astonishing prokaryote, a microscopic, single-celled organism. We celebrated—night and day and wind and me, we sang to the stars, our voices echoing across the no-longer-empty planet.

And more life came, though the wait was, again, agonizingly long, 2.7 billion years ago, though I confess, it might have been earlier since I slipped so often into fantasy, imagining lush life and the music of many. The eukaryotes arrived. How wondrous their cell structures and membrane-bound nucleus, and the brilliance to synthesize protein and produce energy. A huge and significant step, I was convinced more companions were in the wings, a flutter away, but I had to wait and wait and wait—patience became my daily practice as I wrestled my devout desire clamoring inside, like roots pressing against a too-tight pot, terrible and beautiful melody. Years and years piled up like an enormous stone wall until I almost gave up, until finally, 1.1

billion years ago, multicellular life appeared. Cells dividing and working, and then quickly, or so it seemed to me, the beautiful sponge was born. I spent endless days gazing at the sponges.

Time moved glacially, syrupy, a slow breath in, a slow breath out, until 541 million years ago, the lid of a box labeled Life flew off. The sea suddenly swarmed with life, and quickly, 100 million years later, like a dream come true—green! Every shade: light green, dark, forest, emerald, and lime. Land plants graced with the intelligence to use the sun's energy and convert carbon dioxide into sugar. Amazing growth, leaves of every size and shape, teardrops and hearts, circles and ovals and stars. My long-ago fantasies were anemic compared to the reality of this beauty.

I was happy with plants. They were enough, more than enough. These wondrous beings that knew the deep fiber of resilience. Hot sun, pounding rain, blustering dust storms, they twisted and turned and held on for dear life and grew more. It was enough, really, these gorgeous beings, and the great clouds of oxygen and the sea and lakes, but 400 million years ago, I was—there are no other words for it—dumbstruck with awe. I felt as if divine power had taken form. Grand, elegant trees grew and towered over the land, casting long shadows and waving their shiny leaves. How can you not admire a tree? How can you not bow before it? I was never far from them, never wanted them out of my sight. Their solitary forms betray the truth, which is that they should be viewed in the plural. Busy chattering to each other, I loved to listen to them talk through the webbing of fungi in the dirt. They are so kind to each other, so caring, shuttling to each other water, nutrients, and warnings of predators.

Soon the lush green landscape shook with the enormous dinosaurs. Then quickly another stuffed box of life ripped open 65 million years ago, releasing a flurry and frenzy of beings. Mammals, so many of them, I laughed with delight at the burst, the vitality, remembering the empty landscape that now swarmed with what looks like today's rodents, bats, moles, shrews, hedgehogs, badgers, and squirrels. Birds followed and the sky was no longer sad and empty. I watched them for years.

The complexity, the intelligence, from a single-celled organism to this, these beings—the mammals took my breath away. Was I too greedy, eager to have what would come next? I didn't have any power over it, but maybe my imaginings stirred things awake. I found a through line I could easily trace that the beings were becoming smarter, more communicative, more complex, more collaborative, wise. About 55 million years ago, the chimps, monkeys, and gorillas appeared with their larger brains, brilliantly designed to be so very social. Full of play and antics and love and fierce loyalty for each other. They made tools from sticks and rocks, they hunted, and they fought off harm.

I was sated with life, with the green and trees and the many breathing beings, but, yes, I was curious, what form would life take next? I spent years imagining what splendid being would appear. Surely some being with more intelligence, a being that moved beyond the primates' clan loyalty, moving toward the mutual desire for happiness and a habitable world. I was filled with anticipation. It would be an exquisite arrangement. Surely this new being would recognize all it had inherited from the slow beginning 4.5 billion years earlier. Surely this new form of life, given the chimps and apes, would have the capacity for cognition, not only to become aware but to become aware of being aware. Surely they'd have deep humility because of what came before them; surely they'd be awestruck at all that exists.

There are days I want to toss you in an old well.

Or drown you in the triumphant sea.

Or lock the doors of your houses and light them on fire.

Or watch with glee as the wind dismantles your bridges and roads, your buildings and streetlights.

Or the air fills with so much smoke you can't breathe.

Or the earth heats up so hot you keel over from dehydration.

Or gather all the nuts and berries, the green beans and tomatoes, and give them to the animals and let you starve.

Or lock you in a zoo and watch you languish.

Or in a huge warehouse, denying you fresh air and feet touching the ground.

Hog-tie you, burn you, drown you, swallow you up and spit you out, all bones and flesh tattered and in pieces.

I am too full of years, and you are not. I wish it were otherwise: that somewhere lodged in your bones, blood, DNA, you had a deep appreciation of all that has been bequeathed to you. But you don't. Or not enough of you.

I realize now that the voices here are not only for you but for me, because I keep returning to the question: How do I not give up? At this late stage of destruction, what difference does any of it make? The despair is thick and permeates the air. I don't trust humans, but I must, because to mend anything requires them. But it's an angst-ridden, awful, violent relationship. The horrors that have been done and are being done. I'm bruised, I'm broken, I don't want to ache anymore. I've tried to stay upbeat, though with nearly every breath, every thought, I'm in mourning.

Eleanor is walking home with Claire. Eleanor's smile isn't so bright, that's what I see, and she's a little sluggish, a little pale. I'm pretty sure that by the time she makes it home, her spark will have blown out, and she'll be back to slogging through the day.

Our Days of Grace

When Lucinda steps out of her car, she hears them. Four dogs are going at it, and from their baritone bark, she knows they're the big guys because the little ones sound like squeaky chew toys. She grabs her bag and hurries to the building because she knows from the barking that not enough volunteers showed up this morning, and the dogs have been caged too long. She can hear their burning desire to run and sizzle their brains with the smell of tall green grass.

That loud bark with the lift at the end, that's Roger. He's got a thick rope around Lucinda's waist like Vincent when he was a baby and used to wail like a diaper pin stabbing him in the thigh. Man, she'd drop everything. Her husband growled at her not to treat Vinny like a goddamn precious vase or he'd grow up a sissy. He didn't want a sissy. Back then she was a stupid nineteen-year-old, falling for beautiful Frank with his tar-black hair, a man's man. He could yap all he wanted, she knew better: a mother will always protect her baby; it's the law. Besides, Frank was an asshole who left her for that fat whore who lived two blocks away on Mission and Eighteenth. Don't even start, everyone knows that woman had a boob job. Went from a 34 to a 44F in a second, the things so heavy, she tilted so far forward, it was a miracle she didn't fall on her ugly face. Many days Lucinda wished she'd fall. Many, many days. Good riddance, Frank. And on Lucinda's bad days, fuck you.

The little bell rings as she steps into the lobby, smelling of wet dog, ammonia, and gaminess. When she leaves today, she knows this will be her smell, too—her clothes, her hair. She likes it because it reminds her she did something worthwhile, unlike other days that overflow with too much time and nothingness.

"God, I'm glad you're here," says Katie, who's manning the adoption desk. A chestnut-colored Chihuahua is curled up on her lap, and there's a half-eaten ham sandwich and an orange soda on the desk. "Roger is going crazy. He hasn't been out yet, and he probably heard your car. He's got a real thing for you, girl."

Lucinda smiles, clips her lanyard around her neck—VOL UNTEER—and dashes down the hall calling, "I'm coming, hold your horses." When she enters the kennels, Roger changes his bark to quick bits of sound—anxious, ready, happy—which arouses Bucky, Joy, and Lily. Barks bounce off the cement walls, colliding with each other.

"Okay, okay," she says, "but first, Roger."

Eighty pounds of dog, a mix of something and pit bull. Pits get a bad rap, for sure. Men's fault, training the pits to fight, testosterone stinking up the room, the shouting, and soon, blood flying until there is a death. A dog's death, and that gets Lucinda's heart pounding hard. She grew up in LA, and her pop used to go to the dog fights every Saturday night, down at some warehouse in the San Gabriel Valley. He went with a group of neighborhood men and some of his friends from work. He was a garbage man, and that's what they called themselves, The Garbage Men, and after they said it, they'd laugh a sneaky laugh as if they meant something else. Her pop liked to say, "Everyone and everything is garbage." Back then, she thought he meant it all turns to garbage, so pay attention because it'll all be gone someday. When she told him that once, he laughed and said she was an optimist. Later, she came to a different conclusion, but she still likes that earlier meaning the best.

She opens the cage door. Roger jumps up on his hind legs, and his front legs dance in the air.

"Yep," she says. "We're out of here."

Like an eager child, he stands in front of her, head tilted up, wide-eyed, his dark, intense eyes looking at her, only her. She caresses his head and finds the two-inch scar above his right ear, a deep cut that was oozing when he was first brought in. The skin on the scar is now smooth, a raised-up line where no fur will ever grow. Everyone's got battle wounds, she knows, and she, for damn sure, has a lot of them. Life is not for the fainthearted, for sure. He's panting as if he's already running laps and overheating in his mind and will never stop. Lucinda knows that if the pits are raised right, with love and tenderness, they are sweetpeas, like Roger.

Her friends don't understand it. She's at the Humane Society every Saturday and Sunday, and when she gets off work early, on Fridays. Or when she calls in sick as she did today because she needed to be here all Friday because sorrow was starting to lead her by the nose to a place she didn't want to go. She doesn't go to church anymore, no picnics at Dolores Park, or parties at friends' apartments with margaritas and salsa dancing. A lot of Frank's friends sided with her, so they kept her in the loop and kicked him out, but she'd prefer to spend her time with dogs.

"You like dogs more than me," said her friend Gloria, pouting.

Lucinda didn't deny it. They were sitting in Lucinda's kitchen, the sun pouring in, showing off the dust in the corners. Now that she lived alone, she could live the way she wanted. Dust, dirty dishes in the sink, unmade bed.

"You're never going to meet anyone this way," said Gloria.

Lucinda shrugged.

"You're going to be old and alone and sad. What happens when you get sick? Who will take care of you?"

"You will."

Gloria puckered her lips and frowned. "Why are you doing this to yourself? I see Frank with that bitch."

Lucinda ate a bite of her hamburger. "When he tires of her, he'll chuck her for someone shiny and new. It's an old story."

Once a man standing behind Lucinda at the grocery store asked if she was a ballet dancer; her posture was impeccable. She laughed and told him she was standing that way, sucking in her belly, because her lower back hurt like hell. She wished the man had noticed her hands, her long slender fingers that Frank had said held the grace of a ballerina's, how they swept through the air when she spoke. He was convinced she once was a ballet dancer, though she never was—out of her family's price range. Later, Frank made fun of her, how she couldn't speak without waving her hands around like a goddamn retard.

These days, if anyone asks her what's up with the dogs, Lucinda doesn't answer because she's tired of people looking at her like she's got a screw loose. Besides, she can't fully explain it, and, really, she doesn't want to pin it down. She just wants to live it.

Roger is wagging his tail so hard that his backside is penduluming. She slips on his harness, clips on his leash, and they are outside in the blue sky and the soft green grass. As they approach the big lawn, his massive pit hind muscles tremble with excitement. Anticipation has its own beauty. She should tell that to Gloria, who hops into bed with any guy who winks at her.

Lucinda unleashes Roger, and he launches like a rocket, running in circles, round and round, so fast it looks like all four legs are off the ground—airborne! Roger does this every single time, and every time it makes her laugh. It's like hearing the same joke, but you laugh anyway because it's so damn good. His pink tongue hangs out as if he's drunk, and he *is* drunk on running and the smell of dirt and grass.

She stands still in the center, listening to his deep inhales of air pushed down to the very bottom of his lungs. It's one of her favorite places to be, in the center of this euphoric aliveness, Roger running his heart out, all of his wildness on full display, and she is feeling for once that everything is right in the world. He gets to be who he is, which is what everyone wants anyway.

Her job, at least part of it, is to get Roger to like people again, after all the shit he's been through. He came to the Humane Society with a broken back leg, cigarette burns on his head, pink skin showing through patches of fur, scrawny as all hell, ribs poking out, and that oozing cut—barbed wire or a knife, the vet wasn't sure. What the hell is wrong with people? Lucinda's thought long and hard about this socialization stuff because there are some really shitty people out there, and Roger is right to be reluctant. How does a man who used to pull you to him for a hungry kiss, a man who married you—who had real love in his eyes, who had a baby with you, who used to say I think of you all the time, who rolled the end of her toothpaste tube, so it came out smoothly—pick up and leave? Ten years of marriage, then, poof? This is one of the many things in the world that makes her mind stand stock-still. Another one is her son, Vincent, who was once a twig in her arms, who got his tongue stuck in a roller-skate key, and she had to race him to the doctor; her son who jammed a pussy willow bud up his nose and she rushed him to the emergency room, praying, praying—don't let that bud go into his brain—Vincent, who loved to read, his face in a book at breakfast, at dinner, who goes to NYU and sees her, oh, maybe once a year. How can that be?

Her mother had warned her, hadn't she? "Don't marry him, Lucinda. He'll stomp on your heart, and you got a big heart, it's going to bleed all over."

Roger slows to a trot, returning to earth, his chest heaving. Coming over to her, panting, he's got a mix of love and wild in his eyes. He licks her hand, looks at her with real love—there's no other word for it—and she takes him over to the communal water bowl. He laps up the water for a long minute, and when they head back to the big yard, he's ready to go again.

She can't bring him inside yet. He's owed. "Okay, go!"

He takes off, running in a tighter circle, a serenade of her. She laughs and laughs, and with his mouth open like that, he looks like he's laughing too. We get a kick out of each other, she thinks.

Daniel walks by, waves, and calls out, "Traffic is horrible. You may have trouble getting home."

She mimics his little wave. "Okay."

Oh, damn it. He's coming toward her, his daddy longlegs striding through the cut grass, his coolie hat protecting his face from the sun. She should leave right now. Like her, he's here every Saturday and Sunday. Katie told her he's got three kids all grown and gone and a wife who works all the time—a lawyer or something. Separate lives orbiting around each other like different planets. Takes all sorts. He does something like architecture. Harvard MBA, a smarty-pants, he must have bragged about it to Katie, dropped it in some conversation. In his spare time he makes furniture. He once showed Lucinda pictures of his tables and chairs, and she had to admit they were beautiful. Then he got going about wood, types, strength, color, resilience, and on and on; he became a real library, turning pages of himself, filling her with tree facts. She can't tell, though, from his stiffness and formal language, if he's one of those awful Republicans.

Daniel waits until Roger passes by him, then comes over beside her, bringing a smell of Old Spice and dogginess. "How are you?"

His tone is, as always, genuine. She imagines all those hours alone with drawings of buildings and wood makes him greedy for human contact.

She waves her hand at Roger. "I mean, look at Roger. Man, he can live."

Roger is on his back, rolling in the grass, his long legs waving in the air like antennae.

"The dogs save me too," he says. "And the felines. I know you aren't drawn to them, but they can be quite affectionate."

Oh, come off it, felines?

"I suppose you never bother with the rabbits," he says.

"You're a bunny lover?"

He smiles faintly. "Do I hear condescension in your voice?"

"Me? Nah."

"You should see Tulip. White with black spots. She likes to paw a slinky hanging from her cage. She's quite ingenious and clever."

Daniel's voice sounds strangely soft, pulsing with emotion, almost a tremble to it as if tears aren't far behind. She wishes he'd go away and clean a dog cage.

"Do you ever marvel how much of life is an accident?" he says. He's looking out to the faraway distance. "Who you meet? Marry? What happens to you? We don't want to think about it, or I don't, because the veneer of control quickly shatters, and we are left with chaos, which is probably the truth of things. It's too much for us, how immersed we are in the tumult of accident and chance."

"I don't think about that stuff."

"We are biological beings, at the mercy of hormones, the dopamine, serotonin, endorphins."

She waves him off. "You're squeezing the life right out of it."

He laughs sadly. "I like dogs. Their happy dispositions."

"Not true. When Roger first got here, I couldn't get near him. He'd back away in the corner of his cage as if I was going to kick him. Took more than a month for him to not do that."

"He's fortunate his path crossed with yours."

"I'm the lucky one."

Roger bounds up to them, a ball in his mouth. He drops it at her feet and waits, panting, looking from her to the ball. She comes here for this, life reduced to the singular pleasure of a ball thrown, a dog chasing it.

"I think my wife is cheating on me," says Daniel. He's speaking again to the horizon. "I found a receipt in her coat pocket. I wasn't snooping. There was a black stain on her sleeve and I was planning on taking it to the dry cleaner for her. I was clearing out her pockets and found it. A receipt for the Harbor Inn Hotel."

"She's a lawyer, right? Maybe she met a client there for a drink."

"A bill for $250."

"Well, hell."

He doesn't say anything.

She knows she should be kind—that's what women are supposed to do, but she decided a long time ago—when Frank left her—to cut that out. She was going to live the way she wanted to, not let desires unhoused from their owner dump on her because whoever does the dumping walks away lighter, and she's left holding the trash. That's the silver lining of divorce: you are who you are and are no longer a pleaser.

She picks up the slobbery ball and throws it. "My husband cheated on me too," she says. "I got rid of him."

He doesn't say anything.

She's had enough of Daniel. "I'm going to walk Roger now."

Daniel looks tired; his head droops to the right like a bent wire.

"We all die alone," he says.

Christ, she has to get out of here.

Lucinda brought Roger back to life; that's how Katie puts it. To hear Katie tell it, Lucinda is a goddess with a magic touch, but there was no magic. It came down to Lucinda logging in the hours, sitting with Roger in his cage like a Buddha statue. Lucinda told Katie she had nothing better to do. It was true. She didn't want to be at her empty house or read the newspapers and see the face of that terrible president or even hear his voice. Who voted for him anyway? It was probably a Republican who dumped Roger under the freeway.

Katie said the office gossip was all about sending Roger to a sanctuary, one of those places where dogs go when they are unadoptable. Code for unwanted. "At least it's not, you know, death," said Katie.

Immediately a sweat broke out on Lucinda's face, her broad back. While the other dogs in the kennel had a field day barking their heads off, Roger hung his head and paced as if contemplating all the terribleness in the world.

The day before Roger was going to be shipped to New Jersey to some so-called sanctuary, Lucinda sat in the corner of his cage. Two hours of watching him pace. Occasionally he'd whimper as if she were torturing him.

"Oh, for God's sake," she said. "Pull yourself together, or you're going to be booted."

Another hour of this, and with a shaky hand, she opened her book, *The Unbearable Lightness of Being*, and began to read aloud. Katie had given her an article about reading to dogs to calm them down, and Lucinda had thought it was a bunch of baloney. What did Roger care about Tomas and Tereza and Karenin, their dog? But she kept going because she got into the story, and Roger kept pacing and whimpering until she came to the part where Tereza concludes that animals are the last real link to the paradise abandoned by Adam and Eve. Roger stopped. Later, Lucinda told this story to friends, who looked at her as if she was looney. She knows what she saw, and it seems to her that a person's task is to think for herself. Roger tilted his head and looked at her with curious brown eyes as if to ask, is it true?

"It's true," she told him.

He came over and sat beside her, then stretched out and rested his chin on her thigh. She put a hand on his shivering back, and when he didn't leave, when the quivering stopped, she pulled him close and held him.

After Roger ran until he could barely walk, she took out Bucky, Joy, and Lily. With all the shittiness in their lives, it's the least she could do.

Katie comes out to the big yard and hands her a Diet Coke.

"Thanks," says Lucinda.

Katie is in her fifties. She didn't have children, and most of the time she complains about her husband. How he leaves a mess in the kitchen and bathroom, counters with splashes of spaghetti sauce stains, coffee rings, wet towels balled up on the rack, and a toothpaste-blotted sink. He doesn't see it, Katie says, but Lucinda is sure he does and lets her do the cleaning. Hell, she would. Sometimes, like today, she can smell alcohol on Katie's breath. Lucinda guesses she mixes something into her can of Coke. Makes the hours go by.

"Who's staffing the adoption desk?" says Lucinda.

"The Chimney."

That's what they call the guy who has to take a million smoke breaks. They can't ever remember his name. Under his watch, adoption rates plummet. Katie says he can't come tomorrow, so he's doing a shift today.

"He feels obligated," says Katie.

"Well, at least he feels something."

Katie and her husband are heading to Tahoe. To endure the three- to seven-hour drive—you never know about traffic—she went to the library and got a stack of books on tape. "We run out of things to talk about," says Katie. "Thirty years of marriage. It happens."

Lucinda feels a fury run through her. "Well, if you're sick of him, leave him."

"Oh, I'm not sick of him. I think we need to find something new to do together. I read that in *Women's Daily* magazine."

"I don't read those things. All the stuff they tell you to do. I end up with an anxiety attack."

Katie laughs. "Oh, you're a riot, Lucinda."

Lucinda didn't mean it to be funny.

"Did you see how mopey Daniel was today?" said Katie. "I can't imagine what's wrong."

When Frank left her, the neighborhood was a big gossip fest, and Lucinda hated it. "He mentioned something about death," says Lucinda.

"Oh no. I hope he isn't dying," says Katie.

"We're all dying," says Lucinda.

Katie laughs, an irritating giggle. Lily comes over and lies down on the cool grass. She's twelve years old. Her owner gave her up because she didn't want to deal with the vet bills, and she wanted a puppy—new life. At the shelter they call it the Christmas dump, though it isn't even Christmas yet, the unloading of old dogs and replacing them with new ones. Everyone wants young dogs, peppy ones with spunk, who are also friendly and sweet, get along with kids and will chase a ball and bring it back to you, are housetrained, and don't tear up the house. It pisses Lucinda off, these people who think dogs are custom-made, these people who think a dog is a damn toy. With all these mutts waiting in cages, desperately wanting a home, wanting love, she hates even more the people who want pure breeds. Some days Lucinda can't stand it—all the dogs left behind because they don't measure up somehow.

Katie says she better head out. "Dinner, you know," she says. "Someone has to make it."

"Let him do it," she says.

"We'd be having a bowl of cereal."

"Fine. Let him learn something."

Katie laughs and heads to her car. Lily looks like she's fallen asleep on the grass. Lucinda doesn't want to go home, but she's getting hungry. Maybe she'll stop at the Salad Bar Delight and get herself a salad, along with a large chocolate milkshake, and then drive around until the sun sets. She doesn't like driving at night.

"Let's go, Lily," she says.

Lily rouses and Lucinda clips on the leash. When Roger sees Lucinda, he wags his tail, barks a little. She goes into his cage and sits on the concrete floor next to his dog bed. He comes over. She tells him he's magnificent and don't let anyone tell him differently. She strokes his head and says she'll be back tomorrow.

Chimney is at the adoption desk, looking longingly at his pack of Marlboros. She doesn't bother saying goodbye because he never says anything to her.

She steps out the front door and heads to her car. Two cars over from hers, she sees Daniel sitting in his car with that haunted look. She goes over and taps on the window. He turns his head slowly as if it takes a tremendous effort. He doesn't appear surprised that she's there. He rolls down his window.

"I'm heading out," she says.

He nods, barely, looking out the front window.

"Are you heading home?" she says.

"Yes."

On the passenger seat is a pile of balled-up Kleenex. "When?"

He can't seem to make eye contact. "Oh, soon, I suppose."

"Okay," she says. "See you."

She gets in her car and pulls out of the lot. She makes it to the stoplight and sees that the freeway is packed with cars. Nobody moving, as if all the engines stopped working at once. She hits her steering wheel. "Crap! Crapola!" It's going to get dark soon. The last time she drove at night, she almost ran over a man on his bike. She's no good at night. She turns on the radio and finds the traffic report. Everywhere cars lined up, the Bay Area one giganto traffic jam. Major protest on the Golden Gate Bridge. It's going to be hours. A sign stretched across the top of the bridge: STOP THE PIPELINE! END FOSSIL FUEL ADDICTION!

She doesn't know what to think. The nerve of these people, and at the same time, it's about time. Not that she's one of those enviro freakos, but you don't have to look hard to see things are haywire. Weird weather, half the time California's on fire. Now there's something called a fire season.

She turns on her blinker and makes a U-turn back to the Humane Society. Daniel is still in his car, staring into space. When she taps on his window again, he looks at her with eyes of fright, as if he's lost and doesn't know the way home anymore, doesn't know up from down. She saw that look in her eyes after Frank left. How would she manage? Every direction was absolute misery. She asked her friend to help with Vincent, but then her friend got a job, and she had to put Vincent in before-school and after-school care. Broke her heart.

"Traffic up the wazoo," she says.

He nods.

She wants to shake him. You're not the first person in the world to have a cheater spouse. Men can be such babies.

"I don't think I can make it home either," he says.

"Well, I'm going in to say hi to Roger," she says.

"Good idea."

"Why don't you come in too?" she says.

"You think so?"

A bubble of fury. "Yes, I do."

He unlocks his car and gets out. He's wearing a coat that makes his blue eyes bluer, almost periwinkle.

Katie has left—how she made it home is anyone's guess—and Chimney is still at the adoption desk.

"Bad traffic," says Chimney.

"We know," says Lucinda.

"I'm going," says Chimney.

"I'll take care of things," says Lucinda.

Chimney gathers his coat and his pack of cigarettes, and heads out. Immediately he's smoking. We all have something, thinks Lucinda. Though she can't help but look down on him. Killing himself with those things.

She goes to Roger's cage. She can hear Daniel behind her. Roger perks up, tail wagging. Her eyes water—look at him, bursting with warm emotion at the sight of her. That's the nicest welcome. She leashes him and Daniel follows them outside.

"Why don't you adopt him?" he says.

"Wish I could." She explains her work schedule; how she had to do that to her son, long hours away from her, it crushed her. She doesn't want to do that to Roger.

"Sounds hard with your son," says Daniel. "We have a daughter who lives in France. We never see her."

"I never see my son."

He doesn't say anything.

"All that mothering," she says.

"You could say you did a wonderful job. He's able to be on his own, live his life."

"Then I did too good of a job."

"I think my daughter moved far away so she didn't have to see us," he says.

"Because you're a Republican?"

He raises an eyebrow. "What makes you think that?"

She shrugs.

"Not all Republicans are bad, Lucinda."

"Sure," she says because she doesn't want to get into a fight.

Roger is running laps. She imagines he could do this all day.

Boundless energy like her son when he was small. Until he was twelve years old, whenever he left the house he'd call out, "Bye, love you, Mom!"

"It hurts, though," he says. "Not seeing your offspring."

"Damn right."

The sun is setting, the sky turning a peach color, strutting its beauty. But soon it'll be dark, that awful time of day. She hates her reflection in the window—she can't imagine a lonelier image. Her sad, haunted eyes as if she were the only one on the planet. She doesn't know the back roads home, and even if she figures them out, they'll be packed with cars, everyone trying to do the same thing, trying to get around the traffic jam to get home.

"So we beat on," she says.

"Fitzgerald," he says.

"What?"

"F. Scott Fitzgerald. *The Great Gatsby*. 'So we beat on, boats against the current, borne back ceaselessly into the past.'"

She knew that, she just doesn't carry it around like him. "I went to UC Davis, you know."

"Did you enjoy it?"

"I had to drop out. Got pregnant."

"I'm sorry."

She hates when people apologize for something they have nothing to do with. "No need to say that."

"It's an expression," he says. "That's all."

She's ready to take Roger inside because she's had enough of Daniel. She whistles, Roger comes bounding over. She clips on the leash and heads back to the kennel. She hears Daniel tromping behind her. For god's sake!

With Roger back in his cage, she refills his water bowl, which he greedily laps up. "I'm going to clean Lily's cage, then sit with Roger," she says.

Daniel nods, and thankfully, he doesn't follow her. She moves Lily to an empty cage and scrubs the cement floor with soapy water, sloshing it here and there, watching it spiral down the drain. Even this she does willingly, which surprises her since she isn't much of a house cleaner. She can hear Roger whining.

When she's done, she steps into Roger's cage and sits on the floor. He comes over and puts his chin on her thigh. She pets his back, his breathing deepens, his eyelids flutter. Two big runs in one day—he's worn out. So is she.

She must have dozed off because when she wakes, it's dark. No sound except Roger snoring and another dog whimpering in a dream. She can imagine the dog's dream, a field, wind, chasing a squirrel. The simple life, a lovely life. Her neck hurts; her head must have bobbed around, side to side, as though she was on a plane heading who knows where. Her right foot is asleep. Her watch says it's 9:30. She slips out of the cage, careful not to wake Roger; otherwise she'll find herself outside again, watching him run circles.

She heads down the hall to the front lobby and passes by the bunny room. One rabbit is standing on its hind legs, batting at a slinky tied to its cage. Tulip. What's it doing up at this hour playing? She has to admit it's cute.

It's dark in the lobby, and there's the lingering scent of cigarette smoke from Chimney. She can't drive now, it's too dark. She'll crash or run into a ditch, her eyesight is that bad. Setting her bag on the ground, bunching up her coat, she lies down on the old, faded couch, tucking her knees up. She's half asleep when she hears whimpering, and at first she thinks one of the dogs is dreaming loudly. Or got out of its cage and is wandering around. She sits up and looks around in the dark. Not whimpering but muffled crying.

"Hello?" she says, her voice timid.

"It's me," says Daniel.

She looks at the other couch and sees a lump. She comes over to him, looks down. His face is wet from tears.

"I'm sorry I woke you."

She almost says stop apologizing.

"It's just that—" He stops, choking on his words.

When Frank left her, she cried at everything: a dropped

spoon, a broken dish, a pot of daisies, long jags of crying when she didn't have enough money to buy Vincent a new toy, that remote control car he wanted so badly because it spun in wild circles on its back wheel.

"I'm in big trouble," he says.

She nods. "We all are."

He puts his hand over his mouth. Then lets it drop. "I embezzled money from the firm. I shouldn't have, but I did."

His blue eyes are watching her now.

"My uncle Louis embezzled money," she says. "He wanted to buy a house."

"I did it to buy a new car for my wife. She's always wanted a Mercedes. I thought—"

She remembers all the things she did to try to win her husband back. New clothes, lingerie, teeth whitener, a pineapple-only diet, extravagant meals. She signed them up for eight weeks of salsa lessons, booked a trip to Hawaii. Spent all her savings on that, then tapped out credit cards. God, she got in deep, and it took her so long to get out of debt.

Daniel has rolled away from her, showing her his back, but she can see his ribs' jagged rise and fall.

"When my husband strayed, I lost my mind for a while," she says.

The jagged motion stops. She crouches down and puts her hand on his back.

"I don't know what's going to happen," he says.

Her crouch is hurting her knees. "No one does."

"Can you stay here a moment?"

She hears the plea in his tone and doesn't cringe because it cuts straight in, splaying her raw. She murmurs, "It's going to be all right," though she knows no such thing. Who knows anything? But she keeps saying it, over and over, and she climbs in behind him and wraps her arms around him, his coat smelling doggy, because all those nights alone in her crummy apartment, trying not to cry too loudly so she didn't wake her son, so he could dream his sweet childhood dreams and not look at her sad, terrified, puffy face, she wished someone would come and hold her and say these words into the soft pillow of her ear. Maybe, for a peaceful moment, she'd have believed them.

Brethren and Sistren

They've been grinding forever. Evil Bank of Union gave them hella money to find the holes in their security system. Didn't take long to find gaping chasms that tunneled right to pure unencrypted data. Booyah! So fuckin' easy. The bank bozos were like—how did you? Can you fix it? Yeah, we can fix it, morons. Just pay us, dude.

Adam winks at Raj. You look like shit, bro. Hair standing straight up like barbed wire, a green tone to your face. Didn't you wear that red plaid shirt yesterday?

Ah, thank you, Big Man.

Adam rings the big gong. Time to play some ball.

From his chair Raj throws the basketball at the hoop. Misses by a long shot.

Dean picks it up. Nice fadeaway, makes his shot. Whoa. Sick.

Han isn't playing. He's pounding red licorice.

Adam hurls the ball at the wall, catches it, runs to the hoop. Misses.

No hops, says Raj.

Don't talk to me about hops, bro, says Adam. Your legs are ass.

Don't need legs, says Raj, tapping his temple. I've got this beautiful thing.

Wrong, says Dean, grabbing the ball. Breakaway layup.

Adam laughs, chomps a donut.

Adam started coding at age seven. He's an old man at twenty-two. Went to Princeton but dropped out after a year because the US—yeah, the United States of fucking America—paid him a shitload of money to find the holes in the DOD system. Found twenty-one. They said no way; he said yes way, Ultra Top Secret General. The US of A threw money at him and told him to hire a crew—Raj, Dean, and Han—to rectify the situation. Ten months of solid butt-grinding work, they built it airtight. That was three years ago, and now they're working for the Bank and a host of other evil corporations. They will take that money, support themselves, and support the revolution when it comes around.

Raj didn't even bother with college. At the ripe age of fourteen, he built an app that found the closest and cheapest hotel room based on the user's zip code. Hook-ups, he was thinking, his teen body jacked on hormones and porn. Expedia liked his thinking and paid him $8.5 million. So tell me: why go to college? His parents smiled and patted him on the back, and he paid off their mortgage. Financially he, like Adam, is set, but he's not one to lounge on the couch of life. He's a doer, a maker, a self-made man living a self-made life. He's a god with the computer; he dreams in code. The computer is the entire world sitting on his desk, only fingertips away.

One more, says Raj. I got to make it or—

Or you're Buns, says Dean.

Raj pushes back his chair, shoots—swish. Who's Buns?

Adam grins. At least you got some color in those chubby cheeks.

How come all the weight is in your cheeks and nowhere else? says Dean to Raj. You're like a scarecrow, dude.

Simple, says Raj. I live on caffeine. Caffeine in any form.

And Cheez-Its, says Han. Hey, I know about your secret stash.

Raj grins. I'm a vegetarian.

Let's play for real, says Adam.

Let's go! says Dean, clapping his hands.

The new game's fire. Adam found it two weeks ago by poking around his brother's car computer network. He wanted to find a way to put in an endless loop of the song "The End of the World as We Know It" and drive his bro crazy. Such fucking idiots, the car makers. Someone ought to sue their asses because serious damage is going to happen. Who thought connecting the car networks to the internet was a good idea?

Without proper security measures? It made Adam so irate he wanted to teach them a lesson.

Bingo! shouts Raj, tapping into an Audi system.

What's the play? says Dean.

Radio, says Raj.

Station?

Hold on.

I've snagged five, says Adam. This is dope.

Classical is now the dude's hip-hop, says Raj. Here we go. The radio is now blasting Bach. The driver's freakin'.

They laugh and keep hunting because they're the Merry Pranksters 3.0.

How about some rain on this sunshiny day, says Adam.

Is it sunny? says Raj, looking around.

No clue, says Adam. Haven't been outside since, oh, 2010.

Adam taps his keyboard, and the windshield wipers are now on crack, spraying water like a hyper sprinkler.

Hold on, says Han. I got ten cars in one search.

Whoa, bro.

Behold the beauty, says Adam.

Crank the AC, says Han. Make it a blizzard. Icicles dripping from their nose. Turn that California sun-loving, beach-loving dweeb into ice.

Got to be sunny, says Dean. It's California. San Francisco with 260 days of sun. According to weather.com it's a breezy 70 degrees out in lovely San Francisco.

Who knew? says Adam.

Who cares? says Dean.

Raj taps away, swiveling his head right and left, getting out the neck knots. I've got the radio playing so loud the car has to be jumping. Bets on whether he leaps out.

Five bucks, says Dean.

Cheap bastard, says Raj.

Fifty, says Adam.

Let's go! says Raj.

Money-grubber, says Adam.

Adam gets up, turns up his speakers, and blasts Radiohead's "Weird Fishes." He starts dancing, arms overhead, turning circles, his long dark dreadlocks flying like a Ferris wheel. He belts out the high notes, growls the low ones. He's as skinny as a pole, and if he didn't wear a belt, his jeans would fall to his knees, but no one wants to see his pale, frail ugly body. Dude must weigh 150 pounds at six feet. Not a pretty sight. But they're all thin, except for Dean, who pounds the potato chips. None of them shower on a regular basis because they don't remember and/or don't care. Besides, the only people they see are the ones in this big room. A pervasive stench, mostly hidden under hoodies. The fifteen-foot ceiling helps. Only when arms go overhead—Adam dancing—do they catch a whiff. But no one says anything because they know they stink too.

Adam tips back his Coke, eats a Slim Jim.

Okay, says Dean. This is fire.

Raj smiles. Dean's out to shake and shock. He has a whole system to figure out what picture should pop up on the GPS screen to piss the hell out of the driver. He calculates the driver's average speed over a two-week span of time. Fast drivers, he assumes, are young, reckless, so he gives them something sedate, calm, a stream in the middle of nowhere. A cow. Dead leaves whirling. Sometimes he couples it with music: Philip Glass's *The Hours*. Ludovico Einaudi's "Experience." Slow granny drivers get a chick pole dancing or heavy metal rockers with their shirts off, flashing their hairy chests, jamming on electric guitars. AC/DC never gets old. No way to get rid of the image. It sits on the display panel, leering at you like an unwanted passenger.

Whatcha got? says Raj, foot rapid-fire tapping. His screen is gleaming.

Not sure, says Dean.

How about mud wrestling? says Raj.

Think strange, says Han. Snake charmers. Boas wrapped around arms and legs.

Dean frowns. Something weird's happening. Hold on.

Adam stops dancing, turns the music down.

All these cars, zero miles per hour.

What? says Han.

Look at these engines. The speedometer says a big fat zero. Check yours.

Whoa, mine too.

Mine too.

F-ing weird.

Did we hit a parking lot?

Car dealer?

Raj taps on his board. The ones I've got are in a different location from yours. Can't be a parking lot.

Where are yours?

Novato.

Mine are in Berkeley.

I've got San Francisco and Oakland.

All the way down to Burlingame, oh, wait, now down to Palo Alto. Everyone sitting on the highway like roadkill.

Fucking weird, says Adam.

Check their registrations, says Dean.

No, says Adam. No names. We don't work that way.

Why not? says Dean.

A rule, says Adam. We don't poke around in someone else's identity

Uh, dude, we're in someone's car right now, says Raj.

No need for these people's names to infiltrate our minds, says Adam.

Why?

My rule, says Adam.

Because if you had a name, you'd start imagining a life, says Raj, and once you start that, you can imagine where they live, the house, the yard, kids, a dog. A man in a car, just trying to make a living, maybe his wife is dying, maybe he has a sick kid—

Whatever, says Adam, cutting him off. You got to have rules. Got to know where you draw the line. If you don't, you're swimming in an immoral sea, and there will never be a ground, only groundlessness.

Deep, says Raj.

Call someone, says Han.

But don't ask for their name, says Dean snidely.

Hey, I don't care if you understand the rules, says Adam.

Got it, boss, says Dean.

And no boss shit. I don't believe in hierarchy. That's what got us into all this shit.

Raj hacks into the DMV, pulls up the license plate numbers and associated phone numbers. Punches in a number. They hear the cell ringing. Then a recorded message. He tries again. Five rings, then a recording. Again, same thing, as if they're the only ones alive in the world.

The phone is obsolete, says Adam.

Except for grannies, says Dean.

Do grannies have cell phones? says Adam.

Raj tries again. Again. Again. Shit.

Text someone, says Han.

Raj writes: Hey, what's going on? Why are the cars stopped?

Who's this?

Raj smiles, thumbs-ups the others. They crowd around and watch Raj's computer screen.

I'm someone stuck in traffic in lovely Burlingame, writes Raj. Trying to figure out what's going on.

I'm in the Presidio, trying to get to the Golden Gate Bridge. No idea what's happening.

I'm also doing a study, writes Raj.

Dean smacks Raj's shoulder and cackles.

Is this a prank?

No.

What's the study about?

It's about driving and destination.

Adam snorts, takes the basketball, throws it at the wall.

You got the wrong person. I'm not driving anywhere.

What are you doing?

Sitting here.

How long?

Over two hours. Crazy. Never seen traffic like this. Some people are out of their cars milling around.

Did she write *milling*, says Han.

Or he, says Dean.

Smoking, checking their phones, writes he/she/they. Others are talking to one another. Traffic is tangled up. Feels like I'm in NYC again. I sold my car after three weeks living there.

What's going on around you? writes Raj.

The guy next to me in the blue Corolla is smoking one cigarette after another. Must be a nervous tic. He thinks it's a big accident on the bridge. A semi rolled over or something. A big rig plunged over the side. Another guy said someone is about to jump. Oh, wait. A helicopter just flew by. KGO's helicopter. They'll show what's going on.

Dean finds the TV station on his computer and everyone huddles around his screen.

Holy shit, says Adam. People hanging from the top of the bridge, roped in.

That takes some balls.

Women up there.

And breasts.

Down below, thousands of protestors with signs:

NO PIPELINE!

STOP THE MASSACRE

SUN ENERGY

WHO SAID YOU'RE SO FUCKING IMPORTANT?

WE'RE BEING FOSSILIZED

END OIL SUBSIDIES

YOU CAN LIVE WITHOUT PIZZA BUT NOT AIR.

HELP! SOS!

KISS A GOAT

These guys are rock, says Adam.

Why don't you get out of your car? writes Raj. Breathe the salt and briny air.

I'm trying to get to my mom's house. I don't even want to go, but she called and asked me to come by and see her.

I see my mom once a year, writes Raj.

I see my mom once a week.

Wow! Why?

Raj stares at the screen. Sees three pulsing lines, then they disappear.

I believe, says Adam, putting his hand on his heart. I believe in mischief.

They laugh. Just because they're taking the Bank of Union's money doesn't mean they believe in the medieval banking system. They're rebels, they tell themselves, outside the system, ready and willing to mess shit up, if need be.

Brethren, says Adam, putting his hand on his heart. Our brothers and sisters.

Brethren and Sistren on the bridge, says Han.

Raj is still staring at his screen, waiting.

Protesters are gods, says Dean. Hail to the mighty.

A text message appears. Why do I go? Pressure, guilt, I don't know. She needs me. We've got this complicated thing going on. Maybe I'm a pushover. Mother, that's a loaded word. Can you ever get out from under it?

Desire is funny, he writes, making shit up just to keep him/her/them going. Hard to parse out what is a true desire and what isn't. Are you going because you're doing what is expected of an offspring? What is the evolution of desire? Am I sitting here texting you because that's what someone with a phone in his hand does? Who is this, really?

Oh shit. I have to go to the bathroom.

A woman, says Raj to the others. Otherwise, he'd piss in a bottle. He can't remember the last time he spoke to a woman. He's been with these guys, living in a low-lit warehouse for what feels like eternity.

Oh wow, she writes. Found the news on the radio. So many protesters and more on their way. Thousands, they say. Maybe that's why all these people are walking by my car, heading to the bridge. I'm just sitting here feeling outraged, and they're protesting the—yep, the destruction of the earth. I sort of admire them, I mean, pretty ingenious to make the world stop like this.

Raj leans toward his computer screen, wanting to get to know her better. This woman, after sitting two hours, can see the brilliance. That's something.

Pretty fucking cool, he writes.

Yeah, she writes back. Kind of. I mean yes and no.

The others are crowded around Dean's screen, watching the protest.

I can't remember the last time I stood up for something or did something I really wanted to do. I'm sorry I'm going on and on like this, but I've been sitting here for so long. Do you know where I really want to go?

Where? writes Raj. My name is Raj, by the way. No one talks to him like this, none of the guys here talk like this. He feels an intimacy as if he's sitting in the car with her, talking.

Raj, she writes. Okay. I'm Nohemi. I want to walk on that trail at Rodeo Beach. It's above the beach. Do you know it?

When is the last time he walked a trail? Boot on dirt. Dirt in nostrils. His idea of the outside is opening his car window. He writes, No, never done it.

Oh, you should go. A steady climb up on a dusty fire trail. You get to the top of the hill above the surfers riding the waves, and there's this huge stretch of glimmering water, and the city is there, and the pelicans, almost prehistoric birds, flying their great big bodies through the sea air. You're on top of the world. Actually, I just did something I really wanted to do. Yesterday, I quit my job. I couldn't do it anymore. A lawyer, commercial litigation. I couldn't do another interrogatory, another pleading, another trial. Ten, fifteen-hour days. I didn't burn out, I burned up. My hair on fire. Oh, wait. A man is standing on the roof of his pickup, playing *Let it Be* on his guitar. This is beautiful. I'm tearing up. I'm going to open all my windows.

Cool, he writes. He wonders if her eyes water when she thinks of something beautiful. His do, but he's never told anyone that. He's never been in a relationship long enough, with his heart running around in an open field.

He's getting into it, she writes. Eyes closed, singing. He's really fantastic.

Raj closes his eyes. He can picture it, feel it, the man on the roof, his voice ringing out.

What are you listening to? she writes.

The whir of computer fans, he writes.

Ah, the modern worker. I hope it's worth it.

A man has to make a living, he writes. But that's not it, he knows. If he's honest, if he'd say the truth for once, the response would be, what else is there to do? I mean, what should I be doing?

I hear sirens now. No way they're going to get through. Oh god. Now a woman is screaming at the guitar player. This redhead, her face pinched with anger, she looks like she's been living under a rock, maybe surviving on rocks. She's accusing him of egging on the protesters. Boy, she's really yelling as if he's the problem. Good for him! He's just playing and playing.

I can't remember the last time I hiked anywhere, writes Raj.

My dad and I, we used to go out worming.

Worming?

Worms. Creepy crawlers. After dinner, when it was dark and the air cold, we'd head over to our neighbor's farm and dig in the mulch behind their red barn. I grew up in Nebraska, in a little town called Broken Bow. Lots of alfalfa and hay, land flat as a pancake. It smelled like horse manure and that metallic scent of soil. When you start digging, a bouquet of smells envelops you—grass and stench of cow pies, leftover slop from the pigs. I don't know why I'm telling you this. My dad was such a good man. If he were alive he'd be out there protesting for sure. He was recycling before the rest of America. He cut his own hair, and he liked to cook. We'd collect a bucketful of worms and go fishing at Winthrop Lake. Back then you could catch fish big enough to eat. Anyway, we'd bring them home, and I'd debone them.

You can debone a fish? he writes.

Ha! I'm a woman of many talents.

He's never been fishing. Never touched a fish. He has a pale memory of a body of water, let's call it a beach, a memory that his mother hauled out over the years, so for him it would always be true: When you were a little boy, two, three, seven, she'd say, you refused to walk on the sand. You hated how it felt on your bare feet. Scratchy, you'd scream and plop down, refusing to take another step. Someone had to carry you like a little prince, put you on a beach towel where you sat all day. Wouldn't even dig in the sand with your brothers. Wouldn't play in the waves or play catch with your dad. The doctor said it was a hypersensitivity to touch, and we had to desensitize you, so we kept bringing you to the beach, and you cried and cried, refusing to step in the sand, even when you wore your tennis shoes. So, we stopped going. It's not fun to have a sulky kid on the beach towel, whining all the time, asking when are we going to go home.

But hey, Mom, he argues with her in his mind, you were hardly the nature freak parents. No worming adventures for us. An occasional hike that ended in sore feet and blisters and a vow not to do that again. Camping and living in a tent were for the destitute. His parents preferred museums and culture and took him along with his two brothers. He remembers seeing the Monet exhibit at the de Young Museum at age five. He stood in front of the *Water Lilies* painting for so long that his parents were convinced he'd become a painter. Why did he stand there so long? What was he looking at? And when they took him to the Rodin sculptures at Stanford, they decided his destiny was to be a sculptor.

His mother was a professor of classics and wrote lyrical essays and poems, weaving in Greek mythology, though she called it reviving it, breathing life into it again for the modern audience. He'd heard that phrase so many times during her interviews with newspapers. His father was a professor of physics, so there were trips to the Smithsonian National Air and Space Museum and Chabot Space & Science Center. Spring break and summer vacations pinwheeled around museums. When he was twelve, they spent one month in Berlin and visited so many museums that he lost count. Twenty? Twenty-five? The city has 190. He didn't tell any of his friends that fact or that he loved it, every minute of it.

Maybe he can blame his parents for his lack of nature love; maybe he can't since he's eighteen years old. He doesn't write to the woman sitting in the car that there's a hella thick glass between him and dirt. For him, nature is a screen-saver image: flamingos flying in a pink sky; green rolling hills. Nice to look at, but none of it has made him want to put on a pair of hiking boots and hit the trail or go dig for worms.

In all honesty, nature makes him feel uncomfortable, and, well, insignificant. The redwood that will live to maybe 2,000 years, and he, if he's lucky, maybe 80. Rocks, hills, the sky, the sea—all of these represent time spans well beyond the puny time that represents an average human life. He doesn't know exactly why it bothers him except for the abstract idea of death.

Yet he's intrigued that she wants to be on a dirt trail. What does it give her? Why doesn't he have the same desire? It seems hers is a more natural desire, since once upon a time humans were hunters and gatherers, then farmers, and dirt was always under fingernails. He looks at his hands—soft, with only an ink smudge on his thumb. He's in a dingy warehouse, 24/7, always in front of a screen.

My phone is dying, she writes.

Raj feels his throat tighten. Oh, shit. Can't you plug it in?

Forgot my cord.

Who forgets their cord? he writes.

I've opened all the windows and I can smell the ocean. You should come out here, I mean it, you really should. This is just unbelievable.

He likes that she didn't make a big deal out of asking him to join her, as if it's the most natural thing to say, Hey, come see this with me. He writes, Are you going to be okay? From the looks of things, you aren't going anywhere for a long time.

Are you worried? How old do you think I am?

She doesn't want an honest answer, he knows this about women. In your twenties, he writes.

Ha! Thirty-five! And even though America wants me to feel awful about that, I'm not. I'm happy to be older, wiser. Happy I quit my miserable job.

Nice. He decides he likes older women.

Okay, I should—

Okay, but you know—

Adam shoves his face in front of Raj's. Signals—hang up, bro, we got something big planned.

Raj holds up one finger. What are you seeing now?

People are singing "Let it Be." Lots of people. You're stuck in some stupid office, you're missing out.

He can picture it, the crowds, the birds, her. What else? he writes.

This guy just walked by. He's smoking a joint and drinking beer. He's got on a 49ers baseball cap and a Warriors T-shirt. Lots of joy out here, lots of anger too. That woman is still screaming, though now I think she's yelling at the crows.

Can I? he writes.

She sends a smiling emoji.

The connection goes dead.

This is LIT! says Adam. We got a way to help our brethren rebels. Brother Dean figured it out.

Dean is jamming on the keyboard, fingers on fire, bringing something to life where before there was nada. He keeps going, grinding on the board, and he's zeroing in on something. Ten more strings of code, he leans back, a big grin on his face, which looks like a blooming flower.

Here it is, amigos, Dean says.

They see the stream of numbers on his screen. These, my friends, are cars. And here are the pathways to the car engines.

Yay! says Adam.

Dean fist-bumps Adam.

Watch the beautiful magic, says Dean.

Dean makes his way through the list, and they watch him

turn off the car engines, ten, twenty, thirty, forty, on and on, creating a vast sea of deadness, tires stuck to asphalt, no more CO², the engine button defunct. They imagine fingers poking at the button, obscenities flying, and after the umpteenth try, car doors slamming.

Dean sends them the addition to the software, and they all get busy.

So fucking good, says Adam.

What happens next? says Han.

Nothing, says Dean. Nothing will happen. Nothing can happen. A vast sea of nothingness. We are back to the beginning of time.

Can't see a tow truck wedging in there and pulling them out, says Raj.

Full stop, says Dean.

Raj imagines the woman in her dead car. Car radio off, GPS gone. She'll get out of her car, her phone dead and heavy in her pocket, and start walking to the bridge, joining the throngs heading that way. Maybe the wind is blowing, maybe the sun is blazing, maybe the seagulls are crying out and she'll see glimpses of the bridge, and like a beacon, it'll call to her, and the protesters hanging from the top will look like they're waving at her. Festive, laced with outrage and wildness. All bets are off. He imagines her smiling, loving all of it—God, after all those hours stuck in an office, reading briefs, she's out! She'll make her way through the mass of protestors, and she'll keep going all the way across to that trail she's after. Her mother will have to wait because there's the beach and that trail. No hum of engines, only human voices scattered by the wind. She's going to do what she wants.

We're going to see some hot-ass tempers, says Dean. We're a country of Neanderthals.

Hey, I've got some Neanderthal in me, says Adam.

Right. I don't stand corrected.

I'm pure *Homo sapien*, says Han, the species that overpowered you cavemen.

No way, bro, says Dean.

Another hundred cars become something other than car, says Han. What do you call a car that can't move?

A rock, says Adam.

A metal box.

It was always a metal box, says Han.

Raj pushes back his chair, a squeal bouncing off the walls. He stands.

What are you doing? says Dean.

I think we got to go, says Raj.

Where? says Adam.

To the bridge, says Raj.

What? says Han.

Oh yeah, says Dean. That makes a lot of sense. A massive traffic jam. We should get in our cars and go sit in them for endless hours.

We drive as far as we can, then walk, says Raj.

Wait. Did you just say the word "walk"? says Adam. You, a man who despises walking? Did zombies take over your body?

He walks from his car to the warehouse, says Han.

That's five minutes tops. We're talking f-ing miles, says Adam.

I'm going, says Raj.

Are you kidding? says Dean. You're not kidding, are you?

I don't get it, says Han.

Something's happening right now that's greater than all of us, says Raj.

What the hell does that mean? says Adam.

Adam is staring at him as if he's grown a second head. Something pretty great is happening right here. We're going to shut down all the cars in the US of A.

Raj puts on his coat.

We're already part of this, dude, whatever this is, says Adam.

But he needs to be closer, to be in it. Raj can't remember the last time he stepped outside. He jots down her phone number, stuffs it in his pocket, and steps out into the cool, bright air.

The Big Picture

Lincoln zips on his bike, up Arguello Boulevard, a steep hill that makes his lungs burn in a good way, glides through the eucalyptus-scented shade, and pedals to the dirt pullout overlooking the bay. Whoa. Joe and his papa were right. So many people on the bridge, everything at a standstill.

He lets the sight pour over him. Glances at his chewed-off nails from worry about what's going on in the world. Wars, shootings, tornadoes, sea rising, he knows about it all. Baffled by people who aren't worried about it—what are they doing? Why aren't they paying attention? But, he thinks, watching the scene below him, everyone on the bridge is paying attention.

Go, Joe told him, ride your bike to the bridge, see what people can do together. A force, that's what, a force to be reckoned with. Go see that. Joe gave him a lock for his bike. Even his papa said he could go—"This is part of your education because you're a young man with intelligence and integrity, and I see you doing remarkable things."

Which made Lincoln stand taller and puff his chest out, as it does now thinking about that word, "remarkable" coming out of his papa's intelligent mouth. First time Joe and his papa said the same thing, a chorus of go and go. Something clicked inside, pieces of a complicated puzzle fitting together.

But looking at the scene below him, he doesn't need to hear the fusion of their voices. Doesn't want to hear Kevin's voice and the voices of kids his age, concerned about getting ahead, standing out, and getting attention; seems silly, a joke. It's his voice he's listening to—he hopes it doesn't go away or ever get quiet—because it's laughing as an anchor drops inside. He can't explain it except to say this is who he is, this is where he needs to be. Lincoln thinks of John Francis, a Black man his father had never heard of—but now he has—who walked across America protesting the country's dependence on big oil, walking because he would not, could not, pollute by driving a car or riding in a plane. Couldn't do it if he wanted to sleep at night. Twenty years and counting of walking. Calls himself a Planetwalker, someone who walks the planet. Lincoln likes that. Planetwalker.

Someone pulls up beside him on a bike. A woman, maybe in her forties? Sweat shines on her face, and her sunglasses reflect the bridge. "A mess down there," she says.

A beautiful mess, he thinks. He smells the salt in the air. The ocean looks like a wrinkled blue shirt.

"Well, I was going to ride across the bridge to the headlands, but I guess not."

"Guess not," he says.

"Kind of ruins my day."

He looks at her. So many ways to see the world—that's his first thought. Not my way—his second thought.

She turns around, rides away from the bridge.

Lincoln hears the helicopters before he sees them. TV station helicopters—KRON, KGO—written in big letters on their sides. Circling the bridge. People are making news. Cars and people and horns honking, drums beating a rhythm that makes Lincoln nod his head. The bay flashes little pieces of white light, and Lincoln keeps nodding as he flies down the hill to the people-stuffed bridge.

Hugh is pushing his way through the mob, the group of eight on bongo drums. People are a blur, a big lump of flesh blocking his way because this is the last place he wants to be.

"It's going to be all right," shouts Fran, who is trailing behind him.

He grips Gabe's hand tighter, thinking, This doesn't happen to people like us. Other people get stuck in a mob; other people get trapped in a dangerous mass of uncontrollable energy. Hugh can feel the raucous brute aggression in the air, the chaos.

He smells it too—pungent, sharp. Heat rises along the back of his neck and spreads over his skull, and Gabriel tries to yank his hand out of Hugh's, but Hugh won't let go—no way—because he knows his son too well. If Gabe gets away, Hugh will be frantically looking for his son, calling out his name, which will thrill Gabe, thinking it's a game of hide and seek, and he'll be stuck on this damn bridge forever.

Hugh glances back to make sure Fran and Louise are following, and thank god they are, so he keeps making his way through the shouting and chanting, sweat trickling down his face, pushing through the chaos of anger. Or maybe it's his anger because they should be on a plane right now, right now flying over the Pacific, seat belts fastened, chairs in their upright position, a flight attendant demonstrating an air mask, Gabe asking for a flimsy bag of roasted peanuts. He's worked so damn hard, no one handed him a thing, he met each challenge, pushed himself to do more, make it happen, he's owed. He turns; yes, Fran and Louise are behind him.

They are weaving in and out of the trapped cars, stretched all the way across the bridge and beyond. Yellow, white, black, brown, blue, red. But where is he leading them? Hugh hears a woman with disheveled brown hair say she wishes she'd worn her clown outfit. Who are these people?

Gabe asks if Hugh has any gum. Fran thinks gum calms Gabriel but he doesn't have it, and Gabriel whines and yanks hard on Hugh's arm. Sharp pain jolts Hugh's shoulder. He wants to yell at his son, what a thing to do to your father.

"We have to get across," says Hugh.

"Why?" says Gabriel.

He hears Fran's voice in his head: be firm, but friendly, not patronizing. Hugh clenches his jaw. "Because I said so."

"That's a stupid reason."

"We're on a bridge. A bridge is made to cross."

"A bridge can just be here."

"It's a man-made structure connecting two land masses separated by water," says Hugh.

"It's a concrete and metal thing. I can call it anything I want. An oink. A moo. A flying cow."

"Do you see the water?" says Hugh. "We're walking above the water."

"I hate walking."

"Let's go, Gabriel."

"No."

As Hugh looks to Fran for help—she's about four people behind him, and just then, Gabe unleashes an ear-splitting howl, a scream that slices like a serrated knife through the noise, drawing the attention of everyone within a 100-foot radius. A man with sparse hair, a gap between his two front teeth, comes over.

"You need help, kid?" he says to Gabriel.

Gabriel pouts.

"He's my son," says Hugh. "We're trying to cross the bridge."

The man looks Hugh up and down. He points his finger at Hugh. "I got my eye on you."

Hugh flushes; Gabe smiles. Fran is talking to a fairly ample redhead, and now Fran is laughing. A woman near Hugh is speaking of the massive traffic jam with enthusiasm. It isn't until now, listening to this elated woman, that he understands others—maybe everyone on the bridge—is giddy because cars are lined up for miles and miles, engines turned off, no one going anywhere. What kind of world does he live in? Who are these people?

Hugh grips Gabriel's hand and begins moving forward, and what comes to mind is that he's like a camel in a desert, trying to find water in a furious dust storm. It's hard to see, hard to walk. A woman waves her sign in the air—NO PIPELINE, her belly button pierced with a silver heart. A heavy-lidded man with a red 49ers baseball cap and a camouflage coat stands next to her, speaking to her out of the side of his mouth with a sly cat's smile. Hugh hears him say he wished he worked out more. They have to keep going, but it occurs to him that even if he found an Uber, it would be stuck, trapped like a fly in a spider's web. What's on the other side of the bridge that could possibly solve anything? He's a man with a mission, but the mission is empty, laughable.

But he doesn't stop. He's a force, going against the current because he wants out of this mess. He will not be stopped. Hugh turns and looks for Fran, but she's not anywhere. Neither is Louise. "Fran!" He scans the sea of faces and thinks he sees her over by the railing, her back to him, standing there, gazing out at the bay, as if she's not in an unruly uprising but alone, out for a peaceful walk, enjoying the view.

"Fran!" The noise drowns out his voice.

The man who said he'd be keeping an eye on Hugh aims his finger at him again. A group, gray-haired and slightly stooped, stands in a tight circle, singing a hymn. Gabe suddenly turns into a huge boulder, digging in his heels, using all his body weight to halt their progress.

"It's imperative we find your mother and sister," says Hugh.

He watches his son's lips form the words, no, no, no. A man wearing a black plastic garbage bag walks by. His sign reads YOU CAN'T DRINK OIL. In that moment, while Hugh reads the sign again, Gabriel jerks his hand out of Hugh's and he's gone.

"Gabe!"

Hugh tries to run after him, but the throng stops him, so he pushes harder, heading back the way he came, between elbows and shoulders and bodies, dodging a sign, NEGATIVE EMISSIONS, back to the center of the bridge, where the drums are louder, wilder. He's feverishly hunting for his son—Hugh spots him. "Gabe!" Gabe cuts and ducks like a professional basketball player and is gone.

Hugh nears the center of the bridge, where the drummers are sitting on the concrete. People have gathered around the drummers—they've pulled out the meridian separators to make more room—and a flash mob of dancers is wildly waving their arms and swaying their hips, and there is Fran, Fran is with them, her arms overhead, her hips gyrating, her head tossed back, a big smile on her face. Louise is nearby, a replica of her mother.

As he presses his way into the circle of dancers, formulating what he'll say to his wife, he spots his son. Not dancing, but standing stock-still, looking straight up. Hugh follows his gaze to the white gulls circling overhead, then further up to the top of the bridge. Are those people up there? Perched like statues, but not statues, real people who defied the wind and maybe overcame the fear of heights to climb the bridge. What people are willing to do, he thinks, feeling a magnetic wave of excitement. He watches the people on the top of the bridge, his mouth open in awe. But the astonishment vanishes as quickly as it came, and he mutters, "Crazy people. Everyone has gone crazy." He waves frantically at Fran, "Fran!" She doesn't look over; maybe she doesn't hear him. She's dancing, arms waving wildly above her head.

Raj feels like he's been released from serving time, endless years in solitary confinement. Overwhelmed, all of it overwhelming: the air and the grit, people laughing, chanting, cheers, piercing whistles, shouting, and music threaded through it all. Drums—where are they? As if he's stepped into not one of those badass tanks where you float in salt water and dissolve into nothing, but a sensory overload tank, a tank that activates all senses, and you dissolve because you aren't isolated; everything is threaded through you. Fucking unbelievable.

He weaves in and out of cars, taking in the cigarette smoke, the weed, the music, the voices, and part of him is hunting for her, this woman who used to go worming with her dad, who knows how to debone a fish, who wants to hike a dirt trail. Part of him knows the search is futile because the crowd is enormous, and part of him wants to believe the impossible is possible. So he's hunting and not hunting, looking for her and not looking, part of it all and outside of it all. He doesn't even know what she looks like.

Small crowds have collected around certain people who have a message or information or something. He passes by, catching fragments—the system, the entire paradigm. The governor is coming by helicopter. Senators. Got them to listen by shutting it all down.

The energy here—he doesn't feel dystopia in his bones. More like hope. A steely, determined hope. He thinks of the guys back at the warehouse and how they'd laugh at that word. They've already given up, already accepted the dystopia. If enough people want dystopia, will it happen? How many people does it take? What constitutes many? And how many people does it take to make something else happen?

He passes by a girl with a sign, I LOVE ELEPHANTS. His heart lurches. A woman walks by, a dog on a leash.

"Are you by any chance Nohemi?" says Raj.

"Nope." She introduces herself as Lucinda.

Raj pets her dog, and the dog wags his tail.

"I had to see, you know," says Lucinda. "My dog and I walked for miles."

Raj tells her he did the same. He hears applause, a sustained burst of shouting and clapping.

"There's a rumor this protest might go on for days," she says.

He feels like he's walked into someone's dream.

"I think it's good," she says.

He's not certain if he agrees, but then again, what else is there to do but this? He looks around. What if that woman in the purple sweater is her? Or that woman with the white sun hat? Or with long curly brown hair? A man walks around selling bottles of water, soft drinks, and sandwiches. Or what if she's that woman, slightly matronly?

"I think the way out of this is to lose interest in ourselves," says Lucinda.

"True, but that might be impossible," says Raj.

"Even just a little bit." She looks at the dog with what he decides is love.

A man with a big mustache comes over to Raj and holds up his hand. It's right there, in front of Raj's face, and without thinking, Raj gives him a high-five.

"That's it," says the man. "That's exactly it."

"That's right," says Raj.

He smiles a big leonine smile.

A woman walks by; her sign reads NO PIPELINE.

On impulse, he says, "Wait! Are you Nohemi?"

She shakes her head no and moves on.

It's a beautiful day, sun spilling over everything, seagulls like white cutouts on blue. It doesn't matter if he never finds her, he tells himself. He's in the world, part of something bigger than himself. But he keeps walking, looking at each 30ish woman, wondering, is that her, is that her?

When Ava saw her mother on the TV news, her seventy-year-old mother shakily climbing up the Golden Gate Bridge in a pair of white sneakers, she screamed. Then she was out the front door, racing to the bridge, calling Ed and Nelson on her cell, leaving messages to meet her at the bridge. Hurry! They'd have to walk, cars stalled for miles and miles.

At first, Ava was running, but after the second mile, she slowed her pace and noticed the cypress, bent and craggy like old people. Resilient, shaped by memories of wind. The memory of her mother drifts in when Eleanor took the family camping at Crystal Cove Beach. They gathered driftwood and started a fire and roasted marshmallows. They ate roasted hot dogs that were a little gritty with sand. When her father and brother fell asleep, she and her mother were still awake and went down to the ocean. The two of them stood barefoot in the freezing water. What did her mother say? The sea makes me swoon? Was that it?

She tries Nelson's phone—no answer—leaves another message. She is sweating through her shirt. The roads are endless.

She tries Ed.

"Hola, mi amiga," he says cheerily.

Forever the optimist. "Where are you?" she says.

"Almost there. Carnivalesque where I am," he says. In between the stopped cars, people are drinking and smoking, he tells her, music from the radios blasting. Like a big block party.

"I hear chanting and shouting," she says. "You must be closer than me."

They agree to meet by the Round House Café on the south end of the bridge.

"I'll be the one in the top hat," says Ed.

"You're kidding, right?" she says.

He laughs, and she thinks she hears another male voice laughing alongside Ed's.

"She wants to die," she says severely. "That's why she's doing this."

"God, Ava," he says. "Why does your brain always go to the worst possible thing?"

"Did you ever call her? See her? I was there, remember, at the Goldman ceremony. She was out of her mind. Maybe she's gone mad, her grief, her anger. She wants to die, that's why she's doing this. Go out big, with a big dramatic ending, so it all means something."

Nelson is calling. "Hold on," she says to Ed. "Nelson! Come to the bridge. My mom has climbed on it. She's on the bridge!"

"Oh my god," says Nelson. He tells her he'll be there.

She flips back to Ed.

"Like I said," says Ed, "it's pretty much a party here. It feels like people have come together after a long time apart. They miss each other terribly. There's love and zing in the air. There's happy in the air, which you might not know about. It's like they remembered they exist, that they are the ones they've been waiting for."

"I'm not kidding around, but you are, you always are."

If the IVF works, if all goes well, and by that, she means one time, one series of injections, and she becomes pregnant, she wants her mother to be there. A grandmother to hold her grandchild. If her mother jumps—if the wind blows her off the bridge, if she stumbles, slips. She wants her mother alive so she can apologize and tell her mother she forgives her for everything.

"This is serious," she says.

"Maybe this is what she wants. I mean, how courageous, our mother of ours, who has no climbing experience whatsoever. I know she inspires me, even if this is how it ends."

"How can you say that!" Why does she always feel like the older, wiser sister around him? Why can't he ever grow up?

Ava comes to a parting of the eucalyptus trees and sees the bridge and swarms of people, hears the chants, louder and clearer, though she can't make out what they're saying. She spots the people on top of the bridge and gasps. Is her mother on the very top, blowing in this strong wind? She's going to be thrown, tossed to the water.

"I'll be there in ten minutes," she says.

"Roger that," says Ed.

The line goes dead.

Ed looks at Henry. "My sister is hysterical."

"The hysterical woman cliché."

"All her life she wanted to be otherwise. She used to have such self-possession, such reasoning powers. Now, they're shot."

"Look at all these people," says Henry, smiling. "Hundreds of thousands of people. Maybe we should dance for them. Perform right here."

"What if my mother dies?" says Ed.

Henry shrugs. "Then she'll die."

"So cold."

"No, a realist. If someone wants to end it, they will." Henry pulls Ed close, and Ed covers his neck with kisses. Ed will not say what's formed at the back of his throat, will not say he loves Henry because this, he tells himself, is enough, and he doesn't want to scare Henry and be left with nothing, bereft. He doesn't deserve Henry; he does deserve Henry. Colleen is already talking about the next performance, putting them together again on stage. "You two are captivating, two parts of a whole," she said. "You held the audience in the grip of your hands."

Ed takes hold of Henry's hand and they head to the bridge, the wind blowing in their hair, pinning the seagulls in blue sky.

Henry stops. Ed turns and Henry puts his hands on Ed's shoulders. "I don't mean to sound cold, I don't. Your mother may die today." He pulls Ed toward him, chest to chest, and holds him tight.

Ed feels the edifice inside crumble.

❧

"Mom! Get down!" says Ava.

Eleanor looks down and sees her daughter. Her son too. They look so tiny from up here, so fragile and delicate like little creatures. Strange that her body once held them in a pool of water. From up here the cars appear benign, the glint of chrome radiators, the shimmer of paint, like toys. Behind the shouts and chants, Eleanor hears the wind whistle. A ship is far at sea and the pulse of the Pacific enters her.

She hadn't planned to climb the bridge, and she can't quite believe she's up here, holding on to two narrow cables. Though in hindsight she sees it was always in the realm of possibility. For a whole week Eleanor waited for the next meeting with the children. An entire week falling in and out of desolation, the anticipation of being with the children, the room full of exuberance and idealism and action.

When Eleanor showed up for the next meeting, her old heart battering wildly, she said of course she'd go to the protest. Of course, she'd ride a bike—the children, such geniuses with their liberated imaginations, suggested they all ride bikes to get around the lines of stopped cars—and it all sounded fine because she never truly considered the reality of riding from her house to the Golden Gate Bridge, pedaling Claire's mother's red Schwinn.

She chugged up the long hill, gasping for air, her legs rubbery and her lungs burning. The speedy children were far ahead of her, along with the parents, though fortunately, there were a few stragglers. Claire stayed close and kept calling out words of encouragement, "You can do it," she'd say.

Then: "Eleanor! We're almost there!" she said.

Then: "Eleanor!"

Eleanor used the last of her energy to crest the hill, and there, in all its glory, was the bridge and the crowd of people.

"God almighty," said Eleanor.

The young teacher looked at her with an arched eyebrow.

"Aren't you glad you're here?" said Claire.

No, yes. "Yes," she said, her voice out of focus.

She looks down at her children and the growing crowd, the voices growing louder.

"Mom, please!" says Ava.

She tries to imagine what Ava sees—a mother who is unrecognizable, most likely. She's the policy wonk, tucked away in a boardroom where reason and calm voices prevail. But that self is nowhere; it's dismantled. Eleanor feels clearheaded and can't think of any other place she wants to be.

"Doing all right?" says Jake.

"I think I am," she says.

Jake, the young man up on the bridge, called out to her. "Hey! Hey you!"

Eleanor looked around.

"Up here!"

She tilted her head back, gazing at the cable leading to the bridge tower. A young man was standing on the cable. Three others perched on the platform at the top of the bridge on the right tower and another four on the other side. But this young man came walking down closer to her. He said he knew her. She spoke at Berkeley, and he was in the class. She told him she didn't remember him.

"You said you had no good news," said the man.

She had a vague memory of this. Anyway, it sounded like something she'd say. He smiled at her, a smile like a flash of light, a beacon. Bright white teeth. "Here's some good news," he said. "The view is fantastic. Wanna join me?" He pointed to the gate that led to the cable.

He told her they were protesting the pipeline, stretching from Canada to the Bay Area. A big vein of oil that, if the pipeline failed, if there was a leak, devastation for the land, water, creatures, and humans. What the hell, she thought. Then stopped. She'd never climbed anything, except when she was a girl, gingerly stepping up a ladder to a slide, the children below her yelling at her to hurry up. No rock climbing or scaling a ladder to fix a roof. If she lost her footing, that would be the end of her. If her legs gave out, that would be the end of her. The wind might blow too strongly, and that might be the end of her.

She was shaking at first, but Jake told her to grip the two wires and use them as handholds. Terrifying and thrilling; when did she last feel this alive?

Ed and Ava look as if they're arguing. Eleanor gazes to the far hill, at the Robin Williams tunnel, and sees the cars snake all the way up the hill, and she imagines the line of cars down the hill, down through San Rafael and Novato and Rohnert Park, on and on. Cars stopped everywhere in the Bay Area, the Bay Area brought to its knees. Even up and down the coast, Oregon, Washington, Idaho, and Arizona—something about a hack to the cars' computer systems. The eight protesters perched on the top of the bridge look like enormous, prehistoric birds. A sign stretches across the expanse, waving in the wind like a huge sail, as if they, everyone, even she, might lift up and take flight.

The bongo drums beat a pattern, round and round, trance-like, and at the heart of the bridge people are dancing. The wind calms, then blasts her. She feels herself sway. Whatever happens, she's responsible because she's behind this whole thing. The money from the Goldman Prize handed over to Greenpeace. "Do what you will with it," she told Greg.

Angry drivers are out of their cars, but they're the minority. Most people, it seems, are experiencing something close to euphoria. Something sheds from her, and it all rushes in, hitting her like a sudden, unheard wave at the beach. Fifty years of arguing and presenting papers to CEOs, boards of directors, and shareholders, appealing to logic and reason to unearth this passion right in front of her. Fifty years to come to this point, to the beat of the drums, a beat that says it's time, it's time, it's beyond time.

The children have pulled out their homemade signs and are waving them, crayon-colored pictures of apple-green and turquoise-blue earth, signs professing their love of birds and dogs and owls and giraffes. Claire's sign: I LOVE ELEPHANTS.

You're right, Hazel, heaven is on earth. Arthur's words come rushing in; the measure of a good life is how well you care. This is the way to ensure you plunge into the warmth of life.

"Hey!" Jake calls out to her. He points to his phone, tells her protests are happening, not just here, but around the world. Greenpeace organized over 1,000 protests.

She smiles. "I feel like I'm becoming the wind."

He laughs.

It had to come to this, she thinks, one foot sunk in the horror. Crisis precipitates desire and the means. It had to, she thinks, because it's hard to talk about nature and have people listen; because we're swimming in nature, our beings caught up in the vast network of air and water and dirt and sun; because humans are deeply intertwined with the oxygen from the trees and plants and the reciprocated CO^2; it's akin to fish swimming in water. Akin to asking a fish, How's the water?

Until nature, the very substance we are swimming in, changes. Until the water becomes undrinkable; the air fills with smoke or chemicals, and is too hot to breathe; birds fall out of the sky, poisoned by the air; or the dirt is contaminated and depleted or parched and can't grow anything. Bees die. Humans are forced out of nature. They look around—what happened? What happened to the fresh air? Fresh water? Dirt to grow food?

She was fifty years too early, with few ears to hear her, few eyes to see her. But she's here now.

"Look!" says Jake. He points out to the bay. "Whales."

Three, no four humpback whales in the bay.

She feels the breath empty from her lungs.

"Mom, get down!" Ava says. "You're going to fall!"

Nelson is beside Ava now, with the same worried expression as her daughter. At least they have each other, thinks Eleanor.

She and Arthur once walked across the bridge. It must have been twenty years ago. The wind blew as it does today, and they leaned forward into it, her face near his to hear him. What was he talking about? They held hands, they must have. And if they didn't, they should have. Did she stop at some point on the bridge and tell him she loved him? God, she hopes she didn't squander any of it.

She glances up. The woman at the very top of the bridge looks as calm and strong as an eagle. There is nothing Eleanor, who is so many years older, could tell her except let her feeling for life be enormous and know the suffering will be just as great. But she guesses the young woman knows that.

Claire waves at her. "Hi, Eleanor!"

She lets go of the wire and waves back. "Hi, Claire!"

Ava gasps, Ed laughs. Their personalities in a nutshell. They must have been summoned by the TV news cameras pointing their lenses upward, then back to the enormous crowd. Ed puts his arm around another man, the cat in the ballet. They are about the same height, both fit, in tight shirts, tight jeans, and slim hips. Ed kisses the man on the cheek, and the man grabs Ed's earlobe and tugs. Her son is in love, and Eleanor feels flush with happiness for him.

Ava's face is strained with worry. She wants to assure her daughter if she falls and dies today, it'll be fine. A verse from the Bible recited by Hazel floats in her head, *A man goeth to his last home.* "Come down, Mom!" says Ava.

She climbed because the young man clipped to the bridge beckoned and smiled, and she felt the allure; because why should the children bear the burden, so heavy it could crush them, of saving the world? Life itself is shattering enough. Who said she—or anyone—could abdicate their responsibility? Who gave them an out? Small-minded and selfish to surrender to despair. She'll stay up here for days and days if that's what it takes. Let the light come and go, let the night roll over her. To stop the world, so it looks around, becomes aware and astonished by the beauty and the ruin, so it sees it has come to an end and a new beginning. Thank god she wore sneakers.

Will any of this make a difference? But if you think like that, nothing will ever get done. In drifts a bit of wisdom from this expansive moment. Don't depend on results, concentrate on the work. Plant the seeds; you might be planting a redwood, which means you won't see it in your lifetime. But maybe someone else will. Claire or Alexander. Because at some point, you must gamble everything to fill out every inch of your life.

"Way to go, Mom!" says Ed.

Ava is saying something to Ed, and Eleanor supposes it's a reprimand. Eleanor flashes forward and sees in her mind great crowds fleeing from horrific natural disasters. Tornadoes, tsunamis, wildfires, floods. She blinks the tears away.

"You've done enough," Ava said to her once.

Has she? Has anyone?

The sun splashes the water, turning it silvery blue, then pewter. Somewhere all the birds are flying over the grass. A sycamore tree waves its green leaves and a red fox digs in the dirt. Soon the twilight will move up from the ground and swallow the sky. She can taste the water on her lips, this earth, its richness. The children are singing and waving their signs.

It feels like spring when things rise from the dead. New buds and new green, that light apple-green the eye requires to wake something vital inside. When baby raccoons and rabbits, cubs, and squirrels arrive; when people who've been holed up, curled in bed, covers pulled to the chin, the curtain pulled down, feel the itch to move. New life, another breath. Put on a coat, step outside, the glisten of a bare shoulder, thin lines of collarbones, glossy red lips, painted eyes. A deep-seated need for something other than solitude. It's been a long, hard winter.

I am in the grip of this. An awed concentration. I didn't think I'd ever feel this again because I've been in tatters, like a woman in a beautiful flowing dress, with pieces of the fabric ripped off, one section after another, and I'm left with only a shoulder strap, a strip of fabric down my back. I admit I did some of the ripping. I let myself sink too far from the warm rays of hope, the pulse and beat of life. Instead, I've been listening to something like a eulogy, dead and deadly, wanting to bury myself before my time. I watched the fires and floods, the hurricanes and tornadoes and tsunamis with indifference, or worse, sometimes cheering them on. Burn it all down; blow it all away, flood the streets, drown it.

But all that life bursting on the bridge like ripe fruit; a refusal to be indifferent, a refusal to accept the demise. What's happening on the bridge and everywhere, protests popping up like brilliant lights, is bringing this new intoxicating spring feeling.

And there's Eleanor, white-knuckled, gripping the cable wires, shaky legs, and happy. I thought she and I were alike, barely hanging on, up to our necks in despair, but she's done something that's taken her beyond herself, out of herself. Made herself new again. Her spirit is lifted to the sky's ceiling, and the earth is humming with glee. Something necessary is moving through the air.

Raj looks as if he's just woken up, wandering around big-eyed, and Lincoln, he's been awake from the day he was born. He's talking to a woman with a picture of a redwood tree on her T-shirt. I wish this were the moment when Hugh changes his life. It'll come, but not now. Maybe in months, but most likely years and years.

Jake just told Eleanor a joke, and she laughs, her laughter fluttering down to Ed and Ava, landing lightly on them like leaves, and now it belongs to everyone. That laugh all over her,

Ava looks up, and she feels herself crack open to the excitement. Something inside loosens. Her mother is up there! A wave of pride and astonishment engulfs her. Lucinda glances at Eleanor with awe and feels, for a moment, that here on the bridge, in this loud protest, this is where she belongs.

I see the way now. It's sloshed everywhere on the bridge on people's faces, in the seagulls buffeted by the wind, the cypress in the hill growing sideways to the ground, hanging on. I've known this but forgot it, probably like you. To love the world wholeheartedly, unconditionally. That there exists something rather than nothing is astonishing. We might not ever know what caused the world to exist, but we can explain why things are the way they are. The special feature of this world, at least in my mind, is life.

It's risky, though, to love like this. Risky because it's impossible to predict or control what will be required of you. To love like this frees you from yourself and imprisons you with demands.

And what you love will perish, but this is what life adds up to. To live otherwise is to live behind a wall, glass or brick, withholding the heart; and that is not life. I know that, or rather, I remember this now, looking at the glorious congregation of people on the bridge. Everything is sharply in focus. The big grins and bright teeth, the sway of hips to the drumbeat, hair fluffed up by the wind, the children waving their handmade signs, Ava staring at her mother with big eyes of love, Ed kissing Henry. If you love like that, taking the risk and becoming recklessly vulnerable, you are alive. Heaven on earth, it's true.

I want to say love the air and the trees and the animals, and me. Slow down, lie down on the dirt and stare at the stars and fill the world with a similar vastness of love. You are here for a brief moment in cosmic time. I want to say I love you, I want to lie down with you. To have you love me back, always. I want to say, with this chorus of voices, loud and bright and unrelenting, yes, the world as it is will eventually perish, but not now, please, not soon.

ACKNOWLEDGMENTS

During the pandemic, a walk around the block saved me. A hike up a dirt path saved me and my children. The purple of iris, the peach of rose, a woodpecker hammering on a telephone pole, coyotes howling at night. Trees. The scent of laurel. Ocean. Mud. Fog laying the land. So many times, the nonhuman world saved me. This book was born from my desire to do something for the nonhuman world.

I am forever grateful to Elizabeth Stark, Ellen Sussman, Rosemary Graham, Peter Seeger, and Kinye Watson for their invaluable feedback on the early drafts of this book. Their insightful comments blew air on the orange coal of creativity.

Thank you, Dr. Aviva Rossi, for talking to me at great length about the environment and the ethos and culture of environmental studies. Professor Forrest Hartman's class, An Introduction to European Philosophy: From Descartes to Derrida, was critical to my understanding of how humans have reduced the natural world into object and resource. The American philosopher Graham Harman's object-oriented ontology development provided a fascinating lens to look at the nonhuman world. Ursula K. Le Guin's work gave me permission to personify nature since objectifying it has led to where we are now. David Naiman's "Crafting with Ursula" series on his fabulous podcast, *Between the Covers*, contributed to this commitment, helping me explore what it would mean for humans to admit other creatures as kin.

Children for Change, a child-led nonprofit founded by Annelise Bauer, is a huge inspiration to me personally and for this collection. When despair settles in, when all seems lost, I remember this organization; how wise children are, how wonderfully visionary they are, how committed they are to changing the course of devastation and destruction.

Thank you, Gail Collins-Ranadive, who sponsored The Prism Prize for Climate Literature and chose *In This Ravishing World*, as the winner of The Prism Prize for Climate Literature. It means so much to me, as well as your generous words about this collection.

And thank you, Peter Seeger, my husband, who has believed in my writing and me all along.